Beloe William

History Of Herodotus

Translated from the Greek with Notes Vol. 2

Beloe William

History Of Herodotus
Translated from the Greek with Notes Vol. 2

ISBN/EAN: 9783337194987

Printed in Europe, USA, Canada, Australia, Japan

Cover: Foto ©Andreas Hilbeck / pixelio.de

More available books at **www.hansebooks.com**

THE

HISTORY

OF

HERODOTUS,

TRANSLATED

FROM

THE GREEK.

WITH NOTES.

BY

THE REVEREND WILLIAM BELOE.

IN FOUR VOLUMES.

VOL. II.

LONDON:

PRINTED FOR LEIGH AND SOTHEBY,
YORK-STREET, COVENT-GARDEN.

M DCC XCI.

HERODOTUS.

THALIA[1].

CHAP. I.

GAINST this Amafis Cam-byfes, the fon of Cyrus, led an army compofed as well of his other fubjects, as of the Ionic and Æolic Greeks. His induce-ments were thefe : by an ambaf-fador whom he difpatched for this purpofe into Ægypt, he demanded the daughter of Amafis, which

[1] *Thalia.*]—On the commencement of his obfervations on this book, M. Larcher remarks, that the names of the mufes were only affixed to the books of Herodotus at a fubfequent and later period. Porphyry does not diftinguifh the fecond book of our hiftorian by the name of Euterpe, but is fatisfied with calling it the book which treats of the affairs of Ægypt. Athenæus alfo fays, the firft or the fecond book of the hiftories of Herodotus.

I am neverthelefs rather inclined to believe that thefe names were annexed to the books of Herodotus from the fpontaneous impulfe of admiration which was excited amongft the firft hear-ers of them at the Olympic games.

According

which he did at the fuggeftion of a certain Ægyptian who had entertained an enmity againft his mafter. This man was a phyfician, and when Cyrus had once requefted of Amafis the beft medical advice which Ægypt could afford, for a diforder in his eyes, the king had forced him, in preference to all others, from his wife and family, and fent him into Perfia. In revenge for which treatment this Ægyptian inftigated Cambyfes to require the daughter of Amafis, that he might either fuffer affliction from the lofs of his child, or by refufing to fend her, provoke the refentment of

According to Paufanias, there were originally no more than three mufes, whofe names were Μελιτη, Μνημη, and Αοιδη. Their number was afterwards encreafed to nine, their refidence confined to Parnaffus, and the direction or patronage of them, if thefe be not improper terms, affigned to Apollo. Their conteft for fuperiority with the nine daughters of Evippe, and confequent victory, is agreeably defcribed by Ovid. Met. book v. Their order and influence feems in a great meafure to have been arbitrary. The names of the books of Herodotus have been generally adopted as determinate with refpect to their order. This was, however, without any affigned motive, perverted by Aufonius, in the fubjoined epigram:

Clio gefta canens, tranfactis tempora reddit
Melpomene tragico proclamat moeft boatu.
Comica lafcivo gaudet fermone Thalia.
Dulciloquos calamos Euterpe flatibus urget.
Terpfichore aff. ctus citharis movet, imperat, auget.
Plectra gerens Erato faltat pede, carmine vultu.
Carmina Calliope libris heroica mandat
Uranie cœli motus fcrutatur et aftra.
Signat cuncta manu loquitur Polyhymnia geftu
Mentis Apollinee vis has movet undique mufas
In medio refidens complectitur omnia Phœbus.—T.

Cambyfes. Amafis both dreaded and detefted the
power of Perfia, and was unwilling to accept, though
fearful of refufing the overture. But he well knew
that his daughter was meant to be not the wife
but the concubine of Cambyfes, and therefore he
determined on this mode of conduct: Apries, the
former king, had left an only daughter: her name
was Nitetis ᵃ, and fhe was poffeffed of much elegance and beauty. The king, having decorated her
with great fplendour of drefs, fent her into Perfia
as his own child. Not long after, when Cambyfes
occafionally addreffed her as the daughter of Amafis,
" Sir," faid fhe, " you are greatly miftaken, and
" Amafis has deceived you; he has adorned my per-
" fon, and fent me to you as his daughter, but Apries
" was my father, whom he, with his other rebelli-
" ous fubjects, dethroned and put to death." This
fpeech and this occafion immediately prompted
Cambyfes in great wrath to commence hoftilities

ᵃ *Nitetis.*]—Cambyfes had not long been king, ere he refolved upon a war with the Ægyptians, by reafon of fome
offence taken againft Amafis their king. Herodotus tells us it
was becaufe Amafis, when he defired of him one of his daughters
to wife, fent him a daughter of Apries inftead of his own. But
this could not be true, becaufe Apries having been dead above
forty years before, no daughter of his could be young enough
to be acceptable to Cambyfes.—So far Prideaux; but Larcher
endeavours to reconcile the apparent improbability, by faying
that there is great reafon to fuppofe that Apries lived a prifoner
many years after Amafis dethroned him and fucceeded to his
power; and that there is no impoffibility in the opinion that Nitetis might, therefore, be no more than twenty or twenty-two
years of age when fhe was fent to Cambyfes.—*T.*

gainſt Ægypt.—Such is the Perſian account of
ie ſtory.

II. The Ægyptians claim Cambyſes as their
wn, by aſſerting that this incident did not happen
) him, but to Cyrus[1], from whom, and from this
aughter of Apries, they ſay he was born[4]. This,
owever, is certainly not true. The Ægyptians
re of all mankind the beſt converſant with the
'erſian manners, and they muſt have known that a
atural child could never ſucceed to the throne of
'erſia, whilſt a legitimate one was alive. And it
ras equally certain that Cambyſes was not born of
n Ægyptian woman, but was the ſon of Caſſan-
ane, the daughter of Pharnaſpe, of the race of
ie Achæmenides. This ſtory, therefore, was in-
ented by the Ægyptians, that they might from
iis pretence claim a connection with the houſe of
'yrus.

III. Another ſtory alſo is aſſerted, which to me

[3] *But to Cyrus*]—They ſpeak with more probability, who ſay
was Cyrus, and not Cambyſes, to whom this daughter of
pries was ſent.—*Prideaux.*

[4] *They ſay he was born.*]—Polyænus, in his Stratagemata, re-
tes the affair in this manner:—Nitetis, who was in reality the
aughter of Apries, cohabited a long time with Cyrus as the
aughter of Amaſis. After having many children by Cyrus,
ie diſcloſed to him who ſhe really was; for though Amaſi, was
ead, ſhe wiſhed to revenge herſelf on his ſon Pſammenitus.
yrus acceded to her wiſhes, but died in the midſt of his pre-
arations for an Ægyptian war. This, Cambyſes was perſuaded
y his mother to undertake, and revenged on the Ægyptians
ie cauſe of the family of Apries.—*T.*

ſeems

feems improbable. They fay that a Perfian lady once vifiting the wives of Cyrus, faw ftanding near their mother the children of Caffandane, whom fhe complimented in high terms on their fuperior excellence of form and perfon. "Me," replied Caffandane, "who am the mother of thefe children, " Cyrus neglects and defpifes, all his kindnefs is " beftowed on this Ægyptian female." This fhe faid from refentment againft Nitetis. They add that Cambyfes, her eldeft fon, inftantly exclaimed, " Mo- " ther, as foon as I am a man, I will effect the utter " deftruction of Ægypt ⁵ ". Thefe words, from a prince who was then only ten years of age, furprized and delighted the women; and as foon as he be-

---

⁵ *I will effect the utter deftruction of Ægypt.*]—Literally, I will turn Ægypt upfide down.

M. Larcher enumerates, from Athenæus, the various and deftructive wars which had originated on account of women; he adds, what a number of illuftrious families had, from a fimilar caufe, been utterly extinguifhed. The impreffion of this idea, added to the vexations which he had himfelf experienced in domeftic life, probably extorted from our great poet, Milton, the following energetic lines:

Oh why did God,
Creator wife, that peopled higheft heaven
With fpirits mafculine, create at laft
This novelty on earth, this fair defect
Of nature, and not fill the world at once
With men as angels, without feminine,
Or find fome other way to generate
Mankind ? This mifchief had not then befall'n,
And more that fhall befall, innumerable
Difturbances on earth through female fnares.—T.

came

came a man, and fucceeded to the thron♦ he re--
membered the incident, and commenced hoftilities
againft Ægypt.

IV. He had another inducement to this under-.
taking. Among the auxiliaries of Amafis was a
man named Phanes, a native of Halicarnaffus, and
greatly diftinguifhed by his mental as well as military accomplifhments. This perfon being, for I
know not what reafon, incenfed againft Amafis,
fled in a veffel from Ægypt, to have a conference
with Cambyfes. As he poffeffed great influence
among the auxiliaries, and was perfectly acquainted
with the affairs of Ægypt, Amafis ordered him to
be rigoroufly purfued, and for this purpofe equip-
ped, under the care of the moft faithful of his
eunuchs, a three-banked galley. The purfuit was
fuccefsful, and Phanes was taken in Lydia, but he
was not caaried back to Ægypt, for he circum-
vented his guards, and by making them drunk
effected his efcape: He fled inftantly to Perfia :
Cambyfes was then meditating the expedition againft
Ægypt, but was deterred by the difficulty of marching an army over the deferts, where fo little water
was to be procured. Phanes explained to the king
all the concerns of Amafis; and to obviate the
above difficulty, advifed him to fend and afk of the
king of the Arabs a fafe paffage through his territories.

V. This is indeed the only avenue by which
Ægypt can poffibly be entered. The whole country,

try, from Phœnicia to Cadytis, a city which belongs
to the Syrians of Paleſtine, and in my opinion equal
to Sardis, together with all the commercial towns
as far as Jenyſus[6], belong to the Arabians. This
is alſo the caſe with that ſpace of land which from
the Syrian Jenyſus extends to the lake of Serbonis.
from the vicinity of which mount Caſius[7] ſtretches
to the ſea. At this lake, where, as was reported,
Typhon was concealed, Ægypt commences. This
tract, which comprehends the city Jenyſus, mount
Caſius, and the lake of Serbonis, is of no trifling

---

[6] *Jenyſus.*]—Stephanus Byzantinus calls this city Inys, for
that is manifeſtly the name he gives it, if we take away the
Greek termination. But Herodotus, from whom he borrows,
renders it Jenis. It would have been more truly rendered Do-
rice Janis, for that was nearer to the real name. The hiſtorian, however, points it out plainly by ſaying, that it was three
days journey from mount Caſius, and that the whole way was
through the Arabian deſert.—*Bryant.*

Mr. Bryant is certainly miſtaken with reſpect to the ſituation
of this place. It was an Arabian town, on this ſide lake Serbonis compared with Syria, on the other compared with Ægypt.
When Herodotus ſays that this place was three days journey
from mount Caſius, he muſt be underſtood as ſpeaking of the
Syrian ſide; if otherwiſe, Cambyſes could not have been ſo
embarraſſed from a want of water, &c.—See Larcher farther
on this ſubject.

[7] *Mount Caſius.*]—This place is now called by ſeamen mount
Tenère; here anciently was a temple ſacred to Jupiter Caſius;
in this mountain alſo was Pompey the Great buried, as ſome affirm, being murdered at its foot. This, however, is not true, his
body was burnt on the ſhore by one of his freedmen, with the
planks of an old fiſhing-boat, and his aſhes being conveyed to
Rome, were depoſited privately by his wife Cornelia in a vault
of his Alban villa.—*See Middleton's Life of Cicero.*—*T.*

conftantly adopted to provide themfelves with water
in thefe deferts, from the time that they were firft
mafters of Ægypt. But as, at the time of which we
fpeak, they had not this refource, Cambyfes liftened
to the advice of his Halicarnaffian gueft, and folicited of the Arabian prince a fafe paffage through his
territories; which was granted, after mutual pro-
mifes of friendfhip.

VIII. Thefe are the ceremonies which the Arabians obferve when they make alliances, of which no
people in the world are more tenacious?. On thefe
occafions fome one connected with both parties ftands
betwixt them, and with a fharp ftone opens a vein
of the hand, near the middle finger, of thofe who
are about to contract. He then takes a piece of
the veft of each perfon, and dips it in their blood,
with which he ftains feveral ftones purpofely placed
in the midft of the affembly, invoking during the
procefs Bacchus and Urania. ' When this is finifhed, he who folicits the compact to be made

---

? *Tenacious.*]—How faithful the Arabs are at this day, when
they have pledged themfelves to be fo, is a topic of admiration
and of praife with all modern travellers. They who once put
themfelves under their protection have nothing afterwards to
fear, for their word is facred. Singular as the mode here defcribed of forming alliances may appear to an Englifh reader,
that of taking an oath by putting the hand under the thigh, in
ufe amongft the patriarchs, was furely not lefs fo.

f' Abraham faid unto the eldeft fervant of his houfe that ruled
over all that he had, Put, I pray thee, thy hand under my
thigh." Gen. xxiv. 2.—*T.*

pledges

pledges his friends for the fincerity of his engagements to the ftranger or citizen, or whoever it
may happen to be; and all of them conceive an
indifpenfable neceffity to exift of performing what
they promife. Bacchus and Urania are the only
deities whom they venerate. They cut off their
hair round their temples, from the fuppofition that
Bacchus wore his in that form; him they call
Urotalt, Urania, Alilat [19].

IX. When the Arabian prince had made an alliance with the meffengers of Cambyfes, he ordered
all his camels to be laden with camel fkins filled
with water, and to be driven to the deferts, there
to wait the arrival of Cambyfes and his army. Of
this incident the above feems to me the more probable narrative. There is alfo another, which,
however I may difbelieve, I think I ought not to
omit. In Arabia is a large river called Corys,
which lofes itfelf in the Red Sea: from this river
the Arabian is faid to have formed a canal of the
fkins of oxen and other animals fewed together,
which was continued to the above-mentioned deferts, where he alfo funk a number of cifterns to
receive the water fo introduced. From the river
to the defert is a journey of twelve days; and they
fay that the water was conducted by three diftinct
canals into as many different places.

[19] *Alilat.*]—According to Selden, in his treatife de Diis Syris,
the Mitra of the Perfians is the fame with the Alitta or Alilat
of the Arabians.—*T.*

X. At the Pelufian mouth of the Nile Pfammenitus, the fon of Amafis, was encamped, and expected Cambyfes in arms. Amafis himfelf, after a
reign of forty-four years, died before Cambyfes had
advanced to Ægypt, and during the whole enjoyment of his power he experienced no extraordinary
calamity. At his death his body was embalmed,
and depofited in a fepulchre which he had erected
for himfelf in the temple of Minerva ". During
the reign of his fon Pfammenitus Ægypt beheld a
moft remarkable prodigy; there was rain at the
Ægyptian Thebes, a circumftance which never
happened before, and which, as the Thebans themfelves affert, has never occurred fince. In the
higher parts of Ægypt it never rains, but at that
period we read it rained at Thebes in diftinct
drops ".

XI. The Perfians having paffed the deferts, fixed
their camp oppofite to the Ægyptians, as with the
defign of offering them battle. The Greeks and
Carians, who were the confederates of the Ægyp-

" *Temple of Minerva.*]—This is not expreffed in the original
text, but it was evident that it is in the temple of Minerva,
from chap. clxix. of the fecond book.—*T.*

" *In diftinct drops.*]—Herodotus is perhaps thus particular, to
diftinguifh rain from mift.

It is a little remarkable that all the mention which Herodotus
makes of the ancient Thebes, is in this paffage, and in this flight
manner. In book ii. chap. xv. he informs us that all Ægypt
was formerly called Thebes.—*T.*

tians, to fhew their refentment againft Phanes, for introducing a foreign army againft Ægypt, adopted this expedient: his fons, whom he had left behind, they brought into the camp, and in a confpicuous place, in the fight of their father, they put them one by one to death upon a veffel brought thither for that purpofe. When they had done this, they filled the vafe which had received the blood with wine and water; having drank which[1], all the auxiliaries immediately engaged the enemy. The battle was obftinately difputed, but after confiderable lofs on both fides, the Ægyptians fled.

XII. By the people inhabiting the place where this battle was fought a very furprizing thing was pointed out to my attention. The bones of thofe who fell in the engagement were foon afterwards collected, and feparated into two diftinct heaps. It was obferved of the Perfians, that their heads were fo extremely foft as to yield to the flight impreffion even of a pebble; thofe of the Ægyptians, on the contrary, were fo firm, that the blow of a large ftone could hardly break them. The reafon which they

[1] *Having drank which.*]—They probably fwore at the fame time to avenge the treafon of Phanes, or perifh. The blood of an human victim mixed with wine accompanied the moft folemn form of execration among the ancients. Catiline made ufe of this fuperftition to bind his adherents to fecrecy: "He carried round," fays Salluft, "the blood of an human victim, mixed with wine; and when all had tafted it, after a fet form of execration (ficut in folennibus facris fieri confuevit) he imparted his defign."—*T.*

gave

gave for this was very fatisfactory—the Ægyptians from a very early age fhave their heads [14], which by being conftantly expofed to the action of the fun, become firm and hard; this treatment alfo prevents baldnefs, very few inftances of which are ever to be feen in Ægypt. Why the fkulls of the Perfians are fo foft may be explained from their being from their infancy accuftomed to fhelter from the fun, by their conftant ufe of turbans. I faw the very fame fact at Papremis, after examining the bones of thofe who, under the conduct of Achæmenes [15], fon of Darius, were defeated by Inaros the African.

XIII. The Ægyptians after their defeat fled in great diforder to Memphis. Cambyfes difpatched a Perfian up the river in a Mitylenian veffel to treat with them; but as foon as they faw the veffel enter Memphis, they rufhed in a croud from the citadel, deftroyed

[14] *Shave their heads.*]—The fame cuftom ftill fubfifts: I have feen every where the children of the common people, whether running in the fields, affembled round the villages, or fwimming in the waters, with their heads fhaved and bare. Let us but imagine the hardnefs a fkull muft acquire thus expofed to the fcorching fun, and we fhall not be aftonifhed at the remark of Herodotus.—*Savary.*

[15] *Achæmenes.*]—Herodotus and Diodorus Siculus fay, that it was Achæmenes, the brother of Xerxes, and uncle of Artaxerxes, the fame who before had the government of Ægypt in the beginning of the reign of Xerxes, that had the conduct of this war; but herein they were deceived by the fimilitude of names; for it appears by Ctefias, that he was the fon of Hameftris, whom Artaxerxes fent with his army into Ægypt.—*Prideaux.*

the veffel, tore the crew in pieces [16], and afterwards carried them into the citadel. Siege was immediately laid to the place, and the Ægyptians were finally compelled to furrender. Thofe Africans who lived neareft to Ægypt, apprehenfive of a fimilar fate, fubmitted without conteft, impofing a tribute on themfelves, and fending prefents to the Perfians. Their example was followed by the Cyreneans and Barceans, who were ftruck with the like panic. The African prefents Cambyfes received very gracioufly, but he expreffed much refentment at thofe of the Cyreneans, as I think, on account of their meannefs. They fent him five hundred minæ of filver, which, as foon as he received, with his own hands he threw amongft his foldiers.

XIV. On the tenth day after the furrender of the citadel of Memphis, Pfammenitus, the Ægyptian king, who had reigned no more than fix months, was by order of Cambyfes ignominioufly conducted, with other Ægyptians, to the outfide of the walls, and by way of trial of his difpofition, thus treated: His daughter, in the habit of a flave, was fent with a pitcher to draw water; fhe was accompanied by a number of young women clothed in the fame garb, and felected from families of the firft diftinction. They paffed, with much and loud lamentation,

---

[16] *Tore the crew in pieces.*]—They were two hundred in number; this appears from a following paragraph, where we find that for every Mitylenian maffacred on this occafion ten Ægyptians were put to death, and that two thoufand Ægyptians thus perifhed.—*Larcher.*

before

before their parents, from whom their treatment excited a correspondent violence of grief. But when Psammenitus beheld the spectacle, he merely declined his eyes upon the ground; when this train was gone by, the son of Psammenitus, with two thousand Ægyptians of the same age, were made to walk in procession with ropes round their necks, and bridles in their mouths. These were intended to avenge the death of those Mitylenians who, with their vessel, had been torn to pieces at Memphis. The king's counsellors had determined that for every one put to death on that occasion ten of the first rank of the Ægyptians should be sacrificed. Psammenitus observed these as they passed, but although he perceived that his son was going to be executed, and whilst all the Ægyptians around him wept and lamented aloud, he continued unmoved as before. When this scene also disappeared, he beheld a venerable personage, who had formerly partaken of the royal table, deprived of all he had possessed, and in the dress of a mendicant asking charity through the different ranks of the army. This man stopped to beg an alms of Psammenitus, the son of Amasis, and the other noble Ægyptians who were sitting with him; which, when Psammenitus beheld, he could no longer suppress his emotions, but calling on his friend by name, wept aloud [17], and beat his head. This the spies, who

were

---

[17] *Wept aloud.*]—A very strange effect of grief is related by Mr. Gibbon, in the story of Gelimer, king of the Vandals, when after an obstinate resistance he was obliged to surrender himself to Belisarius.

were placed near him to obferve his conduct on
each incident, reported to Cambyfes; who, in aftonifhment at fuch behaviour, fent a meffenger,
who was thus directed to addrefs him, "Your
" lord and mafter, Cambyfes, is defirous to know
" why, after beholding with fo much indifference
" your daughter treated as a flave, and your fon
" conducted to death, you expreffed fo lively a con-
" cern for that mendicant, who, as he has been in-
" formed, is not at all related to you?" Pfammenitus
made this reply: " Son of Cyrus, my domeftic mis-
" fortunes were too great to fuffer me to fhed tears ";
" but

Belifarius. " The firft public interview," fays our hiftorian, "was
in one of the fuburbs of Carthage; and when the royal captive
accofted his conqueror, he burft into a fit of laughter. The
croud might naturally believe that extreme grief had deprived
Gelimer of his fenfes; but in this mournful ftate unfeafonable
mirth infinuated to more intelligent obfervers that the vain and
tranfitory fcenes of human greatnefs are unworthy of a ferious
thought."

" Shed tears.]—This idea of extreme affliction or anger
tending to check the act of weeping, is expreffed by Shakefpeare
with wonderful fublimity and pathos. It is part of a fpeech of
Lear:

You fee me here, ye gods, a poor old man,
As full of grief as age, wretched in both.
If it be you that ftir thefe daughters hearts
Againft their father, fool me not fo much
To bear it tamely: Touch me with noble anger,
And let not women's weapons, water drops,
Stain my man's cheeks. No, you unnatural hags,
I will have fuch revenges on you both
That all the world fhall——I will do fuch things,

What

" but it was confiftent that I fhould weep for my
" friend, who, from a ftation of honour and of wealth,
" is in the laft ftage of life reduced to penury." Cambyfes heard and was fatisfied with his anfwer. The
Ægyptians fay that Crœfus, who attended Cambyfes in this Ægyptian expedition, wept at the incident. The Perfians alfo who were prefent were
exceedingly moved, and Cambyfes himfelf yielded
fo far to compaffion, that he ordered the fon of
Pfammenitus to be preferved out of thofe who had
been condemned to die, and Pfammenitus himfelf
to be conducted from the place where he was, to his
prefence.

XV. The emiffaries employed for the purpofe
found the young prince had fuffered firft, and was
already dead; the father they led to Cambyfes, with
whom he lived, and received no farther ill treatment; and, could he have refrained from ambitious
attempts, would probably have been intrufted with
the government of Ægypt. The Perfians hold the
fons of fovereigns in the greateft reverence, and
even if the fathers revolt they will permit the fons
to fucceed to their authority; that fuch is really
their conduct may be proved by various examples.

> What they are yet I know not, but they fhall be
> The terrors of the earth.——You think I'll weep—
> No, I'll not weep. I have full caufe of weeping;
> But this heart fhall break into a hundred thoufand flaws
> Or e'er I weep. *T.*

Thannyras

Thannyras the fon of Inarus [19], received the kingdom which his father governed; Paufiris alfo, the
fon of Amyrtæus, was permitted to reign after his
father, although the Perfians had never met with
more obftinate enemies than both Inarus and Amyrtæus. Pfammenitus revolted, and fuffered for his
offence: he was detected in ftirring up the Ægyptians to rebel; and being convicted by Cambyfes,
was made to drink a quantity of bullock's blood [20],
which immediately occafioned his death.—Such
was the end of Pfammenitus.

XVI. From Sais, Cambyfes proceeded to Memphis, to execute a purpofe he had in view. As
foon as he entered the palace of Amafis, he ordered
the body of that prince to be removed from his

[19] *Inarus.*]—The revolt of Inarus happened in the firft year
of the 80th Olympiad, 460 before the Chriftian æra. He rebelled againft Artaxerxes Longimanus, and with the affiftance of
the Athenians defied the power of Perfia for nearly five years.
After he was reduced, Amyrtæus held out for fome time longer
in the marfhy country.—The particulars may be found in the
firft book of Thucydides, chap. civ. &c.

[20] *Bullock's blood.*]—Bull's blood, taken frefh from the animal,
was confidered by the ancients as a powerful poifon, and fuppofed to act by coagulating in the ftomach. Themiftocles, and
feveral other perfonages of antiquity, were faid to have died by
taking it.—See Plut. in Themift. and Pliny, book xxviii. ch. ix.
Ariftophanes, in the Ἱππεῖς, alludes to this account of the death
of Themiftocles.

Βίλτιρον ἡμῖν αἷμα ταύρειον πιεῖν
Ὁ Θεμιστοκλέυς γὰρ θάνατος αἱρετώτερος.

tomb.

tomb. When this was done, he commanded it to
be beaten with rods, the hair to be plucked out,
and the flesh to be goaded with sharp instruments,
to which he added other marks of ignominy. As
the body was embalmed, their efforts made but
little impression; when therefore they were fatigued
with these outrages, he ordered it to be burned. In
this last act Cambyses paid no regard to the religion
of his country, for the Persians venerate fire as a
divinity [21]. The custom of burning the dead does
not prevail in either of the two nations; for the reason above mentioned, the Persians do not use it,
thinking it profane to feed a divinity with human
carcases; and the Ægyptians abhor it, being fully
persuaded that fire is a voracious animal, which
devours whatever it can seize, and when saturated
finally expires with what it has consumed. They
hold it unlawful to expose the bodies of the dead [22]

to

[21] *Venerate fire as a divinity.*]—This expression must not be
understood in too rigorous a sense. Fire was certainly regarded
by the Persians as something sacred, and perhaps they might
render it some kind of religious worship, which in its origin referred only to the deity of which this element was an emblem.
But it is certain that this nation did not believe fire to be a
deity, otherwise how would they have dared to have extinguished it throughout Persia, on the death of the sovereign, as we
learn from Diodorus Siculus?—See an epigram of Dioscorides,
Brunk's Analecta, vol. i. 503.—*Larcher.*

[22] *Bodies of the dead.*]—We learn from Xenophon, that the
interment of bodies was common in Greece; and Homer tells us
that the custom of burning the dead was in use before the Trojan war. It is therefore probable that both customs were practised at the same time; this was also the case at Rome, as appears

from

to any animals, for which reason they embalm them, fearing lest, after interment, they might become the prey of worms. The Ægyptians assert, that the above indignities were not inflicted upon the body of Amasis, but that the Persians were deceived, and perpetrated these insults on some other Ægyptian of the same age with that prince. Amasis, they say, was informed by an oracle of the injuries intended against his body, to prevent which he ordered the person who really sustained them, to be buried at the entrance of his tomb, whilst he himself, by his own directions given to his son, was placed in some secret and interior recess of the sepulchre. These assertions I cannot altogether believe, and am rather inclined to impute them to the vanity of the Ægyptians.

---

from many ancient monuments: the custom, however, of interment, seems to have preceded that of burning. " At mihi quidem antiquissimum sepulturæ genus id fuisse videtur quo apud Xenophontem Cyrus utitur. Redditur enim terræ corpus et ita locatum et situm quasi operimento matris obducitur."—*Cicero de legibus*, lib. ii. 22.

" That seems to me to have been the most ancient kind of burial, which, according to Xenophon, was used by Cyrus. For the body is returned to the earth, and so placed as to be covered with the veil of its mother." The custom of burning at Rome, according to Montfaucon, ceased about the time of Theodosius the younger.

Sylla was the first of the Cornelian family whose body was burnt, whence some have erroneously advanced that he was the first Roman; but both methods were mentioned in the laws of the twelve tables, and appear to have been equally prevalent. After Sylla, burning became general.—*T.*

XVII.

XVII. Cambyfes afterwards determined to commence hoftilities againft three nations at once,
the Carthaginians, the Ammonians, and the Macrobian * Æthiopians, who inhabit that part of
Lybia which lies towards the fouthern ocean.
He accordingly refolved to fend againft the Carthaginians a naval armament; a detachment of his
troops was to attack the Ammonians by land; and
he fent fpies into Æthiopia, who, under pretence of
carrying prefents to the prince, were to afcertain the
reality of the celebrated table of the fun ¹¹, and to
examine the condition of the country.

XVIII. What they called the table of the fun
was this:—A plain in the vicinity of the city was
filled to the height of four feet with the roafted
flefh of all kinds of animals, which was carried
there in the night, under the infpection of the magiftrates; during the day whoever pleafed was at
liberty to go and fatisfy his hunger. The natives
of the place affirm, that the earth fpontaneoufly produces all thefe viands: this, however, is what they
term the table of the fun.

---

* i. e. long-lived.

²³ *Table of the fun.*]—Solinus fpeaks of this table of the fun
as fomething marvellous, and Pomponius Mela feems to have
had the fame idea. Paufanias confiders what was reported of
it as fabulous. "If," fays he, "we credit all thefe mar-
vels on the faith of the Greeks, we ought alfo to receive as true
what the Æthiopians above Syene relate of the table of the
fun." In adhering to the recital of Herodotus, a confiderable
portion of the marvellous difappears.—*Larcher.*

C 3

XIX.

XIX. As soon as Cambyfes had refolved on the meafures he meant to purfue, with refpect to the Æthiopians, he fent to the city of Elephantine for fome of the Ichthyophagi who were fkilled in their language. In the mean time he directed his naval forces to proceed againft the Carthaginians; but the Phœnicians refufed to affift him in this purpofe, pleading the folemnity of their engagements with that people, and the impiety of committing acts of violence againft their own defcendants.—Such was the conduct of the Phœnicians, and the other armaments were not powerful enough to proceed. Thus, therefore, the Carthaginians efcaped being made tributary to Perfia, for Cambyfes did not choofe to ufe compulfion with the Phœnicians, who had voluntarily become his dependants, and who conftituted the moft effential part of his naval power, The Cyprians had alfo fubmitted without conteft to the Perfians, and had ferved in the Ægyptian expedition,

XX. As foon as the Ichthyophagi arrived from Elephantine, Cambyfes difpatched them to Æthiopia. They were commiffioned to deliver, with certain prefents, a particular meffage to the prince. The prefents confifted of a purple veft, a gold chain for the neck, bracelets, an alabafter box of perfumes [24], and a cafk of palm wine. The Æthiopians

---

[24] *Alabafter box of perfumes.*]—It feems probable that perfumes in more ancient times were kept in fhells. Arabia is the country of perfumes, and the Red Sea throws upon the coaft a number

Æthiopians to whom Cambyſes ſent, are reported
to be ſuperior to all other men in the perfections
of ſize and beauty : their manners and cuſtoms,
which differ alſo from thoſe of all other nations,
have beſides this ſingular diſtinction ; the ſupreme
authority is given to him who excels all his fellow
citizens [25] in ſize and proportionable ſtrength.

XXI.

number of large and beautiful ſhells, very convenient for ſuch a
purpoſe.—See Horace :

Funde capacibus
Unguenta de conchis.

That to make a preſent of perfumes was deemed a mark of
reverence and honour in the remoteſt times amongſt the Orientals, appears from the following paſſage in Daniel.

" Then the king Nebuchadnezzar fell upon his face and
worſhipped Daniel, and commanded that they ſhould offer an
oblation and ſweet odours to him."

See alſo St. Mark, xiv. 3 :

" There came a woman having an alabaſter box of ointment
of ſpikenard, very precious ; and ſhe brake the box, and poured
it on his head."

See alſo Matth. xxvi. 7.

To ſprinkle the apartments and the perſons of the gueſts with
roſe-water, and other aromatics, ſtill continues in the Eaſt to be
a mark of reſpectful attention.

Alabaſtron did not properly ſignify a veſſel made of the ſtone
now called alabaſter, but one without handles, μη εχον λαϐας.

Alabaſter obtained its name from being frequently uſed for
this purpoſe ; the ancient name for the ſtone was *alabaſtrites,*
and perfumes were thought to keep better in it than in any
other ſubſtance. Pliny has informed us of the ſhape of theſe
veſſels, by comparing to them the pearls called elenchi, which
are known to have been ſhaped like pears, or, as he expreſſes it,
faſtigiatâ longitudine, alabaſtrorum figura, in pleniorem orbem
deſinentes. lib. ix. cap. 35.—*T.*

[25] *Who excels all his fellow citizens, &c.*]—That the quality of

XXI. The Ichthyophagi on their arrival offered the prefents, and thus addreffed the king: " Cambyfes, fovereign of Perfia, from his anxious defire " of becoming your friend and ally, has fent us to " communicate with you, and to defire your accep- " tance of thefe prefents, from the ufe of which he " himfelf derives the greateft pleafure." The Æthiopian prince, who was aware of the object they had in view, made them this anfwer:—" The king of " Perfia has not fent you with thefe prefents, from " any defire of obtaining my alliance; neither do you " fpeak the truth, who, to facilitate the unjuft de- " figns of your mafter, are come to examine the ftate " of my dominions: if he were influenced by prin- " ciples of integrity, he would be fatisfied with his " own, and not covet the poffeffions of another; nor " would he attempt to reduce thofe to fervitude " from whom he has received no injury. Give him " therefore this bow, and in my name fpeak to him " thus: The king of Æthiopia fends this counfel to " the king of Perfia—when his fubjects fhall be " able to bend this bow with the fame eafe that I " do, then with a fuperiority of numbers he may " venture to attack the Macrobian Æthiopians. In

---

ftrength and accomplifhments of perfon were in the firft infti- tution of fociety the principal recommendations to honour, is thus reprefented by Lucretius:

> Condere cæperunt urbeis, arcemque locare
> Præfidium reges ipfi fibi perfugiumque:
> Et pecudes et agros divifere atque dedere
> Pro facie cujufque, et viribus ingenioque
> Nam facies multum valuit, virefque vigebant.　　T.

" the

" the mean time let him be thankful to the gods, that
" the Æthiopians have not been infpired with the
" fame ambitious views of extending their poffef-
" fions."

XXII. When he had finifhed, he unbent the
bow and placed it in their hands; after which, taking the purple veft, he enquired what it was, and
how it was made: the Ichthyophagi properly explained to him the procefs by which the purple
tincture was communicated; but he told them that
they and their vefts were alike deceitful. He then
made fimilar enquiries concerning the bracelets and
the gold chain for the neck: upon their defcribing
the nature of thofe ornaments, he laughed; and conceiving them to be chains [26], remarked, that the
Æthiopians

---

[26] *Conceiving them to be chains.*]—We learn from a paffage
in Genefis, xxiv. 22, that the bracelets of the Orientals were
remarkably heavy; which feems in fome meafure to juftify
the fentiment of the Æthiopian prince, who thought them
chains fimply becaufe they were made of gold, which was ufed
for that purpofe in his country.—See chap. xxiii.

" And it came to pafs as the camels had done drinking, that
the man took a golden ear-ring of half a fhekel weight, and two
bracelets for her hands, of ten fhekels weight of gold."

That the bracelet was formerly an enfign of royalty amongft
the Orientals, Mr. Harmer, in his Obfervations on Paffages of
Scripture, infers from the circumftance of the Amalekites bringing to David the bracelet which he found on Saul's arm, along
with his crown. That it was a mark of dignity there can be
little doubt; but it by no means follows that it was a mark of
royalty, though the remark is certainly ingenious. If it was,
there exifted a peculiar propriety in making it the part of a
prefent from one prince to another. By the Roman generals
they were given to their foldiers, as a reward of bravery. Small
chains

Æthiopians poſſeſſed much ſtronger, He proceeded laſtly to aſk them the uſe of the perfumes;
and when they informed him how they were made
and applied, he made the ſame obſervation as he
had before done of the purple robe [27]. When he
came to the wine, and learned how it was made, he

chains were alſo in the remoteſt times worn round the neck, not
only by women but by the men. That theſe were alſo worn by
princes appears from Judges, viii. 26.

" And the weight of the golden ear-rings that he requeſted,
was a thouſand and ſeven hundred ſhekels of gold; beſide ornaments, and *collars*, and purple raiment that was on the kings of
Midian; and beſide the chains that were about their camels
necks." Which laſt circumſtance tends alſo to prove that they
thus alſo decorated the animals they uſed, which faſhion is to
this day obſerved by people of diſtinction in Ægypt.—*T.*

[27] *Purple robe.*]—It is a circumſtance well known at preſent
that on the coaſt of Guagaquil as well as on that of Guatima,
are found thoſe ſnails which yield the purple dye ſo celebrated
by the ancients, and which the moderns have ſuppoſed to have
been loſt. The ſhell that contains them is fixed to rocks that
are watered by the ſea; it is of the ſize of a large nut. The
juice may be extracted from the animal in two ways; ſome perſons kill the animal after they have taken it out of the ſhell, they
then preſs it from the head to the tail with a knife, and ſeparating from the body that part in which the liquor is collected, they
throw away the reſt. When this operation, repeated upon ſeveral
of the ſnails, hath yielded a certain quantity of the juice, the
thread that is to be dyed is dipped in it, and the buſineſs is done.
The colour, which is at firſt as white as milk, becomes afterwards green, and does not turn purple till the thread is dry.
We know of no colour that can be compared to the one we
have been ſpeaking of, either in luſtre or in permanency.—
Raynal.

Pliny deſcribes the *purpura* as a turbinated ſhell like the buc-
cinum, but with ſpines upon it; which may lead us to ſuſpect the
Abbé's account of the ſnails of a little inaccuracy.—*T.*

drank

drank it with particular fatisfaction; and enquired
upon what food the Perfian monarch fubfifted, and
what was the longeft period of a Perfian's life. The
king, they told him, lived chiefly upon bread; and
they then defcribed to him the properties of corn:
they added, that the longeft period of life in Perfia
was about eighty years. " I am not at all furprized," faid the Æthiopian prince, " that, fubfifting on
" dung, the term of life is fo fhort among them;
" and unlefs," he continued, pointing to the wine,
" they mixed it with this liquor, they would not
" live fo long:" for in this he allowed that they
excelled the Æthiopians.

XXIII. The Ichthyophagi in their turn quef-
tioned the prince concerning the duration of life in
Æthiopia, and the kind of food there in ufe:—They
were told, that the majority of the people lived to
the age of one hundred and twenty years, but that
fome exceeded even that period; that their meat
was baked flefh, their drink milk.   When the fpies
expreffed aftonifhment at the length of life in Æthiopia, they were conducted to a certain fountain, in
which having bathed, they became fhining as if
anointed with oil, and diffufed from their bodies
the perfume of violets.   But they afferted that the
water of this fountain was of fo infubftantial a nature, that neither wood, nor any thing ftill lighter
than wood, would float upon its furface, but every
thing inftantly funk to the bottom.   If their reprefentation of this water was true, the conftant ufe of
it may probably explain the extreme length of life

which the Æthiopians attain.   From the fountain
they were conducted to the public prifon, where all
that were confined were fecured by chains of gold;
for among thefe Æthiopians brafs is the rareft of all
the metals.   After vifiting the prifon they faw alfo
what is called the table of the fun.

XXIV. Finally they wer[e] fhewn their coffins [28],
which are faid to be conftru[ct]ed of cryftal, and in
this manner:—After all the moifture is exhaufted
from

[28] *Coffins.*]—Coffins, though a[s]
confidered as marks of diftinction
the dead either by Turks or Ch[r]

" With us," fays Mr. Ha[rmer]
of Scripture, " the pooreft p[eo]ple have th[ei]r
tions cannot afford them, the p[oor]
Eaft, on the contrary, they ar[e not]
Turks and Chriftians, Thevenot a[ffures]
ancient Jews probably buried their d[ead]
neither was the body of our Lord,
coffin, nor that of Elifha, whofe bon[es]   the
corpfe that was let down a little after into his fepulchre, 2 Kings,
xiii. 21.   That they, however, were anciently made [us]e of in
Ægypt, all agree; and antique coffins, of ftone and fycamore
wood, are ftill to be feen in that country, not to mention thofe
faid to be made of a kind of pafte-board, formed by folding and
glewing cloth together a great number of times, which were cu-
rioufly plaiftered, and then painted with hieroglyphics.   Its being
an ancient Ægyptian cuftom, and its not being ufed in the neighbouring countries, were doubtlefs the caufe that the facred hiftorian exprefsly obferves of Jofeph, that he was not only embalmed, but put into a coffin too, both being managements peculiar in
a manner to the Ægyptians."—*Obfervations on Paffages of Scripture*, vol. ii. 154.

Mr. Harmer's obfervation in the foregoing note is not ftrictly
true.

from the body, by the Ægyptian or some other procefs, they cover it totally with a kind of plafter,
which they decorate with various colours, and make
it convey as near a refemblance as may be of the
perfon of the deceafed. They then inclofe it in a
hollow pillar of cryftal [19], which is dug up in great
abundance,

true. The ufe of coffins might very probably be unknown in
Syria, from whence Jofeph came ; but that they were ufed by all
nations contiguous on one fide at leaft to Ægypt, the paffage before us proves fufficiently. I have not been able to afcertain at
what period the ufe of coffins was introduced in this country, but it appears from the following paffage of our celebrated antiquary Mr. Strutt, that from very remote times
our anceftors were interred in fome kind of coffin. "It was
cuftomary in the Chriftian burials of the Anglo Saxons to
leave the head and fhoulders of the corpfe uncovered till the
time of burial, that relations, &c. might take a laft view of their
deceafed friend." We have alfo the following in Durant, "Corpus totum at fudore obvolutum ac locuto conditum veteres in
cœnaculis, feu tricliniis exponebant."

We learn from a paffage in Strabo, that there was a temple at
Alexandria, in which the body of Alexander was depofited, in
coffin of gold ; it was ftolen by Seleucus Cybiofactes, who
a coffin of glafs in its place. This is the only author, except
Herodotus, in whom I can remember to have feen mention made
of a coffin of glafs. The urns of ancient Rome, in which the
afhes of the dead were depofited, were indifferently made of
gold, filver, brafs, alabafter, porphyry, and marble ; thefe were
externally ornamented according to the rank of the deceafed.
A minute defcription of thefe, with a multitude of fpecimens,
may be feen in Montfaucon.—T.

[19] Pillar of cryftal.]—"Our glafs," fays M. Larcher, "is
not the production of the earth, it muft be manufactured with
much trouble." According to Ludolf, they find in fome parts
of Æthiopia large quantities of foffil falt, which is tranfparent,
and

abundance, and of a kind that is easily worked. The deceased is very conspicuous through the crystal, has no disagreeable smell, nor any thing else that is offensive. This coffin the nearest relations keep for a twelvemonth in their houses, offering before it different kinds of victims, and the first-fruits of their lands; these are afterwards removed and set up round the city.

XXV. The spies, after executing their commission, returned; and Cambyses was so exasperated at their recital, that he determined instantly to proceed against the Æthiopians, without ever providing for the necessary sustenance of his army, or reflecting that he was about to visit the extremities of the earth. The moment that he heard the report of the Ichthyophagi, like one deprived of all the powers of reason, he commenced his march with the whole body of his infantry, leaving no forces behind but such Greeks as had accompanied him to Ægypt. On his arrival at Thebes, he selected from his army about fifty thousand men, whom he ordered to make an incursion against the Ammonians, and to burn the place from whence the oracles of Jupiter were delivered: he himself, with the remainder of his

and which indurates in the air: this is perhaps what they took for glass.

We have the testimony of the Scholiast on Aristophanes, that ὑαλος, though afterwards used for glass, signified anciently crystal: as therefore Herodotus informs us that this substance was digged from the earth, why should we hesitate to translate it crystal?—*T.*

troops,

troops, marched againſt the Æthiopians. Before
he had performed a fifth part of his intended expedition, the proviſions he had with him were totally
conſumed. They proceeded to eat the beaſts which
carried the baggage, till theſe alſo failed. If after
theſe incidents Cambyſes had permitted his paſſions
to cool, and had led his army back again, notwithſtanding his indiſcretion he ſtill might have deſerved
praiſe. Inſtead of this, his infatuation continued,
and he proceeded on his march. The ſoldiers,
as long as the earth afforded them any ſuſtenance,
were content to feed on vegetables; but as ſoon
as they arrived among the ſands and the deſerts,
ſome of them were prompted by famine to proceed
to the moſt horrid extremities. They drew lots,
and every tenth man was deſtined to ſatisfy the
hunger of the reſt [10]. When Cambyſes received
intelligence of this faſt, alarmed at the idea of de-
vouring one another, he abandoned his deſigns upon

---

[10] *Satisfy the hunger of the reſt.*]—The whole of this narrative is tranſcribed by Seneca with ſome little variation, in his
treatiſe *de Irâ*; who in the concluſion adds, though we know not
from what authority, that notwithſtanding theſe dreadful ſuffer-
ings of his troops, the king's table was ſerved with abundance
of delicacies. Servabantur interim illi generoſæ aves et inſtru-
menta epularum camelis vehebantur.

Perhaps the moſt horrid example on record of ſuffering from
famine, is the deſcription given by Joſephus of the ſiege of Je-
ruſalem. Eleven thouſand priſoners were ſtarved to death after
the capture of the city, during the ſtorm. Whilſt the Romans
were engaged in pillage, on entering ſeveral houſes they found
whole families dead, and the houſes crammed with ſtarved car-
caſes; but what is ſtill more ſhocking, it was a notorious faſt,
that a mother killed, dreſſed, and eat her own child.—*T.*

the

the Æthiopians, and returning homeward arrived at length at Thebes, after lofing a confiderable number of his men. From Thebes he proceeded to Memphis, from whence he permitted the Greeks to embark.—Such was the termination of the Æthiopian expedition.

XXVI. The troops who were difpatched againft the Ammonians left Thebes with guides, and penetrated, as it fhould feem, as far as Oafis. This place is diftant from Thebes about a feven days journey over the fands, and is faid to be inhabited by Samians, of the Æfchryonian tribe. The country is called in Greek, " The happy Iflands." The army is reported to have proceeded thus far; but what afterwards became of them it is impoffible to know, except from the Ammonians, or thofe whom the Ammonians have inftructed on this head. It is certain that they never arrived among the Ammonians, and that they never returned[1]. The Ammonians affirm, that as they were marching forwards from Oafis through the fands, they halted at fome place of middle diftance, for the purpofe of taking repaft, which whilft they were doing, a ftrong fouth wind

---

[1] *Never returned.*]—The route of the army makes it plain that the guides, who detefted the Perfians, led them aftray amidft the deferts; for they fhould have departed from the lake Mareotis to this temple, or from the environs of Memphis. The Ægyptians, intending the deftruction of their enemies, led them from Thebes to the great Oafis, three days journey from Abydus; and having brought them into the vaft folitudes of Lybia, they no doubt abandoned them in the night, and delivered them over to death.—*Savary.*

arofe,

arofe, and overwhelmed them beneath a mountain of fand [12], fo that they were feen no more.—
Such, as the Ammonians relate, was the fate of
this army.

XXVII. Soon after the return of Cambyfes to
Memphis, the god Apis appeared, called by the
Greeks Epaphus [13]. Upon this occafion the Ægyptians clothed themfelves in their richeft apparel, and
made great rejoicings. Cambyfes took notice of this,
and imagined it was done on account of his late unfortunate projects. He ordered, therefore, the magiftrates of Memphis to attend him; and he afked
them why they had done nothing of this kind when
he was formerly at Memphis, and had only made

[12] *Mountain of fand.*]—What happens at prefent in performing this journey, proves the event to be very credible. Travellers, departing from the fertile valley lying under the tropic,
march feven days before they come to the firft town in Æthiopia. They find their way in the day-time by looking at marks,
and at night by obferving the ftars. The fand-hills they had
obferved on the preceding journey having often been carried away by the winds, deceive the guides; and if they
wander the leaft out of the road, the camels, having paffed five
or fix days without drinking, fink under their burden, and die:
the men are not long before they fubmit to the fame fate, and
fometimes, out of a great number, not a fingle traveller efcapes;
at others the burning winds from the fouth raife vortexes of duft,
which fuffocate man and beaft, and the next caravan fees the
ground ftrewed with bodies totally parched up.—*Savary.*

[13] *Epaphus.*]—Epaphus was the fon of Io, the daughter of
Inachus. The Greeks pretended he was the fame perfon as the
god Apis; this the Ægyptians rejected as fabulous, and afferted that Epaphus was pofterior to Apis by many centuries.

rejoicings now that he had returned with the loss of so many of his troops. They told him, that their deity [14] had appeared to them, which after a long absence

---

[14] *Their deity.*]—It is probable that Apis was not always confidered as a deity; perhaps they regarded him as a fymbol of Ofiris, and it was from this that the Ægyptians were induced to pay him veneration. Others affert confidently that he was the fame as Ofiris; and fome have faid, that Ofiris having been killed by Typhon, Ifis inclofed his limbs in an heifer made of wood. Apis was facred to the moon, as was the bull Mnevis to the fun. Others fuppofed, that both were facred to Ofiris, who is the fame with the fun. When he died there was an univerfal mourning in Ægypt. They fought for another, and having found him, the mourning ended. The priefts conducted him to Nilopolis, where they kept him forty days. They afterwards removed him in a magnificent veffel to Memphis, where he had an apartment ornamented with gold. During the forty days above mentioned the women only were fuffered to fee him. They ftood round him, and lifting up their garments, difcovered to him what modefty forbids us to name. Afterwards the fight of the god was forbidden them.

Every year they brought him a heifer, which had alfo certain marks. According to the facred books, he was only permitted to live a ftipulated time; when this came he was drowned in a facred fountain.—*Larcher.*

A few other particulars concerning this Apis may not be unacceptable to an Englifh reader.

The homage paid him was not confined to Ægypt; many illuftrious conquerors and princes of foreign nations, Alexander, Titus, and Adrian, bowed themfelves before him. Larcher fays that he was confidered as facred to the moon; but Porphyry exprefsly fays, that he was facred to both fun and moon. The following paffage is from Plutarch: " The priefts affirm that the moon fheds a generative light, with which fhould a cow wanting the bull be ftruck, fhe conceives Apis, who bears the fign of that

abſence it was his cuſtom to do; and that when this happened, it was cuſtomary for all the Ægyptians to hold a ſolemn feſtival. Cambyſes diſbelieved what they told him, and condemned them to death, as guilty of falſhood.

XXVIII. As ſoon as they were executed, he ſent for the prieſts, from whom he received the ſame anſwer. " If," ſaid he, " any deity has ſhown " himſelf familiarly in Ægypt, I muſt ſee and " know him." He then commanded them to bring Apis before him, which they prepared to do. This Apis, or Epaphus, is the calf of a cow which can have no more young. The Ægyptians ſay, that on this occaſion the cow is ſtruck with light-ning, from which ſhe conceives and brings forth Apis. The young one ſo produced, and thus nam-ed, is known by certain marks: The ſkin is black, but on its forehead is a white ſtar of a triangular

that planet." Strabo ſays, that he was brought out from his apartment to gratify the curioſity of ſtrangers, and might al-was be ſeen through a window. Pliny relates with great ſolem-nity that he refuſed food from the hand of Germanicus, who died ſoon after; and one ancient hiſtorian aſſerts, that during the ſeven days when the birth of Apis was celebrated, crocodiles forgot their natural ferocity, and became tame.

The biſhop of Avranches, M. Huet, endeavoured to prove that Apis was a ſymbol of the patriarch Joſeph.

It has been generally allowed, that Oſiris was reverenced in the homage paid to Apis. Oſiris introduced agriculture, in which the utility of the bull is obvious; and this appears to be the moſt rational explanation that can be given of this part of the Ægyptian ſuperſtition. *See Savary, Pococke, &c.—T.*

form,

form. It has the figure of an eagle on the back, the tail [15] is divided, and under the tongue [16] it has an insect like a beetle.

XXIX. When the priests conducted Apis to his presence, Cambyses was transported with rage. He drew his dagger, and endeavouring to stab him in the belly, wounded him in the thigh; then turning to the priests with an insulting smile, " Wretches," he exclaimed, "think ye that gods are " formed of flesh and blood, and thus susceptible of " wounds? This, indeed, is a deity worthy of Ægyp- " tians: but you shall find that I am not to be mock- " ed with impunity." He then called the proper officers, and commanded the priests to be scourged: he directed also that whatever Ægyptian was found celebrating this festival should be put to death. The priests were thus punished, and no further solemnities observed. Apis himself languished and died in the temple, from the wound of his thigh,

---

[15] *The tail.*]—The Scholiast of Ptolemy says, but I know not on what authority, that the tail of the bull encreased or diminished according to the age of the moon.—*Larcher.*

[16] *Under the tongue.*]—In all the copies of Herodotus, it is ἐπὶ δὲ τῇ γλώσσῃ, upon the tongue; but it is plain from Pliny and Eusebius that it ought to be ὑπὸ, under. The former explains what it was, Nodus sub lingua quem cantharum appellant, " a knot under the tongue, which they call cantharus, or the beetle." viii. 46. The spot on the forehead is also changed by the commentators from quadrangular to triangular. Pliny mentions also a mark like a crescent on the right side, and is silent about the eagle. The beetle was considered as an emblem of the sun.—*T.*

and

and was buried [37] by the priefts without the knowledge of Cambyfes.

XXX. The Ægyptians affirm, that in confequence of this impiety Cambyfes became immediately infane, who indeed did not before appear to have
the proper ufe of his reafon. The firft impulfe of
his fury was directed againft Smerdis, his own
brother, who had become the object of his jealoufy,
becaufe he was the only Perfian who had been able
to bend the bow which the Ichthyophagi brought
from Æthiopia, the breadth of two fingers. He
was therefore ordered to return to Perfia, where as
foon as he came Cambyfes faw this vifion: a
meffenger appeared to arrive from Perfia, informing him that Smerdis, feated on the royal throne,
touched the heavens with his head. Cambyfes was
inftantly ftruck with the apprehenfion that Smerdis
would kill him, and feize his dominions; to prevent which he difpatched Prexafpes, a Perfian, and
one of his moft faithful adherents, to put him to
death. He arrived at Sufa, and deftroyed Smerdis, fome fay, by taking him afide whilft engaged
in the diverfion of the chace; others believe that
he drowned him in the Red Sea; this, however,
was the commencement of the calamities of Cambyfes.

XXXI. The next victim of his fury was his

---

[37] *Buried by the priefts.*]—This account is contradicted by
Plutarch, who tells us, that Apis having been flain by Cambyfes,
was by his order expofed and devoured by dogs.—*T.*

fifter,

fister, who had accompanied him to Ægypt. She
was also his wife, which thing he thus accomplished: before this prince, no Perfian had ever been
known to marry his fifter [18]; but Cambyfes, being
paffionately fond of one of his, and knowing that
there was no precedent to juftify his making her
his wife, affembled thofe who were called the royal
judges; of them he defired to know whether there
was any law which would permit a brother to
marry his fifter, if he thought proper to do fo.
The royal judges in Perfia are men of the moft
approved integrity, who hold their places for life,
or till they fhall be convicted of fome crime [19],

[18] *Marry his fifter.*]—Ingenious and learned men of all ages
have amufed themfelves with drawing a comparifon betwixt the
laws of Solon and Lycurgus. The following particularity affords
ample room for conjecture and difcuffion: At Athens a man
was fuffered to marry his fifter by the father, but forbidden
to marry his fifter by the mother. At Lacedæmon things were
totally reverfed, a man was allowed to marry his fifter by the
mother, and forbidden to marry his fifter by the father.—See
what Bayle fays on the circumftance of a man's marrying his
fifter, article *Sarah.*—T.

[19] *Of fome crime.*]—An appointment like this, manifeftly leading to corruption, and the perverfion of juftice, prevailed in this
country with refpect to judges, till the reign of George the
Third, when a law was paffed, the wifdom of which cannot be
fufficiently admired, making the judges independent of the king,
his minifters, and fucceffors. Yet, however this provifion may
in appearance diminifh the ftrength of the executive power, the
riot-act, combined with the affiftance of the ftanding army,
which is always kept up in this country, add as much to the
influence of the crown, as it may at firft fight feem to have loft
in prerogative. Such, however, was the opinion of judge
Blackftone.—T.

Every

Every thing is referred to their decifion, they are
the interpreters of the laws, and determine all private difputes. In anfwer to the enquiry of Cambyfes, they replied fhrewdly, though with truth, that
although they could find no law which would permit
a brother to marry his fifter, they had difcovered
one which enabled a monarch of Perfia to do
what he pleafed. In this anfwer the awe of Cambyfes prevented their adopting literally the fpirit
of the Perfian laws; and to fecure their perfons, they took care to difcover what would juftify
him who wifhed to marry his fifter. Cambyfes,
therefore, inftantly married the fifter whom he
loved [40], and not long afterwards a fecond [41]. The
younger of thefe, who accompanied him to Ægypt,
he put to death,

XXXII. The manner of her death, like that of
Smerdis, is differently related. The Greeks fay
that Cambyfes made the cub of a lionefs and a
young whelp engage each other, and that this princefs was prefent at the combat; and when this latter
was vanquifhed, another whelp of the fame litter
broke what confined it, and flew to affift the other,
and that both together were too much for the young
lion. Cambyfes feeing this, expreffed great fatisfaction; but the princefs burft into tears. Camby-

40 *Whom he loved.*]—Her name, according to the Scholiaft of
Lucian, was Atoffa, who next married Smerdis, one of the magi,
and afterwards Darius, fon of Hyftafpes.—*Larcher.*

41 *Afterwards a fecond.*]—If Libanius may be credited, the
name of this lady was Meroe.—*Weffeling.*

fes

ses observed her weep, and enquired the reason ; she answered, that seeing one whelp assist another of the same brood, she could not but remember Smerdis, whose death she feared nobody would revenge. For which saying, the Greeks affirm, that Cambyses put her to death. On the contrary, if we may believe the Ægyptians, this princess was sitting at table with her husband, and took a lettuce in her hand, dividing it leaf by leaf: "Which," said she, "seems in your eyes most agreeable, this lettuce "whole, or divided into leaves?" He replied, "When whole." "You," says she, "resemble this "lettuce, as I have divided it, for you have thus "torn in sunder the house of Cyrus." Cambyses was so greatly incensed, that he threw her down, and leaped upon her; and being pregnant, she was delivered before her time, and lost her life.

XXXIII. To such excesses in his own family was Cambyses impelled, either on account of his impious treatment of Apis, or from some other of those numerous calamities which afflict mankind. From the first hour of his birth he laboured under what by some is termed the sacred disease. It is, therefore, by no means astonishing that so great a bodily infirmity should at length injure the mind.

XXXIV. His phrenzy, however, extended to the other Persians. He once made a remarkable speech to Prexaspes, for whom he professed the greatest regard, who received all petitions to the king, and whose son enjoyed the honourable office

of

of royal cup-bearer. " What," fays he, upon fome occafion, " do the Perfians think of me, or in what " terms do they fpeak of me ?" " Sir," he replied, " in all other refpe_cts they fpeak of you with honour; " but it is the general opinion that you are too much " addicted to wine." " What!" returned the prince in anger, " I fuppofe they fay that I drink to excefs, and " am deprived of reafon ; their former praife, there- " fore, could not be fincere." At fome preceding period he had afked of thofe whom he ufed moft familiarly, and of Crœfus among the reft, whether they thought he had equalled the greatnefs of his father Cyrus. In reply they told him, that he was the greater of the two, for that to all which Cyrus had poffeffed, he had added the empire of Ægypt and of the ocean. Crœfus, who was prefent, did not affent to this. " Sir," faid he to Cambyfes, " in my opinion you are not equal to your father ; " you have not fuch a fon as he left behind him." Which fpeech of Crœfus was highly agreeable to Cambyfes,

XXXV. Remembering this, he turned with great anger to Prexafpes : " You," faid he, " fhall " prefently be witnefs of the truth or falfhood of " what the Perfians fay. If I hit directly through " the heart [42] your fon, who ftands yonder, it will " be

---

[42] *Through the heart.*]—The ftory of William Tell, the great deliverer of the Swifs cantons from the yoke of the Germans, may be properly introduced in this place. Grifler governed Switzerland for the Emperor Albert. He ordered William Tell,
a Swifs

" be evident that they speak of me maliciously; if
" I miss my aim, they will say true in affirming that
" I am mad." No sooner had he spoken, than he
bent his bow, and struck the young man. When
he fell, the king ordered his body to be opened,
and the wound to be examined. He was rejoiced
to find that the arrow had penetrated his heart; and
turning to the father with a malicious smile, " You
" observe," said he, " that it is not I that am mad,
" but the Persians who are foolish. Tell me,"
he continued, " if you ever saw a man send an arrow
" surer to its mark?" Prexaspes, seeing he was
mad, and fearing for himself, replied, " I do not
" think, Sir, that even a deity could have aimed
" so well."—Such was his treatment of Prexaspes.
At another time, without the smallest provocation,
he commanded twelve Persians of distinction to be
interred alive.

a Swiss of some importance, for a pretended offence, to place
an apple on the head of one of his children, and to hit it,
en pain of death, with an arrow. He was dexterous enough to
do so, without hurting his child. Grisler, when the affair was
over, took notice that Tell had another arrow concealed under
his cloak, and asked him what it was for? " I intended," replied Tell, " to have shot you to the heart, if I had killed
my child." The governor ordered Tell to be hanged; but the
Swiss, defending their countryman, flew to arms, destroyed their
governor, and made themselves independent. See this historical anecdote referred to by Smollet, in his sublime Ode to
Independence.

> Who with the generous rustics sate
> On Uri's rock, in close divan,
> And wing'd that arrow, sure as fate,
> Which ascertain'd the sacred rights of man.—T.

XXXVI.

XXXVI. Whilft he was purfuing thefe extravagancies, Crœfus gave him this advice : " Do not,
" Sir, yield thus intemperately to the warmth of your
" age and of your temper. Reftrain yourfelf, and
" remember that moderation is the part of a wife
" man, and it becomes every one to weigh the
" confequences of his actions. Without any adequate
" offence you deftroy your fellow-citizens, and put
" even children to death. If you continue thefe
" exceffes, the Perfians may be induced to revolt
" from you. In giving you thefe admonitions, I do
" but fulfil the injunctions which the king your
" father repeatedly laid upon me, to warn you of
" whatever I thought neceffary to your welfare."
Kind as were the intentions of Crœfus, he received
this anfwer from Cambyfes : " I am aftonifhed at
" your prefumption in fpeaking to me thus, as if
" you had been remarkable either for the judicious
" government of your own dominions, or for the
" wife advice which you gave my father. I cannot
" forget that, inftead of waiting for the attack of the
" Maffagetæ, you counfelled him to advance and
" encounter them in their own territories. By your
" mifconduct you loft your own dominions, and by
" your ill advice were the caufe of my father's ruin.
" But do not expect to efcape with impunity; in-
" deed I have long wifhed for an opportunity to
" punifh you." He then eagerly fnatched his
bow [43], intending to pierce Crœfus with an arrow,
but

---

[43] Snatched his bow.]—The mental derangement under which
Saul laboured, previous to the elevation of David, bears fome
refemblance

but by an expeditious flight he escaped. Cambyses
instantly ordered him to be seized and put to death;
but as his officers were well acquainted with their
prince's character, they concealed Crœsus, thinking
that if at any future period he should express con-
trition, they might by producing him obtain a reward; but if no farther enquiries were made concerning him, they might then kill him. Not long
afterwards Cambyses expressed regret for Crœsus,
which when his attendants perceived, they told him
that he was alive. He expressed particular satisfac-
tion at the preservation of Crœsus, but he would
not forgive the disobedience of his servants, who
were accordingly executed.

XXXVII. Many things of this kind did he perpetrate against the Persians and his allies, whilst he
stayed at Memphis: neither did he hesitate to vio-
late the tombs, and examine the bodies of the dead.
He once entered the temple of Vulcan, and treated
the shrine of that deity with much contempt. The
statue of this god exceedingly resembles the Pa-
taici which the Phœnicians place at the prow of
their triremes: they who have not seen them, may
suppose them to resemble the figure of a pigmy.
Cambyses also entered the temple of the Cabiri [44],
to which access is denied to all but the priests. He

resemblance to the character here given of Cambyses; and the
escape of the son of Jesse from the javelin of the king of Israel,
will admit of a comparison with that of Crœsus from the arrow of
Cambyses.—T.

[44] Cabiri.]—Concerning these see book ii. chap. li.

burned their ftatues, after exercifing upon them his wit and raillery. Thefe ftatues refemble·Vulcan, whofe fons the Cabiri are fuppofed to be.

XXXVIII. For my own part I am fatisfied that Cambyfes was deprived of his reafon; he would not otherwife have difturbed the fanctity of temples, or of eftablifhed cuftoms. Whoever had the opportunity of choofing for their own obfervance, from all the nations of the world, fuch laws and cuftoms as to them feemed the beft, would, I am of opinion, after the moft careful examination, adhere to their own. Each nation believes that their own laws are by far the moft excellent; no one, therefore, but a madman, would treat fuch prejudices with contempt. That all men are really thus tenacious of their own cuftoms, appears from this, amongft other inftances: Darius once fent for fuch of the Greeks as were dependent on his power, and afked them what reward would induce them to eat the bodies of their deceafed parents; they replied that no fum could prevail on them to commit fuch a deed. In the prefence of the fame Greeks, who by an interpreter were informed of what paffed, he fent alfo for the Callatiæ, a people of India known to eat the bodies of their parents. He afked them for what fum they would confent to burn the bodies of their parents. The Indians were difgufted at the queftion, and intreated him to forbear fuch language.—Such is the force of cuftom; and Pindar [45] feems to me to have fpoken with peculiar

---

[45] *Pindar.*]—The paffage in Pindar which is here referred to,

is

culiar propriety, when he obſerved that custom [46] was the univerſal ſovereign.

XXXIX. Whilſt Cambyſes was engaged in his Ægyptian expedition, the Lacedæmonians were proſecuting a war againſt Polycrates, the ſon of Æaces, who had forcibly poſſeſſed himſelf of Samos. He had divided it into three parts, aſſigning one ſeverally to his brothers Pantagnotus and Syloſon. He afterwards, having killed Pantagnotus, and baniſhed Syloſon, who was the younger, ſeized the whole. Whilſt he was thus circumſtanced, he

is preſerved in the Scholia ad Nem. ix. 35. It is this:—Νομος ὁ παντων βασιλιος θνατοι τε ᾳ αθανατοι αποι δικαιῶι το βαιοτατον ὑπερτατῳ χειρί.—"Cuſtom is the ſovereign of mortals and of gods; with its powerful hand it regulates things the moſt violent." —T.

[46] *Cuſtom.*]—Many writers on this ſubjeĉt appear not to have diſcriminated accurately betwixt cuſtom and habit: the ſovereign power of both muſt be confeſſed; but it will be found, on due deliberation, that cuſtom has reference to the aĉtion, and habit to the aĉtor. That the Athenians, the moſt refined and poliſhed nation of the world, could bear to ſee human ſacrifices repreſented on their theatres, could liſten with applauſe and with delight to the miſery of Œdipus, and the madneſs of Oreſtes, is to be accounted for alone from the powerful operation of their national cuſtoms. The equally forcible ſway of habit, referring to an individual, was never perhaps expreſſed with ſo much beauty as in the following lines of our favourite Shakeſpeare:

> How uſe doth breed a habit in a man!
> This ſhadowy deſert, unfrequented woods,
> I better brook than flouriſhing peopled towns,
> Here I can ſit alone, unſeen of any,
> And to the nightingale's complaining notes
> Tune my diſtreſſes, and record my woes.   T.

x   made

made a treaty of alliance with Amafis, king of
Ægypt, which was cemented by various prefents on
both fides. His fame had fo increafed, that he was
celebrated through Ionia and the reft of Greece.
Succefs attended all his military undertakings; he
had a hundred fifty-oared veffels, and a thoufand
archers. He made no difcrimination in the objeets
of his attacks, thinking that he conferred a greater
favour [47] even on a friend, by reftoring what he had
violently taken, than by not molefting him at all.
He took a great number of iflands, and became
mafter of feveral cities on the continent. The
Lefbians, who with all their forces were proceeding
to affift the Milefians, he attacked and conquered
in a great fea-fight. Thofe whom he made prifoners he put in chains, and compelled to fink the
trench [48] which furrounds the walls of Samos.

XL. The great profperity of Polycrates excited
both the attention and anxiety of Amafis. As his

[47] *A greater favour.*]—This fentiment is falfe, and Libanius
feems to me to have fpoken with truth, when, in a difcourfe which
is not come down to us, he fays, "An inftance of good fortune·
never gives a man fo much fatisfaction as the lofs of it does uneafinefs."—*Larcher.*

[48] *Sink the trench.*]—It would be an interefting labour to in-
veftigate, from ages the moft remote and nations the moft barbarous, the various treatment which prifoners of war have experienced : from the period, and from thofe who put in practice
againft their unfortunate captives every fpecies of oppreffion and
of cruelty, to the prefent period, when the refinement of manners,
and the progrefs of the milder virtues, foftens the afperity, and
takes much from the horrors of war.—*T.*

fuccefs

fuccefs continually encreafed, he was induced to write and fend this letter to Sámos.

" AMASIS to POLYCRATES.

" THE fuccefs of a friend and an ally fills me
" with particular fatisfaction; but as I know the
" invidioufnefs of fortune [49], your extraordinary
" profperity

[49] *Invidioufnefs of fortune.*]—Three very diftinct qualities of mind have been imputed to the three Greek hiftorians, Herodotus, Thucydides, and Xenophon, with refpect to their manner of reflecting on the facts which they relate. Of the firft it has been faid that he feems to have confidered the deity as viewing man with a jealous eye, as only promoting his fucceffes to make the cataftrophe of his fate the more calamitous. This is pointed out by Plutarch with the fevereft reprehenfion. Thucydides, on the contrary, admits of no divine interpofition in human affairs, but makes the good or ill fortune of thofe whofe hiftory he gives us depend on the wifdom or folly of their own conduct. Xenophon, in diftinction from both, invariably confiders the kindnefs or the vengeance of heaven as influencing the event of human enterprizes. " That is," fays the Abbé Barthelemy, " according to the firft, all fublunary things are governed by a fatality; according to the fecond, by human prudence; according to the laft, by the piety of the individual."—The inconftancy of fortune is admirably defcribed in the following paffage from Horace, and with the fentiment with which the lines conclude every ingenuous mind muft defire to be in unifon.

> Fortuna fævo læta negotio
> Ludum infolentem ludere pertinax
> Tranfmutat incertos honores
> Nunc mihi, nunc aliis benigna.
>   Laudo manentem : fi celeres quatit
>   Pennas refigno quæ dedit et meâ

Virtute

" prosperity excites my apprehensions. If I might
" determine for myself, and for those whom I re-
" gard, I would rather have my affairs sometimes
" flattering, and sometimes perverse. I would wish
" to pass through life with the alternate experience
" of good and evil, rather than with uninterrupted
" good fortune. I do not remember to have heard
" of any man remarkable for a constant succession of
" prosperous events, whose end has not been final-
" ly calamitous. If, therefore, you value my coun-
" sel, you will provide this remedy against the excess
" of your prosperity:—Examine well what thing
" it is which you deem of the highest consequence
" to your happiness, and the loss of which would
" most afflict you. When you shall have ascertained
" this, banish it from you, so that there may be no
" possibility of its return. If after this your good
" fortune still continue, without diminution or
" change, you will do well to repeat the remedy
" I propose."

XLI. Polycrates received this letter, and seriously

Virtute me involvo, probamque
Pauperiem sine dote quæro.

It would be inexcusable not to insert Dryden's version, or rather paraphrase, of the above passage.

Fortune, that with malicious joy
Does man her slave oppress,
Proud of her office to destroy,
Is seldom pleas'd to bless :
Still various, and inconstant ft I',
But with an inclination to be ill,

ly deliberated on its contents. The advice of
Amasis appeared sagacious, and he resolved to follow it. He accordingly searched among his trea-
sures for something, the loss of which would most
afflict him. He conceived this to be a seal-
ring [50], which he occasionally wore; it was an
emerald

> Promotes, degrades, delights in strife,
> And makes a lottery of life.
> I can enjoy her while she's kind,
> But when she dances in the wind,
> And shakes the wings, and will not stay,
> I puff the prostitute away:
> The little or the much she gave is quietly resign'd.
> Content with poverty, my soul I arm,
> And virtue, tho' in rags, will keep me warm. *T.*

[50] *A seal-ring.*]—This ring has been the subject of some
controversy amongst the learned, both as to what it represented,
and of what precious stone it was formed.

Clemens Alexandrinus says it represented a lyre. Pliny says
it was a sardonyx; and that in his time there existed one in the
temple of Concord, the gift of Augustus, affirmed to be this of
Polycrates. Solinus asserts also, that it was a sardonyx; but
Herodotus expressly tells us, it was an emerald. At this period
the art of engraving precious stones must have been in its infancy, which might probably enhance the value of his ring to
Polycrates. It is a little remarkable that the moderns have
never been able to equal the ancients in the exquisite delicacy
and beauty of their performances on precious stones. Perhaps
it may not be too much to add, that we have never attained the
perfection with which they executed all works in miniature.
Pliny says, that Cicero once saw the Iliad of Homer written so
very finely, that it might have been contained 'in nuce', in a nut-
shell. Aulus Gellius mentions a pigeon made of wood, which
imitated the motions of a living bird; and Ælian speaks of an
artist, who wrote a distich in letters of gold, which he inclosed
in the rind of a grain of corn. Other instances of a similar kind

emerald fet in gold, and the workmanfhip of Theodorus the Samian, the fon of Telecles. Of this determining to deprive himfelf, he embarked in a
fifty-oared veffel, with orders to be carried into the
open fea: when he was at fome diftance from the
ifland, in the prefence of all his attendants, he took
the ring from his finger and caft it into the fea;
this done he failed back again.

XLII. Returning home he regretted his lofs,
but in the courfe of five or fix days this accident
occurred:—A fifherman caught a fifh of fuch fize
and beauty, that he deemed it a proper prefent for
Polycrates. He went therefore to the palace, and
demanded an audience; being admitted, he prefented his fifh to Polycrates, with thefe words: "Al-
" though, fir, I live by the produce of my induftry,
" I could not think of expofing this fifh which I
" have taken, to fale in the market-place, believing
" it worthy of you to accept, which I hope you
" will." The king was much gratified, and made
him this reply: "My good friend, your prefent
" and your fpeech are equally acceptable to me;
" and I beg that I may fee you at fupper [51]." The
fifherman,

are collected by the learned Mr. Dutens, in his Enquiry into the
Origin of the Difcoveries attributed to the Moderns.—*T.*

[51] *See you at fupper.*]—The circumftance of a fovereign prince
afking a common fifherman to fup with him, feems at firft fight
fo entirely repugnant, not only to modern manners but alfo to
confiftency, as to juftify difguft and provoke fufpicion. But let
it be remembered, that in ancient times the rites of hofpitality
were paid without any diftinction of perfon; and the fame fimplicity of manners, which would allow an individual of the

fisherman, delighted with his reception, returned to his house. The servants proceeding to open the fish, found in its paunch the ring of Polycrates; with great eagerness and joy they hastened to carry it to the king, telling him where they had met with it. Polycrates concluded that this incident bore evident marks of divine interposition; he therefore wrote down every particular of what had happened, and transmitted it to Ægypt.

XLIII. Amasis, after perusing the letter of his friend, was convinced that it was impossible for one mortal to deliver another from the destiny which awaited him; he was satisfied that Polycrates could not terminate his days in tranquillity, whose good fortune had never suffered interruption, and who had even recovered what he had taken pains to lose. He sent therefore a herald to Samos, to disclaim all future connection [51]; his motive for doing which was the

meanest rank to solicit and obtain an audience of his prince, diminishes the act of condescension which is here recorded, and which to a modern reader may appear ridiculous.—T.

[52] *Future connection.*]—This may be adduced as one amongst numerous other instances, to prove, that where the human mind has no solid hopes of the future, nor any firm basis of religious faith, the conduct will ever be wayward and irregular; and although there may exist great qualities, capable of occasionally splendid actions, there will also be extraordinary weaknesses, irreconcileable to common sense or common humanity. Diodorus Siculus, however, gives a very different account of the matter, and ascribes the behaviour of Amasis to a very different motive:—"The Ægyptian," says he, "was so disgusted with

the apprehenſion, that in any future calamity which might befall Polycrates, he, as a friend and ally, might be obliged to bear a part.

XLIV. Againſt this Polycrates, in all things ſo proſperous, the Lacedæmonians undertook an expedition, to which they were induced by thoſe Samians who afterwards built the city of Cydon in Crete [53]. To counteract this blow, Polycrates ſent privately to Cambyſes, who was then preparing for hoſtilities againſt Ægypt, entreating him to demand ſupplies and aſſiſtance of the Samians. With this Cambyſes willingly complied, and ſent to ſolicit, in favour of Polycrates, ſome naval force to ſerve in his Ægyptian expedition. Thoſe whoſe principles and intentions he moſt ſuſpected the Samian prince ſelected from the reſt, and ſent in forty triremes to Cambyſes, requeſting him by all means to prevent their return.

XLV. There are ſome who aſſert that the Samians ſent by Polycrates, never arrived in Ægypt, but that as ſoon as they reached the Carpathian ſea they conſulted together, and determined to proceed

with the tyrannical behaviour of Polycrates, not only to his ſubjeſts but to ſtrangers, that he foreſaw his fate to be unavoidable, and therefore was cautious not to be involved in his ruin."—*T*.

[53] *Cydon in Crete.*]—This place is now called Canea: ſome ſay it was at firſt called Apollonia, becauſe built by Cydon the ſon of Apollo. Pauſanias ſays, it was built by Cydon ſon of Tegetes. It was once a place of great power, and the largeſt city in the iſland; for a deſcription of its preſent condition, ſee *Savary's Letters on Greece.*—*T*.

no further. Others, on the contrary, affirm, that they did arrive in Ægypt, but that they escaped from their guards, and returned to Samos: they add, that Polycrates met and engaged them at sea, where he was defeated; but that landing afterwards on the island, they had a second engagement by land, in which they were totally routed, and obliged to fly to Lacedæmon. They who assert that the Samians returned from Ægypt, and obtained a victory over Polycrates, are in my opinion mistaken; for if their own force was sufficient to overcome him, there was no necessity for their applying to the Lacedæmonians for assistance. Neither is it at all consistent with probability, that a prince who had so many forces under his command, composed as well of foreign auxiliaries as of archers of his own, could possibly be overcome by the few Samians who were returning home. Polycrates, moreover, had in his power the wives and children of his Samian subjects: these were all assembled and confined in his different harbours; and he was determined to destroy them by fire, and the harbours along with them, in case of any treasonable conjunction between the inhabitants and the Samians who were returning.

XLVI. The Samians who were expelled by Polycrates immediately on their arrival at Sparta obtained an audience of the magistrates, and in the language of suppliants spoke a great while. The answer which they first received informed them, that the commencement of their discourse was not remembered, and the conclusion not understood.

At

At the fecond interview they fimply produced a bread-bafket, and complained that it contained no bread; even to this the Lacedæmonians replied, that their obfervation was unnecesfary [54];—they determined neverthelefs to affift them.

XLVII. After the necesfary preparations, the Lacedæmonians embarked with an army againft Samos: if the Samians may be credited, the conduct of the Lacedæmonians in this bufinefs was the effect of gratitude, they themfelves having formerly received a fupply of fhips againft the Messenians. But the Lacedæmonians affert, that they engaged in this expedition not fo much to fatisfy the wifhes of thofe Samians who had fought their affiftance, as to obtain fatisfaction for an injury which they had formerly received. The Samians had violently taken away a goblet which the Lacedæmonians

---

[54] *Obfervation was unneceffary.*]—The Spartans were always remarkable for their contempt of oratory and eloquence. The following curious examples of this are recorded in Sextus Empiricus:—" A young Spartan went abroad, and endeavoured to accomplifh himfelf in the art of fpeaking; on his return he was punifhed by the Ephori, for having conceived the defign of deluding his countrymen. Another Spartan was fent to Tiffaphernes, a Perfian fatrap, to engage him to prefer the alliance of Sparta to that of Athens; he faid but little, but when he found the Athenians employed great pomp and profufion of words, he drew two lines, both terminating in the fame point, but one was ftraight, the other very crooked; pointing thefe out to Tiffaphernes, he merely faid, "Choofe." The ftory here related of the Samians, by Herodotus, is found alfo in Sextus Empiricus, but is by him applied on a different occafion, and to a different people.—T.

were carrying to Crœfus, and a corfelet [55], which was given them by Amafis king of Ægypt. This latter incident took place at the interval of a year after the former : the corfelet was made of linen, but there were interwoven in the piece a great number of animals richly embroidered with cotton and gold ; every part of it deferved admiration : it was compofed of chains, each of which contained three hundred and fixty threads diftinctly vifible. Amafis prefented another corfelet, entirely refembling this, to the Minerva of Lindus.

XLVIII. To this expedition againft Samos the Corinthians alfo contributed with confiderable ardour. In the age which preceded, and about the time in which the goblet had been taken, they had been affronted by the Samians. Periander [56], the

fon

[55] *A corfelet.*]—Some fragments of this were to be feen in the time of Pliny, who complains that fo curious a piece of workmanfhip fhould be fpoiled, by its being unravelled by different people, to gratify curiofity, or to afcertain the fact here afferted.—*T.*

[56] *Periander.*]—The life of Periander is given by Diogenes Laertius ; from which I have extracted fuch particulars as feem moft worthy the attention of the Englifh reader.

He was of the family of the Heraclidæ ; and the reafon of his fending the young Corcyreans, with the purpofe mentioned by Herodotus, was on account of their having killed his fon, to whom he wifhed to refign his power. He was the firft prince who ufed guards for the defence of his perfon. He was by fome efteemed one of the feven wife men ; Plato, however, does not admit him amongft them. His celebrated faying was, that " Perfeverance may do every thing."

In

ſon of Cypſelus, had ſent to Alyattes, at Sardis, three hundred children of the principal families of the Corcyreans to be made eunuchs. They were entruſted to the care of certain Corinthians, who by diſtreſs of weather were compelled to touch at Samos. The Samians ſoon learned the purpoſe of the expedition, and accordingly inſtructed the chil-' dren to fly for protection to the temple of Diana, from whence they would not ſuffer the Corinthians to take them. But as the Corinthians prevented their receiving any food, the Samians inſtituted a feſtival on the occaſion, which they yet obſerve. At the approach of night, as long as the children continued as ſuppliants in the temple, they intro- duced a company of youths and virgins, who in a kind of religious dance, were to carry cakes made of honey and flour [57] in their hands. This was done that the young Corcyreans, by ſnatching them away, might ſatisfy their hunger, and was repeated till 'the Corinthians who guarded the children de-

In an epigram inſerted in Stephens's Anthologia, and tranſ- lated by Auſonius, χολυ κρατεειν is the maxim attributed to Pe- riander, "Reſtrain your anger:" of which rule he muſt have ſeverely felt the neceſſity, if, as Laertius relates, he killed his wife Meliſſa in a tranſport of paſſion, by kicking her or throw- ing a chair at her when pregnant. Her name, according to the ſame author, was Lyſide; Meliſſa was probably ſubſtituted through fondneſs, certain nymphs and departed human ſouls being called *Meliſſæ*.—*Menage.*   T.

[57] *Honey and flour.*]—The cakes of Samos were very famous. See *Athenæus,* book xiv. c. 13,

parted,

parted. The Samians afterwards sent the children
back to Corcyra [58].

XLIX. If after the death of Periander there had
existed any friendship betwixt the Corinthians and
the Corcyreans, it might be supposed that they
would not have assisted in this expedition against
Samos. But notwithstanding these people had the
same origin (the Corinthians having built Corcyra)
they had always lived in a state of enmity. The
Corinthians, therefore, did not forget the affront
which they had received at Samos; and it was in
resentment of injuries formerly received from the
Corcyreans, that Periander had sent to Sardis these
three hundred youths of the first families of Corcyra, with the intention of their being made eunuchs.

[58] *Back to Corcyra.*]—Plutarch, in his Treatise on the Malignity of Herodotus, says, " that the young Corcyreans were not
preserved by the Samians, but by the Cnidians."—This assertion
is examined and refuted by Larcher.

Pliny says, that the fish called echines stopped the vessel going
swift before the wind, on board of which were messengers of
Periander, having it in command to castrate the sons of the
Cnidian noblemen; for which reason these shells were highly reverenced in the temple of Venus at Cnidos. M. Larcher, avow-
edly giving the reader the above passage from Pliny, is guilty of
a misquotation : " these shells," says he, " arreterent le vaisseau
où étoient ces enfans;" whereas the words of Pliny (see Gronovius's edition, vol. i. page 609) are these, " Quibus inhærentibus
stetisse navem portantem nuncios a Periandro ut castrarentur
nobiles pueri."—T.

L.

. L. When Periander had put his wife Meliſſa to death, he was involved in an additional calamity. By Meliſſa he had two ſons, one of whom was ſe-venteen, the other eighteen years old: Procles, their grandfather by the mother's ſide, had ſent for them to Epidaurus, of which place he was prince ; and had treated them with all the kindneſs due to the children of his daughter. At the time appointed for their departure, he took them aſide, and aſked them if they knew who had killed their mother. To theſe words the elder brother paid no attention; but the younger, whoſe name was Lycophron, took it ſo exceedingly to heart, that at his return to Corinth he would neither ſalute his father, con-verſe with, nor anſwer him; in indignation at which behaviour Periander baniſhed him his houſe.

LI. After the above event Periander aſked his elder ſon, what their grandfather had ſaid to them. The youth informed him, that their grandfather had received them very affectionately, but as he did not remember, he could not relate the words he had uſed to them at parting. The father, however, continued to preſs him; ſaying, it was im-poſſible that their grandfather ſhould diſmiſs them without ſome advice. This induced the young man more ſeriouſly to reflect on what had paſſed; and he afterwards informed his father of every par-ticular. Upon this Periander was determined not at all to relax from his ſeverity, but immediately ſent to thoſe who had received his ſon under their
protection,

protection, commanding them to dismiss him. Lycophron was thus driven from one place to another,
and from thence to a third, and from this last also
the severity of Periander expelled him. Yet, fearful
as people were to entertain him, he still found an
asylum, from the confideration of his being the son
of Periander.

LII. Periander at length commanded it to be
publickly proclaimed, that whoever harboured his
son, or held any conversation with him, should pay
a stipulated fine for the use of Apollo's temple.
After this no person presumed either to receive or
converse with him, and Lycophron himself acquief-
ced in the injunction, by retiring to the public por-
tico. On the fourth day Periander himself observed him in this situation, covered with rags and
perishing with hunger: his heart relenting, he approached, and thus addressed him: " My son,
" which do you think preferable, your present ex-
" tremity of distress, or to return to your obedience,
" and share with me my authority and riches? You
" who are my son, and a prince of the happy Co-
" rinth, choose the life of a mendicant, and perse-
" vere in irritating him who has the strongest claims
" upon your duty. If the incident which induces
" you to think unfavourably of my conduct has
" any evil resulting from it, the whole is fallen
" upon myself; and I feel it the more sensibly, from
" the reflection that I was myself the author of it.
" Experience has taught you how much better it is

§   " to

" to be envied than pitied [59], and how dangerous it " is to provoke a fuperior and a parent—return " therefore to my houfe." To this fpeech Periander received no other anfwer from his fon, than that he himfelf, by converfing with him, had incurred the penalty which his edict had impofed. The king, perceiving the perverfenefs of his fon to be immutable, determined to remove him from his fight; he therefore fent him in a veffel to Corcyra, which place alfo belonged to him. After this, Periander made war upon his father-in-law Procles, whom he confidered · as the principal occafion of what had happened. He made himfelf mafter of Epidaurus [60], and took Procles prifoner; whom neverthelefs he preferved alive.

LIII.

[59] *Envied than pitied.*]—Of this M. Larcher remarks, that it is a proverbial expreffion in the French language: it is no lefs fo in our own. The fame fentiment in Pindar is referred to by the learned Frenchman, which is thus beautifully tranflated by Mr. Weft.

> Nor le's diftafteful is exceffive fame
>   To the four palate of the envious mind;
> Who hears with grief his neighbour's goodly name,
>   And hates the fortune that he ne'er fhall find;
> Yet in thy virtue, Hiero, perfevere,
>   *Since to be envied is a nobler fate*
> *Than to be pitied,* and let ftrict juftice fteer
>   With equitable hand the helm of ftate,
> And arm thy tongue with truth: Oh king! beware
>   Of every ftep, a prince can never lightly err.   *T.*

[60] *Epidaurus.*—This was a city of the Peloponnefe, famous for a temple of Æfculapius. When the Romans were once afflicted by a grievous peftilence, they were ordered by the

oracle

LIII. In procefs of time, as Periander advanced
in years, he began to feel himfelf inadequate to the
cares of government; he fent therefore for Lycophron to Corcyra, to take upon him the adminiftration of affairs: his eldeft fon appeared improper
for fuch a ftation, and was indeed dull and ftupid.
Of the meffenger who brought him this intelligence
Lycophron difdained to take the fmalleft notice.
But Periander, as he felt his affection for the young
man to be unalterable, fent to him his fifter, thinking her interpofition moft likely to fucceed. When
fhe faw him, " Brother," faid fhe, " will you fuffer
" the fovereign authority to pafs into other hands,
" and the wealth of our family to be difperfed,
" rather than return to enjoy them yourfelf? Let

oracle to bring Æfculapius to Rome; they accordingly difpatched ambaffadors to Epidaurus to accomplifh this. The
Epidaurians refufing to part with their god, the Romans prepared to depart: as their veffel was quitting the port, an immenfe ferpent came fwimming towards them, and finally
wreathed itfelf round the prow; the crew, thinking it to be Æfculapius himfelf, carried him with much veneration to Rome.
—His entrance is finely defcribed by Ovid:—

> Jamque caput rerum Romanam intraverat urbem
> Erigitur ferpens—fummoque acclivia malo
> Colla movet: fedefque fibi circumfpicit aptas.

Which defcription, fully confidered, would perhaps afford no
mean fubject for an hiftorical painting.

Epidaurus was alfo famous for its breed of horfes.—See
Virgil, Georgic iii. 43, 4.

> Vocat ingenti clamore Cithæron
> Taygetique canes, domitrixque Epidaurus equorum.

The fame is alfo mentioned by Strabo, book viii.—T.

" me

" me entreat you to·punifh yourfelf no more; re-
" turn, to your country and your family: obfti-
" nacy like yours is but an unwelcome gueft, it only
" adds one evil to another. Pity is by many pre-
" ferred to juftice; and many, from their anxiety to
" fulfil their duty to a mother, have violated that
" which a father might expect. Power, which
" many fo affiduoufly court, is in its nature preca-
" rious. Your father is growing old, do not there-
" fore refign to others honours which are properly
" your own." Thus inftructed by her father, fhe
ufed every argument likely to influence her brother;
but he briefly anfwered, " that as long as his father
" lived he would not return to Corinth." When fhe
had communicated this anfwer to Periander, he
fent a third meffenger to his fon, informing him,
that it was his intention to retire to Corcyra; but
that he might return to Corinth, and take poffeffion
of the fupreme authority. This propofition was
accepted, and Periander prepared to depart for
Corcyra, the young man for Corinth. But when
the Corcyreans were informed of the bufinefs, to
prevent the arrival of Periander among them they
put his fon to death.—This was what induced that
prince to take vengeance of the Corcyreans.

LIV. The Lacedæmonians arriving with a powerful fleet, laid fiege to Samos, and advancing towards the walls, they paffed by a tower which ftands
in the fuburbs, not far from the fea. At this juncture Polycrates attacked them, at the head of a
confiderable force, and compelled them to retreat.

He

He was inftantly feconded by a band of auxiliaries; and a great number of Samians, who falling upon the enemy from a fort which was behind the mountain, after a fhort conflict effectually routed them; and continued the purfuit with great flaughter of the Lacedæmonians.

LV. If all the Lacedæmonians in this engagement had behaved like Archias and Lycopas, Samos muft certainly have been taken; for thefe two alone entered the city, with thofe Samians who fought fecurity within the walls, and having no means of retreat were there flain. I myfelf one day met with a perfon of the fame name, who was the fon of Samius, and grandfon of the Archias abovementioned; I faw him at Pitane [61], of which place he was a native. This perfon paid more attention to Samians than to other foreigners; and he told me, that his father was called Samius, as being the

[61] *Pitane.*]—This proper name involves fome perplexity, and has afforded exercife for much acute and ingenious criticifm. Martiniere, from miftaking a paffage of Paufánias, afferts that it was merely a quarter, or rather fuburbs of Lacedæmon, and is confequently often confounded with it. This miftake is ably pointed out and refuted by Bellanger, in his Critique de quelques Articles du Dict. de M. la Martiniere. This word is found in Hefychius, as defcriptive of a diftinct tribe; in Thucydides of a fmall town; and in Herodotus of a whole people :—— See book ix. chap. 52, where he fpeaks of the cohort of Pitane, which in the glorious battle of Platea was commanded by Amompharetus. It is certain that there were feveral places of this name; the one here fpecified was doubtlefs on the banks of the Eurotas, in Laconia.—See *Effais de Critique, &c.* 316.—— *T.*

immediate

immediate defcendant of him, who with fo much honour had loft his life at Samos. The reafon of his thus diftinguifhing the Samians, was becaufe they had honoured his grandfather by a public funeral [61].

LVI. The Lacedæmonians, after remaining forty days before the place without any advantage, returned to the Peloponnefe. It is reported, though

[61] *Public funeral.*]—The manner in which the funerals of thofe who had died in defence of their country were folemnized at Athens, cannot fail of giving the Englifh reader an elevated idea of that polifhed people.

On an appointed day a number of coffins made of cyprefs wood, and containing the bones of the deceafed, were expofed to view beneath a large tent erected for the purpofe ; they who had relations to deplore, affembled to weep over them, and pay the duties dictated by tendernefs or enjoined by religion. Three days afterwards the coffins were placed upon as many cars as there were tribes, and were carried flowly through the town, to the Ceramicus, where funeral games were celebrated. The bodies were depofited in the earth, and their relations and friends paid for the laft time the tribute of their tears ; an orator appointed by the republic from an elevated place pronounced a funeral oration over his valiant countrymen ; each tribe raifed over the graves fome kind of column, upon which was infcribed the names of the deceafed, their age, and the place where they died.

The above folemnities were conducted under the infpection of one of the principal magiftrates.

The moft magnificent public funeral of which we have any account, was that of Alexander the Great, when his body was brought from Babylon to Alexandria ; a minute defcription of which is given by Diodorus Siculus.

For a particular defcription of the ceremonies obferved at public and private funerals, amongft the Romans, confult Montfaucon.—*T.*

abfurdly

abfurdly enough, that Polycrates ftruck off a great
number of pieces of lead cafed with gold [63], like the
coin of the country, and that with thefe he purchaf-
ed their departure.—This was the firft expedition of
the Dorians of Lacedæmon into Afia.

LVII. Thofe Samians who had taken up arms
againft Polycrates, when they faw themfelves for-
faken by the Lacedæmonians, and were diftreffed
from want of money, embarked for Siphnos [64]. At
this

[63] *Lead cafed with gold.*]—Similar to this artifice, was that
practifed on the people of Gortyna in Crete, by Hannibal, as
recorded by Juftin. After the defeat of Antiochus by the Romans, Hannibal retired to Gortyna, carrying with him an immenfe treafure. This circumftance exciting an invidioufnefs
againft him, he pretended to depofit his riches in the temple of
Diana, to which place he carried with much ceremony feveral
veffels filled with lead. He foon took an opportunity of paffing
over into Afia with his real wealth, which he had concealed in
the images of the gods he affected to worfhip.—*T.*

[64] *Siphnos.*]—This was one of thofe fmall iflands lying oppofite to Attica: They were feventeen in number, and called,
from their fituation with refpect to each other, the Cyclades;
they were all eminently beautiful, and feverally diftinguifhed
by fome appropriate excellence. The marble of Paros was of
inimitable whitenefs, and of the fineft grain ; Andros and Naxos
produced the moft exquifite wine; Amengos was famous for a
die made from a lichen, growing there in vaft abundance. The
riches of Siphnos are extolled by many ancient writers; it is
now called Siphanto.

The following account of the modern circumftances of Siphnos, is extracted principally from Tournefort,

It is remarkable for the purity of its air; the water, fruit,
and poultry are very excellent. Although covered with marble
and granite, it is one of the moft fertile iflands of the Archipelago.

this time the power of the Siphnians was very confiderable, and they were the richeft of all the inhabitants of the iflands. Their foil produced both
the gold and filver metals in fuch abundance, that
from a tenth part of their revenues they had a treafury at Delphi, equal in value to the richeft which
that temple poffeffed. Every year they made an
equal diftribution among themfelves, of the value
of their mines : whilft their wealth was thus accu-
mulating, they confulted the oracle, to know whether they fhould long continue in the enjoyment of
their prefent good fortune. From the Pythian they
received this anfwer :

When Siphnos fhall a milk-white fenate fhew,
And all her market wear a front of fnow ;
Him let her prize whofe wit fufpects the moft,
A fcarlet envoy from a wooden hoft.

At this period the prytaneum, and the forum of
Siphnos, were adorned with Parian marble.

LVIII. This reply of the oracle the Siphnians
were unable to comprehend, both before and after

lago. They have a famous manufactory of ftraw hats, which
are fold all over the Archipelago, by the name of Siphanto caf-
tors: though once fo famous for its mines, the inhabitants can
now hardly tell you where they were. They have plenty of
lead, which the rains difcover. The ladies of Siphanto cover
their faces with linen bandages fo dexteroufly, that you can only
fee their mouth, nofe, and white of the eyes.—*T.*

the

the arrival of the Samians. As foon as the Samians touched at Siphnos, they difpatched a meffenger to the town, in one of their veffels. According to the ancient cuftom, all fhips were painted of
a red colour; and it was this which induced the
Pythian to warn the Siphnians againft a wooden
fnare, and a red ambaffador. On their arrival, the
Samian ambaffadors entreated the inhabitants to
lend them ten talents: on being refufed, they plundered the country. The Siphnians hearing of this,
collected their forces, and were defeated in a regular engagement; a great number were in the retreat cut off from the town, and the Samians afterwards exacted an hundred talents.

LIX. Inftead of money the Samians had received
of the Hermionians the ifland of Thyrea, adjacent
to the Peloponnefe: this they afterwards gave as a
pledge to the Træzenians. They afterwards made
a voyage to Crete, where they built Cydonia, although their object in going there was to expel the
Zacynthians. In this place they continued five
years, during which period they were fo exceedingly profperous, that they not only erected all thofe
temples which are now feen in Cydonia, but built
alfo the temple of Dictynna [65]. In the fixth year,
from a junction being made with the Cretans by
the

---

[65] *Dictynna.*]—Diana was worfhipped in Crete, indifferently
under the name of Dyctynna and of Britomartis. *Britu,* in
the Cretan language, meant fweet, and *martis,* a virgin. Britomartis

the Æginetæ, they were totally vanquished in a sea engagement, and reduced to servitude. The prows of their vessels were taken away and defaced, and afterwards suspended in the temple of Minerva at Ægina. To this conduct towards the Samians the Æginetæ were impelled in resentment of a former injury. When Amphicrates reigned at Samos, he had carried on a war against the Æginetæ, by which they materially suffered; this, however, they severely retaliated.

LX. I have been thus particular in my account of the Samians, because this people produced the greatest monuments[66] of art which are to be seen in Greece. They have a mountain which is one hundred and fifty orgyiæ in height; entirely through this they have made a passage, the length of which is seven stadia, it is moreover eight feet high, and

tomartis was the name of a virgin greatly beloved by Diana; and what is said by Diodorus Siculus on the subject seems most worthy of attention. His story is this:—Dictynna was born in Cæron; she invented hunters toils and nets, and thence her name. She was the daughter of Jupiter, which renders it exceedingly improbable that she should be obliged to fly from Minos, and leap into the sea, where she was caught in some fishers nets. The Mons Dictynnæus of Pliny is now called Cape Spada.—*T.*

[66] *The greatest monuments.*]—Of these monuments some vestiges are still to be seen, consult Tournefort, i. 314. Port Tigani is in form of a half moon, and regards the south-east; its left horn is that famous Jettee which Herodotus reckoned amongst the three wonders of Samos. This work, at that time of day, is an evidence of the Samians application to maritime matters.

as

as many wide. By the fide of this there is alfo an
artificial canal, which in like manner goes quite
through the mountain, and though only three feet
in breadth, is twenty cubits deep. This, by the
means of pipes, conveys to the city the waters of a
copious fpring [67]. This is their firft work, and
conftructed by Eupalinus, the fon of Nauftrophus,

[67] *Copious fpring.*]—On the left of the dale, near to the aqueduct
which croffes it, are certain caverns, the entrance of fome of them
artificially cut. In all appearance fome of thefe artificial caverns
were what Herodotus fays were ranked among the moft wonderful
performances of the Greek nation. The beautiful fpring which
tempted them to go upon fo great a work, is doubtlefs that of
Metelinous, the beft in the ifland, the difpofition of the place
proving perfectly favourable, the moment they had conquered
the difficulty of boring it: but in all probability they were not
exact enough in levelling the ground, for they were obliged to
dig a canal of twenty cubits deep for carrying the fpring to the
place defigned. There muft have been fome miftake in this
paffage of Herodotus.

Some five hundred paces from the fea, and almoft the like
diftance from the river Imbrafis to Cape Cera, are the ruins of
the famous temple of the Samian Juno. But for Herodotus we
fhould never have known the name of the architect. He employed a very particular order of columns, as may be now feen.
It is indeed neither better nor worfe than the Ionian order in its
infancy, void of that beauty which it afterwards acquired.
—Thus far Tournefort.

Its ancient names were Parthenias, Anthemus, and Melam-
phiffus. It was the birth-place of Pythagoras, and the fchool
of Epicurus. Pococke fays, that there are no remains which he
could prevail upon himfelf to believe to belong to this canal.
He adds, that the inhabitants are remarkably profligate and
poor. Tournefort makes a fimilar remark. There are no difciples of Pythagoras, obferves the Frenchman, now left in Samos ; the modern Samians are no more fond of fafting, than they
are lovers of filence.—*T.*

an

an inhabitant of Megara. Their fecond is a mole, which projects from the harbour into the fea, and is two ftadia or more in length, and about twenty orgyiæ in height. Their laft performance was a temple, which exceeds in grandeur all that I have feen. This ftructure was firft commenced by a native of the country, whofe name was Rhœcus [63], fon of Phileus.

LXI. Whilft Cambyfes, the fon of Cyrus, paffed his time in Ægypt, committing various exceffes, two magi, who were brothers, and one of whom Cambyfes had left in Perfia the manager of his domeftic concerns, excited a revolt againft him. The death of Smerdis, which had been ftudioufly kept fecret, and was known to very few of the Perfians, who in general believed that he was alive, was a circumftance to which the laft-mentioned of thefe magi had been privy, and of which he determined to avail himfelf. His brother, who, as we have related, joined with him in this bufinefs, not only refembled

---

[63] *Rhœcus.*]—This Rhœcus was not only a fkilful architect, but he farther invented, in conjunction with Theodorus of Samos, the art of making moulds with clay, long before the Bacchiades had been driven from Corinth; they were alfo the firft who made cafts in brafs, of which they formed ftatues. Paufanias relates the fame fact, with this addition, that upon a pedeftal behind the altar of Diana, called Protothenia, there is a ftatue by Rhœcus: it is a woman in bronze, faid by the Ephefians to be that of Night. He had two fons, Telecles and Theodorus, both ingenious ftatuaries.—*Larcher.*

in

in perſon [69] but had the very name of the young prince, the ſon of Cyrus, who had been put to death by the order of his brother Cambyſes. Him Patizithes, the other magus, publicly introduced and placed upon the royal throne, having previouſly inſtructed him in the part he was to perform. Having done this, he ſent meſſengers to different places, and one in particular to the Ægyptian army, ordering them to obey Smerdis, the ſon of Cyrus, alone.

LXII. Theſe orders were every where obeyed. The meſſenger who came to Ægypt found Cambyſes with the army at Ecbatana, in Syria. He entered into the midſt of the troops [70], and executed

the

[69] *Reſembled in perſon.*]—Similar hiſtorical incidents will here occur to the moſt common reader, there having been no ſtate whoſe annals are come down to us, in which, from the ſimilitude of perſon, factious individuals have not excited commotions. In the Roman government a falſe Pompey and a falſe Druſus claim our attention, becauſe one exerciſed the political ſagacity of Cicero, the other employed the pen of Tacitus. Neither have we in our own country been without ſimilar impoſtors, the examples of which muſt be too familiar to require inſertion here. —*T.*

[70] *Into the midſt of the troops.*]—It may to an Engliſh reader at firſt ſight ſeem extraordinary that any perſon ſhould dare to execute ſuch a commiſſion as this, and ſhould venture himſelf on ſuch a buſineſs amongſt the troops of a man whoſe power had been ſo long eſtabliſhed, and whoſe cruelty muſt have been notorious. But the perſons of heralds, as the functions they were to perform were the moſt important poſſible, were on all occaſions ſacred. Homer more than once calls them the ſacred miniſters of gods and men; they denounced war, and proclaimed peace,

the commiſſion which had been given him. When
Cambyſes heard this, he was not aware of any
fallacy, but imagined that Prexaſpes, whom he had
ſent to put Smerdis to death, had neglected to obey
his commands. " Prexaſpes," ſaid the king, " thou
" haſt not fulfilled my orders." " Sir," he replied,
" you are certainly deceived; it is impoſſible that
" your brother ſhould rebel againſt you, or occaſion
" you the ſmalleſt trouble. I not only executed
" your orders concerning Smerdis, but I buried
" him with my own hands. If the dead can riſe
" again, you may expect alſo a rebellion from Aſty-
" ages the Mede; but if things go on in their uſual
" courſe, you can have nothing to apprehend from
" your brother. I would recommend, therefore,
" that you ſend for this herald, and demand by
" what authority he claims our allegiance to Smer-
" dis."

peace. It has been a matter of diſpute amongſt the learned from
whence this ſanctity was conferred on them; they were ſaid to be
deſcended from Cenyx, the ſon of Mercury, and under the protection of that god. This office, in Athens and Sparta, was hereditary. In Athens, as I have obſerved, the heralds were ſaid to
be derived from Cenyx; in Sparta from Talthybius, the celebrated
herald of Agamemnon. They uſually carried a ſtaff of laurel
in their hands, ſometimes of olive, round this two ſerpents
were twiſted. To what an extreme this reverence for the perſons of ambaſſadors or heralds was carried, will appear from
the book Polymnia, chap. 134. It is almoſt unneceſſary to add,
that in modern times the perſons of ambaſſadors are in like
manner deemed ſacred, unleſs the treatment which in caſe of
war they receive at Conſtantinople be deemed an exception.
The moment that war is declared againſt any foreign power,
the repreſentative of that power is ſeized, and ſent as a priſoner
to the Black Tower.—*T.*

LXIII.

LXIII. This advice was agreeable to Cambyfes: the perfon of the herald was accordingly feized,
and he was thus addreffed by Prexafpes : "You
" fay," my friend, "that you come from Smerdis, the
" fon of Cyrus; but I would advife you to be cau-
" tious, as your fafety will depend upon your fpeak-
" ing the truth; tell me, therefore, did Smerdis
" himfelf entruft you with this commiffion, or did
" you receive it from fome one of his officers ?" " I
" muft confefs," replied the herald, " that fince the
" departure of Cambyfes on this Ægyptian expedi-
" tion, I have never feen Smerdis, the fon of Cyrus.
" I received my prefent commiffion from the ma-
" gus to whom Cambyfes entrufted the manage-
" ment of his domeftic affairs; he it was who told
" me that Smerdis, the fon of Cyrus, commanded
" me to execute this bufinefs." This was the fincere anfwer of the herald; upon which Cambyfes
thus addreffed Prexafpes : " I perceive that, like a
" man of integrity, you performed my commands,
" and have been guilty of no crime: but what Per-
" fian, affuming the name of Smerdis, has revolted
" againft me?" " Sir," anfwered Prexafpes, " I be-
" lieve I comprehend the whole of this bufinefs:
" the magi have excited this rebellion againft you,
" namely, Patizithes, to whom you entrufted the
" management of your houfhold, and Smerdis, his
" brother."

LXIV. As foon as Cambyfes heard the name of
Smerdis, he was impreffed with conviction of the
truth;

truth; and he immediately perceived the real signi‑ fication of the dream in which he had feen Smerdis feated on the royal throne, and touching the firmament with his head. Acknowledging that without any juft caufe he had deftroyed his brother, he lamented him with tears. After indulging for a while in the extremeft forrow, which a fenfe of his misfortunes prompted, he leaped haftily upon his horfe, determining to lead his army inftantly to Sufa againft the rebels. In doing this the fheath fell from his fword", which, being thus naked, wounded him in the thigh. The wound was in the very place in which he had before ftruck Apis, the deity of the Ægyptians. As foon as the blow appeared to be mortal, Cambyfes anxioufly enquired the name of the place where he was: they told him it was called Ecbatana. An oracle from Butos had warned him

---

71 *The fheath fell from the fword.*]—The firft fwords were probably made of brafs; for, as Lucretius obferves,

Et prior æris erat quam ferri cognitus ufus.

It has been remarked, on the following paffage of Virgil,

Ærataque micant peltæ, micat æneus enfis,

that the poet only ufes brafs poetically inftead of iron; this, however, feems forced and improbable. More anciently, which indeed appears from Homer, the fword was worn over the fhoulder; if, therefore, the attitude of Cambyfes in the act of mounting his horfe be confidered, his receiving the wound here defcribed does not appear at all unlikely. In contradiction to modern cuftom, the Romans fometimes wore two fwords, one on each fide; when they wore but one it was ufually, though not always, on the right fide. On this fubject, fee Montfaucon, where different fpecimens of ancient fwords may be feen. The Perfian fwords were called acinaces, or fcymetars.—*T*,

that

that he fhould end his life at Ecbatana; this he underftood of Ecbatana [72] of the Medes, where all his
treafures were depofited, and where he conceived
he was in his old age to die. The oracle, however,
fpoke of the Syrian Ecbatana. When he learned the name of the town, the vexation arifing from
the rebellion of the magus, and the pain of his
wound, reftored him to his proper fenfes. "This,"
he exclaimed, confidering the oracle, "is doubt-
"lefs the place in which Cambyfes, fon of Cyrus,
"is deftined to die."

LXV. On the twentieth day after the above
event he convened the more illuftrious of the Perfians who were with him, and thus addreffed them:
"What has happened to me, compels me to dif-
"clofe to you what I anxioufly defired to conceal.
"Whilft I was in Ægypt, I beheld in my fleep a

[72] *Ecbatana.*]—Ctefias makes this prince die at Babylon;
but this is not the only place in which he contradicts Herodotus.
—*Larcher.*

It appears by the context, that this Ecbatana was in Syria; an
obfcure place, probably, and unheard of by Cambyfes till this
moment. A fimilar fiction of a prophecy occurs in our own
hiftory. Henry the Fourth had been told he was to die in Jerufalem, but died in the Jerufalem chamber at Weftminfter. Which
tale Shakefpeare has immortalized by noticing it.

> It hath been prophefy'd to me many years
> I fhould not die but in Jerufalem,
> Which vainly I fuppos'd the Holy Land.
> But bear me to that chamber, there I'll lie,
> In that Jerufalem fhall Harry die.

Batanæa in Paleftine marks the place of this Syrian Ecbatana.
—*See d'Anville.*

T.

"vifion,

" vifion, which I could wifh had never appeared to
" me.   A meffenger feemed to arrive from home,
" informing me that. Smerdis, fitting on the royal
" throne, touched the heavens with his head.   It
" is not in the power of men to counteract deftiny;
" but fearing that my brother would deprive me of
" my kingdom, I yielded to paffion rather than to
" prudence. Infatuated as I was, I difpatched Prex-
" afpes to Sufa, to put Smerdis to death.   After
" this great crime, I lived with more confidence,
" believing that Smerdis being dead, no one elfe
" would rife up againft me.   But my ideas of the
" future were fallacious; I have murdered my bro-
" ther, a crime equally unneceffary and atrocious,
" and am neverthelefs deprived of my power.   It
" was Smerdis the magus [73] whom the divinity
                                            " pointed

[73] *Smerdis the magus*.]—Mr. Richardfon, in his Differtation on
the Language, &c. of Eaftern nations, fpeaking of the difagree-
ment between the Grecian and Afiatic hiftory of Perfia, makes
the following remarks.

From this period (610 before Chrift) till the Macedonian
conqueft, we have the hiftory of the Perfians as given us by the
Greeks, and the hiftory of the Perfians as written by themfelves.
Between thefe claffes of writers we might naturally expect fome
difference of facts, but we fhould as naturally look for a few
great lines which might mark fome fimilarity of ftory : yet from
every refearch which I have had an opportunity to make, there
feems to be nearly as much refemblance between the annals of
England and Japan, as between the European and Afiatic relations of the fame empire.   The names and numbers of their
kings have no analogy; and in regard to the moft fplendid facts
of the Greek hiftorians, the Perfians are entirely filent. We have
no mention of the great Cyrus, nor of any king of Perfia who
                                                        in

" poined out to me in my dream, 'and who has
" now taken arms againſt me. Things being
" thus circumſtanced, it becomes you to remember
" that Smerdis, the ſon of Cyrus, is actually dead,
" and that the two magi, one with whom I left the
" care of my houſhold, and Smerdis his brother, are
" the men who now claim your obedience. He
" whoſe office it would have been to have revenged
" on theſe magi any injuries done to me, has un-
" worthily periſhed by thoſe who were neareſt to
" him: but ſince he is no more, I muſt now tell
" you, oh Perſians! what I would have you do
" when I am dead — I intreat you all, by thoſe gods
" who watch over kings, and chiefly you who are

in the events of his reign can apparently be forced into a ſimilitude. We have no Crœſus, king of Lydia; not a ſyllable of
Cambyſes, or of his frantic expedition againſt the Æthiopians.
Smerdis Magus, and the ſucceſſion of Darius, the ſon of Hy-
ſtaſpes, by the neighing of his horſe, are to the Perſians circumſtances equally unknown, as the numerous aſſaſſinations recorded
by the Greeks, &c.

To do away, at leaſt in part, any impreſſion to the prejudice of
Grecian hiſtory; which may be made by peruſing the above remarks of Mr. Richardſon, the reader is preſented with the following ſentiments of Mr. Gibbon.

" So little has been preſerved of Eaſtern hiſtory before Mahomet, that the modern Perſians are totally ignorant of the victory of Sapor, an event ſo glorious to their nation."

The incident here mentioned is the victory of Sapor over Va-
lerian the Roman emperor, who was defeated, taken priſoner,
and died in captivity. This happened in the year 260 of the
Chriſtian æra. Mahomet was born in the year 571 of the ſame
æra; if, therefore, Mr. Gibbon's obſervation be well founded,
which it appears to be, Mr. Richardſon's objections fall to the
ground.—T.

" of

" of the race of the Achæmenides, that you will
" never permit this empire to revert to the Medes
" If by any ftratagem they fhall have feized it, by
" ftratagem do you recover it. If they have by
" force obtained it, do you by force wreft it from
" them. If you fhall obey my advice, may the
" earth give you its fruits in abundance; may you
" ever be free, and your wives and your flocks pro-
" lific! If you do not obey me, if you neither
" recover nor attempt to recover the empire, may
" the reverfe of my wifhes befal you, and may
" every Perfian meet a fate like mine!"

LXVI. Cambyfes having thus fpoken, bewailed
his misfortunes. When the Perfians faw the king
thus involved in forrow, they tore their garments,
and expreffed their grief aloud. After a very fhort
interval the bone became infected, the whole of the
thigh mortified, and death enfued. Thus died
Cambyfes, fon of Cyrus, after a reign of feven
years and five months[74], leaving no offspring, male or
female. The Perfians who were prefent could not be
perfuaded that the magi had affumed the fupreme authority; but rather believed that what Cambyfes had
afferted concerning the death of Smerdis was prompted by his hatred of that prince, and his wifh to excite the general animofity of the Perfians againft him.
They were, therefore, generally fatisfied that it was
really Smerdis, the fon of Cyrus, who had affumed

[74] *Seven years and five months.*]—Clemens Alexandrinus
makes him reign ten years.—*Larcher.*

§   the

the fovereignty. To which they were the more inclined, becaufe Prexafpes afterwards pofitively denied that he had put Smerdis to death. When
Cambyfes was dead he could not fafely have confeffed that he had killed the fon of Cyrus.

LXVII. After the death of Cambyfes, the magus, by the favour of his name, pretending to be
Smerdis, the fon of Cyrus, reigned in fecurity
during the feven months which completed the eighth
year of the reign of Cambyfes. In this period he
diftinguifhed the various dependents on his power
by his great munificence, fo that after his death he
was ferioufly regretted by all the inhabitants of Afia,
except the Perfians. He commenced his reign by
publifhing every where an edict which exempted his
iubjects for the fpace of three years both from tribute and military fervice.

LXVIII. In the eighth month he was detected
in the following manner: Otanes, fon of Phar-
nafpes, was of the firft rank of the Perfians, both
with regard to birth and affluence. This nobleman
was the firft who fufpected that this was not Smerdis, the fon of Cyrus; and was induced to fuppofe
who he really was, from his never quitting the citadel,
and from his not inviting any of the nobles to his
prefence. Sufpicious of the impofture, he took thefe
meafures:—He had a daughter named Phædyma,
who had been married to Cambyfes, and whom,
with the other wives of the late king, the ufurper
had taken to himfelf. Otanes fent a meffage to
her,

her, to know whether fhe cohabited with Smerdis, the fon of Cyrus, or with any other perfon. She returned for anfwer, "that fhe could not tell, as fhe "had never feen Smerdis, the fon of Cyrus, nor did "fhe know the perfon with whom fhe cohabited." Otanes fent a fecond time to his daughter: "If," fays he, "you do not know the perfon of Smerdis, the "fon of Cyrus, enquire of Atoffa who it is with "whom you and fhe cohabit, for fhe muft neceffarily "know her brother." To which fhe thus replied, "I can neither fpeak to Atoffa, nor indeed fee any "of the women that live with him. Since this "perfon, whoever he is, came to the throne, the "women have all been kept feparate[75]."

LXIX.

---

[75] *Kept feparate.*]—Chardin, fpeaking of the death of a king of Perfia, and the intemperate grief of his wives, fays, that the reafon why the women upon fuch occafions are fo deeply af-flicted, is not only for the lofs of the king their hufband, but for the lofs of that fhadow of liberty which they enjoyed during his life; for no fooner is the prince laid in his tomb, but they are all fhut up in particular houfes. Tournefort tells us, that after the death of the fultan at Conftantinople, the women whom he honoured with his embraces, and their eldeft daughters, are re-moved into the old feraglio of Conftantinople; the younger are fometimes left for the new emperor, or are married to the bafhas.

It appears that in the Eaft from the remoteft times females have been jealoufly fecluded from the other fex. Neverthelefs, we learn from modern travellers, that this is done with fome re-ftrictions, and that they are not only fuffered to communicate with each other, but on certain days to leave the haram or fera-glio, and take their amufements abroad.

Where a plurality of wives is allowed, each, it fhould feem from Tournefort, has a diftinct and feparate apartment. "I was

LXIX. This reply more and more justified the suspicions of Otanes; he sent, therefore, a third time to his daughter: "My daughter," he observed, "it becomes you, who are nobly born, to "engage in a dangerous enterprize, when your "father commands you. If this Smerdis [76] be not "the son of Cyrus, but the man whom I suspect, he "ought not, possessing your person, and the sove- "reignty of Persia, to escape with impunity. Do "this, therefore—when next you shall be admitted "to his bed, and shall observe that he is asleep, "examine whether he has any ears; if he has, you

extremely at a loss," says he, "how to behave to the great men of the East, when I was called in, and visited, as a physician, the apartments of their wives. These apartments are just like the dormitories of our religious, and at every door I found an arm covered with gauze, thrust out through a small loop-hole, made on purpose: at first I fancied they were arms of wood or brass, to serve for sconces to light up candles in at night; but it surprized me when I was told I must cure the persons to whom these arms belonged." The Easterns listen with much astonishment to the familiarity prevailing betwixt the sexes in Europe. When told that no evil results from this, they answer with a proverb, "Bring butter too near the fire, and you will hardly keep it from melting."—T.

[76] If this Smerdis.]—That Cambyses was the Ahasuerus, and Smerdis the Artaxerxes, that obstructed the work of the temple, is plain from hence, that they are said in Scripture to be the kings of Persia that reigned between the time of Cyrus and the time of that Darius by whose decree the temple was finished; but that Darius being Darius Hystaspes, and none reigning between Cyrus and that Darius in Persia, but Cambyses and Smerdis, it must follow from hence, that none but Cambyses and Smerdis could be the Ahasuerus and Artaxerxes, who are said in Ezra to have put a stop to this work.—Prideaux.

"may

" may be fecure you are with Smerdis, the fon of
" Cyrus ; but if he has not, it can be no other than
" Smerdis, one of the magi." To this Phædyma
replied, " That fhe would obey him, notwithftand-
" ing the danger fhe incurred; being well affured,
" that if he had no ears, and fhould difcover her in
" endeavouring to know this, fhe fhould be inftantly
" put to death." Cyrus had in his life-time deprived
this Smerdis of his ears [77] for fome atrocious crime.

Phædyma complied in all refpects with the injunctions of her father. The wives of the Perfians
fleep with their hufbands by turns [78]. When this
lady

[77] *This Smerdis of his ears.*]—The difcovery of this impofture
was long celebrated in Perfia as an annual feftival. By reafon
of the great flaughter of the magians then made, it was called
magophonia. It was alfo from this time that they firft had the
name of magians, which fignified the cropt-eared, which was
then given them on account of this impoftor, who was thus cropt.
Mige-gufh fignified, in the language of the country then in ufe,
one that had his ears cropt; and from a ringleader of that fect who
was thus cropt, the author of the famous Arabic lexicon called Ca-
mus, tells us they had all this name given them ; and what Herodotus and Juftin, and other authors, write of this Smerdis,
plainly fhews that he was the man.—*Prideaux.*

[78] *The wives of the Perfians fleep with their hufbands by turns.*]
—By the Mahometan law, the Perfians, Turks, and indeed all
true believers, are permitted to have wives of three different
defcriptions ; thofe whom they efpoufe, thofe whom they hire,
and thofe whom they purchafe. Of the firft kind they are limited to four, of the two laft they may have as many as they
pleafe or can afford. Amongft the fingularities fanctified by the
Alcoran, the following is not the leaft: a woman legally efpoufed
may infift on a divorce from her hufband, if he is impotent, if
he is given to unnatural enjoyment, or, to ufe Tournefort's ex-

preffion,

lady next flept with the magus, as foon as fhe faw him in a profound fleep, fhe tried to touch his ears, and being perfectly fatisfied that he had none, as foon as it was day fhe communicated the intelligence to her father.

LXX. Otanes inftantly revealed the fecret to Afpathines and Gobryas, two of the nobleft of the Perfians, upon whofe fidelity he could depend, and who had themfelves fufpected the impofture. It was agreed that each fhould difclofe the bufinefs to the friend in whom he moft confided. Otanes therefore chofe Intaphernes, Gobryas Megabyzus, and Afpathines, Hydarnes. The confpirators being thus fix in number, Darius, fon of Hyftafpes, arrived at Sufa, from Perfia, where his father was governor, when they inftantly agreed to make him alfo an affociate.

LXXI. Thefe feven met [79], and after mutual vows of fidelity confulted together. As foon as Darius was to fpeak, he thus addreffed his confederates: " I was of opinion that the death of Smerdis, " fon of Cyrus, and the ufurpation of the magus, " were circumftances known only to myfelf; and my " immediate purpofe in coming here, was to accom-

preffion, if he does not pay his tribute upon Thurfday and Friday night, which are the times confecrated to the conjugal duties. —T.

[79] *Thefe feven met.*]—Mithridates, king of Pontus, who afterwards gave fo much trouble to the Romans, was defcended from one of thefe confpirators: fee book vii. chap. ii.—*Larcher.*

† " plifh

" plilh the ufurper's death. But fince you are alfo
" acquainted with the matter, I think that all delay
" will be dangerous, and that we fhould inftantly
" execute our intentions." " Son of Hyftafpes,"
replied Otanes, " born of a noble parent, you feem
" the inheritor of your father's virtue; neverthelefs,
" be not precipitate, but let us enter on this bufinefs
" with caution: for my own part, I am averfe to
" undertake any thing, till we fhall have ftrengthen-
" ed our party." " My friends," refumed Darius,
" if you follow the advice of Otanes, your ruin is
" inevitable. The hope of reward will induce fome
" one to betray your defigns to the magus. An
" enterprize like this fhould be accomplifhed by
" yourfelves, difdaining all affiftance. But fince
" you have diffufed the fecret, and added me to
" your party, let us this very day put our defigns
" in execution; for I declare, if this day pafs with-
" out our fulfilling our intentions, no one fhall to-
" morrow betray me; I will myfelf difclofe the con-
" fpiracy to the magus."

LXXII. When Otanes obferved the ardour of
Darius; " Since," he replied, " you will not fuffer
" us to defer, but precipitate us to the termination
" of our purpofe, explain how we fhall obtain en-
" trance into the palace, and attack the ufurpers.
" That there are guards regularly ftationed, if you
" have not feen them yourfelf, you muft have known
" from others; how fhall we elude thefe?" " There
" are many circumftances, Otanes," returned Darius, " which we cannot fo well explain by our

" words

" words as by our actions. There are others which
" may be made very plaufible by words, but are ca-
" pable of no fplendour in the execution. You can-
" not fuppofe that it will be difficult for us to pafs
" the guards; who amongft them will not be im-
" pelled by reverence of our perfons, or fear of our
" authority, to admit us? Befides this, I am fur-
" nifhed with an undeniable excufe; I can fay that
" I am juft arrived from Perfia, and have bufinefs
" from my father with the king. If a falfhood muft
" be fpoken [80], let it be fo. They who are fincere,
" and they who are not, have the fame object in
" view. Falfhood is prompted by views of intereft,

[80] *If a falfhood muft be fpoken.*]—This morality, fays Larcher, is
not very rigid ; but it ought, he continues, to be remembered,
that Herodotus is here fpeaking of falfhood which operates to no
one's injury. Bryant, on the contrary, remarks, that we may
reft affured thefe are the author's own fentiments, though
attributed to another perfon; hence, he adds, we muft not wonder if his veracity be fometimes called in queftion. But when
we remember that one of the firft rudiments of Perfian education was to fpeak the truth, the little fcruple with which
Darius here adopts a falfhood, muft appear very remarkable.
Upon this fubject of fincerity, Lord Shaftefbury has fome very
curious remarks. "The chief of ancient critics," fays he,
" extols Homer above all things for underftanding how to lye in
perfection. His lyes, according to that mafter's opinion, and
the judgment of the graveft and moft venerable writers, were in
themfelves the jufteft moral truths, and exhibitive of the beft
doctrine and inftruction in life and manners." It is well remarked by one of the ancients, though I do not remember which,
that a violation of truth implies a contempt of God, and fear of
man. Yet the graveft of our moralifts and divines have allowed
that there may be occafions in which a deviation from ftrict truth
is venial,—*T.*

" and

" and the language of truth is dictated by fome pro-
" mifed benefit, or the hope of infpiring confidence.
" So that, in fact, thefe are only two different paths
" to the fame end: if no emolument were propofed,
" the fincere man would be falfe, and the falfe man
" fincere. As to the guards, he who fuffers us to
" pafs fhall ·hereafter be remembered to his advan-
" tage; he who oppofes us fhall be deemed an ene-
" my: let us, therefore, now haften to· the palace,
" and execute our purpofe."

LXXIII. When he had finifhed, Gobryas fpake
as follows: " My friends, to recover the empire
" will indeed be glorious; but if we fail, it will be
" nobler to die, than for Perfians to live in fubjection
" to a Mede, and he too deprived of his ears. You
" who were prefent at the laft hours of Cambyfes,
" cannot but remember the imprecations which he
" uttered againft the Perfians if they did not attempt
" the recovery of the empire. We then refufed him,
" attention, thinking him influenced by malignity
" and refentment; ·but now I at leaft fecond the
" propofal of Darius, nor would I have this affem-
" bly break up, but to proceed inftantly againft the
" magus." The fentiments of Gobryas gave univerfal fatisfaction.

LXXIV. During the interval of this confultation, the two magi had together determined to make
a friend of Prexafpes : they were aware that he had
been injured by Cambyfes, who had flain his fon
with an arrow; and that he alone was privy to the

death

death of Smerdis, the son of Cyrus, having been
his executioner; they were conscious also that he
was highly esteemed by the Persians. They accordingly sent for him, and made him the most
liberal promises; they made him swear that he
would on no account disclose the fallacy which
they practised on the Persians; and they promised
him, in reward of his fidelity, rewards without number. Prexaspes engaged to comply with their
wishes; they then told him of their intention to
assemble the Persians beneath the tower[81] which
was the royal residence, from whence they desired
him to declare aloud that he who then sate on the
throne of Persia was Smerdis, the son of Cyrus,
and no other. They were induced to this measure,
from a consideration of the great authority of Prexaspes, and because he had frequently declared that
he had never put Smerdis, the son of Cyrus, to
death, but that he was still alive.

LXXV. Prexaspes agreed to comply with all
that they proposed; the magi accordingly assembled
the Persians, and leading Prexaspes to the top of
the tower, commanded him to make an oration.
He, without paying the least attention to the promises he had made, recited the genealogy of the

---

[81] *Beneath the tower.*]—This was the citadel. Anciently the
kings lodged here for security. In chap. lxviii. Herodotus ob-
serves that the magus would not stir from the citadel, and in
chap. lxxix. he says that the conspirators left behind in the citadel such of their friends as were wounded in attacking the
magi.—*Larcher.*

family

family of Cyrus, beginning with Achæmenes. When he came to Cyrus himself, he enumerated the services which that prince had rendered the Persians. He then made a full discovery of the truth, excusing himself for concealing it so long, from the danger which the revealing it would have incurred, but that it was now forced from him. He assured them that he actually had killed Smerdis, by the order of Cambyses, and that the magi now exercised the sovereign authority. When he had imprecated many curses [81] upon the Persians, if they

- did

[81] *Imprecated many curses.*]—In ancient times, and amongst the Orientals in particular, these kind of imprecations were very frequent, and supposed to have an extraordinary influence. The curse of a father was believed to be particularly fatal; and the furies were always thought to execute the imprecations of parents upon disobedient children: see the stories of Œdipus and Theseus. When Joshua destroyed Jericho, he imprecated a severe curse upon whoever should attempt to rebuild it. This was, however, at a distant period of time accomplished. We have two examples of solemn imprecations on record, which have always been deemed worthy of attention. The one occurred in ancient Rome: When Crassus, in defiance of the auspices, prepared to make an expedition against the Parthians. The tribune Ateius waited for him at the gates of the city, with an altar, a fire, and a sacrifice ready prepared, and with the most horrid solemnity devoted him to destruction. The other example is more modern, it is the imprecation which Averroes, the famous Arabian philosopher, uttered against his son. As it is less generally known, I shall recite it at length: Averroes was one day seriously conversing with some grave friends, when his son, in a riotous manner, intruded himself, accompanied by some dissolute companions. The old man, viewing him with great indignation, spoke two verses to the following effect: "Thy own beauties could not content thee, thou hast

stript

did not attempt the recovery of their rights, and to take vengeance upon the ufurpers, he threw himfelf from the tower.—Such was the end of Prexafpes, a man who through every period of his life merited efteem [31].

LXXVI. The feven Perfians having determined inftantly to attack the magi, proceeded, after imploring the aid of the gods, to execute their purpofe. They were at firft ignorant of what related to the fate of Prexafpes, but they learned it as they went along. They withdrew for a while to deliberate together; they who fided with Otanes, thought that their enterprize fhould be deferred, at leaft during the prefent tumult of affairs. The friends of Darius, on the contrary, were averfe to any delay, and were anxious to execute what they had refolved immediately. Whilft they remained in this fufpence, they obferved feven pair of hawks [34], which,

ftript the wild goat of his beauties; and they who are as beautiful as thyfelf admire thee. Thou haft got his wanton heart, his lecherous eyes, and his fenfelefs head; but to-morrow thou fhalt find thy father will have his pufhing horns. Curfed be all extravagancies: when I was young I fometimes punifhed my father, now I am old I cannot punifh my fon; but I beg of God to deprive him rather of life, than fuffer him to be difobedient." It is related that the young man died within ten months.—*T.*

[31] *Merited efteem.*]—Upon this incident M. Larcher remarks, that this laft noble action of his life but ill correfponds with the mean and daftardly behaviour which Prexafpes had before exhibited to the murderer of his fon.

[34] *Seven pair of hawks.*]—The fuperftition of the ancients, with refpect to the fight or flight of birds, has often exercifed

the

which, purfuing two pair of vultures, beat and feverely tore them. At this fight the confpirators
came immediately into the defigns of Darius; and,
relying on the omen of the birds, advanced boldly
to the palace.

LXXVII. On their arrival at the gates, it happened as Darius had forefeen. The guards, unfuf-
picious of what was intended, and awed by their
dignity [85] of rank, who, in this inftance, feemed to

the fagacity and acutenefs of philofophers and fcholars. Some
birds furnifhed omens from their chattering, as crows, owls, &c.
others from the direction in which they flew, as eagles, vultures,
hawks, &c. An eagle feen to the right was fortunate.—See Homer. The fight of an eagle was fuppofed to foretel to Tarquinius
Prifcus, that he fhould obtain the crown; it predicted alfo, the
conquefts of Alexander; and the lofs of their dominions to Tarquin the Proud, and Dionyfius tyrant of Syracufe; innumerable
other examples muft here occur to the moft common reader.
A raven feen on the left hand was unfortunate.

Sæpe finiftra cava prædixit ab ilice cornix.—*Virgil.*

Upon the fubject of the aufpicia, the moft fatisfactory intelligence is to be obtained from the treatife of Cicero de Divina-
tione. From the Latin word *aufpicia,* from *aves infpicere,*
comes our Englifh word *aufpicious.*—*T.*

[85] *Awed by their dignity.*]—The moft memorable inftance in
hiftory, of the effects of this kind of impreffion, is that of the
foldier fent into the prifon to kill Caius Marius:—The ftory is
related at length by Plutarch. When the man entered the prifon
with his fword drawn, "Fellow," exclaimed the ftern Roman,
"dareft thou kill Caius Marius?" Upon which the foldier dropt
his fword, and rufhed out of doors. This fact, however, being
no where mentioned by Cicero, who fpeaks very largely on the
fubject of Marius, has given Dr. Middleton reafon to fuppofe,
that the whole is a fabulous narration.—*T.*

act

act from a divine impulse, without any quions permitted them to enter. As soon as they came to the interior part of the palace, they met with the eunuchs, who were employed as the royal meffengers; thefe afked their bufinefs, and at the fame time threatened the guards for fuffering them to enter. On their oppofing their farther entrance, the confpirators drew their fwords, and encouraging each other, put the eunuchs to death; from hence they inftantly rufhed to the inner apartments.

LXXVIII. Here the two magi happened to be, in confultation about what was to be done in confequence of the conduct of Prexafpes. As foon as they perceived the tumult, and heard the cries of the eunuchs, they ran towards them, and preparing in a manly manner to defend themfelves, the one feized a bow and the other a lance. As the confpirators drew near to the attack, the bow became ufelefs; but the other magus, who was armed with the lance, wounded Afpathines in the thigh, and deprived Intaphernes of one of his eyes, though the blow was not fatal. The magus who found his bow of no fervice retreated to an adjoining apartment, into which he was followed by Darius and Gobryas. This latter feized the magus round the waift[86], but as this happened in the dark, Darius ftood

in

---

[86] *Round the waift.*]—Not unlike to this was the manner in which David Rizio, the favourite of the unfortunate Mary queen

in hefitation, fearing to ftrike, left he fhould wound
Gobryas. When Gobryas perceived this, he enquired why he was thus inactive : when Darius replied,
" that it was from his fear of wounding his friend,"
" Strike," exclaimed Gobryas, "though you fhall
" pierce both."—Darius inftantly complied, and ran
his fword through the magus.

LXXIX. Having thus flain the magi [37], they
inftantly

queen of Scots, was murdered. Rizio was at fupper with his
miftrefs, attended by a few domeftics, when the king, who had
chofen this place and opportunity to fatisfy his vengeance, entered the apartment with Ruthven and his accomplices. The
wretched favourite, conceiving himfelf the victim whofe death
was required, flew for protection to the queen, whom he feized
round the waift. This attitude did not fave him from the dagger of Ruthven ; and before he could be dragged to the next
apartment, the rage of his enemies put an end to his life, pierc-
ing his body with fifty-fix wounds.—See the account in Robert-
fon's Hiftory of Scotland, vol. i. 359.—T.

[37] The magi.]—It may not in this place be impertinent, to
give a fuccinct account of the magi or magians, as felected
from various writers on the fubject. This fect originating in
the Eaft, abominating all images, worfhipped God only by fire.
Their chief doctrine was, that there were two principles, one of
which was the caufe of all good, the other the caufe of all evil.
The former is reprefented by light, the other by darknefs, and
that from thefe two all things in the world were made. The
good god they named Yazdan or Ormund ; the evil god, Ahra-
man : the former is by the Greeks named Oramafdes, the latter Arimanius. Concerning thefe two gods, fome held both of
them to have been from eternity ; others contended the good
being only to be eternal, the other created : both agreed in this,
that there will be a continual oppofition between thefe two till
the end of the world, when the good god fhall overcome the
evil

inftantly cut off their heads. Their two friends who were wounded were left behind, as well to guard the

evil god; and that afterwards each fhall have his world to him-felf, the good god have all good men with him, the evil god all wicked men. Of this fyftem Zoroafter was the firft founder, whom Hyde and Prideaux make cotemporary with Darius Hyftafpes, but whofe æra, as appears from Moyle, the Greek writers of the age of Darius make many hundred years before their own time. After giving a concife but animated account of the theology of Zoroafter, Mr. Gibbon has this remark: " Every mode of religion, to make a deep and lafting impreffion on the human mind, muft exercife our obedience, by enjoining practices of devotion for which we can affign no reafon; and muft acquire our efteem by inculcating moral duties, analogous to the dictates of our own hearts." The religion of Zoroafter was abundantly provided with the former, and poffeffed a fufficient portion of the latter. At the age of puberty the faithful Per-fian was invefted with a myfterious girdle, from which moment the moft indifferent action of his life was fanctified by prayers, ejaculations, and genuflexions, the omiffion of which was a grie-vous fin. The moral duties, however, were required of the difciple of Zoroafter, who wifhed to efcape the perfecution of Arimanius, or as Mr. Gibbon writes it, Ahriman, and to live with Ormund or Ormufd in a blifsful eternity, where the de-gree of felicity will be exactly proportioned to the degree of virtue and piety. In the time of Theodofius the younger, the Chriftians enjoyed a full toleration in Perfia; but Abdas indif-creetly pulling down a temple, in which the Perfians worfhipped fire, a perfecution againft the Chriftians was excited, and profe-cuted with unrelenting cruelty. The magi are ftill known in Perfia, under the name of parfi or parfes; their fuperftition is contained in three books, named Zend, Pazend, and Veftna, faid by themfelves to be compofed by Zerdafcht, whom they confound with the patriarch Abraham. The Oriental Chriftians pretend, that the magi who adored Jefus Chrift, were difciples of Zoroafter, who predicted to them the coming of the Meffiah, and

the citadel, as on account of their inability to follow them. The remaining five ran out into the
public ſtreet, having the heads of the magi in their
hands, and making violent outcries. They called
aloud to the Perſians, explaining what had happened, and expoſing the heads of the uſurpers; at the
ſame time, whoever of the magi appeared was inſtantly put to death. The Perſians hearing what
theſe ſeven noblemen had effected, and learning the
impoſture practiſed on them by the magi, were
ſeized with the deſire of imitating their conduct.
Sallying forth with drawn ſwords, they killed every
magus whom they met; and if night had not checked
their rage, not one would have eſcaped. The an-
niverſary of this day the Perſians celebrate with
great ſolemnity; the feſtival they obſerve is called
the magophonia, or the ſlaughter of the magi. On
this occaſion no magus is permitted to be ſeen in
public, they are obliged to confine themſelves at
home.

LXXX. When the tumult had ſubſided, and an
interval of five days were elapſed, the conſpirators

---

and the new ſtar which appeared at his birth. Upon this latter
ſubject a modern writer has ingeniouſly remarked, that the preſents which the magi made to Chriſt, indicated their eſteeming
him a royal child, notwithſtanding his mean ſituation and appearance: they gave him gold, frankincenſe, and myrrh, ſuch
as the queen of Sheba preſented to Solomon in his glory.

It ſeems almoſt unneceſſary to add, that from theſe magi or
magians the Engliſh word *magic* is derived:—See Prideaux,
Gibbon, Bayle, Bibliotheque Orientale, and Harmer's Obſervations on Paſſages of Scripture.—*T*.

met

met to deliberate on the fituation of affairs. Their fentiments, as delivered on this occafion, however they may want credit with many of the Greeks, were in fact as follows.—Otanes recommended a republican form of government: "It does not," fays he, " feem to me advifeable, that the govern- " ment of Perfia [ss] fhould hereafter be entrufted " to any individual perfon, this being neither po- " pular nor wife. We all know the extreme lengths " to which the arrogance of Cambyfes proceeded, " and fome of us have felt its influence. How can " that form of government poffibly be good, in " which an individual with impunity may indulge " his paffions, and which is apt to tranfport even " the beft of men beyond the bounds of reafon? " When a man, naturally envious, attains great- " nefs, he inftantly becomes infolent : Infolence " and jealoufy are the diftinguifhing vices of ty- " rants, and when combined lead to the moft enor- " mous crimes. He who is placed at the fummit

---

[ss] *Government of Perfia.*]—Machiavel, reafoning upon the conquefts of Alexander the Great, and upon the unrefifting fub- miffion which his fucceffors experienced from the Perfians, takes it for granted, that amongft the ancient Perfians there was no diftinction of nobility. This, however, was by no means the cafe ; and what Mr. Hume remarks of the Florentine fecretary was undoubtedly true, that he was far better acquainted with Roman than with Greek authors :—See the Effay of Mr. Hume, where he afferts that " Politics may be reduced to a fcience;" with his note at the end of the volume, which contains an enu- meration of various Perfian noblemen of different periods, as well as a refutation of Machiavel's abfurd pofition above ftated. —*T.*

" of

" of power, ought indeed to be a ftranger to envy;
" but we know, by fatal experience, that the con-
" trary happens. We know alfo, that the wor-
" thieft citizens excite the jealoufy of tyrants, who
" are pleafed only with the moft abandoned: they
" are ever prompt to liften to the voice of calumny.
" If we pay them temperate refpect, they take um-
" brage that we are not more profufe in our atten-
" tions: if the refpect with which they are treated
" feem immoderate, they call it adulation. The
" fevereft misfortune of all is, that they pervert the
" inftitutions of their country, offer violence to
" our females, and put thofe whom they diflike to
" death, without the formalities of juftice. But a
" democracy in the firft place bears the honourable
" name of an equality [89]; the diforders which pre-
" vail in a monarchy cannot there take place.
" The magiftrate is appointed by lot, he is ac-
" countable for his adminiftration, and whatever is
" done, muft be with the general confent. I am,

---

[89] *Equality.*]—The word in the original is ισονομιην, which
means equality of laws. M. Larcher tranflates it literally ifo-
nomie; but in Englifh, as we have no authority for the ufe of it,
ifonomy would perhaps feem pedantic. The following paffage
from lord Shaftfbury fully explains the word in queftion.—
Speaking of the influence of tyranny on the arts, " The high
fpirit of tragedy," fays he, " can ill fubfift where the fpirit of
liberty is wanting." The genius of this poetry confifts in the
lively reprefentation of the diforders and mifery of the great; to
the end that the people, and thofe of a lower condition, may be
taught the better to content themfelves with privacy, enjoy
their fafer ftate, and prize the *equality* and juftice of their guardian laws.—*T.*

" therefore, of opinion, that monarchy should be
" abolished, and that, as every thing depends on
" the people ", a popular government should be
" established."—Such were the sentiments of Otanes.

LXXXI. Megabyzus, however, was inclined to
an oligarchy; in favour of which he thus expressed
himself: " All that Otanes has urged, concerning
" the extirpation of tyranny, meets with my entire
" approbation; but when he recommends the su-
" preme authority to be entrusted to the people,
" he seems to me to err in the extreme. Tumul-
" tuous assemblies of the people are never distin-
" guished by wisdom, always by insolence; nei-
" ther can any thing be possibly more preposte-
" rous, than to fly from the tyranny of an indivi-
" dual to the intemperate caprice of the vulgar.
" Whatever a tyrant undertakes, has the merit of
" previous concert and design; but the people are
" always rash and ignorant. And how can they
" be otherwise, who are uninstructed, and with no

---

⁹⁰ *Every thing depends on the people.*]—In this place the favourite adage of Vox populi vox Dei, must occur to every reader;
the truth of which, as far as power is concerned, is certainly
indisputable; but with respect to political sagacity, the sentiment
of Horace may be more securely vindicated:

Interdum vulgus rectum videt, est ubi peccat.

Which Pope happily renders,

The people's voice is odd;
It is, and it is not, the voice of God.   *T*.

" internal

" internal fenfe[91] of what is good and right ? Def-
" titute of judgment, their actions refemble the vio-
" lence of a torrent[92]. To me, a democracy feems
" to involve the ruin of our country : let us, there-

[91] *No internal fenfe.*]—The original is fomewhat perplexed;
but the acute Valcnaer, by reading οικοθεν for οικγιον, at once removes all difficulty.—*T.*

[92] *Their actions refemble the violence of a torrent.*]—Upon the
fubject of popular affemblies, the following remarks of M. de
Lolme feem very ingenious, as well as juft.

" Thofe who compofe a popular affembly are not actuated,
in the courfe of their deliberations, by any clear or precife view
of any prefent or pofitive perfonal intereft. As they fee themfelves loft as it were in the crowd of thofe who are called upon
to exercife the fame function with themfelves; as they know that
their individual vote will make no change in the public refolution, and that to whatever fide they may incline, the general
refult will neverthelefs be the fame, they do not undertake to enquire how far the things propofed to them agree with the
whole of the laws already in being, or with the prefent circumftances of the ftate. As few among them have previoufly confidered the fubjects on which they are called upon to determine;
very few carry along with them any opinion or inclination of
their own; and to which they are refolved to adhere. As, however, it is neceffary at laft to come to fome refolution, the major
part of them are determined, by reafons which they would blufh
to pay any regard to on much lefs ferious occafions : an unufual
fight, a change of the ordinary place of affembly, a fudden dif-
turbance, a rumour, are, amidft the general want of a fpirit of
decifion, the *fufficiens ratio* of the determination of the greateft
part; and from this affemblage of feparate wills, thus formed,
haftily and without reflection, a general will refults, which is
alfo without reflection."—*Conftitution of England,* 250, 251.

Quod enim fretum, quem Euripum, tot motus tantas et tam
varias habere putatis agitationes fluctuum quantas perturbationes
et quantos æftus habet ratio comitiorum.—*Cicero Orat. pro Mu-
ræna.*

" fore,

" fore, entruſt the government to a few individu-
" als, ſelected for their talents and their virtues.
" Let us conſtitute a part of theſe ourſelves, and
" from the exerciſe of authority ſo depoſited,
" we may be juſtified in expecting the happieſt
" events."

LXXXII. Darius was the third who delivered
his opinion. " The ſentiments of Megabyzus,"
he obſerved, " as they relate to a popular govern-
" ment, are unqueſtionably wiſe and juſt; but
" from his opinion of an oligarchy, I totally dif-
" ſent. Suppoſing the three different forms of
" government, monarchy, democracy, and an oligar-
" chy, ſeverally to prevail in the greateſt perfec-
" tion, I am of opinion that monarchy has great-
" ly the advantage. Indeed nothing can be bet-
" ter than the government of an individual emi-
" nent for his virtue. He will not only have re-
" gard to the general welfare of his ſubjects, but
" his reſolutions will be cautiouſly concealed from
" the public enemies of the ſtate. In an oligar-
" chy, the majority who have the care of the ſtate,
" though employed in the exerciſe of virtue for the
" public good, will be the objects of mutual envy
" and diſlike. Every individual will be anxious
" to extend his own perſonal importance, from
" which will proceed faction, ſedition, and blood-
" ſhed. The ſovereign power coming by theſe
" means to the hands of a ſingle perſon, conſtitutes
" the ſtrongeſt argument to prove what form of
" government is beſt. Whenever the people poſ-
                                        " ſeſs

" fefs the fupreme authority, diforders in the ftate
" are unavoidable : fuch diforders introduced in a
" republic do not feparate the bad and the profligate
" from each other, they unite them in the clofeft
" bonds of connection. They who mutually injure
" the ftate, mutually fupport each other; this
" evil exifts till fome individual, affuming autho-
" rity, fuppreffes the fedition; he of courfe ob-
" tains popular admiration, which ends in his be-
" coming the fovereign[93]; and this again tends to
" prove, that a monarchy is of all governments the
" moft excellent. To comprehend all that can be
" faid at once, to what are we indebted for our
" liberty; did we derive it from the people, an
" oligarchy, or an individual? For my own part,
" as we were certainly indebted to one man for
" freedom, I think that to one alone the govern-
" ment fhould be intrufted. Neither can we with-
" out danger change the cuftoms of our coun-
" try."

LXXXIII. Such were the three different opinions delivered, the latter of which was approved
by four out of the feven[94]. When Otanes faw his
defire

93 *Ends in his becoming the fovereign.*]—It is probable that the
afcendant of one man over multitudes began during a ftate of
war, where the fuperiority of courage and of genius difcovers itfelf moft vifibly, where unanimity and concert are moft requifite,
and where the pernicious effects of diforder are moft fenfibly
felt.—*Hume.*

94 *Four out of the feven.*]—This majority certainly decided in
favour of that fpecies of government which is moft fimple and

natural;

desire to establish an equality in Persia, rejected, he spoke thus: "As it seems determined that Persia
" shall be governed by one person, whether chosen
" among ourselves by lot, or by the suffrages of the
" people, or by some other method, you shall have
" no opposition from me: I am equally averse to
" govern or obey. I therefore yield, on condition
" that no one of you shall ever reign over me, or
" any of my posterity." The rest of the conspirators assenting to this, he made no farther opposition, but retired from the assembly. At the present period this is the only family in Persia which
retains its liberty, for all that is required of them is
not to transgress the laws of their country.

LXXXIV. The remaining six noblemen continued to consult about the most equitable mode of
electing a king; and they severally determined,

natural; and which would be, if always vested in proper hands,
the best: but the abuse of absolute power is so probable, and so
destructive, that it is necessary by all means to guard against it.
Aristotle inclines to the opinion of those, who esteem a mixed
government the best that can be devised. Of this they considered the Lacedæmonian constitution a good specimen; the
kings connecting it with monarchy, the senate with oligarchy,
and the ephori and syssytia with democracy.—*Arist. Pol.* l. ii,
cap. 4. Modern speculators on this subject, with one accord
allow the constitution of Great Britain, as it stands at present, to
be a much more judicious and perfect mixture of the three
powers, which are so contrived as to check and counterbalance
each other, without impeding that action of the whole machine,
which is necessary to the well-being of the people. The sixth
book of Polybius opens with a dissertation on the different forms
of government, which deserves attention.—*T.*

. that

that if the choice should fall upon any of themselves, Otanes himself and all his posterity should
be annually presented with a Median habit [95], as
well

---

[95] *Presented with a Median habit.*]—The custom of giving
vests or robes in Oriental countries, as a mark of honour and
distinction, may be traced to the remotest antiquity, and still
prevails. On this subject the following passage is given, from
a manuscript of Sir John Chardin, by Mr. Harmer, in his Ob-
servations on Passages of Scripture.

" The kings of Persia have great wardrobes, where there
are always many hundreds of habits, ready designed for presents, and sorted. They pay great attention to the quality or
merit of those to whom these vestments or habits are given:
those that are given to the great men have as much difference
as there is between the degrees of honour they possess in the
state."

All modern travellers to the East speak of the same custom.
We find also in the Old Testament various examples of a
similar kind. Chardin also, in his account of the coronation of
Solyman the Third, king of Persia, has the following passage: .

" His majesty, as every grandee had paid him his submissions,
honoured him with a calate or royal vest. This Persian
word, according to its etymology, signifies entire, perfect, accomplished, to signify either the excellency of the habit, or the
dignity of him that wears it; for it is an infallible mark of
the particular esteem which the sovereign has for the person to
whom he sends it, and that he has free liberty to approach his
person; for when the kingdom has changed its lord and master, the grandees who have not received this vest dare not presume to appear before the king without hazard of their lives."

This Median habit was made of silk; it was indeed, among the
elder Greeks, only another name for a silken robe, as we learn
from Procopius, την ἐσθητα—ἡν παλαι μεν Ἑλληνις Μηδικην εκαλεν,
νυν δε Σηρικην ονομαζουσιν. The remainder of this passage, literally translated, is, " and all that present which in Persia is most
honourable." This gift is fully explained by Xenophon in the

well as with every other diſtinction magnificent in
itſelf, and deemed honourable in Perſia. They de-
creed him this tribute of reſpect, as he had firſt
agitated the matter, and called them together.
Theſe were their determinations reſpecting Otanes;
as to themſelves, they mutually agreed that acceſs
to the royal palace ſhould be permitted to each of
them, without the ceremony of a previous meſſenger [96], except when the king ſhould happen to be
in bed with his wife. They alſo reſolved, that the
king ſhould marry no woman but from the family
of one the conſpirators. The mode they adopted
to elect a king was this:—They agreed to meet on
horſeback at ſun-riſe, in the vicinity of the city,
and to make him king whoſe horſe ſhould neigh
the firſt.

LXXXV. Darius had a groom, whoſe name
was Œbares, a man of conſiderable ingenuity, for
whom on his return home he immediately ſent.
" Œbares," ſaid he, " it is determined that we are to
" meet at ſun-riſe on horſeback, and that he among

---

firſt book of the Anabaſis; it conſiſted of a horſe with a gilt
bridle, a golden collar, bracelets, and a ſword of the kind peculiar to Media, called acinaces, beſides the ſilken veſt. His ex-
preſſions are ſo ſimilar to thoſe of Herodotus, as to ſatisfy us
that theſe ſpecific articles properly made up the gift of honour.—T.

[96] *Previous meſſenger.*]—Viſits to the great in Eaſtern countries are always preceded by meſſengers, who carry preſents,
differing in value according to the dignity of the perſon who is
to receive them. Without ſome preſent or other no viſit muſt
be made, nor favour expected.—T.

" us

" us fhall be king, whofe horfe fhall firft neigh.
" Whatever acutenefs you have, exert it on this
" occafion, that no one but myfelf may attain this
" honour." " Sir," replied Œbares, " if your be-
" ing a king or not depend on what you fay, be
" not afraid; I have a kind of charm, which will
" prevent any one's being preferred to yourfelf."
" Whatever," replied Darius, " this charm may
" be, it muft be applied without delay, as the
" morning will decide the matter." Œbares,
therefore, as foon as evening came, conducted to
the place before the city a mare, to which he
knew the horfe of Darius was particularly inclined:
he afterwards brought the horfe there, and after
carrying him feveral times round and near the
mare, he finally permitted him to cover her.

LXXXVI. The next morning as foon as it was
light the fix Perfians affembled, as had been agreed,
on horfeback. After riding up and down at the
place appointed, they came at length to the fpot
where the preceding evening the mare had been
brought; here the horfe of Darius inftantly began
to neigh, which, though the fky was remarkably
clear, was inftantly fucceeded by thunder and lightning. The heavens thus feemed to favour, and
indeed to act in concert with Darius. Immediately the other noblemen difmounted, and falling at
his feet hailed him king [97].

LXXXVII.

---

[97] *Hailed him king.*]—Darius was about twenty years old
when

LXXXVII. Such, according to some, was the stratagem of Œbares; others, however, relate the matter differently, and both accounts prevail in Persia. These last affirm, that the groom having rubbed his hand against the private parts of the mare, afterwards folded it up in his vest, and that in the morning, as the horses were about to depart, he drew it out from his garment, and touched the nostrils of the horse of Darius, and that this scent instantly made him snort and neigh.

LXXXVIII. Darius the son of Hystaspes [96]

when Cyrus died. Cambyses reigned seven years and five manths; Smerdis Magus was only seven months on the throne; thus Darius was about twenty-nine years old when he came to the crown.—*Larcher.*

This circumstance of thunder and lightning from a cloudless sky, is often mentioned by the ancients, and was considered by them as the highest omen. Horace has left an ode upon it, as a circumstance which staggered his Epicurean notions, and impressed him with awe and veneration, l. i. Od. 34; and the commentators give us instances enough of similar accounts. With us there is no thunder without clouds, except such as is too distant to have much effect; it may be otherwise in hot climates, where the state of the air is much more electrical.—*T.*

[96] *Darius the son of Hystaspes.*]—Archbishop Usher holdeth that it was Darius Hystaspes that was the king Ahasuerus, who married Esther; and that Atossa was the Vashti, and Antyllone the Esther of the holy scriptures. But Herodotus positively tells us, that Antystone was the daughter of Cyrus, and therefore she could not be Esther: and that Atossa had four sons by Darius, besides daughters, all born to him after he was king; and therefore she could not be that queen Vashti, who was divorced from the king her husband in the third year of his reign, nor he that Ahasuerus that divorced her.—*Prideaux.*

was thus proclaimed king; and, except the Arabians, all the nations of Afia who had been fubdued firft by Cyrus, and afterwards by Cambyfes,
acknowledged his authority. The Arabians were
never reduced to the fubjection of Perfia [99], but
were in its alliance: they afforded Cambyfes the
means of penetrating into Ægypt, without which
he could never have accomplifhed his purpofe.
Darius firft of all married two women of Perfia,
both of them daughters of Cyrus, Atoffa who had
firft been married to Cambyfes, and afterwards to

[99] *Never reduced to the fubjection of Perfia.*]—The independence of the Arabs has always been a theme of praife and admiration, from the remoteft ages to the prefent. Upon this fubject the following animated apoftrophe from Mr. Gibbon, in-
cludes all that need be faid. "The arms of Sefoltris and Cyrus,
of Pompey and Trajan, could never atchieve the conqueft of
Arabia. The prefent fovereign of the Turks may exercife a
fhadow of jurifdiction, but his pride is reduced to follicit the
friendfhip of a people whom it is dangerous to provoke, and
fruitlefs to attack. The obvious caufes of their freedom are
infcribed on the character and country of the Arabs; the pa-
tient and active virtues of a foldier are infenfibly nurfed in the
habits and difcipline of a paftoral life. The long memory of
their independence is the firmeft pledge of its perpetuity; and
fucceeding generations are animated to prove their defcent, and
to maintain their inheritance. When they advance to battle,
the hope of victory is in the front, and in the rear the affurance
of a retreat. Their horfes and camels, who in eight or ten days
can perform a march of four or five hundred miles, difappear
before the conqueror: the fecret waters of the defart elude his
fearch; and his victorious troops are confumed with hunger,
thirft, and fatigue, in the purfuit of an invifible foe, who fcorns
his efforts, and fafely repofes in the heart of the burning folitude."

the

the magus, and Antyftone a virgin. He then married Parmys, daughter of Smerdis, fon of Cyrus,
and that daughter of Otanes who had been the inftrument in difcovering the magus. Being firmly
eftablifhed on the throne, his firft work was the
erection of an equeftrian ftatue, with this infcription: "Darius, fon of Hyftafpes, obtained the
" fovereignty of Perfia by the fagacity of his horfe,
" and the ingenuity of Œbares his groom." The
name of the horfe was alfo inferted.

LXXXIX. The next act of his authority was
to divide Perfia into twenty provinces, which they
call fatrapies, to each of which a governor was appointed. He then afcertained the tribute they were
feverally to pay, connecting fometimes many nations together, which were near each other, under
one diftrict; and fometimes he paffed over many
which were adjacent, forming one government of
various remote and fcattered nations. His particular divifion of the provinces, and the mode fixed
for the payment of their annual tribute, was this:
They whofe payment was to be made in filver,
were to take the Babylonian talent [100] for their
                                        ftandard;

<hr/>

[100] *Babylonian talent.*]—What follows on the fubject of the
talent, is extracted principally from Arbuthnot's tables of ancient coins.

The word *talent* in Homer, is ufed to fignify a balance, and
in general it was applied either to a weight or a fum of money,
differing in value according to the ages and countries in which
it was ufed. Every talent confifts of 60 minæ, and every mina
                                                        of

ſtandard; the Euboic talent was to regulate thoſe who made their payment in gold; the Babylonian talent, it is to be obſerved, is equal to ſeventy Euboic minæ. During the reign of Cyrus, and indeed of Cambyſes, there were no ſpecific tributes [101], but preſents were made to the ſovereign. On account of theſe and ſimilar innovations, the Perſians call Darius a merchant, Cambyſes a deſpot, but Cyrus a parent. Darius ſeemed to have no other objeċt in view but the acquiſition of gain; Cambyſes was negligent and ſevere; whilſt Cyrus was of a mild and gentle temper, ever ſtudious of the good of his ſubjeċts.

XC. The Ionians and Magneſians of Aſia, the

of 100 drachmæ, but the talents differed in weight according to the minæ and drachmæ of which they were compoſed.

What Herodotus here affirms of the Babylonian talent, is confirmed by Pollux and by Ælian.

The Euboic talent was ſo called from the iſland Eubœa; it was generally thought to be the ſame with the Attic talent, becauſe both theſe countries uſed the ſame weights; the mina Euboica, and the mina Attica, each conſiſted of 100 drachmæ.

According to the above, the Babylonian talent would amount, in Engliſh money, to about £. 226; the Euboic or Attic talent to £. 193. 15 s.—T.

[101] No ſpecific tributes.]—This ſeemingly contradiċts what was ſaid above, that the magus exempted the Perſians for three years from every kind of impoſt. It muſt be obſerved that theſe impoſts were not for a conſtancy, they only ſubſiſted in time of war, and were rather a gratuity than an impoſt. Thoſe impoſed by Darius were perpetual; thus Herodotus does not appear at all to contradiċt himſelf.—Larcher.

Æolians,

Æolians, Carians, Lycians, Melyeans[102], and Pamphylians, were comprehended under one diftrict; and jointly paid a tribute of four hundred talents of filver; they formed the firft fatrapy. The fecond, which paid five hundred talents, was compofed of the Myfians, Lydians, Alyfonians, Cabalians, and Hygennians [103]. A tribute of three hundred and fixty talents was paid by thofe who inhabit the right fide of the Hellefpont, by the Phrygians and Thracians of Afia, by the Paphlagonians, Mariandynians[104], and Syrians; and thefe nations conftituted the third fatrapy. The Cilicians were obliged to produce every day a white horfe, that is to fay, three hundred and fixty annually, with five hundred talents of filver; of thefe one hundred and forty were appointed for the payment of the cavalry ftationed for the guard of the country; the remaining three

---

[102] *Melyeans.*]—Thefe people are in all probability the fame with the Milyans of whom Herodotus fpeaks, book i. c. clxxiii and book vii. c. clxxvii. They were fometimes called Minyans, from Minos, king of Crete.—*T.*

[103] *Hygennians.*]—For Hygennians Weffeling propofes to read Obigenians.—*T.*

[104] *Mariandynians.*]—Thefe were on the coaft of Bithynia, where was faid to be the Acherufian cave, through which Hercules dragged up Cerberus to light, whofe foam then produced aconite. Thus Dionyfius Periegetes, l. 788.

> That facred plain where erft, as fablers tell,
> The deep-voic'd dog of Pluto, ftruggling hard
> Againft the potent grafp of Hercules,
> With foamy drops impregnating the earth,
> Produc'd dire poifon to deftroy mankind.

hundred

hundred and fixty were received by Darius: thefe
formed the fourth fatrapy.

XCI. The tribute levied from the fifth fatrapy
was three hundred and fifty talents. Under this
diftrict was comprehended the tract of country which
extended from the city Pofideium, built on the
frontiers of Cilicia and Syria, by Amphilochus, fon
of Amphiaraus [105], as far as Ægypt, part of Arabia alone excluded, which paid no tribute. The
fame fatrapy, moreover, included all Phœnicia, the
Syrian Paleftine, and the ifle of Cyprus. Seven
hundred talents were exacted from Ægypt, from
the Africans which border upon Ægypt, from Cyrene and Barce, which are comprehended in the
Ægyptian diftrict. The produce of the fifhery of
the lake Mœris was not included in this, neither
was the corn, to the amount of feven hundred talents
more; one hundred and twenty thoufand meafures
of which were applied to the maintenance of the

---

[105] *Amphilochus, fon of Amphiaraus.*]—For an account of Amphiaraus, fee book the firft, chap. xlvi. The name of the mother
of Amphilochus, according to Paufanias, was Eriphyle. He
appears to have obtained an efteem and veneration equal to
that which was paid to his father. He had an oracle at Mallus,
in Cilicia, which place he built; he had alfo an altar erected to
his honour at Athens. His oracle continued in the time of Plutarch, and the mode of confulting it was this:—The perfon
who wifhed an anfwer to fome enquiry paffed a night in the
temple, and was fure to have a vifion, which was to be confidered as the reply. There is an example in Dion Caffius, of a
picture which was painted in the time of Commodus, defcriptive
of an anfwer communicated by this oracle.—*T.*

Perfians

Perfians and their auxiliary troops garrifoned within
the white caftle of Memphis: this was the fixth
fatrapy. The feventh was compofed of the Satga-
gydæ, the Gandarii, the Dadicæ and Aparytæ, who
together paid one hundred and feventy talents. The
eighth fatrapy furnifhed three hundred talents, and
confifted of Sufa and the reft of the Ciffians.

XCII. Babylon and the other parts of Affy-
ria conftituted the ninth fatrapy, and paid a thoufand talents of filver, with five hundred young
eunuchs. The tenth fatrapy furnifhed four hundred and fifty talents, and confifted of Ecbatana,
the reft of Media, the Parycanii, and the Orthocory-
bantes. The Cafpians, the Paufiæ, the Pantima-
thi, and the Daritæ, contributed amongft them two
hundred talents, and formed the eleventh fatrapy.
The twelfth produced three hundred and fixty talents, and was compofed of the whole country from
the Bactrians to Æglos.

XCIII. From the thirteenth fatrapy four hundred
talents were levied; this comprehended Pactyïca,
the Armenians, with the contiguous nations, as far as
the Euxine. The fourteenth fatrapy confifted of the
Sangatians, the Sarangæans, the Thamanæans, Uti-
ans, and Menci, with thofe who inhabit the iflands
of the Red Sea, where the king fends thofe whom
he banifhes [106]; thefe jointly contributed fix hundred
talents.

[106] *Whom he banifhes.*]—Banifhment feems to have been
adopted

talents. The Sacæ and Cafpii formed the fifteenth
fatrapy, and provided two hundred and fifty talents.
Three hundred talents were levied from the Parthians, Chorafmians, Sogdians, and Arians, who were
the fixteenth fatrapy.

XCIV. The Paricanii and Æthiopians of Afia
paid four hundred talents, and formed the feven-
teenth fatrapy. The eighteenth was taxed at two
hundred talents, and was compofed of the Matieni, the Safpires, and Alarodians. The Mofchi,

adopted as a punifhment at a very early period of the world;
and it may be fuppofed that, in the infancy of fociety, men, re-
luctant to fanguinary meafures, would have recourfe to the expulfion of mifchievous or unworthy members, as the fimpler and
lefs odious remedy. When we confider the effect which exile
has had upon the minds of the greateft and wifeft of mankind,
and reflect on that attractive fweetnefs of the natal foil, which
whilft we admire in poetic defcription we ftill feel to be *ratione
valentior omni*, it feems wonderful that banifhment fhould not
more frequently fuperfede the neceffity of fanguinary punifhments. That Ovid, whofe mind was enervated by licentious
habits, fhould deplore, in ftrains the moft melancholy, the abfence of what alone could make life fupportable, may not perhaps be thought wonderful; but that Cicero, whofe whole life
was a life of philofophic difcipline, fhould fo entirely lofe his
firmnefs, and forget his dignity, may juftify our concluding of
the punifhment of exile, that human vengeance need not inflict
a more fevere calamity. In oppofition to what I have afferted
above, fome reader will perhaps be inclined to cite the example
of Lord Bolingbroke, his conduct, and his reflections upon
exile; but I think I can difcern through that laboured apo-
logy, a fecret chagrin and uneafinefs, which convinces me at
leaft, that whilft he acted the philofopher and the ftoic, he had
the common feelings and infirmities of man.—*T*.

Tibareni, Macrones, Mofynœci, and Mardians, provided three hundred talents, and were the nineteenth fatrapy. The Indians, the moft numerous nation of whom we have any knowledge, were proportionally taxed; they formed the twentieth fatrapy, and furnifhed fix hundred talents in golden ingots.

XCV. If the Babylonian money be reduced to the ftandard of the Euboic talent, the aggregate fum will be found to be nine thoufand eight hundred and eighty talents in filver; and, eftimating the gold at thirteen times [107] the value of filver, there will be found, according to the Euboic talent, four thoufand fix hundred and eighty of thèfe talents. The whole being eftimated together, it will appear that the annual tribute [108] paid to Darius was fourteen thoufand

---

[107] *Thirteen times the value of filver.*]—The proportion of gold to filver varied at different times, according to the abundance of thefe two metals. In the time of Darius it was thirteen to one; in the time of Plato, twelve; and in the time of Menander, the comic poet, it was ten.—*Larcher.*

In the time of Julius Cæfar the proportion of gold to filver at Rome was no more than nine to one. This arofe from the prodigious quantity of gold which Cæfar had obtained from the plunder of cities and temples. It is generally fuppofed amôngft the learned, that in the gold coin of the ancients one-fiftieth part was alloy.—*T.*

[108] *The annual tribute.*]—The comparifon of two paffages in Herodotus (book i. chap. cxcii. and book iii. chaps. lxxxix. xcvi.) reveals an important difference between the *grofs* and the *net* revenue of Perfia, the fums paid by the provinces, and the gold or filver depofited in the royal treafury. The monarch might

thoufand five hundred and fixty talents, omitting many trifling fums not deferving our attention.

XCVI. Such was the fum which Afia principally, and Africa in fome fmall proportion, paid to Darius. In procefs of time the iflands alfo were taxed, as was that part of Europe which extends to Theffaly. The manner in which the king depofited thefe riches in his treafury, was this:—The gold and filver was melted and poured into earthen veffels; the veffel, when full, was removed, leaving the metal in a mafs. When any was wanted, fuch a piece was broken off as the contingence required.

XCVII. We have thus defcribed the different fatrapies, and the impoft on each. Perfia is the only province which I have not mentioned as tributary. The Perfians are not compelled to pay any fpecific taxes, but they prefent a regular gratuity. The Æthiopians who border upon Ægypt, fubdued by Cambyfes in his expedition againft the Æthiopian Macrobians, are fimilarly circumftanced, as are alfo the inhabitants of the facred town of Nyffa, who have feftivals in honour of Bacchus. Thefe Æthiopians, with their neighbours, refemble in their cuftoms the Calantian Indians: they have the fame rites of fepulture [109], and their dwellings are

might annually fave three millions fix hundred thoufand pounds of the feventeen or eighteen millions raifed upon the people.— *Gibbon.*

[109] *The fame rites of fepulture.*]—The word in the text is

σπιρματι,

are subterraneous. Once in every three years these two nations present to the king two chœnices of gold unrefined, two hundred blocks of ebony, twenty large elephants teeth, and five Æthiopian youths, which custom has been continued to my time. The people of Colchos [110] and their neighbours, as far as mount Caucasus, imposed upon themselves the payment of a gratuity. To this latter place the Persian authority extends; northward of this their name inspires no regard. Every five years the nations above-mentioned present the king with an hundred youths and an hundred virgins [111], which also has been continued within my remembrance. The Arabians contribute every year frankincense to the

σπιςματι, which means grains: to say of two different nations that they use the same grain, seems ridiculous enough. Valcnaer proposes to read σηματι, which seems obvious and satisfactory. —*T*.

[110] *The people of Colchos.*]—It was the boast of the Colchians, that their ancestors had checked the victories of Sesostris, but they sunk without any memorable effort under the arms of Cyrus, followed in distant wars the standard of the great king, and presented him every fifth year with a hundred boys and as many virgins, the fairest produce of the land. Yet he accepted this *gift* like the gold and ebony of India, the frankincense of the Arabs, and the negroes and ivory of Æthiopia: The Colchians were not subject to the dominion of a satrap, and they continued to enjoy the name as well as substance of national independence.—*Gibbon.*

[111] *Hundred virgins.*]—The native race of Persians is small and ugly, but it has been improved by the perpetual mixture of Circassian blood. This remark Mr. Gibbon applies to the Persian women in the time of Julian. Amongst modern travellers, the beauty of the Persian ladies is a constant theme of praise and admiration.—*T.*

amount of a thoufand talents.—Independent of the tributes before fpecified, thefe were the prefents which the king received.

XCVIII. The Indians procure the great number of golden ingots, which, as I have obferved, they prefent as a donative to the king, in this manner:— That part of India which lies towards the eaft is very fandy; and indeed, of all nations concerning whom we have any authentic accounts, the Indians are the people of Afia who are neareft the eaft, and the place of the rifing fun. The part moft eaftward, is a perfect defert, from the fand. Under the name of Indians many nations are comprehended, ufing different languages; of thefe fome attend principally to the care of cattle, others not: fome inhabit the marfhes, and live on raw fifh, which they catch in boats made of reeds, divided at the joint, and every joint [112] makes one canoe, Thefe Indians have a drefs made of rufhes [113], which having

---

[112] *Every joint.*]—This affertion feems wonderful; but Pliny, book xvi. chap. 36, treating of reeds, canes, and aquatic fhrubs, affirms the fame, with this precaution indeed, "if it may be credited." His expreffion is this:—Harundini quidem Indicæ arborea amplitudo, quales vulgo in templis videmus.—Spiffius mari corpus, fœminæ capacius. Navigiorumque etiam vicem præftant (fi credimus) *fingula internodia.*—*T.*

[113] *Cloaths made of rufhes.*]—To trace the modern drefs back to the fimplicity of the firft fkins, and leaves, and feathers, that were worn by mankind in the primitive ages, if it were poffible, would be almoft endlefs; the fafhion has been often changed, while the materials remained the fame: the materials have been

I 3   different

having mowed and cut, they weave together like a mat, and wear in the manner of a cuirass.

XCIX. To the east of these are other Indians, called Padæi [114], who lead a pastoral life, live on raw flesh [115], and

---

different as they were gradually produced by successive arts, that converted a raw hide into leather, the wool of the sheep into cloth, the web of the worm into silk, and flax and cotton into linen of various kinds. One garment also has been added to another, and ornaments have been multiplied on ornaments, with a variety almost infinite, produced by the caprice of human vanity, or the new necessities to which man rendered himself subject by those many inventions which took place after he ceased to be, as God had created him, upright.—See historical remarks on dress, prefixed to a collection of the dresses of different nations, ancient and modern.

The canoes and dresses here described, will strike the reader as much resembling those seen and described by modern voyagers to the South Seas.—*T.*

[114] *Padæi.*]—

> Impia nec sævis celebrans convivia mensis
> Ultima vicinus Phœbo tenet arva Padæus.
>
> *Tibull.* l. iv. 144.

[115] *On raw flesh.*]—Not at all more incredible is the custom said to be prevalent among the Abyssinians, of eating a slice of meat raw from the living ox, and esteeming it one of the greatest delicacies. The assertion of this fact by Mr. Bruce, the celebrated traveller, has excited a clamour against him, and by calling his veracity in question, has probably operated, amongst other causes, to the delay of a publication much and eagerly expected. This very fact, however, is also asserted of the Abyssinians by Lobo and Poncet. If it be allowed without reserve, an argument is deducible from it, to prove that bullock's blood, in contradiction to what is asserted by our historian, in ch. 15. of this book, is not a poison; unless we suppose that the quantity thus

taken

and are said to observe these customs : —If any man
among them be diseased, his nearest connections put
him to death, alledging in excuse that sickness would
waste and injure his flesh. They pay no regard to
his assertions that he is not really ill, but without
the smallest compunction deprive him of life. If a
woman be ill, her female connections treat her in
the same manner. The more aged among them are
regularly killed and eaten; but to old age there are
very few who arrive, for in case of sickness they put
every one to death.

C. There are other Indians, who, differing in
manners from the above, put no animal to death [116],
sow no grain, have no fixed habitations, and live
solely upon vegetables. They have a particular grain,
nearly of the size of millet, which the soil spon-
taneously produces, which is protected by a calyx,
the whole of this they bake and eat. If any of these
be taken sick, they retire to some solitude, and there
remain, no one expressing the least concern about
them during their illness, or after their death.

CI. Among all these Indians whom I have speci-
fied, the communication between the sexes is like

taken into the stomach would be too small to produce the
effect. Lobo, as well as Mr. Bruce, affirms, that the
Abyssinians eat beef, not only in a raw state, but reeking from
the ox.—T.

[116] *Put no animal to death*.]—Nicolas Damascenus has preserved the name of this people. He calls them Aritonians.
—*Larcher.*

that

that of the beasts, open and unreftrained.' They are all of the fame complexion, and much refembling the Æthiopians. The femen which their males emit is not, like that of other men, white, but black like their bodies [117], which is alfo the cafe with the Æthiopians. Thefe Indians are very remote from Perfia towards the fouth, and were never in fubjection to Darius.

CII. There are ftill other Indians towards the north, who dwell near the city of Cafpatyrum, and the country of Pactyïca. Of all the Indians thefe in their manners moft refemble the Bactrians; they are diftinguifhed above the reft by their bravery, and are thofe who are employed in fearching for the gold. In the vicinity of this diftrict there are vaft deferts of fand, in which a fpecies of ants [118] is produced, not

---

[117] *Black like their bodies.*]—Semen fi probe concoctum fuerit, colore album et fplendens effe oportet, ut vel hinc pateat quam parum vere Herodotus fcribat femen nigrum Æthiopes promere. *Rodericus a Caftro de univerfa mulierum medicina.*—Ariftotle had before faid the fame thing, in his hiftory of animals.— *Larcher.*

[118] *Species of ants.*]—Of thefe ants Pliny alfo makes mention, in the following terms:

" In the temple of Hercules, at Erythræ, the horns of an Indian ant were to be feen, an aftonifhing object. In the country of the northern Indians, named Dandæ, thefe ants caft up gold from holes within the earth. In colour they refemble cats, and are as large as the wolves of Ægypt. This gold, which they throw up in the winter, the Indians contrive to fteal in the fummer, when the ants, on account of the heat, hide themfelves under ground. But if they happen to fmell them, the ants rufh from

not fo large as a dog, but bigger than a fox. Some of thefe, taken by hunting, are preferved in the palace of the Perfian monarch. Like the ants common in Greece, which in form alfo they nearly refemble, they make themfelves habitations in the ground, by digging under the fand. The fand thus thrown up is mixed with gold duft, to collect which the Indians are difpatched into the deferts. To this expedition they proceed each with three camels faftened together, a female being fecured between two males, and upon her the Indian is mounted, taking particular care to have one which recently has foaled. The females of this defcription are in all refpects as

from their holes, and will often tear them in pieces, though mounted on their fwifteft camels, fuch is the fwiftnefs and fiercenefs they difplay from the love of their gold."

Upon the above Larcher has this remark:—The little communication which the Greeks had with the Indians, prevented their inveftigating the truth with refpect to this animal; and their love of the marvellous inclined them to affent to this defcription of Herodotus. Demetrius Triclinius fays, on the Antigone of Sophocles, doubtlefs from fome ancient Scholiaft which he copies, that there are in India winged animals, named ants, which dig up gold. Herodotus and Pliny fay nothing of their having wings. Moft of our readers will be induced to confider the defcription of thefe ants as fabulous; neverthelefs, de Thou, an author of great credit, tells us, that Shah Thomas, fophi of Perfia, fent, in the year 1559, to Soliman an ant like thefe here defcribed.

They who had feen the vaft nefts of the termites, or white ants, might eafily be perfuaded that the animals which formed them were as large as foxes. The difproportion between the infect, though large, and its habitation, is very extraodinary. —T.

fwift

swift as horses, and capable of bearing much greater burdens [119].

CIII.

[119] *Greater burdens.*]—Of all the descriptions I have met with of this wonderful animal, the following, from Volney, seems the most animated and interesting:—

No creature seems so peculiarly fitted to the climate in which it exists, as the camel. Designing the camel to dwell in a country where he can find little nourishment, nature has been sparing of her materials in the whole of his formation. She has not bestowed upon him the fleshiness of the ox, horse, or elephant, but limiting herself to what is strictly necessary, she has given him a small head without ears, at the end of a long neck without flesh. She has taken from his legs and thighs every muscle not immediately requisite for motion, and in short has bestowed on his withered body only the vessels and tendons necessary to connect its frame together. She has furnished him with a strong jaw, that he may grind the hardest aliments; but, lest he should consume too much, she has straitened his stomach, and obliged him to chew the cud. She has lined his foot with a lump of flesh, which, sliding in the mud, and being no way adapted to climbing, fits him only for a dry, level, and sandy soil, like that of Arabia: she has evidently destined him likewise for slavery, by refusing him every sort of defence against his enemies. So great, in short, is the importance of the camel to the desert, that were it deprived of that useful animal, it must infallibly lose every inhabitant.—*V ʃey.*

With respect to the burdens which camels are capable of carrying, Russel tells us, that the Arab camel will carry one hundred rotoloes, or five hundred pounds weight; but the Turcomans camel's common load is one hundred and sixty rotoloes, or eight hundred pounds weight. Their ordinary pace is very slow, Volney says, not more than thirty-six hundred yards in an hour; it is needless to press them, they will go no quicker. Raynal says, that the Arabs qualify the camels for expedition by matches, in which the horse runs against him; the camel, less active and nimble, tires out his rival in a long course. There is one peculiarity with respect to camels, which not being generally

rally

CIII. As my countrymen of Greece are well acquainted with the form of the camel, I shall not
here describe it; I shall only mention those particulars concerning it with which I conceive them to be
less acquainted [120]. Behind, the camel has four
thighs, and as many knee joints; the member of
generation falls from between the hinder legs, and
is turned towards the tail.

CIV. Having thus connected their camels, the
Indians proceed in search of the gold, choosing the
hottest time of the day as most proper for their purpose, for then it is that the ants conceal themselves
under the ground. In distinction from all other
nations, the heat with these people is greatest, not

rally known, I give the reader, as translated from the Latin of
Father Strope, a learned German missionary. " The camels
which have had the honour to bear presents to Mecca and Medina
are not to be treated afterwards as common animals; they are
considered as consecrated to Mahomet, which exempts them
from all labour and service. They have cottages built for their
abodes, where they live at ease, and receive plenty of food, with
the most careful attention."—*T.*

[120] *To be less acquainted.*]—These farther particulars concerning the camel, are taken from Mr. Pennant.

The one-bunched camel, is the Arabian camel, the two-
bunched, the Bactrian. The Arabian has six callosities on the
legs, will kneel down to be loaded, but rises the moment he
finds the burden equal to his strength. They are gentle always, except when in heat, when they are seized with a sort of
madness, which makes it unsafe to approach them. The Bactrian camel is larger and more generous than the domesticated
race. The Chinese have a swift variety of this, which they call
by the expressive name of Fong Kyo Fo, or camels with feet of
the wind.

at mid-day, but in the morning. They have a
vertical fun till about the time when with us people
withdraw from the forum ¹¹¹; 'during which period
the warmth is more exceffive than the mid-day fun
in Greece, fo that the inhabitants are then faid to
go into the water for refrefhment. Their mid-day
is nearly of the fame temperature as in other places;
after which the warmth of the air becomes like
the morning elfewhere; it then progreffively grows

¹¹¹ *People withdraw from the forum.*]—The times of the
forum were fo exactly afcertained, as to ferve for a notation of
time. The time of full forum is mentioned by many authors,
as Thucydides, Xenophon, Diodorus Siculus, Lucian, and others,
and is faid by Suidas to have been the third hour in the morning
that is, nine o'clock; and Dio Chryfoftom places it as an intermediate point between morning, or furf-rife, and noon, which
agrees alfo with nine o'clock. One paffage in Suidas fpeaks alfo
of the fourth, fifth, and fixth hours; but either they were fora
of different kinds, or the author is there miftaken, or the paffage
is corrupt. See Ælian, xii. 30. and Athenæus, xiv. 1. the
time of breaking up the forum, αλαφης διαλυσις, is not, I believe,
mentioned, except here, by Herodotus; but by this paffage it
appears that it muft have been alfo a ftated time, and before
noon; probably ten or eleven o'clock. This account of a
fun, hotter and more vertical in the morning than at noon, is fo
perfectly unphilofophical, that it proves decifively, what the hypothefis of our author concerning the overflowing of the Nile
gave ftrong reafon to fufpect, that Herodotus was perfectly un-
informed on fubjects of this kind. Mid-day, or noon, can be
only, at all places, when the fun is higheft and confequently
hotteft, unlefs any clouds or periodical winds had been affigned
as caufes of this fingular effect. Whoever fabricated the account he here repeats thought it neceffary to give an appearance of novelty even to the celeftial phenomena of the place.
Herodotus himfelf ufes the term of πληθωρα αγορης in book ii.
ch. 173, and vii. 223.—*T.*

milder,

milder, till at the fetting fun it becomes very cool.

CV. As foon as they arrive at the fpot, the Indians precipitately fill their bags with fand, and return as expeditioufly as poffible. The Perfians fay that thefe ants know and purfue the Indians by their fmell, with inconceivable fwiftnefs. They affirm, that if the Indians did not make confiderable progrefs whilft the ants were collecting themfelves together, it would be impoffible for any of them to efcape. For this reafon, at different intervals [121], they feparate one of the male camels from the female, which are always fleeter than the males, and are at this time additionally incited by the remembrance of their young whom they had left. Thus, according to the Perfians, the Indians obtain their greateft quantity of gold; what they procure by digging is of much inferior importance.

CVI. Thus it appears that the extreme parts of the habitable world are diftinguifhed by the poffeffion of many beautiful things, as Greece is for its agreeable and temperate feafons. India, as I have already remarked, is the laft inhabited country

[121] *At different intervals.*]—This paffage is fomewhat perplexing. The reader muft remember that the Indian rode upon the female camel, which was betwixt two males. This being the fwifteft, he trufted to it for his own perfonal-fecurity; and it may be fuppofed that he untied one or both of the male camels, as the enemy approached, or as his fears got the better of his avarice.—*T.*

towards the eaſt, where every ſpecies of birds and of quadrupeds, horſes excepted [113], are much larger than in any other part of the world. Their horſes are not ſo large as the Niſæan horſes of Media. They have alſo a great abundance of gold, which

[113] *Horſes excepted.*]—Every thing of moment which is involved in the natural hiſtory of the horſe, may be found in M. Buffon. But, as Mr. Pennant obſerves, we may in this country boaſt a variety which no other ſingle kingdom poſſeſſes. Moſt other countries produce but one kind, while ours, by a judicious mixture of the ſeveral ſpecies, by the happy difference of our ſoil, and by our ſuperior ſkill in management, may triumph over the reſt of Europe in having brought each quality of this noble animal to the higheſt perfection. The ſame author tells us, that the horſe is in ſome places found wild; that theſe are leſs than the domeſtic kinds, of a mouſe colour, have greater heads than the tame, their foreheads remarkably arched, go in great herds, will often ſurround the horſes of the Mongals and Kalkas while they are grazing, and carry them away. Theſe are exceſſively vigilant: a centinel placed on an eminence gives notice to the herd of any approaching danger, by neighing aloud, when they all run off with amazing ſwiftneſs. Theſe are ſometimes taken by the means of hawks, which fix on their heads, and diſtreſs them ſo as to give the purſuers time to overtake them. In the interior parts of Ceylon is a ſmall variety of the horſe, not exceeding thirty inches in height, which is ſometimes brought to Europe as a rarity. It may not, in this place, be impertinent to inform the reader, that in the Eaſt the riding on a horſe is deemed very honourable, ſince Europeans are very ſeldom permitted to do it. In the book of Eccleſiaſtes, chap. x. ver. 7. we meet with this expreſſion, " I have ſeen ſervants on horſes," which we may of courſe underſtand to be ſpoken of a thing very unuſual and improper.

To conclude this ſubject, I have only to obſerve, that the Arabian horſes are juſtly allowed to be the fineſt in the world in point of beauty and of ſwiftneſs, and are ſent into all parts to improve the breed of this animal.—*T.*

X

they

they procure partly by digging, partly from the rivers, but principally by the method above defcribed.   They poffefs likewife a kind of plant, which, inftead of fruit, produces wool [114], of a finer and better quality than that of fheep : of this the natives make their cloaths.

CVII. The laft inhabited country towards the fouth, is Arabia, the only region of the earth which produces frankincenfe [115], myrrh, cinnamon [116],

[114] *Produces wool.*]—This was doubtlefs the cotton fhrub, called by the ancients byffus. This plant grows to the height of about four feet: it has a yellow flower, ftreaked with red, not unlike that of the mallow; the piftil becomes a pod of the fize of a fmall egg ; in this are from three to four cells, each of which, on burfting, is found to contain feeds involved in a whitifh fubftance, which is the cotton. The time of gathering the cotton is when the fruit burfts, which happens in the months of March and April. The fcientific name of this plant is goffypium.—*T.*

[115] *Frankincenfe.*]—This, of all perfumes, was the moft efteemed by the ancients; it was ufed in divine worfhip, and was in a manner appropriated to princes and great men. Thofe employed in preparing it were naked, they had only a girdle about their loins, which their mafter had the precaution to fecure with his own feal.—*T.*

[116] *Cinnamon*]—is a fpecies of laurel, the bark of which conftitutes its valuable part. This is taken off in the months of September and February. When cut into fmall flices; it is expofed to the fun, the heat of which curls it up in the form in which we receive and ufe it. The berry, when boiled in water, yields, according to Raynal, an oil, which, fuffered to congeal, acquires a whitenefs. Of this candles are made, of a very aromatic fmell, which are referved for the fole ufe of the king of Ceylon, in which place it is principally found.—*T.*

cafia,

cafia [117], and ledanum [118]. Except the myrrh, the Arabians obtain all thefe aromatics without any confiderable trouble. To colleƈt the frankincenfe, they burn under the tree which produces it a quantity of the ftyrax [119], which the Phœnicians export into Greece; for thefe trees are each of them guarded by a prodigious number of flying ferpents, fmall of body, and of different colours, which are difperfed by the fmoke of the gum. It is this fpecies of ferpent which in an immenfe body infefts Ægypt.

CVIII. The Arabians, moreover, affirm, that their whole country would be filled with thefe ferpents, if the fame thing were not to happen with refpeƈt to them which we know happens, and, as it fhould feem, providentially, to the vipers. Thofe animals, which are more timid, and which ferve for the purpofe of food, to prevent their total confumption are always remarkably proli-

[117] *Cafa.*]—This is, I believe, a baftard kind of cinnamon, called in Europe caffia lignea; the merchants mix it with true cinnamon, which is four times its value; it is to be diftinguifhed by a kind of vifcidity perceived in chewing it.—*T.*

[118] *Ledanum.*]—Ledanum, or ladanum, according to Pliny, was a gum made of the dew which was gathered from a fhrub called lada.—*T.*

[119] *Styrax.*]—This is the gum of the ftorax tree, is very aromatic, and brought to this country in confiderable quantities from the Archipelago. It is obtained by making incifions in the tree. The Turks adulterate it with faw-duft. Another fpecies of ftorax is imported to Europe from America, and is procured from the liquid amber-tree.—*T.*

fic,

fic [110], which is not the cafe with thofe which are fierce and venomous. The hare, for inftance, the prey of every beaft and bird, as well as of man, produces young abundantly. It is the fingular property of this animal [111], that it conceives a fecond time, when it is already pregnant, and at the fame time carries in its womb young ones covered with down, others not yet formed, others juft beginning to be formed, whilft the mother herfelf is again ready to conceive. But the lionefs, of all animals the ftrongeft and moft ferocious, produces but one young one [112] in her life, for at the birth of her cub fhe lofes her matrix. The reafon of this feems to be, that as the claws of the lion are fharper by much than thofe of any other animal, the cub, as foon as it begins to ftir in the womb, injures and tears the matrix, which it does ftill more and more

---

[110] *Remarkably prolific.*]—See Derham's chapter on the balance of animals, *Phyfico-Theology*, b. iv. ch. x. and ch. xiv. §. 3.

[111] *The fingular property of this animal.*]—With refpect to the fuperfœtation of this animal, Pliny makes the fame remark, affigning the fame reafon. Lepus omnium prædæ nafcens, folus præter Dafypodem fuperfœtat, aliud educans, aliud in utero pilis veftitum, aliud implume, aliud inchoatum gerens pariter. This doctrine of fuperfœtation is ftrenuoufly defended by Sir T. Brown, in his Vulgar Errors; and, as far as it refpects the animal in queftion, is credited by Larcher: but Mr. Pennant very fenfibly remarks, that as the hare breeds very frequently in the courfe of the year, there is no *neceffity* of having recourfe to this doctrine to account for their numbers.—*T.*

[112] *But one young one.*]—This affertion is perfectly abfurd and falfe. The lionefs has from two to fix young ones, and the fame lionefs has been known to litter four or five times.—*T.*

as it grows bigger, so that at the time of its birth no part of the womb remains whole.

CIX. Thus, therefore, if vipers and those winged serpents of Arabia were to generate in the ordinary course of nature, the natives could not live. But it happens, that when they are incited by lust to copulate, at the very instant of emission the female seizes the male by the neck, and does not quit her hold till she has quite devoured it [11]. The male thus perishes, but the female is also punished; for whilst the young are still within the womb, as the time of birth approaches, to make themselves a passage they tear in pieces the matrix, thus avenging their father's death. Those serpents which are not injurious to mankind lay eggs, and produce a great quantity of young. There are vipers in every part of the world, but winged serpents are found only in Arabia, where there are great numbers.

CX. We have described how the Arabians procure their frankincense; their mode of obtaining the cassia is this:—The whole of their body, and the face, except the eyes, they cover with skins of different kinds; they thus proceed to the place where it grows, which is in a marsh not very deep, but infested by a winged species of animal much resembling a bat, very strong, and making a hideous noise; they protect their eyes from these, and then gather the cassia.

[11] *Quite devoured it.*]—This narrative must also be considered as entirely fabulous.—*T.*

CXI.

CXI. Their manner of collecting the cinnamon [134] is still more extraordinary. In what particular spot it is produced, they themselves are unable to certify. There are some who assert that it grows in the region where Bacchus was educated, and their mode of reasoning is by no means improbable. These affirm that the vegetable substance, which we, as instructed by the Phœnicians [135], call cinnamon,

---

[134] *Cinnamon.*]—The substance of Larcher's very long and learned note on this subject, may, if I mistake not, be comprised in very few words: by cinnamomum the ancients understood a branch of that tree, bark and all, of which the cassia was the bark only. The cutting of these branches is now prohibited, because found destructive of the tree. I have before observed, that of cinnamon there are different kinds; the cassia of Herodotus was, doubtless, what we in general understand to be cinnamon, of which our cassia, or cassia lignea, is an inferior kind. —*T.*

[135] *As instructed by the Phœnicians.*]—I cannot resist the pleasure of giving at full length the note of Larcher on this passage, which detects and explains two of the most singular and unaccountable errors ever committed in literature.

" The above is the true sense of the passage, which Pliny has mistaken. He makes Herodotus say that the cinnamon and casia are found in the nests of certain birds, and *in particular of the phœnix.* Cinnamomum et casias, fabulose narravit antiquitas, princepsve Herodotus, avium nidis et privatim phœnicis, in quo situ Liber Pater educatus esset, ex inviis rupibus arboribusque decuti. The above passage from Pliny, Dupin has translated, most ridiculously, ' l'antiquité fabuleuse, et *le prince des menteurs,* Herodote, disent,' &c. He should have said Herodotus first of all, for princeps, in this place, does not mean prince, and menteur cannot possibly be implied from the text of Pliny. Pliny had reason to consider the circumstance as fabulous, but he ought not to have imputed it to our historian, who

says

mon, is by certain large birds carried to their nests constructed of clay, and placed in the cavities of inacessible rocks. To procure it thence the Arabians have contrived this stratagem :—they cut in very large pieces the dead bodies of oxen, asses, or other beasts of burden, and carry them near these nests: they then retire to some distance; the birds soon fly to the spot, and carry these pieces of flesh to their nests, which not being able to support the weight, fall in pieces to the ground. The Arabians take this opportunity of gathering the cinnamon, which they afterwards dispose of to different countries.

CXII. The ledanum [116], or, as the natives term it,

says no such thing. But the authority of Pliny has imposed not only on Statius,

> Phariæque exempta volucri
> Cinnama,

where Pharia volucris means the phœnix ; and on Avienus,

> Internis etiam procul undique ab oris
> Ales amica deo largum congessit amomum ;

but also on Van Stapel, in his Commentaries on Theophrastus. Pliny had, doubtless, read too hastily this passage of Herodotus, which is sufficiently clear. Suidas and the Etymologicum Magnum, are right in the word κινᾰμωμον.''

[116] *Ledanum.*]—The following further particulars concerning this aromatic are taken from Tournefort.

It is gathered by the means of whips, which have long handles, and two rows of straps ; with these they brush the plants, and to these will stick the odoriferous glue which hangs on the leaves ; when the whips are sufficiently laden with this glue, they take a knife and scrape it clean off the straps.

In

ịt, ladanum, is gathered in a more remarkable manner than even the cinnamon. In itfelf it is particularly fragạnt, though gathered from a place as
much the contrary. It is found fticking to the
beards of he-goats, like the mucus of trees. It is
mixed by the Arabians in various aromatics, and
indeed it is with this that they perfume themfẹlves
in common.

CXIII. I have thought it proper to be thus minute on the fubjeᵭ of the Arabian perfumes; and
we may add, that the whole of Arabia exhales a
moſt delicious fragrance. There are alfo in this
country two fpeciès of fheep, well deferving admiration, and to be found no where elfe. One of
them is remarkable for an enormous length of
ṭail [137], extending to three cubits, if not more.

In the time of Diofcorides, and before, they ufed to gather
the ledanụm not only with whips, but they alfo were careful in
ϛombing off fuch of it as was found fticking to the beards and
ᵗhighs of the goats, which fed upon nothing but the leaves of the
ϛiſtus.

The ledum is a fpecies of ciftus.

[137] *Enormous length of tail.*]—The following defcription of the
broad-tailed fheep, from Pennant, takes away from the feeming
improbability of this account.

"This fpecies," fays Mr. Pennant, "is common in Syria,
Barbary, and Æthiopia. Some of their tails end in a point, but
are oftener fquare or round. They are fo long as to trail on the
ground, and the fhepherds are obliged to put boards with fmall
wheels under the tails, to keep them from galling. Thefe
tails are efteemed a great delicacy, are of a fubftance between
fat and marrow, and are eaten with the lean of the mutton. Some
of thefe tails weigh 50 lb. each."

If they were permitted to trail them along the ground, they would certainly ulcerate from the friction. But the shepherds of the country are skilful enough to make little carriages, upon which they secure the tails of the sheep: the tails of the other species are of the size of one cubit,

CXIV. Æthiopia, which is the extremity of the habitable world, is contiguous to this country on the south-west. This produces gold in great quantities, elephants with their prodigious teeth, trees and shrubs of every kind, as well as ebony; its inhabitants are also remarkable for their size, their beauty, and their length of life.

CXV. The above are the two extremes of Asia and Africa. Of that part of Europe nearest to the west, I am not able to speak with decision. I by no means believe that the Barbarians give the name of Eridanus [138] to a river which empties itself into the Northern Sea, whence, as it is said, our amber comes. Neither am I better ac-

[138] *Eridanus.*]—Bellanger was of opinion, that Herodotus intended here to speak of the Eridanus, a river in Italy; Pliny thought so too, and expresses his surprize that Herodotus should be unable to meet with a person who had seen this river, although part of his life was spent at Thuria, in Magna Græcia.

But this very reflection ought to have convinced both Pliny and Bellanger, that Herodotus had another Eridanus in view.

The Eridanus here alluded to, could not possibly be any other than the Rho-daune, which empties itself into the Vistula, near Dantzic, and on the banks of which amber is now found in large quantities.—*Larcher.*

quainted

quainted with the iflands called the Caffiterides [139], from which we are faid to have our tin. The name Eridanus is certainly not barbarous, it is of

[139] *Caffiterides.*]—Pliny fays thefe iflands were thus called from their yielding abundance of lead; Strabo fays, that they were known only to the Phœnicians; Larcher is of opinion that Great Britain was in the number of thefe.

The Phœnicians, who were exceedingly jealous of their commerce, ftudioufly concealed the fituation of the Caffiterides, as long as they were able; which fully accounts for the ignorance fo honeftly avowed by Herodotus. Camden and d'Anville agree in confidering the Scilly Ifles as undoubtedly the Caffiterides of the ancients. Strabo makes them ten in number, lying to the north of Spain; and the principal of the Scilly ifles are ten, the reft being very inconfiderable. Dionyfius Periegetes exprefsly diftinguifhes them from the Britifh ifles;

Νισας θ' Εσπεριδας τοθι κασσιτεροιο γινεθλη—

*   *   *   *   *   *   *   *

Αλλαι δ' ωκεανοιο παραι Βορεωτιδας ακ]ας
Δισσαι ν,σοι εασι Βρρ΄ίανιδις.—v. 563.

Yet it is not an improbable conjecture of his commentator Hill, that the promontory of Cornwall might perhaps at firft be confidered as another ifland. Diodorus Siculus defcribes the carrying of tin from the Caffiterides, and from Britain, to the northern coaft of France, and thence on horfes to Marfeilles, thirty days journey; this muft be a new trade eftablifhed by the Romans, who employed great perfeverance to learn the fecret from the Phœnicians. Strabo tells us of one Phœnician captain, who finding himfelf followed by a Roman veffel, purpofely fteered into the fhallows, and thus deftroyed both his own fhip and the other; his life, however, was faved, and he was rewarded by his countrymen for his patriotic refolution.

Euftathius, in his comment on Dionyfius, reckons alfo ten Caffiterides; but his account affords no new proof, as it is manifeftly copied from Strabo, to the text of which author it affords a remarkable correction.—*T.*

K 4 Greek

Greek derivation, and, as I should conceive, introduced by one of our poets. I have endeavoured, but without succefs, to meet with fome one
who from ocular obfervation might defcribe to me
the fea which lies in that part of Europe. It is neverthelefs certain, that both our tin and our amber [140] are brought from thofe extreme regions.

CXVI. It is certain that in the north of Europe
there is a prodigious quantity of gold; but how it
is produced I am not able to tell with certainty.
It is affirmed indeed, that the Arimafpi, a people
who have but one eye, take this gold away violently from the griffins; but I can never perfuade
myfelf that there are any men who, having but one
eye, enjoy in all other refpects the nature and qualities
of other human beings. Thus much feems un-
queftionable, that thefe extreme parts of the world
contain within themfelves things the moft beautiful as well as rare.

CXVII. There is in Afia a large plain, fur-

---

[140] *Amber.*]—Amber takes its name from *ambra*, the Arabian name for this fubftance; the fcience of electricity is fo
called from *electrum*, the Greek word for amber. This term
of electricity is now applied not only to the power of attracting
lighter bodies, which amber poffeffes, but to many other powers
of a fimilar nature. Amber is certainly not of the ufe, and
confequently not of the value, which it has been, but it is ftill
given in medicine, and is, as I am informed, the bafis of all var-
nifhes. It is found in various places, but Pruffia is faid to produce the moft and the beft.—T.

rounded on every part by a ridge of hills, through which there are five different apertures. It formerly belonged to the Chorafmians, who inhabit those hills in common with the Hyrcanians, Parthians, Sarangenfians, and Thomaneans; but after the fubjection of thefe nations to Perfia, it became the property of the great king. From thefe furrounding hills there iffues a large river called Aces: this formerly, being conducted through the openings of the mountain, watered the feveral countries above mentioned. But when thefe regions came under the power of the Perfians, the apertures were clofed, and gates placed at each of them, to prevent the paffage of the river. Thus on the inner fide, from the waters having no iffue, this plain became a fea, and the neighbouring nations, deprived of their accuftomed refource, were reduced to the extremeft diftrefs from the want of water. In winter they, in common with other nations, had the benefit of the rains, but in fummer, after fowing their millet and fefamum, they required water but in vain. Not being affifted in their diftrefs, the inhabitants of both fexes haftened to Perfia, and prefenting themfelves before the palace of the king, made loud complaints. In confequence of this, the monarch directed the gates to be opened towards thofe parts where water was moft immediately wanted; ordering them again to be clofed after the lands had been fufficiently refrefhed : the fame was done with refpect to them all, beginning where moifture was wanted the moft. I have, however, been informed, that this is only granted in

consideration

confideration of a large donative above the usual tribute.

CXVIII. Intaphernes, one of the seven who had conspired against the magus, lost his life from the following act of insolence. Soon after the death of the usurpers, he went to the palace, with the view of having a conference with the king; for the conspirators had mutually agreed, that, except the king should happen to be in bed with his wife, they might any of them have accefs to the royal prefence, without sending a previous mefſenger. Intaphernes, not thinking any introduction necefſary, was about to enter, but the porter and the introducing officer prevented him, pretending that the king was retired with one of his wives. He, not believing their affertion, drew his fword, and cut off their ears and nofes; then taking the bridle from his horſe, he tied them together, and fo difiniffed them.

CXIX. In this condition they prefented themfelves before the king, telling him why they had been thus treated. Darius, thinking that this might have been done with the confent of the other confpirators, fent for them feparately, and defired to know whether they approved of what had happened. As foon as he was convinced that Intaphernes had perpetrated this without any communication with the reft, he ordered him, his fon, and all his family, to be taken into cuſtody; having many reafons to fufpect, that in concert with his friends he might

might excite a fedition : he afterwards commanded
them all to be bound, and prepared for execution.
The wife of Intaphernes then prefented herfelf before the royal palace, exhibiting every demonftration
of grief. As fhe regularly continued this conduct,
her frequent appearance at length excited the compaffion of Darius; who thus addreffed her by a
meffenger : " Woman, king Darius offers you the
" liberty of any individual of your family, whom you
" may moft defire to preferve." After fome deliberation with herfelf, fhe made this reply : " If the
" king will grant me the life of any one of my fami-
" ly, I choofe my brother in preference to the reft."
Her determination greatly aftonifhed the king; he
fent to her therefore a fecond meffage to this ef-
feét : " The king defires to know why you have
" thought proper to pafs over your children and
" your hufband, and to preferve your brother; who
" is certainly a more remote connection than your
" children, and cannot be fo dear to you as your
" hufband ?" She anfwered thus: " Oh king! if
" it pleafe the deity, I may have another hufband;
" and if I be deprived of thefe, may have other
" children ; but as my parents are both of them
" dead, it is certain that I can have no other bro-
" ther [141]." The anfwer appeared to Darius very
judicious;

[141] *I can have no other brother.*]—This very fingular, and I
do not fcruple to add prepofterous fentiment, is imitated very
minutely by Sophocles, in the Antigone. That the reader
may the better underftand, by comparing the different application of thefe words, in the hiftorian and the poet, I fhall fubjoin
a part of the argument of the Antigone.

Eteocles

judicious; indeed he was so well pleased with it, that he not only gave the woman the life of her brother, but also pardoned her eldest son : the rest were all of them put to death. Thus, at no great

Eteocles and Polynices were the sons of Œdipus, and successors of his power; they had agreed to reign year by year alternately ; but Eteocles breaking the contract, the brothers determined to decide the dispute in a single combat : they fought and mutually slew each other. The first act of their uncle Creon, who succeeded to the throne, was to forbid the rites of sepulture, to Polynices, denouncing immediate death upon whoever should dare to bury him. Antigone transgressed this ordinance, and was detected in the fact of burying her brother; she was commanded to be interred alive, and what follows is part of what is suggested by her situation and danger.

> And thus, my Polynices, for my care
> Of thee, am I rewarded, and the good
> Alone shall praise me: for a husband dead,
> Nor, had I been a mother, for my children
> Would I have dar'd to violate the laws.—
> Another husband and another child
> Might sooth affliction; but, my parents dead,
> A brother's loss could never be repair'd.
>
> *Franklin's Sophocles.*

The reader will not forget to observe, that the piety of Antigone is directed to a lifeless corpse, but that of the wife of Intaphernes to her living brother, which is surely less repugnant to reason, and the common feelings of the human heart, not to speak of the superior claims of duty.

There is an incident similar to this in Lucian :—See the tract called Toxaris, or Amicitia, where a Scythian is described to neglect his wife and children, whilst he incurs the greatest danger to preserve his friend from the flames. " Other children," says he, " I may easily have, and they are at best but a precarious blessing, but such a friend I could no where obtain." —*T.*

interval

interval of time, perished one of the seven conspirators.

CXX. About the time of the last illness of Cambyses, the following accident happened. The governor of Sardis was a Persian, named Orœtes, who
had been promoted by Cyrus. This man conceived the atrocious design of accomplishing the death'
of Polycrates of Samos, by whom he had never in
word or deed been injured, and whose person he
never had beheld. His assigned motive was commonly reported to be this : Orœtes one day sitting
at the gates of the palace [142] with another Persian,
whose name was Mitrobates, governor of Dascy-
lium, entered into a conversation with him, which
at length terminated in dispute. The subject about
which they contended was military virtue : " Can
" you," says Mitrobates to Orœtes, " have any pre-
" tensions to valour, who have never added Samos
" to the dominions of your master, contiguous as it

[142] *At the gates of the palace.*]—In the Greek it is at the·
king's gate. The grandees waited at the gate of the Persian
kings :—This custom, established by Cyrus, continued as long as
the monarchy, and at this day, in Turkey, we say the Ottoman
port, for the Ottoman court.—*Larcher.*

Ignorance of this custom has caused several mistakes, particu-·
larly in the history of Mordecai, in the book of Esther, who is
by many authors, and even by Prideaux, represented as meanly
situated when placed there. Many traces of this custom may
be found in Xenophon's Cyropædia. Plutarch, in his life of
Themistocles, uses the expression of *those at the king's gate,*
των ιπι θυραις βασιλιως, as a general designation for nobles and
state officers.—See *Brisson, de Regno Persarum,* lib. i.—*T.*

" is

" is to your province; and which indeed may fo
" eafily be taken, that one of its own citizens made
" himfelf mafter of it, with the help of fifteen men
" in arms, and ftill retains the fupreme authority?"
This made a deep impreffion upon the mind of
Orœtes; but without meditating revenge againft the
perfon who had affronted him, he determined to effect the death of Polycrates, on whofe account he
had been reproached.

CXXI. There are fome, but not many, who affirm
that Orœtes fent a meffenger to Samos, to propofe
fome queftion to Polycrates, but of what nature is
unknown; and that he found Polycrates in the men's
apartment, reclining on a couch, with Anacreon of
Teos [143] by his fide. The man advanced to deliver
his

[143] *Anacreon of Teos.*]—It is by no means aftonifhing to find,
in the court of a tyrant, a poet who is eternally finging in praife
of wine and love; his verfes are full of the encomiums of Polycrates. How different was the conduct of Pythagoras! That
philofopher, perceiving that tyranny was eftablifhed in Samos,
went to Ægypt, and from thence to Babylon, for the fake of
improvement: returning to his country, he found that tyranny
ftill fubfifted; he went therefore to Italy, and there finifhed his
days.—*Larcher.*

This poet was not only beloved by Polycrates, he was the favourite alfo of Hipparchus the Athenian tyrant. And, notwithftanding the inference which Larcher feems inclined to draw,
from contrafting his conduct with that of Pythagoras, he was
called σοφος by Socrates himfelf; and the terms ηθος και αγαθος,
are applied to him by Athenæus. By the way, much as has been
faid on the compofitions of Anacreon by H. Stevens, Scaliger,
M. Dacier, and others, many of the learned are in doubt whether

his meffage; but Polycrates, either by accident, or to demonftrate the contempt [144] in which he held Orœtes, continued all the time he was fpeaking with his face towards to the wall, and did not vouchfafe any reply.

CXXII. Thefe are the two affigned motives for the deftruction of Polycrates: every one will prefer that which feems moft probable. Orœtes, who lived at Magnefia, which is on the banks of the Mæander [145], fent Myrfus the Lydian, fon of Gyges, with a meffage to Polycrates at Samos. With the character of Polycrates Orœtes was well acquainted; for, except Minos [146] the Cnoffian, or whoever before him accomplifhed it, he was the firft Greek

---

ther the works afcribed to him by the moderns are genuine. Anacreontic verfe is fo called, from its being much ufed by Anacreon; it confifts of three Iambic feet and a half, of which there is no inftance in the Lyrics of Horace.—See the Prolegomena to *Barnes's Anacreon*, §. 12.

[144] *Demonftrate the contempt.*]—This behaviour of Polycrates, which was doubtlefs intended to be expreffive of contempt, brings to mind the ftory of Charles the Twelfth of Sweden, who at an interview with the Grand Vizier, expreffed his contempt and indignation by tearing the minifter's robe with his fpur, and afterwards leaving the apartment without faying a word.

[145] *On the banks of the Mæander.*]—This is added in order to diftinguifh that city from the Magnefia on the Sipylus, lying between Sardes and Phocæa.

[146] *Except Minos.*]—What Herodotus fays of the maritime power of Minos, is confirmed by Thucydides and Diodorus Sieulus. His teftimony concerning Polycrates is fupported alfo by Thucydides and Strabo.—*Larcher.*

who

who formed the defign of making himfelf mafter
of the fea.   But as far as hiftorical tradition may
be depended upon, Polycrates is the only individual who projected the fubjection of Ionia and the
iflands.   Perfectly aware of thefe circumftances,
Orœtes fent this meffage.

"Oroetes to Polycrates.

" I underftand that you are revolving fome vaft
" project in your mind, but have not money refpon-
" fible to your views. Be advifed by me, and you
" will at the fame time promote your own advan-
" tage and preferve me.   I am informed, and I be-
" lieve it to be true, that king Cambyfes has de-
" termined on my death.   Receive, therefore, me
" with my wealth, part of which fhall be at your
" difpofal, part at mine: with the affiftance of this
" you may eafily obtain the fovereignty of Greece.
" If you have any fufpicions, fend to me fome one
" who is in your intimate confidence, and he fhall
" be convinced by demonftration."

CXXIII. With thefe overtures Polycrates was
fo exceedingly delighted, that he was eager to comply with them immediately, for his love of money
was exceffive.   He fent firft of all, to examine into
the truth of the affair, Mæandrius his fecretary,
called fo after his father. This Mæandrius, not long
afterwards, placed as a facred donative in the temple
of Juno, the rich furniture of the apartment of Polycrates.   Orœtes, knowing the motive for which
                                                this

this man came, contrived and executed the following artifice : He filled eight chefts nearly to the top
with ftones, then covering over the furface with
gold, they were tied together [147], as if ready to be
removed. Mæandrius on his arrival faw the above
chefts, and returned to make his report to Polycrates.

CXXIV. Polycrates, notwithftanding the pre-
dictions of the foothfayers, and the remonftrances of
his friends, was preparing to meet Orœtes, when his
daughter in a dream faw this vifion : She beheld her
father aloft in the air, wafhed by Jupiter, and
anointed by the fun.   Terrified by this incident, fhe
ufed every means in her power to prevent his going

[147] *Tied together.*]—Before the ufe of locks, it was the cuftom
in more ancient times to fecure things with knots : of thefe fome
were fo difficult, that he alone who poffeffed the fecret was
able to unravel them. The famous Gordian knot muft be
known to every one ; this ufage is often alfo alluded to by
Homer :

> Then bending with full force, around he roll'd
> A labyrinth of bands in fold on fold,
> Clos'd with Circæan art.

According to Euftathius, keys were a more modern invention, for which the Lacedæmonians are to be thanked.

Upon the above paffage from Euftathius, Larcher remarks,
that it is fomewhat fingular, that the Lacedæmonians, whofe
property was in common, fhould be the inventors of keys.

The verfion of Pope which I have given in the foregoing lines
is very defective, and certainly inadequate to the expreffion of

Αυτικ' επηρτυε πωμα θοως δ'επι δ'εσμον ιηλε
Ποικιλον, ον ποτε μιν διδαε Φρεσι ποτνια Κιρκη.—**T**.

to meet Orœtes ; and as he was about to embark for this purpofe, on board a fifty-oared galley, fhe perfifted in auguring unfavourably of his expedition. At this he was fo incenfed, as to declare, that if he returned fafe fhe fhould remain long unmarried. To this fhe expreffed herfelf very defirous to fub- mit; being willing to continue long a virgin [148], rather than be deprived of her father.

CXXV. Polycrates, difregarding all that had been faid to him, fet fail to meet Orœtes. He was accompanied by many of his friends, and amongft the reft by Democedes [149], the fon of Calliphon ; he was a phyfician of Crotona, and the moft fkilful practitioner of his time. As foon as Polycrates ar- rived at Magnefia, he was put to a miferable death, unworthy of his rank and fuperior endowments. Of all the princes who ever reigned in Greece, thofe

---

[148] *Long a virgin.*]—To die a virgin, and without having any children, was amongft the ancients efteemed a very ferious calamity. Electra in Sophocles enumerates this in the cata- logue of her misfortunes:

A τεκνος
Ταλαιν', αμφιυτος αιει οιχω.—166.

Electra makes a fimilar complaint in the Oreftes of Euripi- des ; as does alfo Polyxena at the point of death, in the Hecuba of Euripides.—T.

[149] *Democedes.*]—Of this perfonage a farther account is given in the fourth book. He is mentioned alfo by Ælian, in his Various Hiftory, book viii. chap. 17; and alfo by Athenæus, book xii. chap. 4. which laft author informs us, that the phy- ficians of Crotona were, on account of Democedes, efteemed the firft in Greece.—See alfo chap. 151. of this book.—T.

of

of Syracufe alone excepted, none equalled Polycrates in magnificence. Orœtes having bafely put him
to death [150], fixed his body to a crofs; his attendant
he fent back to Samos, telling them, "They ought
" to be thankful, that he had not made them flaves."
The ftrangers, and the fervants of thofe who had
accompanied Polycrates, he detained in fervitude.
The circumftance of his being fufpended on a crofs,
fulfilled the vifion of the daughter of Polycrates: for
he was wafhed by Jupiter, that is to fay by the rain,
and he was anointed by the fun, for it extracted the
moifture from his body. The great profperity of
Polycrates terminated in this unfortunate death,
which indeed had been foretold him by Amafis
king of Ægypt.

CXXVI. But it was not long before Orœtes
paid ample vengeance to the manes of Polycrates.
After the death of Cambyfes, and the ufurpation of
the magi, Orœtes, who had never deferved well of
the Perfians, whom the Medes had fraudulently deprived of the fupreme authority, took the advan-

---

[150] *Put him to death*]—The Perfians generally beheaded or
flead thofe whom they crucified: fee an account of their treatment of Hiftiæus, book vi. chap. 30. and of Leonidas, book vii.
238.—*T*.

The beautiful and energetic lines which Juvenal applied to
Sejanus, are remarkably appofite to the circumftances and fate
of Polycrates.

> Qui nimios optabat honores,
> Et nimias pofcebat opes, numerofa parabat
> Excelfæ turris tabulata, unde altior effet
> Cafus, et impulfæ præceps immane ruinæ.—*T*.

tage

tage of the diforder of the times [51], to put to death Mitrobates, the governor of Dafcylium, and his fon Cranapes. Mitrobates, was the perfon who had formerly reproached Orœtes; and both he and his fon were highly efteemed in Perfia. In addition to his other numerous and atrocious crimes, he com-paffed the death of a meffenger, fent to him from Darius, for no other reafon but becaufe the pur-port of the meffage was not agreeable to him. He ordered the man to be way-laid in his return, and both he and his horfe were flain, and their bodies concealed.

CXXVII. As foon as Darius afcended the throne, he determined to punifh Orœtes for his various enormities, but more particularly for the murder of Mitrobates and his fon. He did not think it prudent to fend an armed force openly againft him, as the ftate was ftill unfettled, and as his own authority had been fo recently obtained; he was informed, moreover, that Orœtes poffeffed confiderable ftrength: his government extended over Phrygia, Lydia, and Ionia, and he was regu-gularly attended by a guard of a thoufand men. Darius was, therefore, induced to adopt this mode of proceeding: He affembled the nobleft of the Perfians, and thus addreffed them: " Which of " you, Oh Perfians! will undertake for me the " accomplifhment of a project which requires

---

[51] *Diforder of the times.*]—For ι ταυτη τι αρχη, which pre-vailed in preceding editions, Weffeling propofes to read ιι ταυτη ταραχη, which removes all perplexity.—*T.*

" fagacity

" fagacity alone, without military aid, or any kind
" of violence; for where wifdom is required force
" is of little avail? Which of you will bring me
" the body of Orœtes, alive or dead? He has never
" deferved well of the Perfians; and, in addition to
" his numerous crimes, he has killed two of our
" countrymen, Mitrobates and his fon. He has
" alfo, with intolerable infolence, put a meffenger
" of mine to death: we muft prevent, therefore',
" his perpetrating any greater evils againft us, by
" putting him to death."

CXXVIII. When Darius had thus fpoken, thirty Perfians offered to accomplifh what he wifhed.
As they were difputing on the fubject, the king
ordered the decifion to made by lot, which fell upon
Bagæus, the fon of Artontes. To attain the end
which he propofed, he caufed a number of letters
to be written on a variety of fubjects, and prefixing
to them the feal of Darius, he proceed with them
to Sardis. As foon as he came to the prefence of
Orœtes, he delivered the letters one by one to the
king's fecretary; one of whom is regularly attendant upon the governors of provinces. The motive of Bagæus in delivering the letters feparately
was to obferve the difpofition of the guards, and
how far they might be inclined to revolt from
Orœtes. When he faw that they treated the letters with great refpect [151], and their contents with
ftill

ſtill greater, he delivered one to this effect: "Per-
" ſians, king Darius forbids your ſerving any longer
" Orœtes as guards:" in a moment they threw
down their arms. Bagæus, obſerving their prompt
obedience in this inſtance, aſſumed ſtill greater confidence, he delivered the laſt of his letters, of which
theſe were the contents: "King Darius commands
" the Perſians who are at Sardis to put Orœtes to
" death:" without heſitation they drew their ſwords
and killed him. In this manner was the death of
Polycrates of Samos revenged on Orœtes the Perſian.

CXXIX. Upon the death of Orœtes, his effects were all of them removed to Suſa. Not long
after which Darius, as he was engaged in the chace,
in leaping from his horſe twiſted his foot with ſo
much violence, that the ancle-bone was quite diſlo-
cated. Having at his court ſome Ægyptians, ſuppoſed to be the moſt ſkilful of the medical profeſ-
ſion, he truſted to their aſſiſtance. They, however,
encreaſed the evil, by twiſting and otherwiſe violently handling the part affected: from the extreme
pain which he endured, the king paſſed ſeven days
and as many nights without ſleep. In this ſituation,
on the eighth day, ſome one ventured to recommend Democedes of Crotona, having before heard
of his reputation at Sardis. Darius immediately ſent

riod the diſtinction obſerved with regard to letters in the Eaſt is
this. thoſe ſent to common perſons are rolled up, and not ſealed; thoſe ſent to noblemen and princes are ſealed up, and en-
cloſed in rich bags of ſilk or ſattin curiouſly embroidered.—T.

for

for him: he was difcovered amongft the flaves of
Orœtes, where he had continued in negleft, and
was brought to the king juft as he was found, in
chains and in rags.

CXXX. As foon as he appeared, Darius afked
him if he had any knowledge of medicine? In the
apprehenfion that if he difcovered his art, he fhould
never have the power of returning to Greece, Democedes for a while diffembled; which Darius perceiving, he ordered thofe who had brought him to
produce the inftruments of punifhment and torture.
Democedes began then to be more explicit, and
confeffed that, although he poffeffed no great knowledge of the art, yet by his communication with a
phyfician he had obtained fome little proficiency.
The management of the cafe was then entrufted to
him; he accordingly applied fuch medicines and
ftrong fomentations as were cuftomary in Greece,
by which means Darius, who began to defpair of
ever recovering the entire ufe of his foot, was not
only enabled to fleep, but in a fhort time perfeftly
reftored to health. In acknowledgment of his
cure, Darius prefented him with two pair of fetters
of gold! upon which Democedes ventured to afk
the king, whether, in return for his reftoring him to
health, he wifhed to double his calamity [151]? The
king,

---

[151] *Double his calamity.*]—The ancients were very fond of
this play upon words:—See in the Septem contra Thebas of
Æfchylus, a play on the word Polynices:

king, delighted with the reply, sent the man to the apartments of his women: the eunuchs who conducted him informed them, that this was the man who had restored the king to life; accordingly, every one of them taking out a vase of gold [154], gave it to Democedes with the case. The present was so very valuable, that a servant who followed him behind, whose name was Sciton, by gathering up the staters which fell to the ground, obtained a prodigious sum of money.

Οἱ δῆτ' ὀρθῶς κατ' ἐπωνυμιην
Καὶ πολυνιικις
Ωλοιτ' ασιβιι διανοιᾳ.—v. 833.

The particular point in this passage is omitted by Mr. Potter, probably because he did not find it suited to the genius of the English language.

See also Ovid's description of the flower:

Ipse suos gemitus foliis inscribit et ai ai
Flos habet inscriptum.   T.

[154] *Taking out a vase of gold.*]—This is one of the most perplexed passages in Herodotus; and the conjectures of the critics are proportionably numerous. The great difficulty consists in ascertaining what is designed by ὑπολυπησα and θηκη. The φιαλη appears to have been a jar or vase, probably itself of gold. Few have doubted that the passage is corrupt: the best conjectural reading gives this sense, " that each, taking gold out of a chest in a vase, (φιαλη) gave it, vase and all, to Democedes. Υπολυπησα is thus made to signify plunging the vase among the gold to fill it, as a pitcher into water, which sense is confirmed by good authorities. The idea more immediately excited by the word, is, that they struck the bottom of the vase to shake out all the gold; but according to this interpretation, the vase itself is the θηκη, or case.—T.

CXXXI.

CXXXI. The following was what induced Democedes to forfake Crotona, and attach himfelf to
Polycrates.   At Crotona he fuffered continual reftraint from the auftere temper of his father; this becoming infupportable he left him, and went to
Ægina.   In the firft year of his refidence at this
place he excelled the moft fkilful of the medical
profeffion, without having had any regular education, and indeed without the common inftruments
of the art.   His reputation, however, was fo great,
that in the fecond year the inhabitants of Ægina,
by general confent, engaged his fervices at the price
of one talent.   In the third year the Athenians retained him, at a falary of one hundred minæ[155];

[155] *One hundred minæ.*]—Valcnaer fufpects that this place has
been altered by fome copyifts. Athens, in the time of its greateft
fplendor, allowed their ambaffadors but two drachmæ a day, and
a hundred drachmæ make but one mina.   If when the Athenians were rich they gave no more to an ambaffador, how is it
likely that, when they were exceedingly poor, they fhould give
a penfion of a hundred minæ to a phyfician ? Thus far Valcnaer. From this and other paffages in the ancient writers, it appears that in remoter times it was ufual to hire phyficians for
the affiftance of a whole city by the year.   The fees which
were given phyficians for a fingle incidental vifit, was very inconfiderable, as appears from the famous verfes of Crates, preferved by Diogenes Laertius.

Τίθει μαγειρῳ μνᾶς δέκ', ἰατρῷ δραχμὴν
Κόλακι τάλαντα πέντι, συμβόλῳ καπνὸν
Πόρνῃ ταλαντον, φιλοσόφῳ τριώβολον.

"To a cook 30*l*.; to a phyfician two groats; to a flatterer
500 *l*.; to a counfellor nothing; to a whore 180 *l*.; to a philofopher a groat." The above is fuppofed to defcribe part of
the accounts of a man of fortune.—*T.*

and

and in the fourth year Polycrates engaged to give him two talents. His refidence was then fixed at Samos; and to this man the phyficians of Crotona are confiderably indebted for the reputation which they enjoy; for at this period, in point of medical celebrity, the phyficians of Crotona held the firft, and thofe of Cyrene the next place. At this time alfo the Argives had the credit of being the moft fkilful muficians [156] of Greece.

CXXXII. Democedes having in this manner reftored the king to health, had a fumptuous houfe provided him at Sufa, was entertained at the king's own table, and, except the reftriction of not being able to return to Greece, enjoyed all that he could wifh. The Ægyptian phyficians, who had before the care of the king's health, were on account of their inferiority to Democedes, a Greek, condemned to the crofs, but he obtained their pardon. He alfo procured the liberty of an Elean foothfayer, who having followed Polycrates was detained and neglected amongft his other flaves. It may be added, that Democedes remained in the higheft eftimation with the king.

CXXXIII. It happened not long afterwards, that Atoffa, daughter of Cyrus, and wife of Darius,

---

[156] *Muficians.*]—Mufic was an important part of Grecian education. Boys till they were ten years old were taught to read by the grammatiftes; they were then taught mufic three years by the citharistes; after their thirteenth year they learned the gymnaftic exercifes, under the care of the paidotades.—*T.*

had an ulcer upon her breaſt, which finally breaking ſpread itſelf conſiderably. As long as it was
ſmall, ſhe was induced by delicacy to conceal it;
but when it grew more troubleſome ſhe ſent for
Democedes, and ſhewed it to him. He told her
he was able to cure it; but exacted of her an oath,
that in return ſhe ſhould ſerve him in what he might
require, which he aſſured her ſhould be nothing to
diſgrace her.

CXXXIV. Atoſſa was cured by his ſkill, and,
obſervant of her own promiſe and his inſtructions,
ſhe took the opportunity of thus addreſſing Darius,
whilſt ſhe was in bed with him : " It is wonderful,
" my lord, that having ſuch a numerous army at
" command, you have neither encreaſed the power
" of Perſia, nor at all extended your dominions.
" It becomes a man like you, in the vigour of
" your age, and maſter of ſo many and ſuch pow-
" erful reſources, to perform ſome act which may
" ſatisfy the Perſians of the ſpirit and virtue of
" their prince. There are two reaſons which give
" importance to what I recommend :—The one,
" that your ſubjects may venerate the manly ac-
" compliſhments of their maſter; the other, that
" you may prevent the indolence of peace excit-
" ing them to tumult and ſedition. Do not there-
" fore conſume your youth in inactivity, for the
" powers of the mind [157] increaſe and improve
" with

---

[157] *Powers of the mind.*]—This opinion is thus expreſſed
by

" with thofe of the body; and in like manner as
" old age comes on they become weaker and
" weaker, till they are finally blunted to every
" thing." " What you fay [158]," anfwered Darius,
" coincides with what was paffing in my mind. I
" had intended to make war againft Scythia, and
" to conftruct a bridge to unite our continent with
" the other, which things fhall foon be executed."
" Will it not, Sir," returned Atoffa, " be better to
" defer your intentions againft the Scythians, who
" will at any time afford you an eafy conqueft?
" Rather make an expedition againft Greece: I
" wifh much to have for my attendants fome

by Lucretius, which I give the reader from the verfion of
Creech.

> Befides, 'tis plain that fouls are born and grow,
> And all by age decay as bodies do:
> To prove this truth, in infants minds appear
> Infirm and tender, as their bodies are;
> In man the mind is ftrong; when age prevails,
> And the quick vigour of each member fails,
> The mind's pow'rs too decreafe and wafte apace,
> And grave and reverend folly takes the place.   T.

[158] *What you fay.*]—I have not tranflated Ω γυναι, which is in
the original, becaufe I do not think we have any correfpondent
word in our language. Oh woman! would be vulgar; and according to our *norma loquendi*, Oh wife! would not be adequate.
In the Ajax of Sophocles, v. 293, γυναι is ufed to exprefs contempt; but in the paffage before us it certainly denotes tendernefs. The addrefs of our Saviour to his mother proves this
moft fatisfactorily:—See alfo Homer:

Και εμοι ταδε παντα μελει γυναι.   —T.

" women

" women of Sparta, Argos, Athens, and Co-
" rinth, of whom I have heard so much. You
" have, moreover, in the man who healed the
" wound of your foot, the propereſt perſon in the
" world to deſcribe and explain to you every
" thing which relates to Greece." " If it be your
" wiſh," replied Darius, " that I ſhould firſt make a
" military excurſion againſt Greece, it will be pro-
" per to ſend thither previouſly ſome Perſians as
" ſpies, in company with the man to whom you
" allude. As ſoon as they return, and have in-
" formed me of the reſult of their obſervations,
" I will proceed againſt Greece."

CXXXV. Darius having delivered his ſentiments, no time was loſt in fulfilling them. As ſoon
as the morning appeared he ſent for fifteen Perſians
of approved reputation, and commanded them, in
company with Democedes, to examine every part
of the ſea-coaſt of Greece, enjoining them to be
very watchful of Democedes, and by all means to
bring him back with them. When he had done
this, he next ſent for Democedes himſelf, and after
deſiring him to examine and explain to the Perſians every thing which related to Greece, he entreated him to return in their company. All the
valuables which he poſſeſſed he recommended him
to take, as preſents to his father and his brethren,
aſſuring him that he ſhould be provided with a
greater number on his return. He moreover informed
him, that he had directed a veſſel to accompany him,
which

which was to be furnished with various things of value. In these professions Darius, as I am of opinion, was perfectly sincere; but Democedes, apprehending that the king meant to make trial of his fidelity, accepted these proposals without much acknowledgment. He desired, however, to leave his own effects, that they might be ready for his use at his return; but he accepted the vessel which was to carry the presents for his family. Darius, after giving these injunctions to Democedes, dismissed the party to prosecute their voyage.

CXXXVI. As soon as they arrived at Sidon, in Phœnicia, they manned two triremes, and loaded a large transport with different articles of wealth; after this they proceeded to Greece, examining the sea-coasts with the most careful attention. When they had informed themselves of the particulars relating to the most important places in Greece; they passed over to Tarentum [159] in Italy. Here Aristophilides, prince of Tarentum, and a native of Crotona, took away the helms of the Median vessels, and detained the Persians as spies. Whilst his companions were in this predicament, Democedes himself went to Crotona. Upon his arrival at his native place, Aristophilides gave the Persians their

---

[159] *Tarentum.*]—These places, with the slightest variation possible, retain their ancient names. We now say the gulph of Tarento, and Crotona is now called Cottrone.—*T.*

liberty,

liberty, and reftored what he had taken from them.

CXXXVII. The Perfians, as foon as they reco-vered their liberty, failed to Crotona, in pursuit of Democedes, and meeting with him in the forum, feized his perfon. Some of the inhabitants, through fear of the Perfian power, were willing to deliver him up; others, on the contrary, beat the Perfians with clubs; who exclaimed, "Men of Crotona; " confider what ye do, in taking away from us a " fugitive from our king. Do you imagine that " you will derive any advantage from this infult to " Darius; will not rather your city be the firft ob- " ject of our hoftilities, the firft that we fhall plunder " and reduce to fervitude?" Thefe menaces had but little effect upon the people of Crotona, for they not only affifted Democedes to efcape, but alfo deprived the Perfians of the veffel which accompanied them. They were, therefore, under the neceffity of return-ing to Afia, without exploring any more of Greece, being thus deprived of their conductor. On their departure Democedes commiffioned them to inform Darius, that he was married to a daughter of Milo, the name of Milo the wreftler being well known to the Perfian monarch. To me it feems that he ac-celerated his marriage, and expended a vaft fum of money on the occafion, to convince Darius that he enjoyed in his own country no mean reputa-tion.

CXXXVIII. The Perfians, leaving Crotona,

were

were driven by contrary winds to Japygia [160], where
they were made flaves. Gillus, an exile of Tarentum, ranfomed them, and fent them home to Darius.
For this fervice the king declared himfelf willing to
perform whatever Gillus fhould require, who accordingly explaining the circumftances of his misfortune, requefted to be reftored to his country.
But Darius thinking that if, for the purpofe of
effecting the reftoration of this man, a large fleet.
fhould be fitted out, all Greece would take alarm;
he faid that the Cnidians would of themfelves be able
to accomplifh it: imagining that as this people
were in alliance with the Tarentines, it might be
effected without difficulty. Darius acceded to his
wifhes, and fent a meffenger to Cnidos [161], requiring them to reftore Gillus to Tarentum. The
Cnidians were defirous to fatisfy Darius; but their
folicitations had no effect on the Tarentines, and
they were not in a fituation to employ force.—Of
thefe particulars the above is a faithful relation, and
thefe were the firft Perfians who, with the view

[160] *Japygia.*]—This place is now called Cape de Leuca.
—*T*.

[161] *Cnidos.*]—At this remote period, when navigation was
certainly in its infancy, it feems not a little fingular that there
fhould be any communication or alliance between the people of
Tarentum and of Cnidos. The diftance is not inconfiderable,
and the paffage certainly intricate. Ctefias, the hiftorian, was a
native of Cnidos; here alfo was the beautiful ftatue of Venus, by
Praxiteles; here alfo was Venus worfhipped. Oh Venus regina
Cnidi Paphique, &c.

It is now a very miferable place, and called Cape Chio or
Cnio.—*T*.

of

óf examining the ftate of Greece, paffed over thither from Afia.

CXXXIX. Not long afterwards Darius befieged and took Samos. This was the firft city, either of Greeks or barbarians, which felt the force of his arms, and for thefe reafons : Cambyfes, in his expedition against Ægypt, was accompanied by a great number of Greeks. Some, as it is probable, attended him from commercial views, others as foldiers, and many from no other motive than curiofity. Among thefe laft was Sylofon, an exile of Samos, fon of Æaces, and brother of Polycrates. It happened one day very fortunately for this Sylofon, that he was walking in the great fquare of Memphis with a red cloak folded about him. Darius, who was then in the king's guards, and of no particular confideration, faw him, and was fo delighted with his cloak, that he went up to him with the view of purchafing it. Sylofon, obferving that Darius was very folicitous to have the cloak, happily, as it proved for him, expreffed himfelf thus :— " I " would not part with this cloak for any pecuniary " confideration whatever; but if it muft be fo, I will " make you a prefent of it." Darius praifed his generofity, and accepted the cloak.

CXL. Sylofon for a while thought he had foolifhly loft his cloak, but afterwards when Cambyfes died, and the feven confpirators had deftroyed the Magus, he learned that Darius, one of thefe feven, had obtained the kingdom, and was the very man

to whom formerly at his requeſt, in Ægypt, he had
given his cloak.   He went, therefore, to Suſa, and
preſenting himſelf before the royal palace, ſaid that
he had once done a ſervice to the king.   Of this
circumſtance the porter informed the king; who
was much aſtoniſhed, and exclaimed, "To what
"Greek can I poſſibly be obliged for any ſervices?
"I have not long been in poſſeſſion of my authority,
"and ſince this time no Greek has been admitted
"to my preſence, nor can I at all remember being
"indebted to one of that nation.   Introduce him,
"however, that I may know what he has to ſay."
Syloſon was accordingly admitted to the royal preſence; and being interrogated by interpreters who
he was, and in what circumſtance he had rendered
ſervice to the king, he told the ſtory of the cloak,
and ſaid that he was the perſon who had given it. In
reply, Darius exclaimed, "Are you then that ge-
"nerous man, who, at a time when I was poſſeſ-
"ſed of no authority, made me a preſent, which,
"though ſmall, was as valuable to me then, as any
"thing of importance would be to me now?   I
"will give you in return, that you may never re-
"pent of your kindneſs to Darius, the ſon of Hyſ-
"taſpes, abundance of gold and ſilver."   "Sir,"
replied Syloſon, "I would have neither gold nor
"ſilver; give me Samos my country, and deliver
"it from ſervitude.   Since the death of Polycrates
"my brother, whom Orœtes ſlew, it has been in
"the hands of one of our ſlaves. Give me this, Sir,
"without any effuſion of blood, or reducing my
"countrymen to ſervitude."

CXLI.

CXLI. On hearing this Darius fent an army, commanded by Otanes, one of the feven, with orders to accomplifh all that Sylofon had defired. Otanes proceeded to the fea, and embarked with his troops.

CXLII. The fupreme authority at Samos was then poffeffed by Mæandrius, fon of Mæandrius, to whom it had been confided by Polycrates himfelf. He was defirous of proving himfelf a very honeft man, but the times would not allow him. As foon as he was informed of the death of Polycrates, the firft thing he did was to erect an altar to Jupiter Liberator, tracing round it the facred ground, which may now be feen in the neighbourhood of the city. Having done this, he affembled the citizens of Samos, and thus addreffed them : " You are well acquainted that Polycrates confided " to me his fceptre and his power, which if I think " proper I may retain ; but I fhall certainly avoid " doing that myfelf which I deemed reprehenfible " in another. The ambition of Polycrates to rule " over men who were his equals, always feemed to " me unjuft; nor can I approve of a like conduct in " any man. Polycrates has yielded to his deftiny; and " for my part, I lay down the fupreme authority, and " reftore you all to an equality of power. 1 only " claim, which I think I reafonably may, fix talents " to be given me from the wealth of Polycrates, as " well as the appointment in perpetuity to me and " my pofterity of the priefthood of Jupiter Libera- " tor, whofe temple I have traced out; and then 1 re-

" ftore

" ftore you to liberty." When Mæandrius had thus
fpoken, a Samian exclaimed from the midft of the affembly, " You are not worthy to rule over us, your
" principles are bad, and your conduct reproachable.
" Rather let us make you give an account of the
" wealth which has paffed through your hands."
The name of this perfon was Telefarchus, a man
much refpected by his fellow-citizens.

CXLIII. Mæandrius revolved this circumftance
in his mind; and being convinced that if he refigned
his power fome other would affume it, he determined to continue as he was. Returning to the
citadel, he fent for the citizens, as if to give them
an account of the monies which had been alluded to, inftead of which he feized and confined
them. Whilft they remained in imprifonment
Mæandrius was taken ill; his brother Lycaretus,
not thinking he would recover, that he might the
more eafily fucceed in his views upon Samos put
the citizens who were confined to death; indeed
it did not appear that they were defirous of life
under the government of a tyrant [161].

CXLIV. When, therefore, the Perfians arrived
at Samos, with the view of reftoring Sylofon, they
had no refiftance to encounter. The Mæandrian
faction expreffed themfelves on certain conditions
ready to fubmit; and Mæandrius himfelf confented

[161] *The government of a tyrant.*]—See Weffeling's note and
Paw's conjecture upon this paffage.—*T.*

to leave the ifland. Their propofitions were accepted by Otanes ; and whilft they were employed in ratifying them, the principal men of the Perfians had feats brought, on which they placed themfelves in front of the citadel.

CXLV. Mæandrius had a brother, whofe name was Charileus, who was of an untoward difpofition, and for fome offence was kept chained in a dungeon. As foon as he heard what was doing, and beheld from his place of confinement the Perfians fitting at their eafe, he clamoroufly requefted to fpeak with Mæandrius. Mæandrius, hearing this, ordered him to be unbound, and brought before him. As foon as he came into his prefence, he began to reproach and abufe him, earneftly importuning him to attack the Perfians. " Me," he exclaimed, " who am your brother, and who have " done nothing worthy of chains, you have moft " bafely kept bound in a dungeon ; but on the " Perfians, who would afford you an eafy victory, " and who mean to drive you into exile, you dare " not take revenge. If your fears prevent you, give " me your auxiliary troops, who am equally difpofed " to punifh them for coming here, and to expel " you yourfelf from our ifland."

CXLVI. To this difcourfe Mæandrius gave a favourable ear, not, I believe, that he was abfurd enough to imagine himfelf equal to a conteft with the forces of the king, but from a fpirit of envy

M 3

againft

against Sylofon, and to prevent his receiving the government of Samos without trouble or exertion. He wished, by irritating the Perfians, to debilitate the power of Samos, and then to deliver it into their hands; for he well knew that the Perfians would refent whatever infults they might receive upon the Samians, and as to himfelf he was certain that whenever he pleafed he could depart unmolefted, for he had provided a fecret path, which led immediately from the citadel to the fea, by which he afterwards efcaped. In the mean while Charileus, having armed the auxiliaries, opened the gates, and fallied forth to attack the Perfians, who fo far from expecting any thing of the kind, believed that a truce had been agreed upon, and was then in force. Upon thefe Perfians, who were fitting at their eafe, and who were perfons of diftinction, the Samians fallied, and put them to death; the reft of the troops, however, foon came to their affiftance, by whom the party of Charileus was repulfed, and obliged again to feek fhelter in the citadel.

CXLVII. Otanes, the commander in chief, had hitherto obferved the orders of Darius, not to put any Samian to death, or to take any prifoners, but to deliver the ifland to Sylofon, fecure and without injury; but feeing fo great a flaughter of his countrymen, his indignation prevailed, and he ordered his foldiers to put every Samian they could meet with to death, without any diftinction of age. Immediately part of his forces blockaded the citadel, whilft whilſt another part were putting the inhabitants to the ſword, not ſuffering the ſacred places to afford any protection.

CXLVIII. Mæandrius leaving Samos, ſailed to Lacedæmon. On his arrival there with his wealth, he ſet in order his goblets of gold and ſilver, and directed his ſervants to clean them. Having entered into converſation with Cleomenes [163], ſon of Anaxandrides, the king of Sparta, he invited him to his houſe. Cleomenes ſaw his plate, and was ſtruck with aſtoniſhment. Mæandrius deſired him to accept of what he pleaſed [164]; but Cleomenes

was

---

[163] *Cleomenes,*]—Of this Cleomenes a memorable ſaying is preſerved in the Apophthegms of Plutarch. It relates to Homer and Heſiod, the former he called the poet of the Lacedæmonians, the latter the poet of the Helots, or the ſlaves; becauſe Homer gave directions for military conduct, Heſiod about the cultivation of the earth.—*T.*

[164] *To accept of what he pleaſed.*]—This ſelf-denial will appear leſs extraordinary to an Engliſh reader, when he is informed, that according to the inſtitutions of Lycurgus, it was a capital offence for a Spartan to have any gold or ſilver in his poſſeſſion. This we learn from Xenophon; and it is alſo aſcertained by the following paſſage from Athenæus, ſee the ſixth book of the Deipnoſoph: "The divine Plato and Lycurgus of Sparta would not ſuffer in their republics either gold or ſilver, thinking that of all the metals iron and braſs were ſufficient." Plutarch, in the life of Lyſander, tells us of a man named Therax, who, though the friend and colleague of Lyſander, was put to death by the ephori, becauſe ſome ſilver was found in his houſe. The ſelf-denial, therefore, or rather forbearance of the ancient Romans, amongſt whom no ſuch interdiction exiſted, ſeems better entitled to our praiſe. This ſumptuary law with reſpect

M 4

to

was a man of the ftricteft probity, and although Mæandrius perfifted in importuning him to take fomething, he would by no means confent; but hearing that fome of his fellow-citizens had received prefents from Mæandrius, he went to the ephori, and gave it as his opinion, that it would be better for the interefts of Sparta to expel this Samian from the Peloponnefe, left either he himfelf, or any other Spartan, fhould be corrupted by him. The advice of Cleomenes was generally approved, and Mæandrius received a public order to depart.

CXLIX. When the Perfians had taken the Samians as in a net [165], they delivered the ifland to Sylofon almoft without an inhabitant [166]. After a certain interval, however, Otanes, the Perfian general, re-peopled it, on account of fome vifion which he had, as well as from a diforder which feized his privities.

CL. Whilft the expedition againft Samos was on foot, the Babylonians, being very well pre-

to gold and filver, took its rife from an oracle, which affirmed that the deftruction of Sparta would be owing to its avarice :— it was this,

Α' φιλοχςτματια Σπαςταν ελιι.   Τ'.

[165] *As in a net.*]—The Greek is ςαγηνιυσαντις, which was the cuftom of the Perfians, and was alfo done with refpect to the iflands of Chios, Lefbos, and Tenedos, fee book vi. chap. 31, where their manner of doing it is defcribed.—*T.*

[166] *Without an inhabitant.*]—Strabo imputes this want of inhabitants to the cruelty of Sylofon, and not to the feverity of the Perfians.—*Larcher.*

•   pared,

pared, revolted. During the reign of the Magus, and whilft the feven were engaged in their confpiracy againft him, they had taken advantage of the confu- fion of the times to provide againft a fiege, and their exertions had never been difcovered. When they had once refolved on the recovery of their liberties, they took this meafure:—Excepting their mothers, every man chofe from his family the female whom he liked beft, the remainder were all of them affembled to- gether, and ftrangled [167]. Their referve of one wo- man was to bake their bread [168]; the reft were deftroyed to prevent a famine.

CLI. On the firft intelligence of this event, Darius affembled his forces, and marched againft them: on his arrival before the city, he befieged it in form. This, however, made fo little impref- fion upon them, that they affembled upon the ram- parts, amufed themfelves with dancing, and treated Darius and his army with the extremeft contempt. One amongft them exclaimed, " Perfians, why do

[167] *Affembled together and ftrangled.*]—Prideaux, making men- tion of this ftrange and unnatural action, omits informing his readers that the Babylonians made an exception in favour of their mothers; but by this barbarous action the prophecy of Ifaiah againft this people was very fignally fulfilled :—
" But thefe two things fhall come to thee in a moment, in one day, the lofs of children and widowhood; they fhall come upon thee in their perfection, for the multitude of thy forceries, and for the great abundance of thine enchantments." Ifaiah, xlvii. 9.—*T.*
[168] *Bake their bread.*]—This anciently was the employment of the women, fee book vii. chap. 187.—*T.*

" you

" you lofe your time? if you be wife, depart. When
" mules produce young [169] you fhall take Baby-
" lon." This was the fpeech of a Babylonian, not
believing fuch a thing poffible.

CLII. A whole year and feven months having
been confumed before the place, Darius and his
army began to be hopelefs with refpect to the event.
They had applied all the offenfive engines, and
every ftratagem, particularly thofe which Cyrus had
before fuccefsfully ufed againft the Babylonians;
but every attempt proved ineffectual, from the unremitting vigilance of the befieged.

CLIII. In the twentieth month of the fiege, the
following remarkable prodigy happened to Zopyrus,

[169] *Mules produce young.*]—Upon this paffage M. Larcher remarks, that mules but feldom engender. As I have never feen nor
heard of any well-authenticated account of fuch a circumftance,
I give the reader the following paffage from Pennant, with fome
confidence of its being invariably the cafe. " Neither mules, nor
the fpurious offspring of any other animal, generate any farther:
all thefe productions may be looked upon as monfters; therefore,
nature, to preferve the original fpecies of animals entire and
pure, wifely ftops, in inftances of deviation, the powers of pro-
pagation."

What Theophraftus or Pliny may have afferted, in contradiction to the above, will weigh but very little againft the unquali-
fied affertion of fo able a naturalift as Mr. Pennant. The
circumftance was ever confidered as a prodigy, as appears from
the following lines of Juvenal:

Egregium, fanctumque virum fi cerno, bimembri
Hoc monftrum puero, vel miranti fub aratro
Pifcibus inventis et *fatæ* comparo *mulæ.—T.*

fon

fon of Megabyzus, who was one of the feven that dethroned the Magus : one of the mules employed to carry his provifions. produced a young one; which, when it was firft told him, he difbelieved, and defired to fee it; forbidding thofe who had witneffed the fact to difclofe it, he revolved it ferioufly in his mind; and remembering the words of the Babylonian, who had faid the city fhould be taken when a mule brought forth, he from this conceived that Babylon was not impregnable. The faying itfelf, and the mule's having a young one, feemed to indicate fomething preternatural.

CLIV. Having fatisfied himfelf that Babylon might be taken, he went to Darius, and enquired if the capture of this city was of particular importance to him. Hearing that it really was, he began to think how he might have the honour of effecting it by himfelf; for in Perfia there is no more certain road to greatnefs, than by the performance of illuftrious actions. He conceived there was no more probable means of obtaining his end, than firft to mutilate himfelf, and thus pafs over to the enemy. He made no fcruple to wound himfelf beyond the power of being healed, for he cut off his nofe and his ears, and clipping his hair clofe, fo as to give it a mean appearance [170], he fcourged himfelf; and

---

[170] *To give it a mean appearance.*]—I do not remember an inftance of the hair being cut off as a punifhment; it was frequently

and in this condition prefented himfelf before Darius.

CLV. When the king beheld a man of his illuf-trious rank in fo deplorable a condition, he in-ftantly leaped in anger from his throne [17], and afked who had dared to treat him with fuch barbarity? Zopyrus made this reply, "No man, Sir, except "yourfelf, could have this power over my perfon; "I alone have thus disfigured my body, which I "was prompted to do from vexation at beholding "the Affyrians thus mock us."—"Wretched man," anfwered the king, "do you endeavour to difguife "the fhameful action you have perpetrated under "an honourable name? Do you fuppofe that becaufe "you have thus deformed yourfelf, the enemy will "the fooner furrender? I fear what you have done "has been occafioned by fome defect of your rea-

---

quently done as expreffive of mourning in the moft remote times; and it was one characteriftic mark of the fervile condition. See Juvenal, fat. v. book i. 170.

Omnia ferre
Si potes et debes pulfandum *vertice rafo*
Præbebis quandoque caput, nec dura tenebis
Flagra pati, his epulis et tali dignus amico.   *T.*

[17] *Leaped in anger from his throne.*]—This incident, with the various circumftances attending it, properly confidered, would furnifh an artift with an excellent fubject for an hiftorical paint-ing—The city of Babylon at a diftance, the Perfian camp, the king's tent, himfelf and principal nobles in deep confulta-tion, with the fudden appearance of Zopyrus in the mutilated condition here defcribed, might furely be introduced and ar-ranged with the moft admirable effect.—*T.*

"fon."

" fon."   " Sir," anfwered Zopyrus, " if I had
" previoufly difclofed to you my intentions, you
" would have prevented their accomplifhment ; my
" prefent fituation is the refult of my own determi-
" nation only.   If you do not fail me, Babylon is
" our own.   I propofe to go, in the condition in
" which you fee me, as a deferter to the Babyloni-
" ans : it is my hope to perfuade them that I have
" fuffered thefe cruelties from you, and that they
" will, in confequence, give me fome place of mi-
" litary truft.   Do you, on the tenth day after my
" departure, detach to the gate of Semiramis [172] a
" thoufand men of your army, whofe lofs will be of
" no confequence ; at an interval of feven days more
" fend to the Ninian gates other two thoufand ; again,
" after twenty days, let another party, to the number
" of four thoufand, be ordered to the Chaldean gates,
" but let none of thefe detachments have any wea-

[172] *The gate of Semiramis.*]—Mr. Bryant's remark on this
word is too curious to be omitted :—

Semiramis was an emblem, and the name was a compound,
of Sama-Ramas, or Ramis : it fignified the divine token, the
type of providence ; and as a military enfign, it may with fome
latitude be interpreted the ftandard of the Moft High.   It confifted of the figure of a dove, which was probably encircled with
the Iris, as thofe two emblems were often reprefented together.
All who went under that ftandard, or who payed any deference
to that emblem, were ftiled Semarim and Samorim. One of the
gates of Babylon was ftiled the gate of Semiramis, undoubtedly
from having the facred emblem of Sama-Ramas, or the dove,
engraved by way of diftinction over it.   Probably the lofty obe-
lifk of Semiramis, mentioned by Diodorus, was named from the
fame hieroglyphic.

                                        " pons

" pons but their fwords; after this laſt-mentioned
" period, let your whole army advance, and furround
" the walls. At the Belidian and Ciſſian gates be
" careful that Perſians are ſtationed. I think that
" the Babylonians, after witneſſing my exploits in
" the field, will entruſt me with the keys of thoſe
" gates. Doubt not but the Perſians, with my aid,
" will then accompliſh the reſt."

CLVI. After giving theſe injunctions, he proceeded towards the gates; and, to be conſiſtent in
the character which he aſſumed [173], he frequently
ſtopped to look behind him. The centinels on the
watch-towers, obſerving this, ran down to the gate,

---

[173] *The character which he aſſumed.*]—Many circumſtances in
hiſtory of Zopyrus reſemble thoſe of Sinon in the Æneid.

> ——— Qui ſe ignotum venientibus ultro
> Hoc ipſum ut ſtrueret, Trojamque aperiret Achivis,
> Obtulerat, fidens animi, atque in utrumque paratus
> Seu verſare dolos, ſeu certæ occumbere morti.—

Both tell a miſerable tale of injuries received from their countrymen, and both affect an extraordinary zeal to diſtinguiſh themſelves in the ſervice of their natural enemies.

Sinon ſays of himſelf

> Cui neque apud Danaos uſquam locus, & ſuper ipſi
> Dardanidæ infenſi pœnas cum ſanguine poſcunt.—

Again he ſays,

> Fas mihi Graiorum ſacrata reſolvere jura
> Fas odiſſe viros, atque omnia ferre ſub auras
> Si qua tegunt: teneor patriæ nec legibus ullis.   *T.*

which,

which, opening a little, they enquired who he was, and what he wanted? When he told them his name was Zopyrus, and that he had deferted from the Perfians, they conducted him before their magiftrates. He then began a miferable tale of the injuries he had fuffered from Darius, for no other reafon but that he had advifed him to withdraw his army, feeing no likelihood of his taking the city. "And now," fays he, "ye men of Babylon, I come a friend "to you, but a fatal enemy to Darius and his "army. I am well acquainted with all his de- "figns, and his treatment of me fhall not be un- "revenged."

CLVII. When the Babylonians beheld a Perfian of fuch high rank deprived of his ears and his nofe, covered with wounds and blood, they entertained no doubts of his fincerity, or of the friendlinefs of his intentions towards them. They were prepared to accede to all that he defired; and on his requefting a military command, they gave it him without he- fitation. He then proceeded to the execution of what he had concerted with Darius. On the tenth day, at the head of fome Babylonian troops, he made a fally from the town, and encountering the Per- fians, who had been ftationed for this purpofe by Darius, he put every one of them to death. The Babylonians, obferving that his actions correfpond- ed with his profefsions, were full of exultation, and were ready to yield him the moft implicit obedi- ence. A fecond time, at the head of a chofen detachment of the befieged, he advanced front the town at the time appointed, and flew the two thou-fand foldiers of Darius. The joy of the citizens at this fecond exploit was fo extreme, that the name of Zopyrus refounded with praife from every tongue. The third time alfo, after the number of days agreed upon had paffed, he led forth his troops, attacked and flaughtered the four thoufand. Zopyrus, after this, was every thing with the Babylonians, fo that they made him the commander of their army, and guardian of their walls.

CLVIII. At the time appointed Darius ad-vanced with all his forces to the walls. The perfidy of Zopyrus then became apparent; for as foon as the Babylonians mounted the wall to repel the Per-fian affault, he immediately opened to his country-men what are called the Belidian and Ciffian gates. Thofe Babylonians who faw this tranfaction fled for refuge to the temple of Jupiter Belus; they who faw it not, continued in their pofts, till the circum-ftance of their being betrayed became notorious to all.

CLIX. Thus was Babylon a fecond time taken. As foon as Darius became mafter of the place [174];

he

---

[174] *Mafter of the place.*]—Plutarch informs us, in his Apoph-thegms, that Xerxes being incenfed againft the Babylonians for revolting, after having conquered them a fecond time forbad

their

he levelled the walls, and took away the gates, neither of which things Cyrus had done before. Three thousand of the most distinguished nobility he ordered to be crucified; the rest were suffered to continue where they were. He took care also to provide them with women, for the Babylonians, as we have before remarked, to prevent a famine had strangled their wives. Darius ordered the neighbouring nations to send females to Babylon, each being obliged to furnish a stipulated number. These in all amounted to fifty thousand, from whom the Babylonians of the present day are descended.

CLX. With respect to the merit of Zopyrus, in the opinion of Darius it was exceeded by no Persian of any period, unless by Cyrus; to him, indeed, he thought no one of his countrymen could possibly be compared. It is affirmed of Darius, that he used frequently to assert, that he would rather Zopyrus had suffered no injury, than have been master of twenty Babylons more. He rewarded him magnificently: every year he presented him with the gifts deemed most honourable in Persia; he made him also governor of Babylon for life, free from

their carrying arms, and commanded them to employ their time in finging, music, and all kinds of dissipation, &c.

The Babylonians did not revolt under Xerxes. Plutarch assigns to him a fact, which regards Darius; however this may be, after the reduction of Babylon the Persian monarchs fixed their residence in three great cities; the winter they passed at Babylon, the summer at Media, doubtless at Ecbatane, and the greater part of the spring at Sufa.—*Larcher.*

the payment of any tribute, and to these he added
other marks of liberality.   Megabyzus, who commanded in Ægypt against the Athenians and their
allies, was a son of this Zopyrus, which Megabyzus had a son named Zopyrus [175], who deserted from the Persians to the Athenians.

[175] *A son named Zopyrus.*]—Zopyrus, son of Megabyzus, and
grandson of the famous Zopyrus, revolted from Artaxerxes
after the death of his father and mother, and advanced towards
Athens, on account of the friendship which subsisted betwixt his
mother and the Athenians. He went by sea to Caunus, and commanded the inhabitants to give up the place to the Athenians
who were with him. The Caunians replied, that they were willing
to surrender it to him, but they refused to admit any Athenians.
Upon this he mounted the wall; but a Caunian, named Alcides,
knocked him on the head with a stone.   His grandmother
Amestris afterwards crucified this Caunian.—*Larcher.*

HERODOTUS.

HERODOTUS.

BOOK IV.

MELPOMENE.

CHAP. I.

ARIUS, after the capture of Babylon, undertook an expedition againſt Scythia. Aſia was now both populous and rich, and he was deſirous of avenging on the Scythians the injuries they had formerly committed by entering Media, and defeating thoſe who oppoſed them. During a period of twenty-eight years, the Scythians, as I have before remarked, retained the ſovereignty of the Upper Aſia, entering into which, when in purſuit of the Cimmerians ¹, they expelled the Medes, its ancient poſſeſſors.

---

¹ *Cimmerians.*]—From this people came the proverb of Cimmerian darkneſs.

We reach'd old ocean's utmoſt bounds,
Where rocks controul his waves with ever-during mounds;

There

poſſeſſors. After this long abſence from their country, the Scythians were deſirous to return, but here
as great a labour awaited them as they had experienced in their expedition into Media ; for the
women, deprived ſo long of their huſbands, had
connected themſelves with their ſlaves, and they
found a numerous body in arms ready to diſpute
their progreſs.

> There in a lonely land, and gloomy cells,
> The duſky nation f Cimmeria dwells.
> The ſun ne'er views th' uncomfortable ſeats,.
> When radiant he advances or retreats.
> Unhappy rac. ! whom endleſs night invades,
> Clouds the dull air, and wraps them round in ſhades.
>
> *Odyſ.* book xi.

Of this proverb Ammianus Marcellinus makes a happy uſe,
when cenſuring the luxury and effeminacy of the Roman nobility. " If," ſays he, (I uſe the verſion of Mr. Gibbon) " a
fly ſhould preſume to ſettle in the ſilken folds of their gilded
umbrellas, ſhould a ſun-beam penetrate through ſome unguard-
ed and imperceptible chink, they deplore their intolerable hard-
ſhips, and lament in affected language that they were not born
in the land of the Cimmerians, the regions of eternal darkneſs."

Ovid alſo chooſes the vicinity of Cimmeria as the propereſt
place for the palace of the god of ſleep.

> Eſt prope Cimmerios, longo ſpelunca receſſu,
> Mons cavus, ignavi domus et penetralia Somni,
> Quo nunquam radiis oriens, mediuſve, cadenſve
> Phœbus adire poteſt, nebulæ caligine mixtæ
> Exhalantur humo, dubiæque crepuſcula lucis.

The region aſſigned to this people in ancient geography was
part of European Scythia, now called Little Tartary.—*T.*

II.

II. It is a cuſtom with the Scythians to deprive all their ſlaves of ſight ² on account of the
milk ³, which is their cuſtomary drink: They have
a parti-

² *Deprive all their ſlaves of ſight.*]—Barbarous as this conduct
will appear to every humane reader, although practiſed amongſt
an uncivilized race of men, he will be far more ſhocked when I
remind him that in the moſt refined period of the Roman empire thoſe who were deemed the wiſeſt and moſt virtuous of
mankind did not ſcruple to uſe their ſlaves with yet more atrocious cruelty. It was cuſtomary at Rome to expoſe ſlaves who
were ſick, old, and uſeleſs, to periſh miſerably in an iſland of
the Tyber. Plutarch tells us, in his Life of Cato, that it was his
cuſtom to ſell his old ſlaves for any price, to get rid of the burden.
They were employed, and frequently in chains, in the moſt la-
borious offices, and for trivial offences, and not ſeldom on mere
ſuſpicion, were made to expire under the moſt horrid tortures
that can be imagined.—*T.*

³ *On account of the milk.*]—Of this people Homer ſpeaks in
the following lines.

> And where the far-fam'd Hippomolgian ſtrays,
> Renown'd for juſtice and for length of days,
> Thrice happy race, that, innocent of blood,
> From milk innoxious ſeek their ſimple food.—*Il.* xiii.

Upon this ſubject Larcher gives the following paſſage from
Niebuhr :—

" J'entendis et vis moi-même, à Baſra, que lorſq'un Arabe
trait la femelle du buſle, un autre lui fourre la main et le bras
juſqu'au coude, dans la vulva, parce qu'on prétend ſavoir par
expérience qu'étant chatouillée de la ſorte, elle donne plus de
lait. Cette methode réſſemble beaucoup a celle des Scythes."—
We learn, from ſome lines of Antiphanes, preſerved in Athenæus,
that the Scythians gave this milk to their children as ſoon as
they were born.

Ειτ ȣ ϲοφοι δητ ειϲιν οι Σκυθαι ϲφοδρα ;
Οι γινομενοιϲιν ευθεως τοις παιδιοις
Διαδιδοαϲιν ιππων κJ βοων πινειν γαλα.

" De

a particular kind of bone, shaped like a flute: this is applied to the private parts of a mare, and blown into from the mouth. It is one man's office to blow, another's to milk the mare. Their idea is, that the veins of the animal being thus inflated, the dugs are proportionably filled. When the milk is thus obtained, they place it in deep wooden vessels, and the slaves are directed to keep it in continual agitation. Of this that which remains at top[4] is most esteemed, what subsides is of inferior value. This it is which induces the Scythians to deprive all their captives of sight, for they do not cultivate the ground, but lead a pastoral life[5].

III.

" Do not those Scythians appear to you remarkably wise who give to their children, as soon as ever they are born, the milk of mares and cows ?"—*T.*

[4] *Remains at the top.*]—Is it not surprising, asks M. Larcher in this place, that neither the Greeks nor the Latins had any term in their language to express cream ?

Butter also was unknown to the Greeks and Romans till a late period. Pliny speaks of it as a common article of food among barbarous nations, and used by them as an unction. The very name of butter (βυτυρον) which signifies cheese, or coagulum of cows milk, implies an imperfect notion of the thing. It is clear that Herodotus here describes the making of butter, though he knew no name for the product. Pliny remarks, that the barbarous nations were as peculiar in neglecting cheese, as in making butter. *Spuma lactis*, which that author uses in describing what butter is, seems a very proper phrase for cream. Butter is often mentioned in Scripture; see Harmer's curious accounts of the modes of making it in the East, vol. i. and iii.—*T.*

[5] *Lead a pastoral life.*]—The influence of food or climate, which

III. From the union of thefe flaves with the Scythian women, a numerous progeny was born, who, when informed of their origin, readily advanced to oppofe thofe who were returning from Media. Their firft exertion was to interfect the country by a large and deep trench, which extended from the mountains of Tauris to the Palus Mœotis. They then encamped oppofite to the Scythians endeavouring to effect their paffage. Various engagements enfued, in which the Scythians obtained no advantage. " My countrymen," at length one of them exclaimed, " what are we " doing? In this conteft with our flaves, every " action diminifhes our number, and by killing " thofe who oppofe us, the value of victory de- " creafes: let us throw afide our darts and our " arrows, and rufh upon them only with the whips " which we ufe for our horfes. Whilft they fee " us with arms, they think themfelves our equals " in birth and importance; but as foon as they " fhall perceive the whip in our hands, they will be " impreffed with the fenfe of their fervile condition, " and refift no longer."

IV. The Scythians approved the advice; their

---

which in a more improved ftate of fociety is fufpended or fubdued by fo many moral caufes, moft powerfully contributes to form and to maintain the national character of barbarians. In every age the immenfe plains of Scythia or Tartary have been inhabited by vagrant tribes of hunters and fhepherds, whofe indolence refufes to cultivate the earth, and whofe reftlefs fpirit difdains the confinement of a fedentary life.—*Gibbon.*

opponents

opponents forgot their former exertions, and fled : so did the Scythians obtain the sovereignty of Asia ; and thus, after having been expelled by the Medes, they returned to their country. From the above motives Darius, eager for revenge, prepared to lead an army against them,

V. Of their country the Scythians affirm that it was of all others the last formed [a], and in this manner :—When this region was in its original and desart state, the first inhabitant was named Targitaus, a son, as they say (but which to me seems incredible) of Jupiter, by a daughter of the Borysthenes. This Targitaus had three sons, Lipoxais, Arpoxais, and lastly Colaxais. Whilst they possessed the country there fell from heaven into the Scythian district a plough, a yoke, an ax, and a goblet, all of gold. The eldest of the brothers was the first who saw them; who running to take them, was burnt by the gold. On his retiring, the second brother approached, and was burnt also. When these two had been repelled by the burning gold, last of all the youngest brother advanced ; upon him the gold had no effect, and he carried it to his house. The two elder brothers, observing what had happened, resigned all authority to the youngest.

VI. From Lipoxais those Scythians were descended who are termed the Auchatæ ; from Arpoxais, the second brother, those who are called the Catiari and

---

[a] *Last formed.*]—Justin informs us, that the Scythians pretended to be more ancient than the Ægyptians.—*T.*

the Trafpies; from the youngeft, who was king, came
the Paralatæ [7]. Generally fpeaking, thefe people
are named Scoloti, from a furname of their king,
but the Greeks call them Scythians.

VII. This is the account which the Scythians
give of their origin; and they add, that from their
firft king Targitaus, to the invafion of their country
by Darius, is a period of a thoufand years, and no
more. The facred gold is preferved by their kings
with the greateft care; it is every year carried
with great folemnity to every part of the kingdom,
and upon this occafion there are facrifices, with
much pomp, at which the prince prefides. They
have a tradition, that if the perfon in whofe cuftody
this gold remains fleeps in the open air during
the time of their annual feftival, he dies before the
end of the year; as much land is therefore given
him,[8] as he can pafs over on horfeback in the
courfe of a day [9]. As this region is extenfive, king
Colaxais

[7] *Paralatæ.*]—This paffage will be involved in much perplexity, unlefs for τες βασιληας be read του βασιληος.—*T.*

[8] *As much land is therefore given him.*]—This is, beyond
doubt, a very perplexed and difficult paffage; and all that the
different annotators have done has been to intimate their conjectures. I have followed that which to my judgment feemed
the happieft.—*T.*

[9] *On horfeback in the courfe of a day.*]—Larcher adduces, from
Pliny, Ovid, and Seneca, the three following paffages, to prove
that anciently this was the mode of rewarding merit:

Dona ampliffima imperatorum et fortium civium quantum quis
uno die plurimum circumaraviffet.—*Pliny.*

This

Colaxais divided the country into three parts, which he gave to three fons, making that portion the largeſt in which the gold was depoſited. As to the diſtrict which lays farther to the north, and beyond the extreme inhabitants of the country, they ſay that it neither can be paſſed, nor yet diſcerned with the eye, on account of the feathers [10] which are continually falling: with theſe both the earth and the air are ſo filled, as effectually to obſtruct the view.

VIII. Such is the manner in which the Scythians deſcribe themſelves and the country beyond them. The Greeks who inhabit Pontus ſpeak of both as follows: Hercules, when he was driving away the heifers of Geryon [11], came to this region, now

This from Ovid is more pertinent:

> At proceres ——— ———
> Ruris honorati tantum tibi Cipe dedere
> Quantum depreſſo ſubjectis bobus aratro
> Complecti poſſes ad finem ſolis ab ortu.—

See alſo Seneca:—

Illi ob virtutem et bene geſtam rempublicam tantum agri decerneretur, quantum arando uno die circuire potuiſſet.

[10] *On account of the feathers.*]—It muſt immediately occur to the reader that theſe feathers can be nothing elſe but ſnow. —*T.*

[11] *Geryon.*]—To this perſonage the poets aſſigned three heads and three bodies. Heſiod calls him τρικεφαλον and Euripides τρισωματον. See alſo Horace:—

> Qui ter amplum
> Geryonem, Tityonique triſti
> Compeſcit undâ.—

Virgil

now inhabited by the Scythians, but which then was a defert. This Geryon lived beyond Pontus, in an ifland which the Greeks call Erythia, near Gades, which is fituate in the ocean, and beyond the columns of Hercules. The ocean, they fay, commencing at the eaft, flows round all the earth [12]; this, however, they affirm without proving it. Hercules coming from thence, arrived at this country, now called Scythia, where, finding himfelf overtaken by a fevere ftorm, and being exceedingly cold, he wrapped himfelf up in his lion's fkin, and went to fleep. They add, that his mares, which he had detached from his chariot to feed, by fome divine interpofition difappeared during his fleep.

IX. As foon as he awoke, he wandered over all

Virgil calls him Tergeminus; but the minuteft defcription is found in Silius Italicus, the moft fatisfactory in Palæphatus de incredibilibus :—

> Qualis Atlantiaco memoratur litore quondam
> Monftrum Geryones immane tricorporis iræ,
> Cui tres in pugna dextræ varia arma gerebant
> Una ignes fævos, aft altera pone fagittas
> Fundebat, validam torquebat tertia cornum,
> Atque uno diverfa dabat tria vulnera nifu.—
>
> *Punic. Bell.* 13. 200.

Palæphatus, fays he, lived at Tricarenia; and that, being called the Tricarenian Geryon, he was afterwards faid to have had three heads.—*T.*

[12] *Flows round the earth.*]—Upon this paffage the following remark occurs in Stillingfleet's *Origin. Sacr.* book i. c. 4.—

It cannot be denied but a great deal of ufeful hiftory may be fetched out of Herodotus; yet who can excufe his ignorance, when he not only denies there is an ocean compaffing the land, but condemns the geographers for afferting it ?

the

the country in fearch of his mares, till at length he
came to the diftrict which is called Hylæa: there in
a cave he difcovered a female of moft unnatural appearance, refembling a woman as far as the thighs,
but whofe lower parts were like a ferpent [1].   Hercules beheld her with aftonifhment, but he was not
deterred from afking her whether fhe had feen, his
mares? She made anfwer, that they were in her cuftody; fhe refufed, however, to reftore them, but upon
condition of his cohabiting with her. The terms propofed induced Hercules to confent; but fhe ftill deferred reftoring his mares, from the wifh of retaining
him longer with her, whilft Hercules was equally
anxious to obtain them and depart.   After a while
fhe reftored them with thefe words: "Your mares,
" which wandered here, I have preferved; you have
" paid what was due to my care, I have conceived
" by you three fons; I wifh you to fay how I fhall dif-
" pofe of them hereafter; whether I fhall detain them
" here, where I am the fole fovereign, or whether I
" fhall fend them to you."   The reply of Hercules
was to this effect : " As foon as they fhall be grown
" up to man's eftate, obferve this, and you cannot
" err; whichever of them you fhall fee bend this
" bow, and wear this belt [4] as I do, him detain in this
                                            " country;

[1] *Like a ferpent.*]—M. Pelloutier calls this monfter a fyren,
but Homer reprefents the Syrens as very lovely women.

Diodorus Siculus fpeaks alfo of this monfter, defcribing it
like Herodotus. He makes her the miftrefs of Jupiter, by
whom fhe had Scythes, who gave his name to the nation.—
Larcher.

[4] *This belt.*]—It was affigned Hercules as one of his labours
                                                        by

" country: the others, who fhall not be able to
" do this, you may fend away. By minding what
" I fay you will have pleafure yourfelf, and will
" fatisfy my wifhes."

X. Having faid this, Hercules took one of his
bows, for thus far he had carried two, and fhewing
her alfo his belt, at the end of which a golden cup was
fufpended, he gave her them and departed. As
foon as the boys of whom fhe was delivered grew
up, fhe called the eldeft Agathyrfus, the fecond
Gelonus, and the youngeft Scytha. She remembered alfo the injunctions fhe had received; and
two of her fons, Agathyrfus and Gelonus, who
were incompetent to the trial which was propofed,
were fent away by their mother from this country.
Scytha the youngeft was fuccefsful in his exertions,
and remained. From this Scytha, the fon of Hercules, the Scythian monarchs are defcended; and
from the golden cup the Scythians to this day have
a cup at the end of their belts.

XI. This is the ftory which the Greek inhabi-

by Euryftheus, to whom he was fubject, to deprive Hippolyta,
queen of the Amazons, of her belt. Aufonius, in the infcription which he probably wrote for fome ancient relievo, mentions it as the fixth labour.

Threïciam fexto fpoliavit Amazona baltheo.

This labour is alfo mentioned thus by Martial:

Peltatam Scythico difcinxit Amazona nodo.

Whether Herodotus means to fpeak of this belt I pretend not
to determine.—T.

tants of Pontus relate; but there is alſo another, to
which I am more inclined to aſſent:—The Scythian
Nomades of Aſia, having been haraſſed by the
Maſſagetæ in war, paſſed the Araxis, and ſettled
in Cimmeria; for it is to be obſerved, that the
country now poſſeſſed by the Scythians belonged
formerly to the Cimmerians. This people, when
attacked by the Scythians, deliberated what it was
moſt adviſeable to do againſt the inroad of ſo vaſt
a multitude. Their ſentiments were divided;
both were violent, but that of the kings appears
preferable. The people were of opinion, that it
would be better not to hazard an engagement, but
to retreat in ſecurity; the kings were at all events
for reſiſting the enemy. Neither party would recede from their opinions, the people and the princes
mutually refuſing to yield; the people wiſhed to
retire before the invaders, the princes determined
rather to die where they were, reflecting upon what
they had enjoyed before, and alarmed by the fears
of future calamities. From verbal diſputes they
ſoon came to actual engagement, and they happened
to be nearly equal in number. All thoſe who periſhed by the hands of their countrymen were
buried by the Cimmerians near the river Tyré,
where their monuments may ſtill be ſeen. The
ſurvivors fled from their country, which in its abandoned ſtate was ſeized and occupied by the Scythians.

XII. There are ſtill to be found in Scythia walls
and bridges which are termed Cimmerian; the
ſame

fame name is alfo given to a whole diftrict, as
well as to a narrow fea. It is certain that when
the Cimmerians were expelled their country by the
Scythians, they fled to the Afiatic Cherfonefe, where
the Greek city of Sinope [15] is at prefent fituated.
It is alfo apparent, that whilft engaged in the purfuit, the Scythians deviated from their proper courfe,
and entered Media. The Cimmerians in their
flight kept uniformly by the fea coaft; but the Scythians, having Mount Caucafus to their right, continued the purfuit, till by following an inland direction they entered Media.

XIII. There is ftill another account, which has
obtained credit both with the Greeks and barbarians. Arifteas [16] the poet, a native of Proconnefus,
and

---

[15] *Sinope.*]—There were various opinions amongft the ancients concerning this city. Some faid it was built by an Amazon fo called; others affirm it was founded by the Milefians;
Strabo calls it the moft illuftrious city of Pontus. It is thus
mentioned by Valerius Flaccus, an author not fo much read as
he deferves.

> Affyrios complexa finus ftat opima Sinope
> Nympha prius, blandofque Jovis quæ luferat ignes
> Cœlicolis immota procis.

There was alfo a celebrated courtefan of this name, from
whom Sinopiffare became a proverb for being very lafcivious.

The modern name of the place is Sinub, and it ftands at the
mouth of a river called Sinope.—*T.*

[16] *Arifteas.*]—This perfon is mentioned alfo by Pliny and
Aulus Gellius; it is probable that he lived in the time of Cyrus
and Crœfus. Longinus has preferved fix of his verfes; fee
chap. 10, of which he remarks, that they are rather florid than
fublime.

and fon of Cauftrobius, relates, that under the influence of Apollo he came to the Iffedones, that
beyond this people he found the Arimafpi[17], a nation
who have but one eye; farther on the Gryphins[18],
the guardians of the gold; and beyond thefe the
Hyperboreans[19], who poffefs the whole country
quite

sublime. Tzetzes has preferved fix more. The account given
of him by Herodotus is far from fatisfactory.

[17] *Arimafpi*.]—The Arimafpians were Hyperborean Cyclo-
peans, and had temples named Charis or Charifia, in the top of
which were preferved a perpetual fire. They were of the fame
family as thofe of Sicily, and had the fame rites, and particularly worfhipped the Ophite deity under the name of Opis. Arifteas Proconnefius wrote their hiftory, and among other things
mentioned that they had but one eye, which was placed in their
graceful forehead. How could the front of a Cyclopean, one
of the moft hideous monfters that ever poetic fancy framed, be
ftyled graceful? The whole is a miftake of terms, and what this
writer had mifapplied related to Charis a tower, and the eye
was a cafement in the top of the edifice, where a light and fire
were kept up.—*Bryant*.

[18] *Gryphins*.]—

Thus the Gryphins,
Thofe dumb and ravenous dogs of Jove, avoid
The Arimafpian troops, whofe frowning foreheads
Glare with one blazing eye: along the banks
Where Pluto rolls his ftreams of gold, they rein
Their foaming fteeds.
                    Prometheus Vinctus. Æfchy. Potter's Tranflation.

Paufanias tell us, that the Gryphins are reprefented by Arifteas as monfters refembling lions, with the beaks and wings of
eagles. By the way, Dionyfius of Halicarnaffus is of opinion
that no fuch poem as this of Arifteas ever exifted.—*T*.

[19] *Hyperboreans*.]—The ancients do not appear to have had
any precife ideas of the country of this people. The Hyperbo-

quite to the fea, and that all thefe nations, except the Hyperboreans, are continually engaged in war with their neighbours. Of thefe hoftilities the Arimafpians were the firft authors, for that they drove out the Iffedones, the Iffedones the Scythians : the Scythians compelled the Cimmerians, who poffeffed the country towards the fouth, to abandon their native land. Thus it appears, that the narrative of Arifteas differs alfo from that of the Scythians.

XIV. Of what country the relater of the above account was, we have already feen ; but I ought not to omit what I have heard of this perfonage, both at Proconnefus and Cyzicus [20]. It is faid of this Arifteas, that he was of one of the beft families of his country, and that he died in the workfhop of a fuller, into which he had accidentally gone. The fuller immediately fecured his fhop, and went to in-

rean mountains are alfo frequently mentioned, which, as appears from Virgil, were the fame as the Ryphean :

Talis Hyperboreo feptem fubjecta trioni
Gens effraena virum Rhipæo tunditur Euro
Et pecudum fulvis velatur corpora fatis. T.

[20] *Cyzicus.*]—This was one of the moft flourifhing cities of Myfia, fituate in a fmall ifland of the Propontis, and built by the Milefians. It is thus mentioned by Ovid :

Inde Propontiacis hærentem Cyzicon oris
Cyzicon Æmoniæ nobile gentis opus.

The people of this place were remarkable for their effeminacy and cowardice, whence tinctura Cyzicena became proverbial for any daftardly character. It has now become a peninfula, by the filling up of the fmall channel by which it was divided from the continent.—*T.*

form the relations of the deceased of what had happened. The report having circulated through the
city, that Aristeas was dead, there came a man of
Cyzicus, of the city of Artaces, who affirmed that
this assertion was false, for that he had met Aristeas
going to Cyzicus [21], and had spoken with him. In
confequence of his positive affertions, the friends of
Aristeas hastened to the fuller's shop with every
thing which was necessary for his funeral, but when
they came there, no Aristeas was to be found, alive
or dead. Seven years afterwards it is said that he
re-appeared at Proconnesus, and composed those
verses which the Greeks call Arimaspian, after
which he vanished a second time.

XV. This is the manner in which these cities
speak of Aristeas: but I am about to relate a circumstance which to my own knowledge happened
to the Metapontines of Italy, three hundred and
forty years after Aristeas had a second time disappeared, according to my conjecture, as it agrees
with what I heard at Proconnesus and Metapon-
tus. The inhabitants of this latter place affirm,
that Aristeas having appeared in their city, directed
them to construct an altar to Apollo, and near it a

[21] *Going to Cyzicus.*]—Upon this story Larcher remarks, that
there are innumerable others like it, both among the ancients
and moderns. A very ridiculous one is related by Plutarch, in
his Life of Romulus:—A man named Cleomedes, seeing himself pursued, jumped into a great chest, which closed upon him:
after many ineffectual attempts to open it, they broke it in
pieces, but no Cleomedes was to be found, alive or dead.—*T.*

statue

ftatue to Arifteas of Proconnefus. He told them that they were the only people of Italy whom Apollo had ever honoured by his prefence, and that he himfelf had attended the god under the form of a crow [22] : having faid this he difappeared. The Metapontines relate, that in confequence of this they fent to Delphi, to enquire what that unnatural appearance might mean ; the Pythian told them in reply, to perform what had been directed, for that they would find their obedience rewarded ; they obeyed accordingly, and there now ftands near the ftatue of Apollo himfelf, another bearing the name of Arifteas : it is placed in the public fquare of the city, furrounded with laurels.

XVI. Thus much of Arifteas. — No certain knowledge is to be obtained of the places which lie remotely beyond the country of which I before fpake : on this fubject I could not meet with any perfon able to fpeak from his own knowledge. Arifteas above-mentioned confeffes, in the poem which he wrote, that he did not penetrate beyond the Iffe-

[22] *Under the form of a crow.*]—Pliny relates this fomewhat differently. He fays, it was the foul of Arifteas, which having left his body appeared in the form of a crow. His words are thefe : Ariftex etiam vifam evolantem ex ore in Proconnefo, corvi effigie magna quæ fequitur fabulofitate.—*Larcher.*

The crow was facred to Apollo, as appears from Ælian de Animalibus, book vii. 18. We learn alfo from Scaliger, in his Notes on Manilius, that a crow fitting on a tripod was found on fome ancient coins, to which Statius alfo alludes in the following line :

Non comes obfcurus tripodum.   *T.*

dones ;

dones; and that what he related of the countries more remote he learned of the Iſſedones themſelves. For my own part, all the intelligence which the moſt aſſiduous reſearches, and the greateſt attention to authenticity have been able to procure, ſhall be faithfully related.

XVII. As we advance from the port of the Boryſthenites, which is unqueſtionably the centre of all the maritime parts of Scythia, the firſt people who are met with are the Callipidæ [23], who are Greek Scythians: beyond theſe is another nation, called the Halizones [24]. Theſe two people in general obſerve the cuſtoms of the Scythians, except that for food they ſow corn, onions, garlick, lentils, and millet. Beyond the Halizones dwell ſome Scythian huſbandmen, who ſow corn not to eat, but for ſale. Still more remote are the Neuri [25], whoſe country towards the north, as far as I have been able to learn, is totally uninhabited. All theſe nations dwell near the river Hypanis, to the weſt of the Boryſthenes.

XVIII. Having croſſed the Boryſthenes, the firſt

[23] *Callipidæ.*]—Solinus calls theſe people Callipodes.—*T.*

[24] *Halizones.*]—So called becauſe ſurrounded on all ſides by the ſea, as the word itſelf obviouſly teſtifies.—*T.*

[25] *Neuri.*]—Mela, book ii. 1, ſays of this people, that they had the power of transforming themſelves into wolves, and reſuming their former ſhape at pleaſure.—Neuris ſtatum ſingulis tempus eſt, quo ſi velint in lupos, iterumque in eos qui fuere mutentur.—*T.*

country

country towards the fea is Hylæa, contiguous to which are fome Scythian hufbandmen, who call themfelves Olbiopolitæ, but who, by the Greeks living near the Hypanis, are called Boryfthenites [16]. The country poffeffed by thefe Scythians towards the eaft is the fpace of a three days journey, as far as the river Panticapes; to the north, their lands extend to the amount of an eleven days voyage along the Boryfthenes. The fpace beyond this is a vaft inhofpitable defert; and remoter ftill are the Androphagi, or men-eaters, a feparate nation, and by no means Scythian. As we pafs farther from thefe, the country is altogether defert, not containing, to our knowledge, any inhabitants.

XIX. To the eaft of thefe Scythians, who are hufbandmen, and beyond the river Panticapes, are the Scythian Nomades or fhepherds, who are totally unacquainted with agriculture: except Hylæa, all this country is naked of trees. Thefe Nomades inhabit a diftrict to the extent of a fourteen days journey towards the eaft, as far as the river Gerrhus.

XX. Beyond the Gerrhus is fituate what is termed the royal province of Scythia, poffeffed by the more numerous part and the nobleft of the Scythians, who confider all the reft of their countrymen

---

[16] *Boryfthenites.*]—Thefe people are called by Propertius the Boryfthenidæ:

Gloria ad hybernos lata Boryfthenidas. *T.*

as

as their flaves. From the fouth they extend to
Tauris, and from the eaft. as far as the trench
which was funk by the defcendants of the blinded
flaves, and again as far as the port of the Palus
Mœotis, called Chemni, and indeed many of them
are fpread as far as the Tanais. Beyond thefe, to
the north, live the Melanchlæni, another nation
who are not Scythians. Beyond the Melanchlæni
the lands are low and marfhy, and as we believe
entirely uninhabited.

XXI. Beyond the Tanais the region of Scythia
terminates, and the firft nation we meet with are
the Sauromatæ, who, commencing at the remote
parts of the Palus Mœotis, inhabit a fpace to the
north, equal to a fifteen days journey ; the country
is totally deftitute of trees, both wild and cultivated.
Beyond thefe are the Budini, who are hufbandmen,
and in whofe country trees are found in great
abundance.

XXII. To the north, beyond the Budini, is an
immenfe defert of an eight days journey ; paffing
which to the eaft are the Thyffagetæ, a fingular
but populous nation, who fupport themfelves by
hunting. Contiguous to thefe, in the fame region, are
a people called Iyrcæ [17] ; they alfo live by the chace,
which

---

[17] *Iyrcæ.*]—It is in vain that Meffieurs Falconnet and Mallet are defirous of reading here Τυρκοι, the Turks, the fame as
it occurs in Pomponius Mela ; it would be better, with Pintianus,
to

which they thus purfue :—Having afcended the tops of the trees, which every where abound, they watch for their prey. Each man has a horfe, inftructed to lie clofe to the ground, that it may not be feen; they have each alfo a dog. As foon as the man from the tree difcovers his game, he wounds it with an arrow, then mounting his horfe he purfues it, fol-lowed by his dog. Advancing from this people ftill nearer to the eaft, we again meet with Scythians, who having feceded from the Royal Scythians, eftablifhed themfelves here.

XXIII. As far as thefe Scythians the whole country is flat, and the foil excellent; beyond them it becomes barren and ftony. After travelling over a confiderable fpace, a people are found living at the foot of fome lofty mountains, who, both male and female, are faid to be bald from their birth, having large chins, and noftrils like the ape fpecies. They have a language of their own, but their drefs is Scythian; they live chiefly upon the produce of a tree which is called the ponticus, it is as large as a fig, and has a kernel not unlike a bean : when it is ripe they prefs it through a cloth, it produces a thick black liquor which they call afchy, this they drink, mixing it with milk; the groffer parts which remain they form into balls and eat. They have but few cattle, from the want of proper pafturage. Each man dwells under his tree; this

to correct the text of the geographer by that of Herodotus. Pliny alfo joins this people with the Thyffagetæ.—*Larcher.*

during

during the winter they cover with a thick white cloth, which in the summer is removed; they live unmolested by any one, being considered as sacred, and having amongst them no offensive weapon. Their neighbours apply to them for decision in matters of private controversy; and whoever seeks an asylum amongst them is secure from injury. They are called the Argippæi [23].

XXIV. As far as these people who are bald, the knowledge of the country and intermediate nations is clear and satisfactory; it may he obtained from the Scythians, who have frequent communication with them, from the Greeks of the port on the Borysthenes, and from many other places of trade on the Euxine. As these nations have seven different languages, the Scythians who communicate with them have occasion for as many interpreters.

XXV. Beyond these Argippæi, no certain intelligence is to be had, a chain of lofty and inaccessible mountains precluding all discovery. The people who are bald assert, what I can by no means believe, that these mountains are inhabited

[23] *Argippæi.*]—These people are said to have derived their name from the white horses with which their country abounded. The Tartars of the present day are said to hold white horses in great estimation; how much they were esteemed in ancient times, appears from various passages of different writers, who believed that they excelled in swiftness all horses of a different colour.

Qui candore nives anteirent, cursibus auras.   *T.*

by

by men, who in their lower parts refemble a goat;
and that beyond thefe are a race who fleep away
fix months of the year: neither does this feem at all
more probable. To the eaft of the Argippæi it is beyond all doubt that the country is poffeffed by the
Iffedones; but beyond them to the north neither
the Iffedones nor the Argippæi know any thing
more than I have already related.

XXVI. The Iffedones have thefe among other
cuftoms:—As often as any one lofes his father, his
relations feverally provide fome cattle; thefe they
kill, and having cut them in pieces, they difmem-
ber alfo the body of the deceafed, and, mixing the
whole together, feaft upon it; the head alone is
preferved, from this they carefully remove the hair,
and cleanfing it thoroughly fet it in gold [29]: it is
afterwards efteemed facred, and produced in their
folemn annual facrifices. Every man obferves the
above rites in honour of his father, as the Greeks
do theirs in memory of the dead [30]. In other refpects

[29] *Set it in gold.*]—We learn from Livy, that the Boii, a people
of Gaul, did exactly the fame with refpect to the fculls of their
enemies.—Purgato inde capite ut mos iis eft, calvam auro cæla-
vere: idque facrum vas iis erat, quo folemnibus libarent.—*See
Livy*, chap. xxiv. book 23.

[30] *In memory of the dead.*]—The Greeks had anniverfary days
in remembrance of departed friends. Thefe were indifferently
termed Νιμισια, as being folemnized on the feftival of Nemefis,
Ωραια, and Γινισια. This latter word feems to intimate that thefe
were feafts inftituted to commemorate the birth-days; but thefe,
it appears, were obferved by furviving relations and friends upon
the

spects it is said that they venerate the principles of justice; and that their females enjoy equal authority with the men.

XXVII. The Issedones themselves affirm, that the country beyond them is inhabited by a race of men who have but one eye, and by Gryphins who
are

the anniversary of a person's death. Amongst many other customs which distinguished these Γενεσια, some were remarkable for their simplicity and elegance. They strewed flowers on the tomb, they encircled it with myrtle, they placed locks of their hair upon it, they tenderly invoked the names of those departed, and lastly they poured sweet ointments upon the grave.

These observances, with little variation, took place both in Greece and Rome.—See the beautiful Ode of Anacreon:

> Τι σε δει λιθον μυρι ζειν
> Τι δι γη χειν ματαια;
> Εμι μαλλον, ως ετι ζω
> Μυρισον, ροδοις δι κρατα
> Πυκασον.

Thus rendered by Cowley:

> Why do we precious ointments show'r,
> Noble wines why do we pour,
> Beauteous flowers why do we spread
> Upon the mon'ments of the dead?
> Nothing they but dust can shew,
> Or bones that hasten to be so;
> Crown me with roses whilst I live.

See also the much-admired apostrophe addressed by Virgil to the memory of Marcellus:

> Heu miserande puer, si qua fata aspera rumpas,
> Tu Marcellus eris: manibus date lilia plenis,
> Purpureos spargam flores, animamque nepotis
> His saltem accumulem donis.   T.

See

are guardians of the gold.—Such is the information which the Scythians have from the Iſſedones,
and we from the Scythians; in the Scythian tongue
they are called Arimaſpians, from Arima, the Scythian word for one, and ſpu, an eye.

XXVIII. Through all the region of which we
have been ſpeaking, the winter ſeaſon, which continues for eight months, is intolerably ſevere and
cold. At this time if water be poured upon the
ground, unleſs it be near a fire, it will not make
clay. The ſea itſelf[31], and all the Cimmerian Boſphorus, is congealed; and the Scythians who live
within the trench before mentioned make hoſtile
incurſions upon the ice, and penetrate with their
waggons as far as India. During eight months the
climate is thus ſevere, and the remaining four are
ſufficiently cold. In this region the winter is by no

[31] *The ſea itſelf.*]—The Greeks, who had no knowledge of
this country, were of opinion that the ſea could not be congealed; they conſequently conſidered this paſſage of Herodotus
as fabulous. The moderns, who are better acquainted with the
regions of the north, well know that Herodotus was right.—
Larcher.

Upon this ſubject the following whimſical paſſage occurs in
Macrobius.—Nam quod Herodotus hiſtoriarum ſcriptor, contra
omnium ferme qui hæc quæſiverunt, opinionem ſcripſit, mare
Boſporicum, quod et Cimmerium appellat, earumque partium
mare omne quod Scythicum dicitur, id gelu conſtringi et con-
ſiſtere, aliter eſt quam putatur; nam non marina aqua contra-
hitur, ſed quia plurimum in illis regionibus fluviorum eſt, et pa-
ludum in ipſa maria influentium, ſuperficies maris cui dulces
aquæ innatant, congelaſcit, et incolumi aqua-marina videtur in
mari gelu, ſed de advenis undis coactum, &c.

means

means the fame as in other climates; for at this
time, when it rains abundantly elfewhere, it here
fcarcely rains at all, whilft in the fummer the rains
are inceffant.   At the feafon when thunder is common in other places, here it is never heard, but during the fummer it is very heavy.   If it be ever
known to thunder in the winter, it is confidered as
ominous.   If earthquakes happen in Scythia, in
either feafon of the year, it is thought a prodigy.
Their horfes are able to bear the extremeft feverity
of the climate, which the affes and mules frequently
cannot [12]; though in other regions the cold which
deftroys the former has little effect upon the latter.

XXIX. This circumftance of their climate feems
to explain the reafon why their cattle are without
horns [13]; and Homer in the Odyffey has a line

[12] *Affes and mules frequently cannot.*]—This affertion of Herodotus is confirmed by Pliny, who fays, " Ipfum animal (afinus)
frigoris maxime impatiens: ideo non generatur in Ponto, nec
æquinoctis verno, etcætera pecua admittitur fed folftitio." The
afs is a native of Arabia; the warmer the climate in which they
are produced, the larger and the better they are.   " Their fize
and their fpirit," fays Mr. Pennant, " regularly decline as they
advance into colder regions." Hollingfhed fays, that in his time
" our lande did yeelde no affes."   At prefent they appear to be
naturalized in our country; and M. Larcher's obfervation, that
they are not common in England, muft have arifen from mif-
information.   That the Englifh breed of affes is comparatively
lefs beautiful muft be acknowledged.—*T*.

[13] *Without horns.*]—Hippocrates, fpeaking of the Scythian
chariots, fays, they are drawn by oxen which have no horns,
and that the cold prevents their having any.—*Larcher*.

which

which confirms my opinion :—" And Libya, where the sheep have always horns [14] ;" which is as much as to say, that in warm climates horns will readily grow; but in places which are extremely cold they either will not grow at all, or are always diminutive.

XXX. The peculiarities of Scythia are thus explained from the coldness of the climate; but as I have accustomed myself from the commencement of this history to deviate occasionally from my subject, I cannot here avoid expressing my surprize, that the district of Elis never produces mules; yet the air is by no means cold, nor can any other satisfactory reason be assigned. The inhabitants themselves believe that their not possessing mules is the effect of some curse [15]. When their mares require

the

---

[14] *Always horns.*]—The line here quoted from Homer is thus rendered by Pope :

> And two fair crescents of translucent horn
> The brows of all their young increase adorn. *T.*

[15] *Of some curse.*]—The following passage is found in Plutarch's Greek questions.

Q. Why do the men of Elis lead their mares beyond their borders when they would have them covered?

A. Was it because Ænomaus, being remarkable for his great love of horses, imprecated many horrid curses upon mares that should be (thus) covered in Elis, and that the people in terror of his curses will not suffer it to be done within their district?

It is indisputably evident, that something is omitted or corrupted in this passage of Plutarch. As it stands at present it appears that the mares were to be covered by horses, and so

the

the male, the Eleans take them out of the limits of their own territories, and there suffer asses to cover them; when they have conceived they return.

XXXI. Concerning those feathers, which, as the

the translators have rendered it; but the love of Ænomaus for horses, would hardly lead him to so absurd an inconsistency as that of cursing the breed of them within his kingdom. The truth is, it was the breed of mules which he loaded with imprecations; and it was only when the mares were to be covered by asses, that it was necessary to remove them, to avoid falling under his curse. Some word expressing this ought therefore to be found in Plutarch, and the suspicion of corruption naturally falls at once on the unintelligible word ἱέλας, which is totally omitted in the Latin version, and given up by Xylander as inexplicable; Wesseling would change it to ἱνϐοϱϛ, but that does not remove the fault: if we read ὀνοδόκϛς all will be easy. The question will then stand thus: "Why do the men of Elis lead those mares *which are to receive asses*, beyond their borders to be covered?" And we must render afterwards, "that should be *thus* covered," instead of *covered* only: ονοδοκος, being a compound formed at pleasure, according to the genius of the Greek language, but not in common use, might easily be corrupted by a careless or ignorant transcriber. I should not have dwelt so long on a verbal criticism of this kind, had not the emendation appeared important, and calculated to throw additional light on this passage of Herodotus.

Conformable to this is the account of Pausanias:—" In Elis," says he, " mares will not produce from asses, though they will in the places contiguous: this the people impute to some curse." book v. p. 384.—*Kuhnias Edition.*

And Eustathius has a similar remark in his Comment on Dionysius, l. 409.

Upon the above Larcher remarks, that this doubtless was the reason why the race of chariots drawn by mules was abolished at the Olympic games, which had been introduced there in the seventieth Olympiad by Thersias of Thessaly.—*T.*

Scythians

Scythians fay, fo cloud the atmofphere that they cannot penetrate nor even difcern what lies beyond them, my opinion is this :—In thofe remoter regions there is a perpetual fall of fnow, which, as may be fuppofed, is lefs in fummer than in winter. Who-ever obferves fnow falling continually, will eafily conceive what I fay; for it has a great refemblance to feathers. Thefe regions, therefore, whrch are thus fituated remotely to the north, are uninhabita-ble from the unremitting feverity of the climate; and the Scythians, with the neighbouring nations, miftake the fnow for feathers [16].—But on this fub-ject I have faid quite enough.

XXXII. Of the Hyperboreans [17] neither the Scythians nor any of the neighbouring people, the Iffedones alone excepted, have any knowledge; and indeed what they fay merits but little attention. The Scythians fpeak of thefe as they do of the Arimafpians. It muft be confeffed that Hefiod

[16] *Snow for feathers.*]—The comparifon of falling fnow to fleeces of wool, as being very obvious and natural, is found in abundance of writers, ancient and modern.

See Pfalm cxlvii. ver. 5.—Who fendeth his fnow like wool.
Martial beautifully calls fnow denfum tacitarum vellus aquarum.

> In whofe capacious womb
> A vapoury deluge lies to fnow congeal'd;
> Heavy they roll their fleecy world along.—*Thomfon.*

[17] *Hyperboreans.*]—It appears from the Scholiaft on Pindar, that the Greeks called the Thracians Boreans; there is therefore great probability that they called the people beyond thefe the Hyperboreans.—*Larcher.*

mentions

mentions thefe Hyperboreans, as does Homer alfo in
the Epigonoi [18], if he was really the author of thofe
verfes.

XXXIII. On this fubject of the Hyperboreans
the Delians are more communicative. They affirm, that fome facred offerings of this people, carefully folded in ftraw, were given to the Scythians,
from whom defcending regularly through every
contiguous nation [19], they arrived at length at the
Adriatic. From hence, tranfported towards the
fouth, they were firft of all received by the Dodo-
neans of Greece; from them again they were tranf-
mitted to the gulph of Melis; whence paffing into
Euboea, they were fent from one town to another,
till they arrived at Caryftus; not ftopping at Andros,

[18] *Epigonoi.*]—That Homer was the author of various poems
befides the Iliad and the Odyffey, there feems little reafon to
doubt; that he was the author of thefe in queftion can hardly be
made appear. The Scholiaft of Ariftophanes affigns them to
Antimachus; but Antimachus of Colophon was later than Herodotus, or at leaft his cotemporary. The fubject of thefe verfes
were the fuppofed authors of the fecond Theban war. At the
time in which Homer flourifhed, the wars of Thebes and of Troy
were the fubjects of univerfal curiofity and attention.—*T.*

[19] *Through every contiguous nation.*]—On this fubject the
Athenians have another tradition.—*See Paufanias, c. xxxi. p. 77.*

According to them, thefe offerings were given by the Hyperboreans to the Arimafpians, by the Arimafpians to the Scythians, by the Scythians carried to Sinope. The Greeks from
thence paffed them from one to another, till they arrived at
Prafis, a place dependant on Athens; the Athenians ultimately
fent them to Delos. "This," fays M. Larcher, "feems to me
a lefs probable account than that of the Delians."

the

the Caryftians carried them to Tenos, the Tenians
to Delos; at which place the Delians affirm they
came as we have related. They farther obferve,
that to bring thefe offerings the Hyperboreans[40]
fent two young women, whofe names were Hyperoche and Laodice: five of their countrymen accompanied them as a guard, who are held in great
veneration at Delos, and called the Peripheres[41].

[40] *Hyperboreans.*]—Upon the fubject of the Hyperboreans, our
learned mythologift Mr. Bryant has a very curious chapter.
The reader will do well to confult the whole; but the following
extract is particularly applicable to the chapter before us.

Of all other people the Hyperboreans feem moft to have refpected the people of Delos. To this ifland they ufed to fend
continually myftic prefents, which were greatly reverenced: in
confequence of this, the Delians knew more of their hiftory than
any other community of Greece. Callimachus, in his hymn to
Delos, takes notice both of the Hyperboreans and their offerings.

This people were efteemed very facred; and it is faid that
Apollo, when exiled from heaven, and had feen his offspring
flain, retired to their country. It feems he wept; and there
was a tradition that every tear was amber.

See Apollonius Rhodius, book iv. 611.

> The Celtic fages a tradition hold,
> That every drop of amber was a tear
> Shed by Apollo, when he fled from heaven;
> For forely did he weep, and forrowing pafs'd
> Thro' many a doleful region, till he reach'd
> The facred Hyperboreans.

See Bryant, vol. iii. 491.

[41] *Peripheres.*]—Thofe whom the different ftates of Greece
fent to confult Apollo, or to offer him facrifice in the name of their
country, they called Theoroi. They gave the name of Deliaftci
to thofe whom they fent to Delos; and of Pythaftoi to thofe
who went to Delphi.—*Larcher.*

As thefe men never returned, the Hyperboreans were greatly offended, and took the following method to prevent a repetition of this evil:—They carried to their frontiers their offerings, folded in barley-ftraw, and committing them to the care of their neighbours, directed them to forward them progreffively, till, as is reported, they thus arrived at Delos. This fingularity obferved by the Hyperboreans is practifed, as I myfelf have feen, amongft the women of Thrace and Pæonia, who in their facrifices to the regal Diana make ufe of barley-ftraw.

XXXIV. In honour of the Hyperborean virgins who died at Delos, the Delian youth of both fexes celebrate certain rites, in which they cut off their hair [41]; this ceremony is obferved by virgins previous to their marriage, who, having deprived themfelves of their hair, wind it round a fpindle, and place it on the tomb. This ftands in the

---

[41] *Cut off their hair.*]—The cuftom of offering the hair to the gods is of very great antiquity. Sometimes it was depofited in the temples, as in the cafe of Berenice, who confecrated hers in the temple of Venus; fometimes it was fufpended upon trees.—*Larcher.*

When the hair was cut off in honour of the dead, it was done in a circular form. Allufion is made to this ceremony in the Electra of Sophocles, line 52. See alfo Ovid:

　　　　Sciffæ cum vefte capillos.

This cuftom, by the way, was ftrictly forbidden by the Jews. Pope has a very ludicrous allufion to it:—

　　When fortune or a miftrefs frowns,
　Some plunge in bufinefs, others fhave their crowns.—*T.*

　　　　　　　　　　　　vestibule

veſtibule of the temple of Diana, on the left-ſide of
the entrance, and is ſhaded by an olive, which
grows there naturally. The young men of Delos
wind ſome of their hair round a certain herb, and
place it on the tomb.—Such are the honours which
the Delians pay to theſe virgins.

XXXV. The Delians add, that in the ſame age,
and before the arrival of Hyperoche and Laodice at Delos, two other Hyperborean virgins came
there, whoſe names were Argis and Opis [43]; their
object was to bring an offering to Lucina, in
acknowledgment of the happy delivery of their
females ; but that Argis and Opis were accompanied by the deities themſelves. They are, therefore, honoured with other ſolemn rites. The women aſſemble together, and in a hymn compoſed
for the occaſion by Olen of Lycia [44], they call on
the names of Argis and Opis. Inſtructed by theſe
the

[43] *Opis.*]—Orion, who was beloved by Aurora, and whom
Pherecydes aſſerts to have been the ſon of Neptune and Eu-
ryale, or, according to other authors, of Terra, endeavouring
to offer violence to Opis, was ſlain with an arrow by Diana.

The firſt Hyperboreans who carried offerings to Delos were,
according to Callimachus, named Oupis, Loxo, and Hecaerge,
daughter of Boreas.—*Larcher.*

Opis is thus mentioned by Virgil:

Opis ad Ætherium pennis aufertur Olympum.

According to Servius, Opis, Loxo, and Hecaerge, were ſy-
nonymous terms for the moon. Opis was alſo the name of a
city on the Tigris.—*T.*

[44] *Olen of Lycia.*]—Olen, a prieſt and very ancient poet, was
before Homer; he was the firſt Greek poet, and the firſt alſo

the iflanders and Ionians hold fimilar .affemblies, introducing the fame two names in their hymns. This Olen was a native of Lycia, who compofed other ancient hymns in ufe at Delos. When the thighs of the victims are confumed on the altar, the afhes are collected and fcattered over the tomb of Opis and Argis. This tomb is behind the temple of Diana, facing the eaft, and near the place where the Ceians celebrate their feftivals.

XXXVI. On this fubject of the Hyperboreans we have fpoken fufficiently at large, for the ftory of Abaris [45], who was faid to be an Hyperborean, and to have made a circuit of the earth without

who declared the oracles of Apollo.   The inhabitants of Delphi chaunted the hymns which he compofed for them. In one of his hymns he called Ilithya the mother of Love ; in another he affirmed that Juno was educated by the Hours, and was the mother of Mars and Hebe.—*Larcher.*

The word Olen was properly an Ægyptian facred term, and expreffed Olen, Olenus, Ailinus, and Linus, but is of un-known meaning.   We read of Olenium fidus, Olenia capella, and the like.

Nafcitur Oleniæ fidus pluviale capellæ.—*Ovid.*

A facred ftone in Elis was called Petra Olenia. If then this Olen, ftyled an Hyperborean, came from Lycia and Ægypt, it makes me perfuaded of what I have often fufpected, that the term Hyperborean is not of that purport which the Grecians have affigned to it.   There were people of this family from the north, and the name has been diftorted, and adapted folely to people of thofe parts.   But there were Hyperboreans from the eaft, as we find in the hiftory of Olen.—See Bryant farther on this fubject, vol. iii. 492-3.

[45] *Abaris.*]—Jamblicus fays of this Abaris, that he was the
difciple

out food, and carried on an arrow [46], merits no
attention.   As there are Hyperboreans, or inhabitants of the extreme parts of the north, one
would fuppofe there ought alfo to be Hyper-
notians, or inhabitants of the correfponding parts
of the fouth. For my own part I cannot but
think it exceedingly ridiculous to hear fome
men talk of the circumference of the earth, pretending, without the fmalleft reafon or probability, that the ocean encompaffes the earth; that
the earth is round, as if mechanically formed fo; and
that Afia is equal to Europe. I will, therefore,
concifely defcribe the figure and the fize of each of
thefe portions of the earth.

XXXVII. The region occupied by the Perfians
extends fouthward to the Red Sea; beyond thefe
to the north are the Medes, next to them are the
Sapirians. Contiguous to the Sapirians, and where
the Phafis empties itfelf into the Northern Sea, are
the Colchians. Thefe four nations occupy the fpace
between the two feas.

difciple of Pythagoras; fome fay he was older than Solon; he
foretold earthquakes, plagues, &c. Authors differ much as to
the time of his coming into Greece : Harpocration fays it was
in the time of Crœfus.—*T*.

[46] *On an arrow.*]—There is a fragment preferved in the Anec-
dota Græca, a tranflation of which Larcher gives in his notes,
which throws much light upon this fingular paffage; it is this:
a famine having made its appearance amongft the Hyperboreans,
Abaris went to Greece, and entered into the fervice of Apollo.
The deity taught him to declare oracles. In confequence of
this, he travelled through Greece, declaring oracles, having in
his hand an arrow, the fymbol of Apollo.—*T*.

XXXVIII.

XXXVIII. From hence to the weſt two tracts of land ſtretch themſelves towards the ſea, which I ſhall deſcribe: The one on the north ſide commences at the Phaſis, and extends to the ſea along the Euxine and the Helleſpont, as far as the Sigeum of Troy. On the ſouth ſide it begins at the Marandynian bay, contiguous to Phœnicia, and is continued to the ſea as far the Triopian promontory; this ſpace of country is inhabited by thirty different nations.

XXXIX. The other diſtrict commences in Perſia, and is continued to the Red Sea [47]. Beſides Perſia, it comprehends Aſſyria and Arabia, naturally terminating in the Arabian Gulph, into which Darius introduced [48] a channel of the Nile. The interval from Perſia to Phœnicia is very extenſive. From Phœnica it again continues beyond Syria of Paleſtine, as far as Ægypt, where it terminates.

[47] *The Red Sea.*]—It is neceſſary to be obſerved, that not only the Arabian Gulph was known by this name, but alſo the Perſian Gulph and the Southern Ocean, that is to ſay, that vaſt tract of ſea which lies between the two gulphs.—*Larcher.*

What Herodotus calls the Erythrean Sea, he carefully diſtinguiſhes from the Arabian Gulph.

Both Herodotus and Agathemenus induſtriouſly diſtinguiſh the Erythrean Sea from the Arabian Gulph, though the latter was certainly ſo called, and had the name of Erythrean. The Parthic empire, which included Perſis, is by Pliny ſaid to be bounded to the ſouth by the Mare Rubrum, which was the boundary alſo of the Perſians: by Mare Rubrum he here means the great ſouthern ſea.—*Bryant.*

[48] *Darius introduced.*]—See book the ſecond, chap. 158.

The

The whole of this region is occupied by three nations only.—Such is the divifion of Afia from Perfia
weftward.

XL. To the eaft beyond Perfia, Media, the
Sapinians and Colchians, the country is bounded
by the Red Sea; to the north by the Cafpian and
the river Araxes, which directs its courfe towards
the eaft. As far as India, Afia is well inhabited;
but from India eaftward the whole country is one
vaft defert, unknown and unexplored.

XLI. The fecond tract comprehends Libya,
which begins where Ægypt ends. About Ægypt
the country is very narrow. One hundred thoufand
orgyiæ, or one thoufand ftadia, comprehend the
fpace between this and the Red Sea[49]. Here the
country expands, and takes the name of Libya.

XLII. I am much furprized at thofe who have
divided and defined the limits of Libya, Afia, and
Europe, betwixt which the difference is far from
fmall. Europe, for inftance, in length much exceeds the other two, but is of far inferior breadth:

[49] *This and the Red Sea.*]—Here we muft neceffarily underftand the ifthmus between the Mediterranean and the Arabian
Gulph or Red Sea. Heredotus fays, book ii. chap. 158, that
the fhorteft way betwixt one fea and the other was one thoufand
ftadia. Agrippa fays, on the authority of Pliny, that from Pe-
lufium to Arfinöe on the Red Sea was one hundred and twenty-
five miles, which comes to the fame thing, that author always
reckoning eight ftadia to a mile.—*Larcher.*

except

except in that particular part which is contiguous
to Asia, the whole of Africa is surrounded by the
sea. The first person who has proved this, was, as
far as we are able to judge, Necho king of Ægypt.
When he had desisted from his attempt to join by a
canal the Nile with the Arabian Gulph, he difpatched some vessels [50], under the conduct of Phœnicians, with directions to pass by the columns of
Hercules, and after penetrating the Northern Ocean
to return to Ægypt. These Phœnicians, taking
their course from the Red Sea, entered into the
Southern Ocean: on the approach of autumn they
landed in Libya, and planted some corn in the
place where they happened to find themselves; when
this was ripe, and they had cut it down, they again

---

[50] *Dispatched some vessels.*]—This Necho is the same who in
scripture is called Pharaoh Necho. He made an attempt to join
the Nile and the Red Sea, by drawing a canal from the one to
the other; but after he had consumed an hundred and twenty
thousand men in the work, he was forced to desist from it. But
he had better success in another undertaking; for having got-
ten some of the expertest Phœnician sailors into his service, he
sent them out by the Red Sea, through the straits of Babelman-
del, to discover the coasts of Africa, who having sailed round it
came home the third year through the straits of Gibraltar and
the Mediterranean Sea, which was a very extraordinary voyage
to be made in those days, when the use of the loadstone was not
known. This voyage was performed about two thousand one
hundred years before Vasquez de Gama, a Portugueze, by difcovering the Cape of Good Hope in 1497, found out the same
way from hence to the Indies by which these Phœnicians came
from thence. Since that it hath been made the common paffage thither from all these western parts of the world.—*Prideaux.*

departed.

departed. Having thus confumed two years, they
in the third doubled the columns of Hercules, and
returned to Ægypt. Their relation may obtain
attention from others, but to me it feems incredible [11], for they affirmed, that having failed round
Africa, they had the fun on their right hand.——
Thus was Africa for the firft time known.

XLIII. If the Carthaginian account may be
credited, Satafpes, fon of Teafpes, of the race of the
Achæmenides, received a commiffion to circumna-
vigate Africa, which he never executed: alarmed
by the length of the voyage, and the folitary appearance of the country, he returned without accomplifhing the tafk enjoined him by his mother.
This man had committed violence on a virgin,
daughter of Zopyrus, fon of Megabyzus, for
which offence Xerxes had ordered him to be crucified ; but the influence of his mother, who was
fifter to Darius, faved his life. She avowed, however, that it was her intention to inflict a ftill
feverer punifhment upon him, by obliging him to
fail round Africa, till he fhould arrive at the Ara-

[11] *To me it feems incredible.*]—Herodotus does not doubt that
the Phœnicians made the circuit of Africa, and returned to
Ægypt by the ftraits of Gibraltar; but he could not believe
that in the courfe of the voyage they had the fun on their right
hand. This, however, muft neceffarily have been the cafe after
the Phœnicians had paffed the line; and this curious circumftance,
which never could have been imagined in an age when aftro-
nomy was yet in its infancy, is an evidence to the truth of a
voyage, which without this might have been doubted.——
Larcher,

bian

bian Gulph. To this Xerxes affented, and Satafpes accordingly departed for Ægypt; he here embarked with his crew, and proceeded to the columns
of Hercules ; paffing thefe, he doubled the promontory which is called Syloes, keeping a fouthern
courfe. Continuing his voyage for feveral months,
in which he paffed over an immenfe tract of fea,
he faw no probable termination of his labours, and
therefore failed back to Ægypt. Returning to the
court of Xerxes, he amongft other things related,
that in the moft remote places he had vifited he
had feen a people of diminutive appearance, cloath-
ed in red garments [52], who on the approach of his
veffel

---

[52] *Red garments.*]—This paffage has been indifferently rendered Phœnician garments and red garments ; the original is
ισθητι φοινικηιη.—Larcher, diffenting from both thefe, tranflates
it "des habits de palmier :" his reafoning upon it does not appear
quite fatisfactory. "It feems very fufpicious," fays he, "that
people fo favage as thefe are defcribed by Herodotus, fhould
either have cloth or ftuff, or if they had fhould poffefs the means
of dying it red." But in the firft place, Herodotus does not
call thefe a favage people; and in the next, the narrative of
Satafpes was intended to excite aftonifhment, by reprefenting
to Xerxes what to him at leaft feemed marvellous. That a
race of uncivilized men fhould cloath themfelves with fkins, or
garments made of the leaves or bark of trees, could not appear
wonderful to a fubject of Xerxes, to whom many barbarous nations were perfectly well known. His furprize would be much
more powerfully excited, at feeing a race of men of whom they
had no knowledge, habited like the members of a civilized fociety;
add to this, that granting them to be what they are not here reprefented, Barbarians, they might ftill have in their country fome
natural or prepared fubftances, communicative of different colours. I therefore accede to the interpretation of rubrâ utentes
vefte,

veſſel to the ſhore, had deſerted their habitations,
and fled to the mountains. But he affirmed, that his
people, ſatisfied with taking a ſupply of proviſions,
offered them no violence. He denied the poſſibility of his making the circuit of Africa, as his veſſel was totally unable to proceed [53]. Xerxes gave
no credit to his aſſertions; and, as he had not fulfilled the terms impoſed upon him, he was executed according to his former ſentence. An eunuch belonging to this Sataſpes, hearing of his maſter's death,
fled with a great ſum of money to Samos, but he was
there plundered of his property by a native of the
place, whoſe name I know, but forbear to mention.

XLIV. Of Aſia, a very conſiderable part was firſt
diſcovered by Darius. He was very deſirous of
aſcertaining where the Indus meets the ocean, the
only river but one in which crocodiles are found;
to effect this, he ſent, amongſt other men in whom
he could confide, Scylax of Caryandia [54]. Departing

veſte, which is given by Valla and Gronovius, and which the
word φοινικηΐη will certainly juſtify.—*T.*

[53] *Unable to proceed.*]—This was, according to all appear-
ances, the eaſt wind which impeded the progreſs of the veſſel,
which conſtantly blows in that ſea during a certain period.—
Larcher.—See the note of Weſſeling.

[54] *Scylax of Caryandia.*]—About this time, Darius being deſirous to enlarge his dominions eaſtward, in order to the con-
quering of thoſe countries laid a deſign of firſt making a diſco-
very of them. for which reaſon, having built a fleet of ſhips at
Caſpatyrus, a city on the river Indus, and as far upon it as the
borders

ing from Cafpatyrus in the Pactyian 'territories,
they followed the eaftern courfe of the river, till
they came to the fea; then failing weftward, they
arrived, after a voyage of thirty months, at the very
point from whence, as I have before related, the
Ægyptian prince difpatched the Phœnicians to cir-
cumnavigate Africa. After this voyage Darius fubdued the Indians, and became mafter of that ocean:
whence it appears that Afia in all its parts, except
thofe more remotely to the eaft, entirely refembles
Africa.

XLV. It is certain that Europe has not hitherto
been carefully examined; it is by no means certain
whether to the eaft and north it is limited by the

borders of Scythia, he gave the command of it to Scylax, a
Grecian of Caryandia, a city in Caria, and one well fkilled in
maritime affairs, and fent him down the river to make the beft
difcoveries he could of all the parts which lay on the banks of
it on either fide; ordering him for this end to fail down the current till he fhould arrive at the mouth of the river; and that then,
paffing through it into the Southern Ocean, he fhould fhape his
courfe weftward, and that way return home. Which orders he
having exactly executed, he returned by the ftraits of Babel-
mandel and the Red Sea; and on the thirtieth month after
his firft fetting out from Cafpatyrus landed in Ægypt, at the
fame place from whence Necho king of Ægypt formerly fent
out his Phœnicians to fail round the coafts of Africa, which it
is moft likely was the port where now the town of Suez ftands,
at the hither end of the faid Red Sea.—*Prideaux.*

There were three eminent perfons of this place, and of this
name:—The one flourifhed under Darius Hyftafpes, the fecond
under Darius Nothus, the third lived in the time of Polybius.
This was alfo the name of a celebrated river in Cappadocia.
—*T.*

ocean.

ocean. In length it unqueſtionably exceeds the two other diviſions of the earth; but I am far from ſatisfied, why to one continent three different names, taken from women, have been aſſigned. To one of theſe diviſions ſome have given as a boundary the Ægyptian Nile, and the Colchian Phaſis; others the Tanais, the Cimmerian Boſphorus, and the Palus Mœotis. The names of thoſe who have thus diſ-tinguiſhed the earth, or the firſt occaſion of their different appellations, I have never been able to learn. Libya, or Africa, is by many of the Greeks ſaid to have been ſo named from Libya, a woman of the country; and Aſia from the wife of Pro-metheus. The Lydians contradict this, and af-firm that Aſia [55] was ſo called from Aſias, a ſon of Cotys, and grandſon of Manis, and not from the wife of Prometheus; to confirm this, they ad-duce the name of a tribe at Sardis, called the Aſian tribe. It has certainly never been aſcertained, whether Europe be ſurrounded by the ocean: it is a matter of equal uncertainty, whence or from

---

[55] *Aſia.*]—In reading the poets of antiquity, it is neceſſary carefully to have in mind the diſtinction of this diviſion of the earth into Aſia Major and Minor.—When Virgil ſays

Poſtquam res Aſiæ, Priamique evertere gentem
Immeritam viſum ſuperis,

it is evident that he can only mean to ſpeak of a ſmall por-tion of what we now underſtand to be Aſia; neither may it be amiſs to remember, that there was a large lake of this name near mount Tmolus, which had its firſt ſyllable long.

Longa canoros
Dant per colla modos, ſonat amnis et Aſia longe
Pulſat palus.   *T.*

whom

whom it derives its name. We cannot willingly
allow that it took its name from the Syrian Europa, though we know that, like the other two, it
was formerly without any. We are well affured that
Europa was an Afiatic, and that fhe never faw the
region which the Greeks now call Europe; fhe
only went from Phœnicia to Crete, from Crete to
Lycia.—I fhall now quit this fubject, upon which
I have given the opinions generally received.

XLVI. Except Scythia, the countries of the
Euxine, againſt which Darius undertook an expedition, are of all others the moſt barbarous; amongſt
the people who dwell within theſe limits we have
found no individual of ſuperior learning and ac-
compliſhments, but Anacharſis [56] the Scythian.
Even of the Scythian nation I cannot in general

---

[56] *Anacharſis.*]—Of Anacharſis the life is given at ſome
length by Diogenes Laertius; his moral character was of ſuch
high eſtimation, that Cicero does not ſcruple to call him ſobrius,
continens, abſtinens, et temperans. He gave riſe to the proverb
applicable to men of extraordinary endowments, of Anacharſis
inter Scythas: he flouriſhed in the time of Solon. The idea of
his ſuperior wiſdom and defire of learning, has given riſe to an
excellent modern work by the Abbé Barthelemy, called the
Voyage du jeune Anacharſis. With reſpect to what Herodotus
here ſays concerning Anacharſis, he ſeemingly contradicts himſelf in chap. xciv. and xcv. of this book, where he confeſſes his
belief that Zamolxis, the ſuppofed deity of the Scythians, was a
man eminent for his virtue and his wiſdom.

Dicenus alſo was a wife and learned Scythian; and one of
the moſt beautiful and intereſting of Lucian's works is named
from a celebrated Scythian phyſician, called Toxaris.

It muſt be remembered, that ſubſequent to the Chriſtian æra
many exalted and accompliſhed characters were produced from
the Scythians or Goths.—T.

speak

ſpeak with extraordinary commendation; they have however, one obſervance, which for its wiſdom excels every thing I have met with.   The poſſibility of eſcape is cut off from thoſe who attack them; and if they are averſe to be ſeen, their places of retreat can never be diſcovered : for they have no towns nor fortified cities, their habitations they conſtantly carry along with them, their bows and arrows they manage on horſeback, and they ſupport themſelves not by agriculture, but by their cattle [57]; their conſtant abode may be ſaid to be in

[57] *By their cattle.*]—" The ſkilful practitioners of the medical art," ſays Mr. Gibbon, " may determine, if they are able to determine, how far the temper of the human mind may be affected by the uſe of animal or of vegetable food; and whether the common aſſociation of carnivorous and cruel, deſerves to be conſidered in any other light than that of an innocent, perhaps a ſalutary prejudice of humanity.   Yet if it be true, that the ſentiment of compaſſion is imperceptibly weakened by the ſight and practice of domeſtic cruelty, we may obſerve that the horrid objects which are diſguiſed by the arts of European refinement are exhibited in their naked and moſt diſguſting ſimplicity in the tent of a Tartarian ſhepherd.   The ox or the ſheep are ſlaughtered by the ſame hand from which they were accuſtomed to receive their daily food; and the bleeding limbs are ſerved with very little preparation at the table of their unfeeling murderer."   Mr. Gibbon afterwards gives the reader the following curious quotation from the Emile of Rouſſeau.

" Il eſt certain que les grands mangeurs de viande ſont en general cruels et feroces plus que les autres hommes.   Cette obſervation eſt de touts les lieux, et de touts les tems : la barbarité Angloiſe eſt connue," &c.—I hope this reproach has long ceaſed to be applied to England by thoſe who really know it, and that the diſpoſitions of our countrymen may furniſh a proof againſt the ſyſtem, in favour of which they were thus adduced.

their

their waggons [58]. How can a people so circum-
stanced afford the means of victory, or even of
attack ?

XLVII. Their particular mode of life may be
imputed partly to the situation of their country,
and the advantage they derive from their rivers;
their lands are well watered, and well adapted for
pasturage. The number of the rivers is almost
equal to the channels of the Nile; the more celebrated of them, and those which are navigable to
the sea, I shall enumerate; they are these:—The
Danube, having five mouths, the Tyres, the Hypa-

[58] *In their waggons.*]—See the advice of Prometheus to Io,
in Æschylus :—

> First then, from hence
> Turn to the orient sun, and pass the height
> Of these uncultur'd mountains : thence descend
> To where the wandering Scythians, train'd to bear
> The distant-wounding bow, on wheels aloft
> Roll on their wattl'd cottages.   *Potter.*

See also Gibbon's description of the habitation of more modern Scythians. " The houses of the Tartars are no more than
small tents of an oval form, which afford a cold and dirty habitation for the promiscuous youth of both sexes. The palaces of
the rich consist of wooden huts, of such a size that they may be
conveniently fixed on large waggons, and drawn by a team, perhaps of twenty or thirty oxen." The same circumstance re-
specting the Scythians is thus mentioned by Horace:—

> Campestres melius Scythæ,
> Quorum plaustra vagas rite trahunt domos,
> Vivunt et rigidi Getæ
> Immetata quibus jugera, liberas
> Fruges et Cererem ferunt,
> Nec cultura placet longior annua.   *T.*

nis,

his, the Boryfthenes, Panticapes, Hypacyris, Gerrhus, and the Tanais.

XLVIII. No river of which we have any knowledge is fo vaft as the Danube; it is always of the
fame depth, experiencing no variation from fummer
or from winter. It is the firft river of Scythia to
the eaft, and it is the greateft of all, for it is
fwelled by the influx of many others: there are five
which particularly contribute to encreafe its fize;
one of thefe the Greeks call Pyreton, the Scythians
Porata; the other four are the Tiarantus, Ararus,
Naparis, and the Ordeffus. The firft of thefe rivers
is of immenfe fize, flowing towards the eaft it
mixes with the Danube; the fecond, the Tiarantus,
is fmaller, having an inclination to the weft; betwixt
thefe the Ararus, Naparis, and Ordeffus have their
courfe, and empty themfelves into the Danube.
Thefe rivers have their rife in Scythia, and fwell
the waters of the Danube [59].

XLIX.

59 *Waters of the Danube.*]—Mr. Bryant's obfervations on this
river are too curious to be omitted.

The river Danube was properly the river of Noah, expreffed
Da-Nau, Da-Nauos, Da-Nauvas, Da-Naubus. Herodotus
plainly calls it the River of Noah, without the prefix; but ap-
propriates the name only to one branch, giving the name of
Ifter to the chief ftream.

It is mentioned by Valerius Flaccus:—

Quas Tanais, flavufque Lycus, Hypanifque Neafque.

This fome would alter to Novafque, but the true reading is
afcertained from other paffages where it occurs; and particularly by this author, who mentions it in another place:—

XLIX. The Maris alfo, commencing amongſt the Agathyrſi, is emptied into the Danube, which is likewife the cafe with the three great rivers, Atlas, Auras, and Tibiſis; theſe flow from the ſummits of Mount Hæmus, and have the fame termination. Into the fame river are received the waters of the Athres, Noes, and Artanes, which flow through Thrace, and the country of the Thracian Crobyzi. The Cius, which, riſing in Pæonia, near Mount Rhodope, divides Mount Hæmus, is alfo poured into the Danube. The Angrus comes from Illyria, and with a northward courfe paſſes over the Tribalian plains, and mixes with the Brongus; the Brongus meets the Danube, which thus receives the waters of thefe two great rivers. The Carpis, moreover, which rifes in the country beyond the Umbrici, and the Alpis, which flows towards the north, are both loſt in the Danube. Commencing with the Celtæ, who, except the Cynetæ, are the moſt remote inhabitants in the weſt of Europe, this river paſſes directly through the center of Europe, and by a certain inclination enters Scythia.

L. By the union of thefe and of many other waters, the Danube becomes the greateſt of all

Hyberna qui terga Noæ, gelidumque fecuri
Haurit, et in totà non audit Amazona ripâ.

Moſt writers compound it with the particle Da, and expreſs it Da-Nau, Da-Nauvis, Da-Naubis. Stephanus Byzantinus fpeaks of it both by the name of Danoubis, and Danouſis, &c.— vol. ii. 339.

rivers; but if one be compared with another, the preference muſt be given to the Nile, into which no ſtream nor fountain enters. The reaſon why in the two oppoſite ſeaſons of the year the Danube is uniformly the ſame, ſeems to me to be this:—In the winter it is at its full natural height, or perhaps ſomewhat more, at which ſeaſon there is in the regions through which it paſſes abundance of ſnow, but very little rain; but in the ſummer all this ſnow is diſſolved, and emptied into the Danube, which together with frequent and heavy rains greatly augment it. But in proportion as the body of its waters is thus multiplied, are the exhalations of the ſummer ſun. The reſult of this action and reaction on the Danube, is that its waters are conſtantly of the ſame depth.

LI. Thus of the rivers which flow through Scythia, the Danube is the firſt; next to this is the Tyres, which riſing in the north from an immenſe marſh, divides Scythia from Neuris. At the mouth of this river thoſe Greeks live who are known by the name of the Tyritæ.

LII. The third is the Hypanis; this comes from Scythia, riſing from an immenſe lake, round which are found wild white horſes, and which is properly enough called the mother of the Hypanis [60]. This river through a ſpace of five days journey

---

[60] *The Hypanis.*]—There were three rivers of this name :— One in Scythia, one in the Cimmerian Boſphorus, and a third

journey from its firſt riſe, is ſmall, and its waters
are ſweet, but from thence to the ſea, which is a
journey of four days more, it becomes exceedingly
bitter. This is occaſioned by a ſmall fountain,
which it receives in its paſſage, and which is of ſo
very bitter a quality[61], that it infects this river,
though by no means contemptible in point of ſize:
this fountain riſes in the country of the ploughing Scythians *, and of the Alazones. It takes the
name of the place where it ſprings, which in the
Scythian tongue is Exampæus, correſponding in
Greek to the " Sacred Ways." In the diſtrict of the
Alazones the ſtreams of the Tyres and the Hypanis have an inclination towards each other, but
they ſoon ſeparate again to a conſiderable diſtance.

LIII. The fourth river, and the largeſt next to
the Danube, is the Boryſthenes[62]. In my opinion

in India, the largeſt of that region, and the limits of the con-
queſts of Alexander the Great.—This laſt was ſometimes called
the Hypaſis.—_T._

[61] _Bitter a quality._]—This circumſtance reſpecting the Hypanis is thus mentioned by Ovid :—

> Quid non et Scythicis Hypanis a montibus ortus
> Qui fuerat dulcis ſalibus vitiatur amaris.

It is mentioned alſo by Pomponius Mela, book ii. c. 1.—_T._

[62] _Boryſthenes._]—The emperor Hadrian had a famous horſe,
to which he gave this name; when the horſe died, his maſter,
not ſatisfied with erecting a ſuperb monument to his memory,
inſcribed to him ſome elegant verſes, which are ſtill in being.
—_T._

* Herodotus diſtinguiſhes the Σκυθαι αροτηρις, from the Σκυθαι
γιωργοι; and the reader is deſired to correct Scythian huſbandmen for the ploughing Scythians, page 196.

"this

this river is more productive, not only than all
the rivers of Scythia, but than every other in the
world, except the Ægyptian Nile. The Nile, it
muſt be confeſſed, diſdains all compariſon; the Boryſthenes nevertheleſs affords moſt agreeable and
excellent paſturage, and contains great abundance
of the more delicate fiſh. Although it flows in the
midſt of many turbid rivers, its waters are perfectly
clear and ſweet; its banks are adorned by the
richeſt harveſts, and in thoſe places where corn is
not ſown the graſs grows to a ſurpriſing height;
at its mouth a large maſs of ſalt is formed of itſelf.
It produces alſo a ſpecies of large fiſh, which is
called the Antacæus; theſe, which have no prickly
fins, the inhabitants ſalt: it poſſeſſes various other
things which deſerve our admiration. The courſe
of the ſtream may be purſued as far as the country
called Gerrhus, through a voyage of forty days, and
it is known to flow from the north. But of the remoter places through which it paſſes, no one can
ſpeak with certainty; it ſeems probable that it runs
towards the diſtrict of the Scythian huſbandmen,
through a pathleſs deſert. For the ſpace of a
ten days journey theſe Scythians inhabit its
banks. The ſources of this river only, like thoſe
of the Nile, are to me unknown, as I believe
they are to every other Greek. This river, as
it approaches the ſea, is joined by the Hypanis,
and they have both the ſame termination; the
neck of land betwixt theſe two ſtreams is called
the Hippoleon promontory, in which a temple is

Q 3   erected

erected to Ceres [61]. Beyond this temple as far as the
Hypanis, dwell the Borysthenites.—But on this fubject enough has been faid.

LIV. Next to the above, is a fifth river, called
the Panticapes; this alfo rifes in the north, and
from a lake. The interval betwixt this and the
Borysthenes is poffeffed by the Scythian hufbandmen. Having paffed through Hylæa, the Panticapes mixes with the Borysthenes.

LV. The fixth river is called the Hypacyris:
this, rifing from a lake, and paffing through the
midft of the Scythian Nomades, empties itfelf into
the fea near the town of Carcinitis [64]. In its
courfe it bounds to the right Hylæa, and what is
called the courfe of Achilles.

LVI. The name of the feventh river is the Gerrhus;
it takes it name from the place Gerrhus, near which
it feparates itfelf from the Borysthenes, and where
this latter river is firft known. In its paffage to-

---

[63] *To Ceres.*]—Some manufcripts read to "Ceres," others to
"the Mother;" by this latter expreffion Ceres muft be underftood,
and not Vefta, as Gronovius would have it. In his obfervation,
that the Scythians were acquainted neither with Ceres nor
Cybele, he was perfectly right; but he ought to have remembered that the Borysthenites or Olbiopolitæ were of Greek origin, and that they had retained many of the cuftoms and ufages
of their anceftors.—*Larcher.*

[64] *Carcinitis.*]—Many are of opinion that this is what is now
called Golfo di Mofcovia.—*T.*

/

wards

wards the fea, it divides the Scythian Nomades from the Royal Scythians, and then mixes with the Hypacyris.

LVII. The eighth river is called the Tanais[65]; rifing from one immenfe lake, it empties itfelf into another ftill greater, named the Mœotis, which fe⸗ parates the Royal Scythians from the Sauromatæ. —The Tanais is encreafed by the waters of ano-ther river, called the Hyrgis.

LVIII. The Scythians have thus the advantage of all thefe celebrated rivers. The grafs which this country produces is of all that we know the fulleft of moifture, which evidently appears from the dif-fection of their cattle.

LIX. We have fhewn that this people poffefs the greateft abundance; their particular laws and

[65] *Tanais.*]—This river is now called the Don. According to Plutarch, in his Treatife of celebrated Rivers, it derived its name from a young man called Tanis, who avowing an hatred of the female fex, was by Venus caufed to feel an unnatural paffion for his own mother; and he drowned himfelf in confe-quence in this river. It was alfo called the river of the Ama-zons; and, as appears from an old fcholiaft on Horace, was fometimes confounded with the Danube.—It divides Europe from Afia.

Ευρωπην δ' Ασιης Ταναις δια μισσον οριζει.—
                                             Dionyfius.

See alfo Quintus Curtius.—Tanais Europam et Afiam me-dius interfluit. l. vi. c. 2. Of this river very frequent mention is made by ancient writers; by Horace very elegantly, in the Ode beginning with " Extremum Tanaim fi biberes Lyce, &c."—*T.*

obfervances

obfervances are thefe:—Of their divinities [66], Vefta is without competition the firft, then Jupiter, and Tellus, whom they believe to be the wife of Jupiter; next to thefe are Apollo, the Cœleftial Venus, Hercules, and Mars. All the Scythians revere thefe as deities, but the Royal Scythians pay divine rites alfo to Neptune. In the Scythian tongue Vefta is called Tabiti; Jupiter, and, as I think very properly, Papæus [*]; Tellus, Apia; Apollo, Œtofyrus; the Cœleftial Venus, Artimpafa; and Neptune, Thamimafadas. Amongft all thefe deities Mars is the only one to whom they think it proper to erect altars, fhrines, and temples.

LX. Their mode of facrifice in every place appointed for the purpofe is precifely the fame, it is this:—The victim is fecured with a rope, by its two fore feet; the perfon who offers the facri-

[66] *Of their divinities.*]—It is not unworthy the attention of the Englifh reader, that Herodotus is the firft author who makes any mention of the religion of the Scythians. In moft writings on the fubject of ancient mythology, Vefta is placed next to Juno, whofe fifter fhe was generally fuppofed to be: Montfaucon alfo remarks, that the figures which remain of Vefta have a great refemblance to thofe of Juno. With refpect to this goddefs, the ancients were much divided in opinion; Euripides and Dionyfius Halicarnaffenfis, agree in calling her Tellus.— Ovid feems alfo to have had this in his mind when he faid "Stat vi terra fuâ, vi ftando Vefta vocatur." Moft of the difficulties on this fubject may be folved, by fuppofing there were two Veftas.—*T.*

[*] *Papæus*]—or Pappæus, fignifying father; as being, according to Homer, πατηρ ανδρων τι θιων τι, the *father* of gods and men.

fice,

fice [67], ſtanding behind, throws the animal down by means of this rope; as it falls he invokes the name of the divinity to whom the ſacrifice is offered; he then faſtens a cord round the neck of the victim, and ſtrangles it, by winding the cord round a ſtick; all this is done without fire, without libations, or without any of the ceremonies in uſe amongſt us. When the beaſt is ſtrangled, the ſacrificer takes off its ſkin, and prepares to dreſs it.

LXI. As Scythia is very barren of wood, they have the following contrivance to dreſs the fleſh of the victim:—Having flayed the animal, they ſtrip the fleſh from the bones, and if they have them at hand, they throw it into certain pots made in Scythia, and reſembling the Leſbian caldrons, though ſomewhat larger; under theſe a fire is made with the bones [68]. If theſe pots cannot be procured, they encloſe

[67]. *Who, offers the ſacrifice.*]—Montfaucon, in his account of the gods of the Scythians, apparently gives a tranſlation of this paſſage, except that he ſays " the ſacrificing prieſt, after having turned aſide part of his veil:" Herodotus ſays no ſuch thing, nor does any writer on this ſubject which I have had the opportunity of conſulting.—*T.*

[68] *Fire is made with the bones.*]—Montfaucon remarks on this paſſage, that he does not ſee how this could be done. Reſources equally extraordinary ſeem to be applied in the eaſtern countries, where there is a great ſcarcity of fuel. In Perſia it appears from Sir John Chardin they burn heath; in Arabia they burn cow-dung; and according to Dr. Ruſſel they burn parings of fruit, and ſuch like things. The prophet Ezekiel was ordered to bake his food with human dung. See Ezekiel, chap. iv.

enclofe the flefh with a certain quantity of water in the paunch of the victim, and make a fire with the bones as before. The bones being very inflammable, and the paunch without difficulty made to contain the flefh feparated from the bone, the ox is thus made to drefs itfelf, which is alfo the cafe with the other victims. When the whole is ready, he who facrifices throws with fome folemnity before him the entrails, and the more choice pieces.— They facrifice different animals, but horfes in particular.

LXII. Such are the facrifices and ceremonies obferved with refpect to their other deities; but to the god Mars the particular rites which are paid are thefe—In every diftrict they conftruct a temple to this divinity of this kind; bundles of fmall wood are heaped together, to the length of three ftadia, and quite as broad, but not fo high; the top is a regular fquare, three of the fides are fteep and broken, but the fourth is an inclined plane forming

12. "Thou fhalt bake it with dung that cometh out of man." Voltaire, in his remarks on this paffage, pretends to underfland that the prophet was to eat the dung with his food.—"Comme il n'eft point d'ufage de manger de telles confitures fur fon pain, la plupart des hommes trouvent ces commandemens indignés de la Majefté divin." The paffage alluded to admits of no fuch inference: but it may be concluded, that the burning of bones for the purpofe of fuel was not a very unufual circumftance, from another paffage in Ezekiel.— See chap. xxiv. 5. "Take alfo the choice of the flock, and burn the bones under it, and make it boil well."— T.

the

the afcent, To this place are every year brought·
one hundred and fifty waggons full of thefe bundles
of wood, to repair the ftructure, which the feverity
of the climate is apt to deftroy. Upon the fummit
of fuch a pile each Scythian tribe places an ancient
fcymetar [69], which is confidered as the fhrine of
Mars, and is annually honoured by the facrifice of
fheep and horfes; indeed to this deity more victims
are offered than to all the other divinities. It is
their cuftom alfo to facrifice every hundredth captive, but in a different manner from their other
victims. Having poured libations upon their
heads, they cut their throats into a veffel placed
for the purpofe. With this, carried to the fummit
of the pile, they befmear the above-mentioned fcymetar. Whilft this is doing above, the following
ceremony is obferved below;—From thefe human
victims they cut off the right arms clofe to the
fhoulder, and throw them up into the air. This

---

[69] *Ancient fcymetar.*]—It was natural enough that the Scythians fhould adore with peculiar devotion the god of war; but
as they were incapable of forming either an abftract idea, or a
corporeal reprefentation, they worfhipped their tutelar deity
under the fymbol of an iron cimeter.—*Gibbon.*

In addition to this iron cymetar or cimeter, Lucian tells us
that the Scythians worfhipped Zamolxis as a god. See alfo
Ammianus Marcellinus, xxx. 2.—Nec templum apud eos vifi-
tur, aut delubrum, ne tugurium quidem culmo tectum cerni
ufquam poteft, fed *gladius* Barbarico ritu humi figitur nudus,
eumque et Martem regionem quas circumcircant præfulem
verecundius colunt.

Larcher, who quotes the above paffage from Am. Mar. tells
us from Varro, that anciently at Rome the point of a fpear was
confidered as a reprefentation of Mars.—*T.*

ceremony

ceremony being performed on each victim feverally, they depart: the arms remain where they
happen to fall, the bodies elfewhere.

LXIII. The above is a defcription of their facrifices. Swine are never ufed for this purpofe, as
they will not fuffer them to be kept in their country.

LXIV. Their military cuftoms are · thefe :—
Every Scythian drinks the blood of the firft perfon he flays ; the heads of all the enemies who fall
by his hand in battle he prefents to his king :
this offering entitles him to a fhare of the plunder,
which he could not otherwife claim. Their mode
of ftripping the fkin from the head[70] is this:
they

---

[70] *The fkin from the head.*]—To cut off the heads of enemies
flain in battle, feems no unnatural action amongft a race of
fierce and warlike barbarians. The art of fcalping the head
was probably introduced to avoid the trouble and fatigue of
carrying thefe fanguinary trophies to any confiderable diftance.
Many incidents which are here related of the Scythians, will
neceffarily remind the reader of what is told of the native
Americans. The following war fong, from Boffu's Travels
through Louifiana, places the refemblance in a ftriking point of
view :—" I go to war to revenge the death of my brothers—I
fhall kill—I fhall exterminate—I fhall burn my enemies—I
fhall bring away flaves—I fhall devour their hearts, dry their
flefh, drink their blood—I fhall tear off their fcalps, and make
cups off their fculls."

The quicknefs and dexterity with which the Indians perform
the horrid operation of fcalping, is too well known to require
any defcription. This coincidence of manners is very ftriking,
and

they make a, circular incifion behind the ears, then taking hold of the head at the top, they gradually flay it, drawing it towards them. They next foften it in their hands, removing every flefhy part which may remain, by rubbing it with an ox's hide; they afterwards fufpend it, thus prepared, from the bridles of their horfes, when they both ufe it as a napkin, and are proud of it as a trophy. Whoever poffeffes the greater number of thefe is deemed the moft illuftrious. Some there are who few together feveral of thefe portions of human fkin, and convert them into a kind of fhepherd's garment. There are others who preferve the fkins of the right arms, nails and all, of fuch enemies as they kill, and ufe them as a covering for their quivers. The human fkin is of all others certainly the whiteft, and of a very firm texture; many Scythians will take the whole fkin of a man, and having ftretched it upon wood, ufe it as a covering to their horfes.

LXV. Such are the cuftoms of this people: this treatment, however, of their enemies heads, is not univerfal, it is only perpetrated on thofe whom they moft deteft.—The fcull, below the eye-brows, they cut off, and having cleanfed it thoroughly, if they are poor they merely cover it with a piece of leather; if they are rich, in addition to this they de-

and ferves greatly to corroborate the hypothefis, that America was peopled originally from the northern parts of the old continent.—*T.*

corate

corate the infide with gold ; it is afterwards ufed as
a drinking cup. They do the fame with refpect
to their neareft connections, if any diffenfions have
arifen, and they overcome them in combat before
the king. If any ftranger whom they deem of
confequence happen to vifit them, they make a
difplay of thefe heads [71], and relate every circumftance of the previous connection, the provocations
received, and their fubfequent victory : this they
confider as a teftimony of their valour.

LXVI. Once a year the prince or ruler of every
diftrict mixes a goblet of wine, of which thofe

---

[71] *Difplay of thefe heads.*]—Many inftances may be adduced
from the Roman and Greek hiftorians, of the heads of enemies
vanquifhed in battle being carried in triumph, or expofed as
trophies ; examples alfo occur in fcripture of the fame cuftom.
Thus David carried the Philiftine's head in triumph ; the head
of Ifhbofheth was brought to David as a trophy ; why did
Jael *fmite off* the head of Sifera, but to prefent it triumphantly
to Barak ? It is at the prefent day practifed in the Eaft, many
examples of which occur in Niebuhr's Letters. This is too well
known to require further difcuffion ; but many readers may
perhaps want to be informed, that it was alfo ufual to cut off the
hands and the feet of vanquifhed enemies.—The hands and feet
of the fons of Remmon, who flew Ifhbofheth, were cut off and
hanged up over the pool of Hebron.—See alfo *Lady Wortley
Montague*, vol. ii. p. 19.

" If a minifter difpleafes the people, in three hours time he
is dragged even from his mafter's arms : they cut off his hands,
head, and feet, and throw them before the palace gate with all
the refpect in the world ; while the fultan, to whom they all pro-
fefs unlimited adoration, fits trembling in his apartment."—
T.

Scythians drink [72] who have deftroyed a public
enemy. But of this they who have not done fuch
a thing

[72] *Thofe Scythians drink.*]—Thefe, with many other cuftoms
of the ancient Scythians, will neceffarily bring to the mind of
the reader various circumftances of the Gothic mythology, as
reprefented in the poems imputed to Offian, and as may be feen
defcribed at length in Mallet's Introduction to the Hiftory of
Denmark. To fit in the Hall of Odin, and quaff the flowing
goblets of mead and ale, was an idea ever prefent to the minds
of the Gothic warriors; and the hope of attaining this glorious
diftinction, infpired a contempt of danger, and the moft daring
and invincible courage. See Gray's Defcent of Odin :—

> O. Tell me what is done below ;
>   For whom yon glittering board is fpread,
>   Dreft for whom yon golden bed.
> Pr. Mantling in the goblet fee
>   The pure beverage of the bee ;
>   O'er it hangs the fhield of gold,
>   'Tis the drink of Balder bold.   T.

See alfo in the Edda, the Ode of king Regner Lodbrog.
" Odin fends his goddeffes to conduct me to his palace.—I am
going to fit in the place of honour, to drink ale with the gods.—
The hours of my life are paffed away, I die in rapture." Some
of my readers may probably thank me for giving them a fpecimen of the original ftanzas, as preferved by Olaus Wormius.

> 25.
> Pugnavimus enfibus
> Hoc ridere me facit femper
> Quod Balderi patris fcamna
> Parata fcio in aula.
> Bibemus cerevifiam
> Ex concavis crateribus craniorum
> Non gemit vir fortis contra mortem
> Magnifici in Odini domibus
> Non venis defperabundus
> Verbis ad Odini aulam.

29.

a thing are not permitted to taste; these are obliged to sit apart by themselves, which is considered as a mark of the greatest ignominy [71]. They who have killed a number of enemies, are permitted on this occasion to drink from two cups joined together.

LXVII. They have amongst them a great number who practise the art of divination; for this purpose they use a number of willow twigs [74], in this manner:—They bring large bundles of these

ig.

Fert animus finire
Invitant me Dyfæ
Quas ex Odini aula
Odinus mihi mifit
Lætus cerevifiam cum Afis
In fumma fede bibam
Vitæ elapfæ funt horæ
Ridens moriar.

[71] *Greatest ignominy.*]—Ut quifque plures intercmenit, ita apud eos habetur eximius, cæterum expertem effe cædis inter opprobria vel maximum.—*Pomp. Mela.* l. ii c. 1.

[74] *Willow twigs.*]—Ammianus Marcellinus, in fpeaking of the Huns, fays, " Futura miro præfagiunt modo; nam rectiores virgas vimineas colligentes, eafque cum Incantamentis quibufdam fecretis præftituto tempore difcernentes, aperte quid portendatur norunt.—Larcher, in quoting the above paffage, remarks, that he has fomewhere in the country feen fome traces of this fuperftition practifed. There is an animated fragment of Ennius remaining, in which he exprefies a moft cordial contempt for all foothfayers: as it is not perhaps familiar to every reader, I may be excufed inferting it.

Non

thefe together, and having untied them, difpofe them one by one on the ground, each bundle at a diftance from the reft. This done, they pretend to foretell the future, during which they take up the bundles feparately, and tie them again together. —This mode of divination is hereditary amongft them. The enaries, or "effeminate men," affirm that the art of divination [75] was taught them by the goddefs Venus. They take alfo the leaves of the lime-tree, which dividing into three parts they twine round their fingers; they then unbind it, and exercife the art to which they pretend.

Non vicinos arufpices, non de circo aftrologos,
Non Ifiacos conjectores, non interpretes fomnium,
Non enim funt ii aut fapientia aut arte divina
Sed fuperftitiofi vates, impudentefque harioli,
Aut inertes, aut infani, aut quibus egeftas imperat.

A fimilar contempt for diviners, is expreffed by Jocafta, in the Œdipus Tyrannus of Sophocles:

Εμϐ' πακυσον, κỳ μαθ' ὑιικ' ερι σοι
Βροτιον ὑδιν μαιτικης εχον τεχνης.

Let not a fear perplex thee, Œdipus;
Mortals know nothing of futurity,
And thefe prophetic feers are all impoftors.—T.

[75] *Art of divination.*]—To enumerate the various modes of divination which have at different times been practifed by the ignorant and fuperftitious, would be no eafy tafk. We read of hydromancy, libaromancy, onyctomancy, divinations by earth, fire, and air: we read in Ezekiel of divination by a rod or wand. To fome fuch mode of divination, in all probability, the following paffage from Hofea alludes: " My people afk counfel at their flocks, and their ftaff declareth unto them."

LXVIII. Whenever the Scythian monarch happens to be indifpofed, he fends for three of the moft celebrated of thefe diviners.   When the Scythians defire to ufe the moft folemn kind of oath, they fwear by the king's throne [76]: thefe diviners, therefore, make no fcruple of affirming, that fuch or fuch individual, pointing him out by name, has forfworn himfelf by the royal throne.—Immediately the perfon thus marked out is feized, and informed that by their art of divination, which is infallible, he has been indirectly the occafion of the king's illnefs, by having violated the oath which we have mentioned. If the accufed not only denies the charge, but expreffes himfelf enraged at the imputation, the king convokes a double number of diviners, who, examining into the mode which has been purfued in criminating him, decide accordingly.   If he be found guilty, he immediately lofes his head, and the three diviners who were firft confulted fhare his effects.   If thefe laft diviners acquit the accufed, others are at hand, of whom if the greater number abfolve him, the firft diviners are put to death.

LXIX. The manner in which they are executed is this :—Some oxen are yoked to a waggon filled with faggots, in the midft of which, with their feet tied, their hands faftened behind, and their mouths gagged, thefe diviners are placed; fire is

[76] *King's throne.*]—" The Turks at this day," fays Larcher, " fwear by the Ottoman Porte."   Reifke has the fame remark : " Adhuc obtinet apud Turcas, per Portam Ottomanicam, hoc eft domicilium fui principis, jurare."—*T.*.

then

then set to the wood, and the oxen terrified to make them run violently away. It sometimes happens that the oxen themselves are burned; and often when the waggon is consumed, the oxen escape severely scorched. This is the method by which, for the above-mentioned or similar offences, they put to death those whom they call false diviners.

LXX. Of those whom the king condemns to death, he constantly destroys the male children, leaving the females unmolested. Whenever the Scythians form alliances [77], they observe these ceremonies:—A large earthen vessel is filled with wine, into this is poured some of the blood of the contracting parties, obtained by a slight incision of a knife or a sword; in this cup they dip a scymetar, some arrows, a hatchet, and a spear. After this they pronounce some solemn prayers, and the parties who form the contract, with such of their friends as are of superior dignity, finally drink the contents of the vessel.

LXXI. The sepulchres of the kings are in the district of the Gerrhi. As soon as the king dies [78] a large trench of a quadrangular form is sunk, near where the Borysthenes begins to be navigable. When this has been done, the body is enclosed in

---

[77] *Form alliances.*]—See book i. c. 74.

[78] *King dies.*]—A minute and interesting description of the funeral ceremonies of various ancient nations may be found in Montfaucon, vol. v. 126, &c.—*T.*

wax,

wax, after it has been thoroughly cleanſed, and the entrails taken out; before it is ſown up they fill it with aniſe, parſley-ſeed, bruiſed cypreſs, and various aromatics. They then place it on a carriage, and remove it to another diſtrict, where the perſons who receive it, like the Royal Scythians, cut off a part of their ear, ſhave their heads in a circular form, take a round piece of fleſh from their arm, wound their foreheads, noſes, and pierce their left hands with arrows. The body is again carried to another province of the deceaſed king's realms, the inhabitants of the former diſtrict accompanying the proceſſion. After thus tranſporting the dead body through the different provinces of the kingdom, they come at laſt to the Gerrhi, who live in the remoteſt parts of Scythia, and amongſt whom the ſepulchres are. Here the corpſe is placed upon a couch, round which at different diſtances daggers are fixed; upon the whole are diſpoſed pieces of wood covered with branches of willow. In ſome other part of this trench they bury one of the deceaſed's concubines, whom they previouſly ſtrangle, together with the baker, the cook, the groom, his moſt confidential ſervant, his horſes, the choiceſt of his effects, and finally ſome golden goblets, for they poſſeſs neither ſilver nor braſs: to conclude all, they fill up the trench with earth, and ſeem to be emulous in their endeavours to raiſe as high a mound as poſſible.

LXXII. The ceremony does not here terminate.—They ſelect ſuch of the deceaſed king's attendants,

tendants, in the following year, as have been moſt
about his perſon; theſe are all native Scythians,
for in Scythia there are no purchaſed ſlaves, the
king ſelecting ſuch to attend him as he thinks
proper: fifty of theſe they ſtrangle [79], with an equal
number of his beſt horſes.   Of all theſe they open
and cleanſe the bodies, which having filled with ſtraw,
they ſew up again: then upon two pieces of wood
they place a third of a ſemicircular form, with its
concave ſide uppermoſt, a ſecond is diſpoſed in like
manner, then a third, and ſo on, till a ſufficient number have been erected. Upon theſe ſemicircular pieces
of wood they place the horſes, after paſſing large
poles through them, from the feet to the neck.

[79] *They ſtrangle.*]—Voltaire ſuppoſes that they impaled alive
the favourite officers of the khan of the Scythians, round the
dead body; whereas Herodotus expreſsly ſays that they ſtrangled
them firſt.—*Larcher.*

Whoever has occaſion minutely to examine any of the more
ancient authors, will frequently feel his contempt excited, or his
indignation provoked, from finding a multitude of paſſages ig-
norantly miſunderſtood, or wilfully perverted.   This remark is
in a particular manner applicable to M. Voltaire, in whoſe
work falſe and partial quotations, with ignorant miſconceptions
of the ancients, obviouſly abound. The learned Pauw cannot in
this reſpect be entirely exculpated; and I have a paſſage now
before me, in which the fault I would reprobate is eminently
conſpicuous.—Speaking of the Chineſe laws, he ſays, " they
puniſh the relations of a criminal convicted of a capital offence
with death, excepting the females, *whom they ſell as ſlaves*, following in this reſpect the maxim of the Scythians, recorded by
Herodotus."   On the contrary, our hiſtorian ſays, chap. 70,
tha the females are not moleſted.   A ſimilar remark, as it reſpects M. Pauw, is ſomewhere made by Larcher.—*T.*

One part, of the ſtructure, formed as we have deſcribed, ſupporting the ſhoulders of the horſe, the
other his hinder parts, the legs are left to project
upwards. The horſes are then bridled, and the
reins faſtened to the legs ; upon each of theſe they
afterwards place one of the youths who have been
ſtrangled, in the following manner : a pole is
paſſed through each quite to the neck, through the
back, the extremity of which is fixed to the piece
of timber with which the horſe has been ſpitted ;
having done this with each, they ſo leave them.

LXXIII. The above are the ceremonies obſerved in the interment of their kings : as to the people in general, when any one dies the neighbours
place the body on a carriage, and carry it about to
the different acquaintance of the deceaſed ; theſe
prepare ſome entertainment for thoſe who accompany the corpſe, placing before the body the ſame
as before the reſt. Private perſons, after being thus
carried about for the ſpace of forty days, are then
buried[10]. They who have been engaged in the
performance

[10] *Are then buried.*]—The Scythians did not all of them obſerve
the ſame cuſtoms with reſpect to their funerals : there were ſome
who ſuſpended the dead bodies from a tree, and in that ſtate left
them to putrefy. " Of what conſequence," ſays Plutarch, " is
it to Theodorus, whether he rots in the earth or upon it ?—
Such with the Scythians is the moſt honourable funeral."
Silius Italicus mentions alſo this cuſtom :

At gente in Scythicâ ſuffixa cadavera truncis
Lenta dies ſepelit, putri liquentia tabo.

It

performance of thefe rites, afterwards ufe the following mode of purgation:—After thoroughly wafhing the head, and afterwards drying it, they do thus with regard to the body : they place in the ground three ftakes, inclining towards each other, round thefe they bind fleeces of wool as thickly as poffible, and finally, into the fpace betwixt the ftakes they throw red-hot ftones.

LXXIV. They have amongft them a fpecies of hemp refembling flax, except that it is both thicker and larger ; it is indeed fuperior to flax, whether it is cultivated or grows fpontaneoufly. Of this the Thracians [81] make themfelves garments, which fo nearly refemble thofe of flax, as to require a fkilful eye to diftinguifh them : they who had never feen this hemp, would conclude thefe vefts to be made of flax.

LXXV. The Scythians take the feed of this hemp, and placing it beneath the woollen fleeces

It is not perhaps without its ufe to obferve, that barbarous nations have cuftoms barbarous like themfelves, and that thefe cuftoms much refemble each other, in nations which have no communication. Captain Cook relates, that in Otaheite they leave dead bodies to putrefy on the furface of the ground, till the flefh is entirely wafted, they then bury the bones.—*Larcher.* See *Hawkfworth's Voyages.*

[81] *Of this the Thracians.*]—Hefychius fays that the Thracian women make themfelves garments of hemp : confult him at the word Καναβις:—" Hemp is a plant which has fome refemblance to flax, and of which the Thracian women make themfelves vefts."—*T.*

which

which we have before defcribed, they throw it upon the red-hot ftones, immediately a perfumed vapour [82] afcends ftronger than from any Grecian
ftove. This to the Scythians is in the place of a
bath, and it excites from them cries of exultation.
It is to be obferved, that they never bathe themfelves : the Scythian women bruife under a ftone
fome wood of the cyprefs, cedar, and frankincenfe ;
upon this they pour a quantity of water, till it
becomes of a certain confiftency, with which they
anoint the body [83] and the face ; this at the time
imparts

[82] *A perfumed vapour.*]—As the ftory of the magic powers
imputed to Medea feem in this place particularly applicable,
I tranflate, for the benefit of the reader, what Palæphatus fays
upon the fubject.

Concerning Medea, who was faid by the procefs of boiling
to make old men young agein, the matter was this : fhe firft of
all difcovered a flower which could make the colour of the
hair black or white ; fuch therefore as wifhed to have black
hair rather than white, by her means obtained their wifh.
Having alfo invented baths, fhe nourifhed with warm vapours
thofe who wifhed it, but not in public, that the profeffors of the
medical art might not know her fecret. The name of this
application was πϵριψησις, or " the boiling." When therefore
by thefe fomentations men became more active, and improved
in health, and her apparatus, namely the caldron, wood, and fire,
was difcovered, it was fuppofed that her patients were in
reality boiled. Pelias, an old and infirm man, ufing this operation, died in the procefs.—T.

[83] *Anoint the body.*]—When we read in this place of the
cuftom of anointing the body amongft an uncivilized race,
in a cold climate, and afterwards find that in warmer
regions it became an indifpenfable article of luxury and
elegance with the politeft nations, we paufe to admire the
caprice and verfatility of the human mind. The motive of the
Scythians

imparts an agreable odour, and when removed on the following day gives the skin a soft and beautiful appearance,

LXXVI. The Scythians have not only a great abhorrence of all foreign customs, but each province seems unalterably tenacious of its own, Those of the Greeks they particularly avoid, as appears both from Anacharsis and Scyles. Of Anacharsis it is remarkable, that having personally

---

Scythians was at first perhaps only to obtain agility of body, without any views to cleanliness, or thoughts of sensuality. In hot climates fragrant oils were probably first used to disperse those fœtid smells which heat has a tendency to generate; precious ointments therefore soon became essential to the enjoyment of life; and that they really were so, may be easily made appear from all the best writers of antiquity. See Anacreon, Ode xv.

Εμοι μελει μυροισι
Καταβρεχειν υπηνην ,
Εμοι μελει ροδοισι
Καταστεφειν καρηνα.

Let my hair with unguents flow,
With rosy garlands crown my brow.

See also Horace:

———— funde capacibus
Unguenta de conchis.

The same fact also appears from the sacred scriptures; see the threat of the prophet Micah: "Thou shalt tread the olive, but thou shalt not anoint thee with oil."—These instances are only adduced to prove that fragrant oils were used in private life for the purposes of elegant luxury; how they were applied in athletic exercises, and always before the bath, is sufficiently notorious.—*T*.

vifited

viſited a large part of the habitable world, and
acquired great wiſdom, he at length returned to
Scythia. In his paſſage over the Helleſpont, he
touched at Cyzicus [34], at the very time when the
inhabitants were celebrating a ſolemn and magnificent feſtival to the mother of the gods. He
made a vow, that if he ſhould return ſafe and
without injury to his country, he would inſtitute, in
honour of this deity, the ſame rites he had ſeen
performed at Cyzicus, together with the ſolem-
nities obſerved on the eve of her feſtival [35]. Arriving therefore in Scythia, in the diſtrict of Hylæa,
near the Courſe of Achilles, a place abounding with
trees, he performed all the particulars of the above-
mentioned ceremonies, having a number of ſmall
ſtatues ſecured together [36], with a cymbal in his
hand.

[34] *Cyzicus.*]—An account of the ruins of this place may be
found in Pococke. It now produces a quantity of rich wine in
great repute at Conſtantinople.

This city was once poſſeſſed of conſiderable territory, and
was governed by its own laws. There was here a temple built
to Dindymene by the Argonauts. This muſt not be confounded
with the Cyzicus, a city of Myſia, on the Propontis, built by
the Mileſians.—*T.*

[35] *Eve of her feſtival.*]—Theſe feſtivals probably commenced early on the evening before the day appointed for their
celebration; and it ſeems probable that they paſſed the night
in ſinging hymns in honour of the god or goddeſs to whom the
feaſt was inſtituted. See the Pervigilium Veneris.—*Larcher.*

The Pervigilia were obſerved principally in honour of Ceres
and of Venus, and as appears from Aulus Gellius, and other
writers, were converted to the purpoſes of exceſs and debauch-
ery.—*T.*

[36] *Statues ſecured together.*]—Theſe particularities are related
at

hand. In this fituation he was obferved by one
of the natives, who gave intelligence of what he
had feen to Saulius, the Scythian king. The king
went inftantly to the place, and feeing Anacharfis
fo employed, killed him with an arrow.—If any
one now make enquiries concerning this Anacharfis, the Scythians difclaim all knowledge of
him, merely becaufe he vifited Greece, and had
learned fome foreign cuftoms: but as I have been
informed by Timnes, the tutor of Spargapithes,
Anacharfis was the uncle of Idanthyrfus, a Scythian
king, and that he was the fon of Gnurus, grandfon
of Lycus, and great-grandfon of Spargapithes. If
therefore this genealogy be true, it appears that
Anacharfis was killed by his own brother; for
Saulius, who killed Anacharfis, was the father of
Idanthyrfus.

LXXVII. It is proper to acknowledge that
from the Peloponnefians I have received a very
different account: they affirm that Anacharfis'
was fent by the Scythian monarch to Greece, for
the exprefs purpofe of improving himfelf in fcience;

at length in Apollonius Rhodius, book i. 1139.—This circumftance of the fmall figures tied together, is totally omitted by
Mr. Fawkes in his verfion, who fatisfies himfelf by faying,

> The Phrygians ftill their goddefs' favour win
> By the revolving wheel and timbrel's din.

The trueft idea perhaps of the rites of Cybele, may be obtained from a careful perufal of the Atys of Catullus, one of
the moft precious remains of antiquity, and perhaps the only
perfect fpecimen of the old dithyrambic verfe.—*T*.

and

and they add, that at his return he informed his
employer, that all the people of Greece were occupied in scientific pursuits, except the Laceda-
monians; but they alone endeavoured to perfect
themselves in discreet and wise conversation. This
however, is a tale of Grecian invention; I am
convinced that Anacharsis was killed in the manner which has been described, and that he owed
his destruction to the practice of foreign customs
and Grecian manners,

LXXVIII. Not many years afterwards, Scyles,
the son of Aripithes, experienced a similar fortune.
Aripithes, king of Scythia, amongst many other
children, had this son Scyles by a woman of Istria,
who taught him the language and sciences of Greece.
It happened that Aripithes was treasonably put to
death by Spargapithes, king of the Agathyrsi. He
was succeeded in his dominions by this Scyles, who
married one of his father's wives, whose name was
Opæa. Opæa was a native of Scythia, and had a
son named Oricus by her former husband. When
Scyles ascended the Scythian throne, he was exceedingly averse to the manners of his country, and
very partial to those of Greece, to which he had
been accustomed from his childhood. As often
therefore as he conducted the Scythian forces to the
city of the Borysthenites, who affirm that they are
descended from the Milesians, he left his army before the town, and entering into the place secured
the gates. He then threw aside his Scythian dress,
and assumed the habit of Greece. In this, without

x

guards

guards or attendants, it was his cuftom to parade
through the public fquare, having the caution to
place guards at the gates, that no one of his countrymen might difcover him. He not only thus
fhewed his partiality to the cuftoms of Greece, but
he alfo facrificed to the gods in the Grecian manner. After continuing in the city for the fpace of
a month, and fometimes for more, he would refume his Scythian drefs, and depart. This he frequently repeated, having built a palace in this town,
and married an inhabitant of the place.

LXXIX. It feemed however ordained [87] that his
end fhould be unfortunate, which accordingly happened. It was his defire to be initiated into the
myfteries of Bacchus; and he was already about
to take fome of the facred utenfils in his hands,
when the following prodigy appeared to him. I
have before mentioned the palace which he had in
the city of the Boryfthenites; it was a very large

---

[87] *It feemed however ordained.*]—This idea, which occurs repeatedly in the more ancient writers, is moft beautifully expreffed in the Perfæ of Æfchylus; which I give the reader in
the animated verfion of Potter.

> For when misfortune's fraudful hand
> Prepares to pour the vengeance of the fky,
> What mortal fhall her force withftand,
> What rapid fpeed th' impending fury fly?
> Gentle at firft, with flattering fmiles,
> She fpreads her foft enchanting wiles;
> So to her toils allures her deftin'd prey,
> Whence man ne'er breaks unhurt away.   T.

and magnificent ſtructure, and the front of it was
decorated with ſphinxes and griffins of white marble: the lightning[11] of heaven deſcended upon
it, and it was totally conſumed. Scyles nevertheleſs perſevered in what he had undertaken. The
Scythians reproach the Greeks on account of their
Bacchanalian feſtivals, and aſſert it to be contrary to
reaſon to ſuppoſe that any deity ſhould prompt
men to acts of madneſs. When the initiation of
Scyles was completed, one of the Boryſthenites
diſcovered to the Scythians what he had done—
" You Scythians," ſays he, " cenſure us on ac-
" count of our Bacchanalian rites, when we yield
" to the impulſe of the deity. This ſame deity
" has taken poſſeſſion of your ſovereign, he is
" now obedient in his ſervice, and under the in-
" fluence of his power. If ye diſbelieve my words,
" you have only to follow me, and have ocular
" proof that what I ſay is true." The principal
Scythians accordingly followed him, and by a ſecret avenue were by him conducted to the citadel.
When they beheld Scyles approach with his thiaſus,

---

[11] *The lightning.*]—The ancients believed that lightning never
fell but by the immediate interpoſition of the gods ; and whatever thing or place was ſtruck by it, was ever after deemed
ſacred, and ſuppoſed to have been conſecrated by the deity to
himſelf. There were at Rome, as we learn from Cicero de Di-
vinatione, certain books called " Libri Fulgurales," expreſsly
treating on this ſubject. In Ammianus Marcellinus this expreſſion occurs, " contacta loca nec intueri nec calcari debere
pronuntiant libri fulgurales." The Greeks placed an urn over
the place where the lightning fell : the Romans had a ſimilar
obſervance.

and

and in every other refpect acting the Bacchanal, they deemed the matter of moft calamitous importance, and returning informed the army of all that they had feen.

LXXX. As foon as Scyles returned an infurrection was excited againft him; and his brother Octomafades, whofe mother was the daughter of Tereus, was promoted to the throne. Scyles having learned the particulars and the motives of this revolt, fled into Thrace; againft which place, as foon as he was informed of this event, Octomafades advanced with an army. The Thracians met him at the Ifter; when they were upon the point of engaging, Sitalces fent an herald to Octomafades, with this meffage: " A conteft betwixt us " would be abfurd, for you are the fon of my " fifter. My brother is in your power; if you " will deliver him to me, I will give up Scyles to " you, thus we fhall mutually avoid all danger." As the brother of Sitalces had taken refuge with Octomafades, the above overtures effected a peace. The Scythian king furrendered up his uncle, and received the perfon of his brother. Sitalces immediately withdrew his army, taking with him his brother; but on that very day Octomafades deprived Scyles of his head. Thus tenacious are the Scythians of their national cuftoms, and fuch the fate of thofe who endeavour to introduce foreign ceremonies amongft them.

LXXXI.

LXXXI. On the populousnefs of Scythia I
am not able to fpeak with decifion; they have
been reprefented to me by fome as a numerous
people, whilft others have informed me, that of real
Scythians there are but few. I fhall relate however what has fallen within my own obfervation.
Betwixt the Boryfthenes and the Hypanis there is
a place called Exampæus: to this I have before made fome allufion, when fpeaking of a
fountain which it contained, whofe waters were
fo exceedingly bitter as to render the Hypanis,
into which it flows, perfectly impalatable. In this
place is a veffel of brafs, fix times larger than that
which is to be feen in the entrance of Pontus, confecrated there by Paufanias [89] the fon of Cleombrotus. For the benefit of thofe who may not

[89] *Confecrated there by Paufanias.*]—Nymphis of Heraclea
relates, in the fixteenth book of his hiftory of his country, that
Paufanias, who vanquifhed Mardonius at Platea, in violation of
the laws of Sparta, and yielding to his pride, confecrated,
whilft he was near Byzantium, a goblet of brafs to thofe gods
whofe ftatues may be feen at the mouth of the Euxine, which
goblet may ftill be feen. Vanity and infolence had made him
fo far forget himfelf, that he prefumed to fpecify in the infcription, that it was he himfelf who had confecrated it: " Paufanias of Lacedæmon, fon of Cleombrotus, and of the ancient
race of Hercules, general of Greece, has confecrated this
goblet to Neptune, as a monument of his valour."—*Athenæus.*

What would have been the indignation of this or any hiftorian of that period, if he could have forefeen the bafe and
fervile infcriptions dedicated in after-times, in almoft all parts
of the habitable world, to the Cæfars and their vile defcendants ? Many of thefe have been preferved, and are an outrage
againft all decency.—*T.*

have

have feen it, I fhall here defcribe it. This veffel
which is in Scythia, is of the thicknefs of fix digits,
and capable of containing fix hundred amphoræ.
The natives fay that it was made of the points of arrows, for that Ariantas [90], one of their kings, being
defirous to afcertain the number of the Scythians,
commanded each of his fubjects, on pain of death,
to bring him the point of an arrow: by thefe
means fo prodigious a quantity were collected, that
this veffel was compofed from them. It was left
by the prince as a monument of the fact, and by
him confecrated at Exampæus.—This is what I
have heard of the populoufnefs of Scythia.

LXXXII. This country has nothing remarkable except its rivers, which are equally large and
numerous. If befides thefe and its vaft and extenfive plains, it poffeffes any thing worthy of admiration, it is an impreffion which they fhew of
the foot of Hercules [91]. This is upon a rock, two
cubits

[90] *Ariantas.*]—I have now a remarkable inftance before me,
how dangerous it is to take upon truft what many learned men
put down upon the authority of ancient writers. Hoffman, whofe
Lexicon is a prodigy of learning and of induftry, fpeaking of this
Ariantas, fays, " that he made each of his fubjects bring him
every year the point of an arrow." For the truth of this he
refers the reader to Herodotus, and the paffage before us. Herodotus fays no fuch thing.—*T.*

[91] *Foot of Hercules.*]—The length of the foot of Hercules
was afcertained by that of the ftadium at Olympia, which was
faid to have been meafured by him to the length of 600 of his
own feet: hence Pythagoras eftimated the fize of Hercules by
the rule of proportion; and hence too the proverb, *ex pede Her-*

cubits in fize, but refembling the footftep of a man; it is near the river Tyras.

LXXXIII. I fhall now return to the fubject from which I originally digreffed.—Darius preparing to make an expedition againft Scythia, difpatched emiffaries different ways, commanding fome of his dependants to raife a fupply of infantry, others to prepare a fleet, and others to throw a bridge over the Thracian Bofphorus. Artabanus, fon of Hyftafpes, and brother of Darius, endeavoured to perfuade the prince from his purpofe, urging with great wifdom the indigence of Scythia; nor did he defift till he found all his arguments ineffectual. Darius having completed his preparations, advanced from Sufa with his army.

LXXXIV. Upon this occafion a Perfian, whofe name was Œbazus, and who had three fons in the army, afked permiffion of the king to detain one of them.' The king replied, as to a friend, that the petition was very modeft, " and that he would " leave him all the three." Œbazus was greatly delighted, and confidered his three fons as exempted from the fervice: but the king commanded his guards to put the three young men to death; and thus were the three fons of Œbazus left, deprived of life.

LXXXV. Darius marched from Sufa to where

culem, a more modern fubftitution for the ancient one of ἐξ ονυχαν λεοντα.—See Aul. Gell. l. i. and Erafmus's Adagia, in which the proverb of *ex pede Herculem* has no place.—*T.*

the

the bridge had been thrown over the Bofphorus at Chalcedon. Here he embarked and fet fail for the Cyanean iflands, which, if the Greeks may be believed, formerly floated[91]. Here, fitting in the temple[93]; he caft his eyes over the Euxine, which of all feas moft deferves admiration. Its length is eleven thoufand one hundred ftadia; its breadth, where it is greateft, is three thoufand two hundred. The breadth of the entrance is four ftadia; the length of the neck, which is called the Bofphorus, where the bridge had been erected, is about one

[91] *Formerly floated.*]—The Cyanean rocks were at fo little diftance one from the other, that viewed remotely they appeared to touch. This optic illufion probably gave place to the fable, and the fable gained credit from the dangers encountered on this fea.—*Larcher.*

See a defcription of thefe rocks in Apollonius Rhodius: I give it from the verfion of Fawkes.

> When hence your deftin'd voyage you purfue,
> Two rocks will rife, tremendous to the view,
> Juft in the entrance of the watery wafte,
> Which never mortal yet in fafety paft.
> Not firmly fix'd, for oft, with hideous fhock,
> Adverfe they meet, and rock encounters rock.
> The boiling billows dafh their airy brow,
> Loud thundering round the ragged fhore below.

The circumftance of their floating is alfo mentioned by Valerius Flaccus.

>   Errantefque per altum
>   Cyaneas ——— —   *T.*

[93] *In the temple.*]—Jupiter was invoked in this temple, under the name of Urius, becaufe this deity was fuppofed favourable to navigation, *ugos* fignifying a favourable wind. And never could there be more occafion for his affiftance than in a fea remarkably tempeftuous.—*Larcher.*

hundred

hundred and twenty ftadia. The Bofphorus is connected with the Propontis [94], which flowing into the Hellefpont [95], is five hundred ftadia in breadth, and four hundred in length. The Hellefpont itfelf, in its narroweft part, where it enters the Ægean fea, is forty ftadia long, and feven wide.

[94] *Propontis.*]—Between the Bofphorus and the Hellefpont, the fhores of Europe and Afia, receding on either fide, inclofe the fea of Marmara, which was known to the ancients by the denomination of Propontis. The navigation from the iffue of the Bofphorus to the entrance of the Hellefpont, is about one hundred and twenty miles. Thofe who fteer their weftward courfe through the middle of the Propontis may at once defcry the high lands of Thrace and Bithynia, and never lofe fight of the lofty fummit of mount Olympus, covered with eternal fnows. They leave on the left a deep gulf, at the bottom of which Nicomedia was feated, the imperial refidence of Diocletian; and they pafs the fmall iflands of Cyzicus and Proconnefus, before they caft anchor at Gallipoli, where the fea which feparates Afia from Europe is again contracted into a narrow channel.—*Gibbon.*

[95] *Hellefpont.*]—The geographers, who, with the moft fkilful accuracy, have furveyed the form and extent of the Hellefpont, affign about fixty miles for the winding courfe, and about three miles for the ordinary breadth of thefe celebrated ftreights. But the narroweft part of the channel is found to the northward of the old Turkifh caftles, between the cities of Ceftus and Abydos. It was here that the adventurous Leander braved the paffage of the flood for the poffeffion of his miftrefs:—It was here likewife, in a place where the diftance between the oppofite banks cannot exceed five hundred paces, that Xerxes compofed a ftupendous bridge of boats for the purpofe of tranfporting into Europe an hundred and feventy myriads of Barbarians. A fea contracted within fuch narrow limits may feem but ill to deferve the epithet of *broad*, which Homer as well as Orpheus has frequently beftowed on the Hellefpont.—*Gibbon.*

LXXXVI. The exact menfuration of thefe feas is thus determined; in a long day [96] a fhip will fail the fpace of feventy thoufand orgyæ, and fixty thoufand by night. From the entrance of the Euxine to Phafis, which is the extreme length of this fea, is a voyage of nine days and eight nights, which is equal to eleven hundred and ten thoufand orgyæ, or eleven thoufand one hundred ftadia. The broadeft part of this fea, which is from Sindica [97] to Themifcyra, on the river Thermodon, is a voyage of three days and two nights, which is equivalent to three thoufand three hundred ftadia, or three hundred and thirty thoufand orgyæ. The Pontus, the Bofphorus, and the Hellefpont, were thus feverally meafured by me; and circumftanced as I have already defcribed. The Palus Mœotis flows into the Euxine, which in extent almoft equals it, and which is juftly called the mother of the Euxine.

LXXXVII. When Darius had taken a furvey of the Euxine, he failed back again to the bridge

---

[96] *In a long day.*]—That is, a fhip in a long day would fail eighty miles by day, and feventy miles by night. See Weffeling's notes on this paffage.—*T.*

[97] *Sindica.*]—The river Indus was often called the Sindus. There were people of this name and family in Thrace. Some would alter it to Sindicon, but both terms are of the fame purport. Herodotus fpeaks of a regio Sindica, upon the Pontus Euxinus, oppofite to the river Thermodon. This fome would alter to Sindica, but both terms are of the fame amount. The Ind or Indus of the eaft is at this day called the Sind; and was called fo in the time of Pliny.—*Bryant.*

conftructed

conftructed by Mandrocles the Samian. He then examined the Bofphorus, near which [98] he ordered two columns of white marble to be erected; upon one were infcribed in Affyrian, on the other in Greek characters, the names of the different nations which followed him. In this expedition he was accompanied by all the nations which acknowledged his authority, amounting, cavalry included, to feventy thoufand men, independent of his fleet, which confifted of fix hundred fhips. Thefe columns the Byzantines afterwards removed to their city, and placed before the altar of the Orthofian Diana [99], excepting only one ftone, which they depofited in their city before the temple of Bacchus, and which was covered with Affyrian characters. That part of the Bofphorus where Darius ordered the bridge to be erected is as I conjecture nearly at the point of middle diftance between Byzan-

[98] *Near which.*]—The new caftles of Europe and Afia are conftructed on either continent upon the foundations of two celebrated temples of Serapis, and of Jupiter Urius. The old caftles, a work of the Greek emperors, command the narroweft part of the channel, in a place where the oppofite banks advance within five hundred paces of each other. Thefe fortreffes were reftored and ftrengthened by Mahomet the Second, when he meditated the fiege of Conftantinople: but the Turkifh conqueror was moft probably ignorant that near two thoufand years before his reign Darius had chofen the fame fituation to connect the two continents by a bridge of boats.— *Gibbon.*

[99] *Orthofian Diana.*]—We are told by Plutarch, that in honour of the Orthofian Diana, the young men of Lacedæmon permitted themfelves to be flagellated at the altar with the extremeft feverity, without uttering the fmalleft complaint.—*T.*

tium·

tium and the temple at the entrance of the Euxine.

LXXXVIII. With this bridge Darius was fo much delighted, that he made many valuable prefents [100] to Mandrocles the Samian, who conftructed it: with the produce of thefe the artift caufed a reprefentation to be made of the Bofphorus, with the bridge thrown over it, and the king feated on a throne, reviewing his troops as they paffed. This he afterwards confecrated in the temple of Juno, with this infcription:

> Thus was the fifhy Bofphorus inclos'd,
> When Samian Mandrocles his bridge impos'd:
> Who there, obedient to Darius' will,
> Approv'd his country's fame, and private fkill.

LXXXIX. Darius having rewarded the artift, paffed over into Europe: he had previoufly ordered the Ionians to pafs over the Euxine to the Ifter, where having erected a bridge, they were to wait his arrival. To affift this expedition, the Ionians and Æolians, with the inhabitants of the Hellefpont, had affembled a fleet; accordingly, having paffed the Cyanean iflands, they failed directly to the Ifter; and arriving after a paffage of two days from the fea at that part of the river where it begins to branch off, they conftructed a bridge. Darius

---

[100] *Valuable prefents.*]—Gronovius retains the reading of πασι δικα, which is very abfurd in itfelf, and ill agrees with the context: the true reading is πασι δικα, that is, ten of each article prefented.—See Cafaubon on Athenæus, and others.—T.

croffed

croffed the Bofphorus, and marched through
Thrace; and arriving at the fources of the river
Tearus, he encamped for the fpace of three
days..

XC. The people who inhabit its banks affirm
the waters of the Tearus to be an excellent remedy for various difeafes, and particularly for
ulcers, both in men and horfes. Its fources are
thirty-eight in number, iffuing from the fame rock,
part of which are cold, and part warm; they are
at an equal diftance from Heræum, a city near
Perinthus [101], and from Apollonia on the Euxine,
being a two days journey from both. The Tearus flows into the Contadefdus, the Contadefdus
into the Agrianis, the Agrianis into the Hebrus,
the Hebrus into the fea, near the city Ænus.

XCI. Darius arriving at the Tearus, there fixed
his camp: he was fo delighted with this river, that
he caufed a column to be erected on the fpot, with
this infcription: " The fources of the Tearus afford
" the beft and cleareft waters in the world:—In
" profecuting an expedition againft Scythia, Da-
" rius fon of Hyftafpes, the beft and moft ami-
" able of men, fovereign of Perfia, and of all the
" continent, arrived here with his forces."

XCII. Leaving this place, Darius advanced to-

[101] *Perinthus.*]—This place was anciently known by the different names of Mygdonia, Heraclea, and Perinthus.—It is now
called Pera.—*T.*

wards another river, ·called A*t*ifcus, which flows
through the country of the Odryfians [102]. On his
arrival here he fixed upon one certain fpot, on
which he commanded every one of his foldiers to
throw a ftone as he paffed: this was accordingly
done, and Darius, having thus raifed an immenfe
pile of ftones, proceeded on his march.

XCIII. Before he arrived at the Ifter, he firft of
all fubdued the Getæ, a people who pretend to
immortality. The Thracians of Salmydeffus, and
they who live above Apollonia, and the city of
Mefambria, with thofe who are called Cyrmiani-
ans, and Mypfæans, fubmitted themfelves to Darius without refiftance. The Getæ obftinately defended themfelves, but were foon reduced; thefe of
all the Thracians are the braveft and the moft upright.

XCIV. They believe themfelves to be immortal [103]; and whenever any one dies they are of opinion that he is removed to the prefence of their
god

[102] *Odryfians,*]—Thefe people are fuppofed to be the Molda-
vians: they had a city named Odryfa. Mention is made of
them by Claudian in his Gigantomachia:

Primus terrificum Mavors non fegnis in hoftem
Odrifios impellit equos.

Silius Italicus alfo fpeaks of Odrifius Boreas.—*T.*

[103] *They believe themfelves to be immortal.*]—Arrian calls thefe
people Dacians. "The firft exploits of Trajan," fays Mr.
Gibbon, "were againft the Dacians, the moft warlike of men,
who

god Zamolxis [104], whom some believe to be the same with Gebeleizes. Once in every five years they choose one by lot, who is to be dispatched as a messenger to Zamolxis, to make known to him their several wants. The ceremony they observe on this occasion is this :—Three amongst them are appointed to hold in their hands three javelins, whilst others seize by the feet and hands the person who is appointed to appear before Zamolxis ; they throw him up, so as to make him fall upon the javelins. If he dies in consequence, they imagine that the deity is propitious to them ; if not, they

who dwelt beyond the Danube, and who, during the reign of Domitian, had infulted with impunity the majefty of Rome. To the ftrength and fierceneſs of Barbarians, they added a contempt for life, which was derived from a vain perſuaſion of the immortality of the ſoul."

The Getæ are repreſented by all the claffic writers as the moſt daring and ferocious of mankind ; in the Latin language particularly, every harſh term has been made to apply to them : Nulla Getis toto gens eſt trucilentior orbe, ſays Ovid. Hume ſpeaks thus of their principles of belief, with reſpeɛt to the ſoul's immortality :—" The Getes, commonly called immortal from their ſteady belief of the ſoul's immortality, were genuine Theiſts and Unitarians. They affirmed Zamolxis, their deity, to be the only true God, and aſſerted the worſhip of all other nations to be addreſſed to mere fiɛtions and chimæras : but were their religious principles any more refined on account of theſe magnificent pretenſions ?"—T.

[104] Zamolxis.]—Larcher, in conformity to Weſſeling, prefers the reading of Zalmoxis.—In the Thracian tongue, Zalmos means the ſkin of a bear ; and Porphyry, in the life of Pythagoras, obſerves, that the name of Zalmoxis was given him, becauſe as ſoon as he was born he was covered with the ſkin of that animal.

accuſe

accuse the victim of being a wicked man. Having disgraced him, they proceed to the election of another, giving him, whilst yet alive, their commands. This same people, whenever it thunders or lightens, throw their weapons into the air, as if menacing their god; and they seriously believe that there is no other deity.

XCV. This Zamolxis, as I have been informed by those Greeks who inhabit the Hellespont and the Euxine, was himself a man, and formerly lived at Samos, in the service of Pythagoras, son of Mnesarchus; having obtained his liberty, with considerable wealth, he returned to his country. Here he found the Thracians distinguished equally by their profligacy and their ignorance; whilst he himself had been accustomed to the Ionian mode of life, and to manners more polished than those of Thrace; he had also been connected with Pythagoras, one of the most celebrated philosophers of Greece. He was therefore induced to build a large mansion, to which he invited the most eminent of his fellow-citizens: he took the opportunity of the festive hour to assure them, that neither himself, his guests, nor any of their descendants, should ever die, but should be removed to a place where they were to remain in the perpetual enjoyment of every blessing. After saying this, and conducting himself accordingly, he constructed a subterranean edifice: when it was compleated, he withdrew himself from the sight of his countrymen, and resided for three years beneath the earth.—During this period, the Thracians regretted

gretted his lofs, and lamented him as dead. In the fourth year he again appeared amongft them, and by this artifice gave the appearance of probability to what he had before afferted.

XCVI. To this ftory of the fubterraneous apartment I do not give much credit, though I pretend not to difpute it; I am, however, very certain that Zamolxis muft have lived many years before Pythagoras: whether, therefore, he was a man, or the deity of the Getæ, enough has been faid concerning him. Thefe Getæ, ufing the ceremonies I have defcribed, after fubmitting themfelves to the Perfians under Darius, followed his army.

XCVII. Darius, when he arrived at the Ifter, paffed the river with his army; he then commanded the Ionians to break down the bridge, and to follow him with all the men of their fleet. When they were about to comply with his orders, Coes, fon of Erxander, and leader of the Mytelenians, after requefting permiffion of the king to deliver his fentiments, addreffed him as follows:

" As you are going, Sir, to attack a country,
" which, if report may be believed, is without cities
" and entirely uncultivated, fuffer the bridge to
" continue as it is, under the care of thofe who
" conftructed it:—By means of this our return will
" be fecured, whether we find the Scythians, and
" fucceed againft them according to our wifhes, or
" whether they elude our endeavours to difcover
" them. I am not at all apprehenfive that the
" Scythians

" Scythians will overcome us; but I think that if
" we do not meet them, we fhall fuffer from
" our ignorance of the country. It may be faid,
" perhaps, that I fpeak from felfifh confiderations,
" and that I am defirous of being left behind; but
" my real motive is a regard, for your intereft,
" whom at all events I am determined to follow."

With this counfel Darius was greatly delighted,
and thus replied:—" My Lefbian friend, when I
" fhall return fafe and fortunate from this expedi-
" tion, I beg that I may fee you, and I will not
" fail amply to reward you, for your excellent
" advice."

XCVIII. After this fpeech, the king took a
cord, upon which he tied fixty knots [105], then
fending

---

[105] *Sixty knots.*]—Larcher obferves that this mode of notation proves extreme ftupidity on the part of the Perfians. It
is certain, that the fcience of arithmetic was firft brought to
perfection in Greece, but when or where it was firft introduced
is entirely uncertain; I fhould be inclined to imagine, that
fome knowledge of numbers would be found in regions the moft
barbarous, and amongft human beings the moft ignorant, had I
not now before me an account of fome American nations, who
have no term in their language to exprefs a greater number than
three, and even this they call by the uncouth and tedious name
of patarrarorincourfac. In the Odyffey, when it is faid that
Proteus will count his herd of fea-calves, the expreffion ufed is
πεμπασσεται, *he will reckon them by fives*, which has been remarked, as being probably a relick of a mode of counting practifed in fome remote age, when five was the greateft numeral. To
count the fingers of one hand, was the firft arithmetical effort:
to carry on the account through the other hand was a refinement, and required attention and recollection.

                                        M. Goguet

ſending for the Ionian chiefs, he thus addreſſed them :—

"Men of Ionia, I have thought proper to
"change my original determination concerning
"this bridge: do you take this cord, and ob-
"ſerve what I require; from the time of my
"departure againſt Scythia, do not. fail to
"untie every day one of theſe knots. If they
"ſhall be all looſened before you ſee me again,

M. Goguet thinks, that in all numerical calculations pebbles were firſt uſed : ψηφιζω, to calculate, comes from ψηφος, a little ſtone, and the word *calculation* from *calculi*, pebbles. This is probably true; but between counting by the five fingers and ſtanding in need of pebbles to continue a calculation, there muſt have been many intervening ſteps of improvement. A more complicated mode of counting by the fingers was alſo uſed by the ancients, in which they reckoned as far as 100 on the left hand, by different poſtures of the fingers; the next hundred was counted on the right hand, and ſo on, according to ſome au-thors, as far as 9000. In alluſion to this, Juvenal ſays of Neſtor,

—— Atque ſuos jam *dextrâ* computat annos.

Sat. x. 249.

and an old lady is mentioned by Nicarchus, an Anthologic poet, who made Neſtor ſeem young, having returned to the *left* hand again :

—————— η χερι λαιη
Γηρας αριθμειεσθαι δευτερον αρξαμενην.——

Anthobeg. l. ii.

This, however, muſt be an extravagant hyperbole, as it would make her above 9000 years old, or there is ſome error in the modern accounts.—There is a tract of Bede's on this ſubject which I have not ſeen; it is often cited. Macrobius and Pliny tell us, that the ſtatues of Janus were ſo formed, as to mark the number of days in the year by the poſition of his fingers, in Numa's time 355, after Cæſar's correction 365. —*Saturn.* i. 9. and *Nat. Hiſt.* xxxiv. 7.—7.

"you

4

" you are at liberty to return to your country;
" but in the mean time it is my defire that you
" preferve and defend this bridge, by which means
" you will effectually oblige me." As foon as
Darius had fpoken, he proceeded on his march.

XCIX. That part of Thrace [106] which ftretches
to the fea, has Scythia immediately contiguous:
where, Thrace ends Scythia begins, through which
the Ifter paffes, commencing at the fouth-eaft, and
emptying itfelf into the Euxine. It fhall be my
bufinefs to defcribe that part of Scythia which is continued from the mouth of the Ifter to the fea-coaft.
Ancient Scythia extends from the Ifter weftward,
as far as the city Carcinitis. The mountainous
country above this place, in the fame direction, as
far as what is called the Trachean Cherfonefe, is
poffeffed by the people of Taurus; this place is
fituate near the fea to the eaft. Scythia, like Attica,
is in two parts limited by the fea, weftward and to
the eaft. The people of Taurus are circumftanced
with refpect to Scythia, as any other nation would
be with refpect to Attica, who, inftead of Athenians, fhould inhabit the Sunian promontory,
ftretching from the diftrict of Thonicus, as far as
Anaphlyftus. Such, comparing fmall things with

[106] *That part of Thrace.*]—This chapter will, doubtlefs, appear perplexed on a firft and cafual view, but whoever will be at
the trouble to examine M. d'Anville's excellent maps, illuftra-
tive of ancient geography, will in a moment find every difficulty
refpecting the fituation of the places here defcribed effectually
removed.—*T.*

great, is the diſtrict of Tauris; but as there may
be ſome who have not viſited theſe parts of Attica,
I ſhall endeavour to explain myſelf more intelligibly.
Suppoſe, that beginning at the port of Brunduſium [107], another nation, and not the Iapyges [108],
ſhould occupy that country, as far as Tarentum,
ſeparating it from the reſt of the continent: I mention theſe two, but there are many other places
ſimilarly ſituated, to which Tauris might be compared.

[107] *Brunduſium*.]—This place, which is now called Brindiſi,
was very memorable in the annals of ancient Rome; here Au-
guſtus firſt took the name of Cæſar, here the poet Pacuvius was
born, and here Virgil died:—It belongs to the king of Naples;
and it is the opinion of modern travellers, that the kingdom of
Naples poſſeſſes no place ſo advantageouſly ſituated for trade.
—*T.*

[108] *Iapyges*.]—The region of Iapygia has been at different
times called Meſſapia, Calabria, and Salentum; it is now called
Terra d'Otranto: it derived its name of Iapyges from the
wind called Iapyx:

> Sed vides quanto trepidet tumultu
> 'Pronus Orion. Ego quid ſit ater
> Adriæ novi ſinus et quid albus
>   Peccet Iapyx.

Where I ſuppoſe the Albus, contraſted to Ater, means that this
wind ſurprized the unwary mariner, during a very ſevere
ſky.

Others are of opinion, that the Iapyges were ſo named from
Iapyx, the ſon of Dædalus, and that the wind was named Iapyx, from blowing in the direction of that extremity of Italy,
which is indeed more conformable to the analogy of the Latin
names for ſeveral other winds.

C, The

C. The country above Tauris, as well as that towards the fea to the eaft [109], is inhabited by Scythians, who poffefs alfo the lands which lie to the weft of the Cimmerian Bofphorus, and the Palus Mœotis, as far as the Tanais, which empties itfelf into this lake; fo that as you advance from the Ifter inland, Scythia is terminated firft by the Agathyrfi, then by the Neuri, thirdly by the Androphagi, and laft of all by the Melanchlæni.

CI. Scythia thus appears to be of a quadrangular form, having two of its fides terminated by the fea, to which its other two towards the land are perfectly equal: from the Ifter to the Boryfthenes is a ten days journey, which is alfo the diftance from the Boryfthenes to the Palus Mœotis. Afcending from the fea inland, as far as the country of the Melanchlæni, beyond Scythia, is a journey of twenty days: according to my computation, a day's journey is equal to two hundred fta-

[109] *To the eaft.*]—This defcription of Scythia is attended with great difficulties; it is not, in the firft place, eafy to feize the true meaning of Herodotus; in the fecond, I cannot believe that the defcription here given accords correctly with the true pofition of the places. I am, neverthelefs, aftonifhed that it fhould be generally faithful, when it is confidered how fcanty the knowledge of this country was: the hiftorian muft have laboured with remarkable diligence to have told us what he has. By the phrafe of " the fea to the eaft," Bellanger underftands the Palus Mœotis; but I am convinced that when he defcribes the fea which is to the fouth, and to the weft, he means only to fpeak of different points of the Euxine.—*Larcher.*

dia

dia [110] : thus the extent of Scythia, along its sides, is four thousand stadia ; and through the midst of it inland, is four thousand more.

CII. The Scythians, conferring with one another, conceived that of themselves they were unable to repel the forces of Darius ; they therefore made application to their neighbours. The princes also to whom they applied held a consultation concerning the powerful army of the invader ; at this meeting were assembled the princes of the Agathyrsi,

[110] *Two hundred stadia.*]—Authors do not agree with each other, nor indeed with themselves, about the length of the day's journey ; Herodotus here gives two hundred stadia to a day's journey ; but in the fifth book he gives no more than one hundred and fifty.

Strabo and Pliny make the length of the Arabian Gulph a thousand stadia, which the first of these authors says will take up a voyage of three or four days : what Livy calls a day's journey, Polybius describes as two hundred stadia. The Roman lawyers assigned to each day twenty miles, that is to say, one hundred and sixty stadia.—See *Casaubon on Strabo*, page 61 of the Amsterdam edition, page 23 of that of Paris.

The evangelist Luke tells us, that Joseph and Mary went a day's journey before they sought the child Jesus ; now Maundrel, page 64, informs us, that according to tradition this happened at Beer, which was no more than ten miles from Jerusalem ; according, therefore, to this estimation, a day's journey was no more than eighty stadia. When we recollect that the day has different acceptations, and has been divided into the natural day, the artificial day, the civil day, the astronomical day, &c. we shall the less wonder at any apparent want of exactness in the computations of space passed over in a portion of time by no means determinate.—*T*.

Tauri,

Tauri, Neuri, Androphagi, Melanchlæni, Geloni, Budini, and Sauromatæ.

CIII. Of thefe nations, the Tauri are diftinguifh-ed by thefe peculiar cuftoms [111]: All ftrangers fhip-wrecked on their coafts, and particularly every Greek who falls into their hands, they facrifice to a virgin, in the following manner: after the cere-monies of prayer, they ftrike the victim on the head with a club. Some affirm, that having fixed the head upon a crofs, they precipitate the body from the rock, on the craggy part of which the temple ftands: others again, allowing that the head is thus expofed, deny that the body is fo treated; but fay that it is buried. The facred perfonage to whom this facrifice is offered, the Taurians them-felves affert to be Iphigenia, the daughter of Aga-memnon. The manner in which they treat their captives is this:—Every man cuts off the head of his prifoner, and carries it to his houfe, this he fixes on a ftake, which is placed generally at the top of the chimney; thus fituated, they affect to confider it as the protection of their families: their whole

---

[111] *Peculiar cuftoms.*]—Thefe cuftoms, as far as they relate to the religious ceremonies defcribed in the fubfequent para-graphs of this chapter, muft have been rendered by the Iphi-genia of Euripides, and other writers, too familiar to require any minute difcuffion. The ftory of Iphigenia alfo, in all its particulars, with the fingular refemblance which it bears to the account of the daughter of Jephtha in the facred fcriptures, muft be equally well known.—*T.*

fubfiftence

fnbfiftence is procured by acts of plunder and hoftility.

CIV. The Agathyrfi [112] are a people of very effeminate manners, but abounding in gold; they
have their women in common, fo that, being all
connected by the ties of confanguinity, they know
nothing of envy or of hatred: in other refpects they
refemble the Thracians.

CV. The Neuri obferve the Scythian cuftoms.
In the age preceding this invafion of Darius, they
were compelled to change their habitations, from
the multitude of ferpents which infefted them:
befides what their own foil produced, thefe came
in far greater numbers from the deferts above
them; till they were at length compelled to take
refuge with the Budini; thefe people have the
character of being magicians. It is afferted by the
Scythians, as well as by thofe Greeks who dwell
in Scythia, that once in every year they are all of

---

[112] *Agathyrfi.*)—The country inhabited by this people is
now called Vologhda, in Mufcovy: the Agathyrfi were by
Juvenal called cruel.

Sauromatæque truces aut inumanes Agathyrfi.

Virgil calls them the painted Agathyrfi:

Cretefque Dryopefque fremunt pictique Agathyrfi.

They are faid to have received the name of Agathyrfi from
Agathyrfus, a fon of Hercules.—*T.*

them

them changed into wolves [113]; and that after remaining fo for the fpace of a few days, they refume
their former fhape; but this I do not believe,
although they fwear that it is true.

CVI. The Androphagi are perhaps, of all mankind, the rudeft: they have no forms of law or
juftice, their employment is feeding of cattle; and
though their drefs is Scythian, they have a dialect
appropriate to themfelves.

CVII. The Melanchlæni [114] have all black garments, from whence they derive their name: thefe
are the only people known to feed on human
flefh [115]; their manners are thofe of Scythia.

CVIII. The Budini [116] are a great and nume-

[113] *Into wolves.*]—Pomponius Mela mentions the fame fact,
as I have obferved in page 196. It has been fuppofed by
fome, that this idea might arife from the circumftance of thefe
people cloathing themfelves in the fkins of wolves during the
colder months of winter; but this is rejected by Larcher, without his giving any better hypothefis to folve the fable.—*T.*

[114] *Melanchlæni.*]—

Melanchlænis atra veftis & ex ea nomen.—
Pomp. Mela.

[115] *Human flefh.*]—M. Larcher very naturally thinks this a
paffage tranfpofed from the preceding chapter, as indeed the
word Androphagi literally means eaters of human flefh.

[116] *Budini.*]—The diftrict poffeffed by this people is now
called Podolia: Pliny fuppofes them to have been fo called
from ufing waggons drawn by oxen.—*T.*

rous people; their bodies are painted of a blue and red colour; they have in their country a town called Gelonus, built entirely of wood. Its walls are of a surprising height: they are on each side three hundred stadia in length; the houses and the temples are all of wood. They have temples built in the Grecian manner to Grecian deities, with the statues, altars, and shrines of wood. Every three years [117] they have a festival in honour of Bacchus. The Geloni are of Grecian origin; but being expelled from the commercial towns, they established themselves amongst the Budini. Their language is a mixture of Greek and Scythian.   .

CIX. The Budini are distinguished equally in their language and manner of life from the Geloni: they are the original natives of the country, feeders of cattle, and the only people of the country who eat vermin. The Geloni [118], on the con-

[117] *Every three years.*]—This feast, celebrated in honour of Bacchus, was named the Trieterica, to which there are frequent allusions in the ancient authors.—See Statius.

——— Non hæc Trieterica vobis
Nox patrio de more venit.

From which we may presume that this was kept up throughout the night.

[118] *Geloni.*]—These people are called Picti by Virgil:

Pictosque Gelonos.   *Georg.* ii. 115.

And by Lucan fortes:

Massagetes quo fugit equo fortesque Gelonos.—L. iii. 283.

trary,

trary, pay attention to agriculture, live on corn, cultivate gardens, and refemble the Budini neither in appearance nor complexion. The Greeks however are apt, though erroneoufly, to confound them both under the name of Geloni. Their country is covered with trees of every fpecies; where thefe are the thickeft, there is a large and fpacious lake with a marfh furrounded with reeds. In this lake are found otters, beavers, and other wild animals, who have fquare fnouts: of thefe the fkins are ufed to border the garment [119]; and their tefticles are efteemed ufeful in hyfteric difeafes.

CX. Of the Sauromatæ [120] we have this account. In a conteft which the Greeks had with
the

---

[119] *Border the garment.*]—It is perhaps not unworthy remark, that throughout the facred fcriptures we find no mention made of furs: and this is the more remarkable, as in Syria and Ægypt, according to the accounts of modern travellers, garments lined and bordered with coftly furs are the dreffes of honour and of ceremony. Purple and fine linen are what we often read of in fcripture; but never of fur. —*T.*

[120] *Sauromatæ.*]—This people were alfo called Sarmatæ or Sarmatians. It may perhaps tend to excite fome novel and interefting ideas in the mind of the Englifh reader, when he is informed, that amongft a people rude and uncivilized as thefe Sarmatians are here defcribed, the tender and effeminate Ovid was compelled to confume a long and melancholy exile. It was on the banks of the Danube that he wrote thofe nine books of epiftles, which are certainly not the leaft valuable of his works. The following lines are eminently harmonious and pathetic:

At

the Amazons, whom the Scythians call Oiorpata [111],
or, as it may be interpreted, men-flayers (for Oeor
fignifies a man, and pata to kill) they obtained a
victory over them at Thermodon.   On their return, as many Amazons [112] as they were able to
take

At puto cum requies medicinaque publica curæ
　　Somnus adeft, folitis nox venit orba malis,
Somnia me terrent veros imitantia cafus,
　　Et vigilant fenfus in mea damna mei;
Aut ego Sarmaticas videor vitare fagittas
　　Aut dare captivas ad fera vincla manus :
Aut ubi decipior melioris imagine fomni,
　　Afpicio patriæ tecta relicta meæ,
Et modo vobifcum quos fum veneratus amici,
　　Et modo cum cara conjuge multa loquor.   T.

Herodotus relates the origin of this people in this and
the fubfequent chapters.   The account of Diodorus Siculus
differs materially; the Scythians, fays this author, having
fubdued part of Afia, drove feveral colonies out of the country, and amongft them one of the Medes; this, advancing
towards the Tanais, formed the nation of the Sauromatæ.—
Larcher.

　[111] *Oiorpata.*]—This etymology is founded upon a notion
that the Amazons were a community of women who killed
every man with whom they had any commerce, and yet fubfifted as a people for ages.   This title was given them from
their worfhip, for Oiorpata, or as fome manufcripts have it
Aorpata, is the fame as Patah-Or, the prieft of Orus, or in a
more lax fenfe the votaries of that god.   They were Ανδροκ-
τονοι, for they facrificed all ftrangers whom fortune brought
upon their coaft : fo that the whole Euxine fea, upon which
they lived, was rendered infamous from their cruelty.—
Bryant.

　[112] *Amazons.*]—The more ftriking peculiarities relating to
this fancied community of women, are doubtlefs familiar to the
moft

take captive, they diftributed in three veffels : thefe, when they were out at fea, rofe againft their conquerors, and put them all to death. But as they were totally ignorant of navigation, and knew nothing at all of the management either of helms, fails, or oars, they were obliged to refign themfelves to the wind and the tide, which carried them to Cremnes, near the Palus Mœotis, a place inhabited by the free Scythians. The Amazons here difembarked, and advanced towards the part which was inhabited, and meeting with a ftud of horfes in their route, they immediately feized them, and, mounted on thefe, proceeded to plunder the Scythians.

CXI. The Scythians were unable to explain what had happened, being neither acquainted with the language, the drefs, nor the country of the invaders. Under the impreffion that they were a body of men nearly of the fame age, they offered them battle. The refult was, that having taken fome as prifoners, they at laft difcovered them to be women. After a confultation amongft themfelves, they determined not to put any of them to death, but to feleft a detachment of their youngeft

moft common reader. The fubjeft, confidered in a fcientific point of view, is admirably difcuffed by Bryant. His chapter on the Amazons is too long to tranfcribe, and it would be injurious to mutilate it. " Among barbarous nations," fays Mr. Gibbon, " women have often combated by the fide of their hufbands : but it is *almoft* impoffible that a fociety of Amazons fhould ever have exifted in the old or new world."—*T.*

men,

men, equal in number, as they might conjecture, to the Amazons. They were directed to encamp opposite to them, and by their adversaries motions to regulate their own: if they were attacked, they were to retreat without making resistance; when the pursuit should be discontinued, they were to return, and again encamp as near the Amazons as possible. The Scythians took these measures, with the view of having children by these invaders.

CXII. The young men did as they were ordered. The Amazons, seeing that no injury was offered them, desisted from hostilities. The two camps imperceptibly approached each other. The young Scythians, as well as the Amazons, had nothing but their arms and their horses; and both obtained their subsistence from the chace.

CXIII. It was the custom of the Amazons, about noon, to retire from the rest, either alone or two in company, to ease nature. The Scythians discovered this, and did likewise. One of the young men met with an Amazon, who had wandered alone from the rest, and who, instead of rejecting his caresses, suffered him to enjoy her person. They were not able to converse with each other, but she intimated by signs, that if on the following day he would come to the same place, and bring with him a companion, she would bring another female to meet him. The young man returned, and told what had happened: he was punctual to his engagement,

ment, and the next day went with a friend to the place, where he found the two Amazons waiting to receive them.

CXIV. This adventure was communicated to the Scythians, who foon conciliated the reft of the women. The two camps were prefently united, and each confidered as his wife her to whom he had firft attached himfelf. As they were not able to learn the dialect of the Amazons, they taught them theirs; which having accomplifhed, the hufbands thus addreffed their wives:—" We have re-
" lations and property, let us therefore change this
" mode of life; let us go hence, and communicate
" with the reft of our countrymen, where you and
" you only fhall be our wives." To this the Amazons thus replied: " We cannot affociate with
" your females, whofe manners are fo different
" from our own; we are expert in the ufe of the
" javelin and the bow, and accuftomed to ride on
" horfeback, but we are ignorant of all feminine
" employments: your women are very differently
" accomplifhed; inftructed in female arts, they pafs
" their time in their waggons [121], and defpife the
" chace, with all fimilar exercifes; we cannot
" therefore live with them. If you really defire to
" retain us as your wives, and to behave your-

[121] *In their waggons.*]—Thefe waggons ferved them inftead of houfes. Every one knows that in Greece the women went out but feldom; but I much fear that Herodotus attributes to the Scythian women the manners of thofe of Greece.—*Larcher.*

" felves

" felves honeftly towards us, return to your parents,
" difpofe of your property, and afterwards come
" back to us, and we will live together, at a dif-
" tance from your other connections."

CXV. The young men approved of their advice; they accordingly took their fhare of the property which belonged to them, and returned to
the Amazons, by whom they were thus addreffed.
" Our refidence here occafions us much terror and
" uneafinefs: we have not only deprived you of
" your parents, but have greatly wafted your coun-
" try. As you think us worthy of being your
" wives, let us leave this place, and dwell beyond
" the Tanais."

CXVI. With this alfo the young Scythians complied, and having paffed the Tanais, they marched
forwards a three days journey towards the eaft,
and three more from the Palus Mœotis towards
the north. Here they fixed themfelves, and now
remain. The women of the Sauromatæ ftill retain their former habits of life; they purfue the
chace on horfeback, fometimes with and fometimes
without their hufbands, and, dreffed in the habits
of the men, frequently engage in battle.

CXVII. The Sauromatæ ufe the Scythian language, but their dialect has always been impure,
becaufe the Amazons themfelves had learned it but
imperfectly. With refpect to their inftitutions
concerning marriage, no virgin is permitted to
marry

marry till fhe fhall firft have killed an enemy [114].
It fometimes therefore happens that many women.
die fingle at an advanced age, having never been
able to fulfil the conditions required.

CXVIII. To thefe nations, which I have defcribed affembled in council, the Scythian ambaffadors were admitted—they informed the princes,
that the Perfian, having reduced under his authority all the nations of the adjoining continent, had
thrown a bridge over the neck of the Bofphorus,
in order to pafs into theirs: that he had already
fubdued Thrace, and conftructed a bridge over the
Ifter, ambitioufly hoping to reduce them alfo.
" Will it be juft," they continued, " for you to
" remain inactive fpectators of our ruin? Rather,
" having the fame fentiments, let us advance to-
" gether againft this invader: unlefs you do this,
" we fhall be reduced to the laft extremities, and
" be compelled either to forfake our country, or to
" fubmit to the terms he may impofe. If you
" withhold your affiftance, what may we not dread?
" Neither will you have reafon to expect a diffe-
" rent or a better fate; for are not you the object

[114] *Killed an enemy.*]—The account which Hippocrates gives
is fomewhat different: the women of the Sauromatæ mount on
horfeback, draw the bow, lance the javelin from on horfeback,
and go to war as long as they remain unmarried: they are not
fuffered to marry till they have killed three enemies; nor do
they cohabit with their hufbands till they have performed the
ceremonies which their laws require. Their married women do
not go on horfeback, unlefs indeed it fhould be neceffary to
make a national expedition.

" of

" of the Perſian's ambition as well as ourſelves ? or
" do you ſuppoſe that, having vanquiſhed us, he
" will leave you unmoleſted ? That we reaſon
" juſtly, you have ſufficient evidence before you.
" If his hoſtilities were directed only againſt us,
" with the view of revenging upon us the former
" ſervile condition of his nation, he would immedi-
" ately have marched into our country, without at
" all injuring or moleſting others ; he would have
" ſhewn by his conduct, that his indignation was
" directed againſt the Scythians only. On the con-
" trary, as ſoon as ever he ſet foot upon our con-
" tinent, he reduced all the nations which he met,
" and has ſubdued the Thracians, and our neigh-
" bours the Getæ."

CXIX. When the Scythians had thus delivered
their ſentiments, the princes of the nations who were
aſſembled deliberated among themſelves, but great
difference of opinion prevailed ; the ſovereigns of
the Geloni, Budini, and Sauromatæ were unani-
mous in their inclination to aſſiſt the Scythians; but
thoſe of the Agathyrſi, Neuri, Androphagi, Melanchlæni, and Tauri, made this anſwer to the ambaſſadors : " If you had not been the firſt aggreſ-
" ſors in this diſpute, having firſt of all commenced
" hoſtilities againſt Perſia, your deſire of aſſiſtance
" would have appeared to us reaſonable ; we ſhould
" have liſtened to you with attention, and yielded
" the aid which you require : but without any in-
" terference on our part, you firſt made incurſions
" into their territories, and as long as fortune fa-
" voured

" voured you, ruled over Perfia. The fame for-
" tune now feems propitious to them, and they
" only retaliate your own conduct upon you. We
" did not before offer any injury to this people,
" neither without provocation fhall we do fo now :
" but if he attack our country, and commence
" hoftilities againft us, he will find that we fhall
" not patiently endure the infult. Until he fhall
" do this we fhall remain neuter. We cannot.
" believe that the Perfians intend any injury to us,
" but to thofe alone who firft offended them."

CXX. When the Scythians heard this, and
found that they had no affiftance to expect, they
determined to avoid all open and decifive encounters: with this view they divided themfelves
into two bodies, and retiring gradually before the
enemy, they filled up the wells and fountains which
lay in their way, and deftroyed the produce of
their fields. The Sauromatæ were directed to advance to the diftrict under the authority of Scopafis,
with orders, upon the advance of the Perfians, to
retreat towards the Mœotis, by the river Tanais.
If the Perfians retreated, they were to harrafs and
purfue them. This was the difpofition of one part
of their power. The two other divifions of their
country, the greater one under Indathyrfus, and the
third under Taxacis, were to join themfelves to the
Geloni and Budini, and advancing a day's march
before the Perfians, were gradually to retreat, and
in other refpects perform what had been previoufly
determined in council. They were particularly

§ .   enjoined

enjoined to allure the enemy to pass the dominions of those nations who had withheld their assistance, in order that their indignation might be provoked; that as they were unwilling to unite in any hostilities before, they should now be compelled to take arms in their own defence. They were finally to retire into their own country, and to attack the enemy, if it could be done with any prospect of success [115].

CXXI. The Scythians having determined upon these measures, advanced silently before the forces of Darius, sending forwards as scouts a select detachment of their cavalry: they also dispatched before them the carriages in which their wives and children usually live, together with their cattle, reserving only such a number as was necessary to their subsistence, giving directions that their route should be regularly towards the north.

CXXII. These carriages accordingly advanced as they were directed; the Scythian scouts, finding that the Persians had proceeded a three days journey from the Ister, encamped at the distance of one day's march from their army, and destroyed all the produce of the lands. The Persians, as soon

---

[115] *Prospect of success.*]—The very judicious plan of operation here pourtrayed seems rather to belong to a civilized nation, acquainted with all the subterfuges of the most improved military discipline, than to a people so rude and barbarous as the Scythians are elsewhere represented. The conduct of the Roman Fabius, who, to use the words of Ennius, cunctando restituit rem, was not very unlike this.—*T.*

as they came in fight of the Scythian cavalry, commenced the purfuit; whilft the Scythians regularly retired before them. Directing their attention to one part of the enemy in particular, the Perfians continued to advance eaftward towards the Tanais. The Scythians having croffed this river, the Perfians did the fame, till paffing over the country of the Sauromatæ, they came to that of the Budini.

CXXIII. As long as the Perfians remained in Scythia and Sarmatia, they had little power of doing injury, the country around them was fo vaft and extenfive; but as foon as they came amongft the Budini, they difcovered a town built entirely of wood, which the inhabitants had totally ftripped and deferted; to this they fet fire. This done, they continued their purfuit through the country of the Budini, till they came to a dreary folitude. This is beyond the Budini, and of the extent of a feyen days journey, without a fingle inhabitant. Farther on are the Thyffagetæ[116], from whofe country four great rivers, after watering the intermediate plains, empty themfelves into the Palus Mœotis. The names of thefe rivers are the Lycus, the Oarus, the Tanais, and the Syrgis.

[116] *Thyffagetæ.*]—This people are indifferently named the Thyffagetæ, the Thyrfagetæ, and the Tyrregetæ; mention is made of them by Strabo, Pliny, and Valerius Flaccus.—This latter author fays,

> Non ego fanguineis geftantem tympana bellis
> Thyrfagetem, cinctumque vagis poft terga filebo
> Pellibus. *T.*

CXXIV. As foon as Darius arrived at the above folitude, he halted, and encamped his army upon the banks of the Oarus: he then conftructed eight large forts, at the diftance of fixty ftadia from each other, the ruins of which have been vifible to. my time. Whilft he was thus employed, that detachment of the enemy which he had purfued, making a circuit by the higher parts of the country, returned into Scythia. When thefe had difappeared, and were no more to be difcovered, Darius left his forts in an unfinifhed ftate, and directed his march weftward, thinking that the Scythians whom he had purfued were the whole of the nation, and had fled towards the weft: accelerating therefore his march, he arrived in Scythia, and met with two detachments of Scythians; thefe alfo he purfued, who took care to keep from him at the diftance of one day's march.

CXXV. Darius continued his purfuit, and the Scythians, as had been previoufly concerted, led him into the country of thofe who had refufed to accede to their alliance, and firft of all into that of the Melanchlæni. When the lands of this people had been effectually haraffed by the Scythians, as well as the Perfians, the latter were again led by the former into the diftrict of the Androphagi. Having in like manner diftreffed thefe, the Perfians were allured on to the Neuri: the Neuri being alfo alarmed and haraffed, the attempt was made to carry the Perfians amongft the Agathyrfi. This people however had obferved, that before their own country

§   had

had fuffered any injury from the invaders, the Scythians had taken care to diftrefs the lands óf their
neighbours; they accordingly difpatched to them
a meffenger, forbidding their nearer approach, and
threatening that any attempt to advance fhould
meet with their hoftile refiftance : with this determination the Agathyrfi appeared in arms upon their
borders. But the Melanchlæni, the Androphagi,
and the Neuri, although they had fuffered equally
from the Perfians and the Scythians, neither made
any exertions, nor remembered what they had before menaced, but fled in alarm to the deferts of
the north. The Scythians, turning afide from the
Agathyrfi, who had refufed to affift them, retreated
from the country of the Neuri, towards Scythia,
whither they were purfued by the Perfians.

CXXVI. As they continued to perfevere in the
fame conduct, Darius was induced to fend a meffenger to Indathyrfus, the Scythian prince. " Moft
" wretched man," faid the ambaffador, " why do
" you thus continue to fly, having the choice of
" one of thefe alternatives—If you think yourfelf
" able to contend with me, ftop and let us engage:
" if you feel a confcious inferiority, bring to me,
" as to your fuperior, earth and water [127]; let us.
" come to a conference."

CXXVII.

[127] *Earth and water.*]—Amongft the ancient nations of the
weft, to fhew that they confeffed themfelves overcome, or that
they furrendered at difcretion, they gathered fome grafs, and
prefented it to the conqueror. By this action they refigned all
the claims they poffeffed to their country. In the time of
Pliny, the Germans ftill obferved this cuftom. Summum apud.

CXXVII. The Scythian monarch made this reply: "It is not my difpofition, Oh Perfian, to fly
" from any man through fear; neither do I now
" fly from you. My prefent conduct differs not
" at all from that which I purfue in a ftate of peace.
" Why I do not contend with you in the open
" field, I will explain: we have no inhabited towns
" nor cultivated lands of which we can fear your
" invafion or your plunder, and have therefore no
" occafion to engage with you precipitately: but
" we have the fepulchres of our fathers, thefe you
" may difcover; and if you endeavour to injure
" them, you fhall foon know how far we are able
" or willing to refift you; till then we will not
" meet you in battle. Remember farther, that I

antiquos fignum victoriæ erat herbam porrigere victos, hoc eft
terra et altrice ipfa humo et humatione etiam cedere, quem
morem etiam nunc durare apud Germanos fcio.—Feftus and
Servius, upon verfe 128, book viii. of the Æneid of Virgil,

Et vitta comptos voluit prætendere ramos,

affirm, that herbam do, is the fame thing as victum me fateor
et cedo victoriam. The fame ceremony was obferved, or fomething like it, when a country, a fief, or a portion of land, was
given or fold to any one.—See Du Cange, Gloffary, at the
word Inveftitura. In the Eaft, and in other countries, it was
by the giving of earth and water, that a prince was put in
poffeffion of a country; and the inveftiture was made him in
this manner. By this they acknowledged him their mafter
without controul, for earth and water involve every thing.—
Ariftotle fays, that to give earth and water, is to renounce one's
liberty —Larcher.

Amongft the Romans, when an offender was fent into banifhment, he was emphatically interdicted the ufe of fire and water,
which was fuppofed to imply the abfence of every aid and comfort.—T.

" acknowledge

" acknowledge no mafter or fuperior, but Jupi-
" ter, who was my anceftor, and Hiftia the Scy-
" thian queen. Inftead of the prefents which you
" require of earth and water, I will fend you fuch
" as you better deferve: and in return for your
" calling yourfelf my mafter, I only bid you weep."
—Such was the anfwer of the Scythian *, which
the ambaffador related to Darius.

CXXVIII. The very idea of fervitude exafperated the Scythian princes; they accordingly difpatched that part of their army which was under
Scopafis, together with the Sauromatæ, to folicit a
conference with the Ionians who guarded the
bridge over the Ifter; thofe who remained did not
think it neceffary any more to lead the Perfians
about, but regularly endeavoured to furprize them
when at their meals; they watched, therefore, their
proper opportunities, and executed their purpofe.
The Scythian horfe never failed of driving back
the cavalry of the Perfians, but thefe laft, in falling
back upon their infantry, were always fecured and
fupported. The Scythians, notwithftanding their
advantage over the Perfian horfe, always retreated

---

* *Anfwer of the Scythian.*]—To bid a perfon weep, was a kind
of proverbial form of wifhing him ill; thus Horace,

——— Demetri, teque Tigelli
Difcipularum inter *jubeo plorare* cathedras.

Afterwards, *the anfwer of the Scythians* became a proverb to exprefs the fame wifh; as was alfo the bidding a perfon eat
onions.—See *Diog. Laert.* in the Life of Bias, and Erafmus in
Scythanim oratio, and *cepas edere.*—*T.*

from the foot; they frequently, however, attacked them under cover of the night.

CXXIX. In these attacks of the Scythians upon the camp of Darius, the Persians had one advantage, which I shall explain—it arose from the braying of the asses, and appearance of the mules: I have before observed, that neither of these animals are produced in Scythia [128], on account of the extreme cold. The braying, therefore, of the asses greatly distressed the Scythian horses, which as often as they attacked the Persians pricked up their ears and ran back, equally disturbed by a noise which they had never heard, and figures they had never seen: this was of some importance in the progress of hostilities.

CXXX. The Scythians discovering that the Persians were in extreme perplexity, hoped that by detaining them longer in their country, they should finally reduce them to the utmost distress: with this view, they occasionally left exposed some of their cattle with their shepherds, and artfully retired; of these, with much exultation, the Persians took possession.

CXXXI. This was again and again repeated;

---

[128] *Are produced in Scythia.*]—The Scythians nevertheless, if Clemens Alexandrinus may be believed, sacrificed asses; but it is not improbable that he confounded this people with the Hyperboreans, as he adduces in proof of his assertion a verse from Callimachus, which obviously refers to this latter people. We are also informed by Pindar, that the Hyperboreans sacrificed hecatombs of asses to Apollo.—*Larcher.*

Darius

Darius neverthelefs became gradually in want of almoft every neceffary : the Scythian princes, knowing this, fent to him a meffenger, with a bird, a moufe, a frog, and five arrows [119], as a prefent. The Perfians enquired of the bearer, what thefe might

[119] *A bird, a moufe, a frog, and five arrows.*]—This naturally brings to the mind of an Englifhman a fomewhat fimilar prefent, intended to irritate and provoke, beft recorded and expreffed by our immortal Shakefpeare.—See his Life of Henry the Fifth :—

French Ambaffador.——Thus then, in few ;—
 Your highnefs lately fending into France,
 Did claim fome certain dukedoms, in the right
 Of your great predeceffor Edward the Third ;
 In anfwer of which claim, the prince our mafter
 Says, that you favour too much of your youth,
 And bids you be advifed—There's nought in France
 That can be with a nimble galliard won,
 You cannot revel into dukedoms there ;
 He therefore fends you, meeter for your fpirit,
 This tun of treafure, and in lieu of this
 Defires you, let the dukedoms that you claim
 Hear no more of you.—Thus the Dauphin fpeaks.
K. Henry. What treafure, uncle ?
  Exet.   Tennis-balls, my liege.
K. Henry. We are glad the Dauphin is fo pleafant with us:
 His prefent and your pains we thank you for.
 When we have match'd our rackets to thefe balls,
 We will in France, by God's grace, play a fet
 Shall ftrike his father's crown into the hazard.
 Tell him he hath made a match with fuch a wrangler,
 That all the courts of France will be difturb'd
 With chaces.

It may not be improper to remark, that of this enigmatical way of fpeaking and acting, the ancients appear to have been remarkably fond. In the Pythagorean fchool, the precept to ab-

tain

might mean; but the man declared, that his orders were only to deliver them and return: he advifed them, however, to exert their fagacity, and interpret the myftery.

CXXXII. The Perfians accordingly held a confultation on the fubject. Darius was of opinion, that the Scythians intended by this to exprefs fubmiffion to him, and give him the earth and the water which he required. The moufe, as he explained it, was produced in the earth, and lived on the fame food as man; the frog was a native of the water; the bird bore great refemblance to a horfe [130]; and in giving the arrows they intimated the furrender of their power: this was the interpretation of Darius. Gobryas, however, one of the feven who had dethroned the Magus, thus interpreted the prefents: " Men of Perfia, unlefs like " birds ye fhall mount into the air, like mice " take refuge in the earth, or like frogs leap into " the marfhes, thefe arrows fhall prevent the pof- " fibility of your return to the place from whence

ftain from beans, κυαμων απιχισθαι, involved the command of refraining from unlawful love; and in an epigram imputed to Virgil, the letter Y intimated a fyftematic attachment to virtue; this may be found in Lactantius, book vi. c. iii. The act of Tarquin, in ftriking off the heads from the talleft poppies in his garden is fufficiently notorious; and the fables of Æfop and of Phædrus may ferve to prove that this partiality to allegory was not more univerfal than it was founded in a delicate and juft conception of things.—T.

[130] *To a horfe.*]—It is by no means eafy to find out any refemblance which a bird bears to a horfe, except, as Larcher obferves, in fwiftnefs, which is, however, very far-fetched.—T.

" you

" you came." This explanation was generally accepted.

CXXXIII. That detachment of the Scythians who had before been entrusted with the defence of the Palus Mœotis, but who were afterwards sent to the Ionians at the Ister, no sooner arrived at the bridge, than they thus spake: " Men of Ionia, if " you will but hearken to our words, we come to " bring you liberty: we have been told, that Da- " rius commanded you to guard this bridge for " sixty days only; if in that time he should not " appear, you were permitted to return home. " Do this, and you will neither disobey him nor " offend us: stay, therefore, till the time which he " has appointed, and then depart." With this in- junction the Ionians promising to comply, the Scy- thians instantly retired.

CXXXIV. The rest of the Scythians having sent the present to Darius which we have describ- ed, opposed themselves to him, both horse and foot, in order of battle. Whilst they were in this situa- tion a hare was seen in the space betwixt the two armies; the Scythians immediately pursued it with loud cries. Darius enquiring the cause of the tu- mult which he heard, was informed that the ene- my were pursuing a hare; upon this, turning to some of his confidential attendants, " These men," he exclaimed, " do, indeed, seem greatly to despise " us; and Gobryas has properly interpreted the " Scythian presents: I am now of the same opi- " nion

" nion myfelf, and it becomes us to 'exert all our
" fagacity to effect a fafe return to the place from
" whence we came." "Indeed, Sir," anfwered
Gobryas, " I had before heard of the poverty of
" this people, I have now clearly feen it, and can
" perceive that they hold us in extreme con-
" tempt. I would therefore advife, that as foon
" as the night fets in we light our fires as ufual "';
" and, the farther to delude the enemy, let us tie all
" the affes together, and leave behind us the more
" infirm of our forces; this done, let us retire, be-
" fore the Scythians fhall advance towards the
" Ifter, and break down the bridge, or before the
" Ionians fhall come to any refolution which may
" caufe our ruin."

CXXXV. To this opinion of Gobryas Darius
having acceded, as foon as the evening approached, the more infirm of the troops, and thofe whofe
lofs was deemed of little importance, were left
behind; all the affes alfo were fecured together:
the motive for this was, the expectation that the
prefence of thofe who remained would caufe the
affes to bray as ufual. The fick and infirm were de-

---

¹¹ *Fires as ufual.*]—This incident is related, with very little
variation, in the Stratagemata of Polyænus, a book which I may
venture to recommend to all young ftudents in Greek, from its
entertaining matter, as well as from the eafy elegance and purity of its ftyle; indeed I cannot help expreffing my furprize,
that it fhould not yet have found its way into our public fchools;
it might, I think, be read with much advantage as preparatory
to Xenophon.—*T.*

ferted, under the pretence, that whilft the king was marching with his beft troops to engage the Scythians, they were to defend the camp. After circulating this report, the fires were lighted, and Darius with the greateft expedition directed his march towards the Ifter: the affes, miffing the ufual multitude, made fo much the greater noife, by hearing which the Scythians were induced to believe that the Perfians ftill continued in their camp.

CXXXVI. When morning appeared, they who were left, perceiving themfelves deferted by Darius, made fignals to the Scythians, and explained their fituation; upon which intelligence, the two divifions of the Scythians, forming a junction with the Sauromatæ, the Budini, and Geloni, advanced towards the Ifter, in purfuit of the Perfians; but as the Perfian army confifted principally of foot, who were ignorant of the country, through which there were no regular paths; and as the Scythians were chiefly horfe, and perfectly acquainted with the ways, they mutually miffed of each other, and the Scythians arrived at the bridge much fooner than the Perfians. Here, finding that the Perfians were not yet come, they thus addreffed the Ionians, who were on board their veffels:—"Ionians,
" the number of days is now paft, and you do
" wrong in remaining here; if motives of fear
" have hitherto detained you, you may now break
" down the bridge, and having recovered your

" liberties,

" liberties, be thankful to the gods· and to us:
" we will take care that he who was formerly
" your mafter, fhall never again make war upon
" any one."

CXXXVII. The Ionians being met in council
upon this fubject, Miltiades, the Athenian leader,
and prince of the Cherfonefe [131], on the Hellefpont,
was of opinion that the advice of the Scythians
fhould be taken, and Ionia be thus relieved from
fervitude. Hiftiæus, the Milefian, thought differently; he reprefented, that through Darius each
of them now enjoyed the fovereignty of their feveral cities; that if the power of Darius was once
taken away, neither he himfelf fhould continue fupreme at Miletus, nor would any of them be able
to retain their fuperiority: for it was evident that
all their fellow-citizens would prefer a popular government to that of a tyrant. This argument
appeared fo forcible, that all they who had before
affented to Miltiades, inftantly adopted it.

CXXXVIII. They who acceded to this opinion were alfo in great eftimation with the king.—
Of the princes of the Hellefpont, there were Daph-

[131] *Prince of the Cherfonefe*]—All thefe petty princes had impofed chains upon their country, and were only fupported in
their ufurpations by the Perfians, whofe intereft it was to prefer
a defpotic government to a democracy; this laft would have
been much lefs obfequious, and lefs prompt to obey their pleafure.—*Larcher*.

nis

nis of Abydos, Hippoclus of Lampſacus [133], Hero-
phantus of Parium [134], Metrodorus the Proconneſian [135], Ariſtagoras of Cyzicum, and Ariſton the
Byzantian [136]. Amongſt the Ionian leaders were
Stratias

[133] *Lampſacus.*]—Lampſacus was firſt called Pityuſa, on the
Aſia ſhore, nearly oppoſite to Gallipoli; this place was given to
Themiſtocles, to furniſh him with wine. Several great men
amongſt the ancients were natives of Lampſacus, and Epicurus
lived here for ſome time.—*Pococke.*

From this place Priapus, who was here worſhipped, took one
of his names:

Et te ruricola Lampſace tuta deo.—*Ovid.*

and from hence Lampſacius was made to ſignify wanton; ſee
Martial, book ii. ep. 17.—

Nam mea Lampſacio laſcivit pagina verſu: *T.*

[134] *Parium.*]—Parium was built by the Mileſians, Erythre-
ans, and the people of the iſle of Paros; it flouriſhed much
under the kings of Pergamus, of the race of Attalus, on account of the ſervices this city did to that houſe.—*Pococke.*

It has been diſputed whether Archilochos, the celebrated
writer of iambics, was a native of this place, or of the iſland of
Paros. Horace ſays,

Parios ego primus iambos
Oſtendi Latio, numeros animoſque ſecutus
Archilochi. *T.*

[135] *Metrodorus the Proconneſian.*]—This perſonage muſt not be
confounded with the celebrated philoſopher of Chios, who aſſerted
the eternity of the world. The ancients make mention of the
old and new Proconneſus; the new Proconneſus is now called
Marmora, the old is the iſland of Alonia.—*T.*

[136] *Ariſton the Byzantian.*]—This is well known to be the
modern Conſtantinople, and has been too often and too correctly
deſcribed to require any thing from my pen. Its ſituation was
perhaps

4

Stratias of Chios, Æacides of Samos, Laodamas
the Phocean, and Hiſtiæus the Mileſian, whoſe
opinion prevailed in the aſſembly, in oppoſition to
that of Miltiades: the only Æolian of conſequence
who was preſent on this occaſion, was Ariſtagoras
of Cyme.

CXXXIX. Theſe leaders, acceding to the opinion of Hiſtiæus, thought it would be adviſeable to
break down that part of the bridge which was towards Scythia, to the extent of a bow-ſhot. This,
although it was of no real importance, would prevent the Scythians from paſſing the Iſter on the
bridge, and might induce them to believe that no
inclination was wanting on the part of the Ionians,
to comply with their wiſhes: accordingly, in the
name of the reſt, Hiſtiæus thus addreſſed them:
" Men of Scythia, we conſider your advice as of
" conſequence to our intereſt, and we take in good
" part your urging it upon us. You have ſhewn
" us the path which we ought to purſue, and we
" are readily diſpoſed to follow it; we ſhall break
" down the bridge as you recommend, and in all
" things ſhall diſcover the moſt earneſt zeal to ſe-

perhaps never better expreſſed, than in theſe two lines from
Ovid:

Quaque tenent ponti Byzantia littora fauces
Hic locus eſt gemini janua vaſta maris.

This city was originally founded by Byzas, a reputed ſon of
Neptune, 656 years before Chriſt. Perhaps the moſt minute
and ſatisfactory account of every thing relating to Byzantium,
may be found in Mr. Gibbon's hiſtory.—T.

" cure

" cure our liberties : in the mean time, whilft we
" fhall be thus employed, it becomes you to go in'
" purfuit of the enemy, and having found them,
" revenge yourfelves and us."

CXL. The Scythians, placing an entire confidence in the promlfes of the Ionians, returned to
the purfuit of the Perfians; they did not, however,
find them, for in that particular diftrict they themfelves had deftroyed all the fodder for the horfes, and
corrupted all the fprings, they might otherwife
eafily have found the Perfians: and thus it happened,
that the meafure which at firft promifed them fuccefs became ultimately injurious. They directed
their march to thofe parts of Scythia where they
were fecure of water and provifions for their horfes,
thinking themfelves certain of here meeting with
the enemy; but the Perfian prince, following the
track he had before purfued, found, though with
the greateft difficulty, the place he aimed at : arriving at the bridge by night, and finding it broken
down, he was exceedingly difheartened, and conceived himfelf abandoned by the Ionians.

CXLI. There was in the army of Darius an
Ægyptian very remarkable for the loudnefs of his
voice [137] : this man Darius ordered to advance to
the

---

[137] *Loudnefs of his voice.*]—By the ufe here made of this
Ægyptian, and the particular mention of Stentor in the Iliad, it
may be prefumed that it was a cuftomary thing for one or more
fuch perfonages to be prefent on every military expedition. At
the

the banks of the Ifter, and to pronounce with all his ftrength the name of "Hiftiæus the Milefian;" Hiftiæus immediately heard him, and approaching with all the fleet, enabled the Perfians to repafs, by again forming a bridge.

CXLII. By thefe means the Perfians efcaped, whilft the Scythians were a fecond time engaged in a long and fruitlefs purfuit. From this period the Scythians confidered the Ionians as the bafeft and moft contemptible of mankind, fpeaking of them as men attached to fervitude, and incapable of freedom; and always ufing towards them the moft reproachful terms.

the prefent day, perhaps, we may feel ourfelves inclined to dif-pute the utility, or ridicule the appearance of fuch a charaƈter; but before the invention of artillery, and when the firm but filent difcipline of the ancients, and of the Greeks in particular, is confidered, fuch men might occafionally exert their talents with no defpicable effeƈt.

> Heaven's emprefs mingles with the mortal crowd,
> And fhouts in Stentor's founding voice aloud;
> Stentor the ftrong, endued with brazen lungs,
> Whofe throat furpafs'd the force of fifty tongues.

The fhouting of Achilles from the Grecian battlements, is reprefented to have had the power of impreffing terror on the hearts of the boldeft warriors, and of fufpending a tumultuous and hard fought battle:

> Forth march'd the chief, and diftant from the crowd
> High on the rampart rais'd his voice aloud;
> With her own fhout Minerva fwells the found;
> Troy ftarts aftonifh'd, and the fhores rebound;
> So high his brazen voice the hero rear'd,
> Hofts drop their arms, and tremble as they heard.   T.

CXLIII.

CXLIII. Darius proceeding through Thrace, arrived at Seftos of the Cherfonefe, from whence he paffed over into Afia: he left, however, fome troops in Europe, under the command of Megabyzus [138], a Perfian, of whom it is reported, that one day in converfation the king fpoke in terms of the higheft honour.—He was about to eat fome pomegranates, and having opened one, he was afked by his brother Artabanus, what thing there was which he would defire to poffefs in as great a quantity as there were feeds in the pomegranate [139]? " I would " rather," he replied, " have fo many Megabyzi, " than fee Greece under my power." This compliment he paid him publicly, and at this time he left him at the head of eighty thoufand men.

CXLIV. This fame perfon alfo, for a faying which I fhall relate, left behind him in the Hellefpont a name never to be forgotten. Being at Byzantium, he learned upon enquiry that the Chalcedonians [140] had built their city feventeen years before

the

[138] *Megabyzus.*]—The text reads Megabazus, but Herodotus elfewhere fays Megabyzus, which is fupported by the beft manufcripts.—*T.*

[139] *Seeds in the pomegranate.*]—Plutarch relates this incident in his apophthegms of kings and illuftrious generals, but applies it to Zopyrus, who by mangling his nofe, and cutting off his ears, made himfelf mafter of Babylon.—*T.*

[140] *The Chalcedonians.*]—The promontory on which the ancient Chalcedon ftood, is a very fine fituation, being a gentle rifing ground from the fea, with which it is almoft bounded on three fides ; further on the eaft fide of it, is a fmall river which

the Byzantians had founded theirs : he obferved, that the Chalcedonians muft then have been blind, or otherwife, having the choice of a fituation in all refpects better, they would never have preferred one fo very inferior.—Megabyzus being thus left with the command of the Hellefpont, reduced all thofe who were in oppofition to the Medes [44].

CXLV. About the fame time another great expedition was fet on foot in Africa, the occafion of which I fhall relate; it will be firft neceffary to premife this—The pofterity of the Argonauts [44] having been expelled from Lemnos, by the Pelafgians, who had carried off from Brauron fome Athenian women, failed to Lacedæmon; they difembarked at Taygetus [44], where they made a great fire.

falls into the little bay to the fouth, that feems to have been their port; fo that Chalcedon would be efteemed a moft delightful fituation, if Conftantinople was not fo near it, which is indeed more advantageoufly fituated.—*Pococke.*

[44] *The Medes.*]—Herodotus, and the greater part of the ancient writers, almoft always comprehend the Perfians under the name of Medes. Claudian fays,

Remige Medo
Sollicitatus Athos. *Larcher.*

[44] *Pofterity of the Argonauts.*]—An account of this incident, with many variations and additions, is to be found in Plutarch's Treatife on the Virtues of Women.—*T.*

[44] *Taygetus.*]—This was a very celebrated mountain of antiquity; it was facred to Bacchus, for here, according to Virgil, the Spartan virgins acted the Bacchanal in his honour.

Virginibus

fire. The Lacedæmonians perceiving this, fent to enquire of them who and whence they were; they returned for anfwer that they were Minyæ, defcendants of thofe heroes who, paffing the ocean in the Argo, fettled in Lemnos, and there begot them. When the Lacedæmonians heard this account of their defcent, they fent a fecond meffenger, enquiring what was the meaning of the fire they had made, and what their intentions by coming among them. Their reply was to this effect, that being expelled by the Pelafgians, they had returned, as was reafonable, to the country of their anceftors, and were defirous to fix their refidence with them, as partakers of their lands and honours. The Lacedæmonians expreffed themfelves willing to receive them upon their own terms; and they were induced to this as well from other confiderations, as becaufe the Tyndaridæ [144] had failed in the Argo; they accordingly admitted the Minyæ among them, affigned them lands, and diftributed them among their tribes. The Minyæ in return parted with the women whom they had brought from Lemnos, and connected themfelves in marriage with others.

> Virginibus Bacchata Lacænis
> Taygeta.

Its dogs are alfo mentioned by Virgil, Taygetique canes; though perhaps this may poetically be ufed for Spartan dogs. —*T.*

[144] *Tyndaridæ.*]—Caftor and Pollux, fo called from Tyndarus, the hufband of their mother Leda.—*T.*

CXLVI. In a very fhort time thefe Minyæ became diftinguifhed for their intemperance, making themfelves not only dangerous from their ambition, but odious by their vices. The Lacedæmonians conceived their enormities worthy of death, and accordingly caft them into prifon : it is to be remarked, that this people always inflict capital punifhments by night, never by day. When things were in this fituation, the wives of the prifoners, who were natives of the country, and the daughters of the principal citizens, folicited permiffion to vifit their hufbands in confinement ; as no ftratagem was fufpected, this was granted. The wives of the Minyæ [145] accordingly entered the prifon, and exchanged dreffes with their hufbands : by this artifice they effected their efcape, and again took refuge on Taygetus.

CXLVII. It was about this time that Theras [146], the fon of Autefion, was fent from Lacedæmon to eftablifh a colony : Autefion was the fon of Tifamenus, grandfon of Therfander, great-grandfon of Polynices. This Theras was of the Cadmean family, uncle of Euryfthenes and Procles, the fons of Ariftodemus : during the minority of his

[145] *The wives of the Minyæ.*]—This ftory is related at fome length by Valerius Maximus, book iv. chap. 6, in which he treats of conjugal affection. The fame author tells us of Hipficratea, the beloved wife of Mithridates, who to gratify her hufband, affumed and conftantly wore the habit of a man.—*T.*

[146] *Theras.*]—This perfonage was the fixth defcendant from Œdipus.—*T.*

nephews

nephews the regency of Sparta was confided to him. When his fifters fons grew up, and he was obliged to refign his power, he was little inclined to acknowledge fuperiority where he had been accuftomed to exercife it; he therefore refufed to remain in Sparta, but determined to join his relations. In the ifland now called Thera, but formerly Callifta, the pofterity of Membliares, fon of Pœciles [147] the Phœnician, refided: to this place Cadmus, fon of Agenor, was driven, when in fearch of Europa; and either from partiality to the country, or from prejudice of one kind or other, he left there, among other Phœnicians, Membliares [148] his relation. Thefe men inhabited the ifland of Callifta eight years before Theras arrived from Lacedæmon.

CXLVIII. To this people Theras came, with a felect number from the different Spartan tribes: he

[147] *Pœciles.*]—M. Larcher makes no fcruple of tranflating this Procles; and in a very elaborate note attempts to eftablifh his opinion, that this muft be an abbreviation for Patroclus: but as, by the confeffion of this ingenious and learned Frenchman, the authorities of Herodotus, Paufanias, Apollodorus, and Porphyry, are againft the reading, even of Procles for Pœciles, it has too much the appearance of facrificing plain fenfe and probability at the fhrines of prejudice and fyftem, for me to adopt it without any thing like conviction.—*T.*

[148] *Membliares.*]—Paufanias differs from Herodotus in his account of the defcent of Membliares; he reprefents him as a man of very mean origin: to mark thefe little deviations, may not perhaps be of confequence to the generality of Englifh readers, but none furely will be difpleafed at being informed, where, if they think proper, they may compare what different authors have faid upon the fame fubject.—*T.*

X 3 had

had no hoſtile views, but a ſincere wiſh to dwell
with them on terms of amity.   The Minyæ having eſcaped from priſon, and taken refuge on mount
Taygetus, the Lacedæmonians were ſtill determined to put them to death ; Theras, however, inter-
ceeded in their behalf, and engaged to prevail on
them to quit their ſituation.   His propoſal was accepted, and accordingly, with three veſſels of thirty
oars, he ſailed to join the deſcendants of Membliares, taking with him only a ſmall number of the
Minyæ.   The far greater part of them had made
an attack upon the Paroreatæ, and the Caucons,
and expelled them from their country; dividing
themſelves afterwards into ſix bodies, they built the
ſame number of towns, namely, Lepreus, Magiſtus,
Thrixas, Pyrgus, Epius, and Nudius : of theſe, the
greater part have in my time been deſtroyed by the
Eleans.—The iſland before mentioned is called
Theras, from the name of its founder.

CXLIX. The ſon of Theras refuſing to ſail with
him, his father left him, as he himſelf obſerved, a
ſheep amongſt wolves; from which ſaying the young
man got the name of Oiolycus, which he ever afterwards retained.   Oiolycus had a ſon named
Ægeus, who gave his name to the Ægidæ, a conſiderable Spartan tribe, who finding themſelves in
danger of leaving no poſterity behind them, built,
by the direction of the oracle, a ſhrine to the Furies[149]

of

---

[149] *The Furies.*]—With a view to the information and amuſe-

ment

of Laius and Œdipus; this fucceeded to their
wifh. A circumftance fimilar to this happened
afterwards

ment of the Englifh reader, I fubjoin a few particulars concerning the Furies.

They were three in number, the daughters of Night and
Acheron: fome have added a fourth; their names Alecto, Ti-
fiphone, and Megæra; their refidence in the infernal regions;
their office to torment the wicked.

They were worfhipped at Athens, and firft of all by Oreftes,
when acquitted by the Areopagites of matricide. Æfchylus
was the firft perfon who reprefented them as having fnakes inftead of hair. Their name in heaven was Diræ, from the Greek
word Δυραι, tranfpofing ρ for ν: on earth they were called
Furiæ and Eumenides; their name in the regions below was
Stygiæ Canes. The ancient authors, both Greek and Latin,
abound with paffages defcriptive of their attributes and influence: the following animated apoftrophe to them, is from
Æfchylus—Mr. Potter's verfion.

> See this griefly troop,
> Sleep has opprefs'd them, and their baffled rage
> Shall fail.—Grim-vifag'd hags, grown old
> In loath'd virginity: nor god nor man
> Approach'd their bed, nor favage of the wilds;
> For they were born for mifchiefs, and their haunts
> In dreary darknefs, 'midft the yawning gulphs
> Of Tartarus beneath, by men abhorr'd,
> And by the Olympian gods.

After giving the above quotation from Æfchylus, it may not
be unneceffary to add, that the three whom I have fpecified
by name, were only the three principal, or fupreme of many
furies. Here the furies of Laius and Œdipus are mentioned,
becaufe particular furies were, as it feems, fuppofed ready to
avenge the murder of every individual;

> Thee may th' Erinnys of thy fons deftroy.
> > *Eurip. Medea. Potter,* 1523.

X 4   Or

afterwards in the island of Thera, to the defcendants of this tribe.

CL. Thus far the accounts of the Lacedæmonians and Thereans agree; what follows, is related
on the authority of the latter only:—Grinus, fon of
Æfanius, and defcended from the above Theras,
was prince of the ifland; he went to Delphi, carrying with him an hecatomb for facrifice, and accompanied, amongft other of his citizens, by Battus the fon of Polymneftus, of the family of Euthy-
mus a Minyan; Grinus, confulting the oracle about
fomewhat of a different nature, was commanded by
the Pythian to build a city in Africa. " I," replied
the prince " am too old and too infirm for fuch an
" undertaking; fuffer it to devolve on fome of
" thefe younger perfons who accompany me;" at
the fame time he pointed to Battus. On their return they paid no regard to the injunction of the
oracle, being both ignorant of the fituation of
Africa, and not caring to fend from them a colony
on fo precarious an adventure.

Or the manes themfelves became furies for that purpofe:

> Their fhades fhall pour their vengeance on thy head.
>
> *Ib.* 1503.

Oreftes in his madnefs calls Electra one of his furies; that is,
one of thofe which attended to torment him:

> Off, let me go: I know thee who thou art,
> One of *my* furies, and thou grappleft with me,
> To whirl me into Tartarus.—Avaunt !
>
> *Oreftes,* 270.

It ftands at prefent in the verfion *the* furies, which is wrong.

CLI.

CLI. For feven years after the above event it never rained in Thera; in confequence of which every tree in the place perifhed, except one. The inhabitants confulted the oracle, when the fending a colony to Africa was again recommended by the Pythian: as therefore no alternative remained, they fent fome emiffaries into Crete, to enquire whether any of the natives or ftrangers refiding amongft them had ever vifited Africa. The perfons employed on this occafion, after going over the whole ifland, came at length to the city Itanus [150], where they became acquainted with a certain dyer of purple, whofe name was Corobius; this man informed them, that he was once driven by contrary winds into Africa, and had landed there, on the ifland of Platea: they therefore bargained with him for a certain fum, to accompany them to Thera. Very few were induced to leave Thera upon this bufi- nefs; they who did go were conducted by Coro- bius, who was left upon the ifland he had defcrib- ed, with provifions for fome months; the reft of the party made their way back by fea as expedi- tioufly as poffible, to acquaint the Thereans with the event.

CLII. By their omitting to return at the time appointed, Corobius was reduced to the greateft

[150] *Itanus.*]—Some of the dictionaries inform, that this place is now called Paleo-Caftro; but Savary, in his Letters on Greece, remarks, that the modern Greeks give this name to all ancient places.—*T.*

diftrefs;

diftrefs ; it happened, however, that a Samian veffel, whofe commander's name was Colæus, was, in
its courfe towards Ægypt, driven upon the ifland of
Platea ; thefe Samians, hearing the ftory of Corobius, left him provifions for a twelvemonth. On
leaving this ifland, with a wifh to go to Ægypt, the
winds compelled them to take their courfe weftward, and continuing without intermiffion, carried
them beyond the columns of Hercules, till, as it
fhould feem by fomewhat more than human interpofition, they arrived at Tarteffus [51]. As this was
a port then but little known, their voyage ultimately proved very advantageous; fo that, excepting
Softrates, with whom there can be no competition,
no Greeks were ever before fo fortunate in any
commercial undertaking. With fix talents, which
was a tenth part of what they gained, the Samians
made a brazen vafe, in the fhape of an Argolic
goblet, round the brim of which the heads of
griffins [52] were regularly difpofed : this was depofited

---

[51] *Tarteffus.*]—This place is called by Ptolemy, Cateia, and
is feen in d'Anville's maps under that name, at the entrance of
the Mediterranean : mention is made in Ovid of Tarteffia littora.—*T*.

[52] *Griffins.*]—In a former note upon this word I neglected
to inform the reader, that in Sir Thomas Brown's Vulgar
Errors there is a chapter upon the fubject of grifins, very
curious and entertaining, p. 142. This author fatisfactorily
explains the Greek word Γρυψ or Gryps, to mean no more than
a particular kind of eagle or vulture : being compounded of a
lion and an eagle, it is a happy emblem of valour and magnani-
mity, and therefore applicable to princes, generals, &c. and
from

fited in the temple of Juno, where it is fupported by three coloffal figures, feven cubits high, refting on their knees. . This was the firft occafion of the particular intimacy, which afterwards fubfifted between the Samians and the people of Cyrene and Thera.

CLIII. The Thereans having left Corobius behind, returned and informed their countrymen that they had made a fettlement in an ifland belonging to Africa: they, in confequence, determined, that from each of their feven cities a felect number fhould be fent, and that if thefe happened to be brothers, it fhould be determined by lot who fhould go; and that finally, Battus fhould be their prince and leader: they fent accordingly to Platea two fhips of fifty oars.

CLIV. With this account, as given by the Thereans, the Cyreneans agree, except in what relates to Battus; here they differ exceedingly, and tell, in contradiction, the following hiftory:—There is a town in Crete, named Oaxus, where Etearchus was once king; having loft his wife, by whom he had a daughter, called Phronima, he married a fecond time: no fooner did his laft wife take poffeffion of his houfe, than fhe proved herfelf to Phronima a ftep-mother indeed. Not content with injuring her by every fpecies of cruelty and ill-treat-

from this it is borne in the coat of arms of many noble families in Europe.—T.

ment,

ment, fhe at length upbraided her with being un-
chafte, and perfuaded her hufband to believe fo.
Deluded by the artifice of his wife, he perpetrated
the following act of barbarity againft his daughter:
there was at Oaxus a merchant of Thera, whofe
name was Themifon; of him, after fhewing him
the ufual rites of hofpitality, he exacted an oath that
he would comply with whatever he fhould require;
having done this, he delivered him his daughter,
ordering him to throw her into the fea.　Themifon
reflected with unfeigned forrow on the artifice
which had been practifed upon him, and the obligation impofed; he determined, however, what to
do: he took the damfel, and having failed to fome
diftance from land, to fulfil his oath, fecured a rope
about her, and plunged her into the fea; but he
immediately took her out again, and carried her to
Thera.

CLV. Here Polymneftus, a Therean of fome
importance, took Phronima to be his concubine,
and after a certain time had by her a fon, remarkable for his fhrill and ftammering voice: his name,
as the Thereans and Cyreneans affert, was Battus [153], but I think it was fomething elfe.　He was
not,

---

[153] *Battus.*]—Battus, according to Hefychius, alfo fignifies, in
the Lybian tongue, a king: from this perfon, and his defect of
pronunciation, comes, according to Suidas, the word Βατταϱιζειν,
to ftammer. There was alfo an ancient foolifh poet of this name,
from whom, according to the fame authority, Βαττολογια fignified an unmeaning redundance of expreffion. Neither muft the
Battus

not, I think, called Battus till after his arrival in
Africa; he was then so named, either on account of
the answer of the oracle, or from the subsequent dignity which he attained. Battus, in the African
tongue, signifies a prince; and I should think that
the Pythian, foreseeing he was to reign in Africa,
distinguished him by this African title. As soon as
he grew up he went to Delphi, to consult the oracle
concerning the imperfection of his voice: the answer he received was this:

Hence, Battus! of your voice enquire no more;
But found a city on the Lybian shore.

This is the same as if she had said in Greek,
" Enquire no more, Oh king, concerning your
" voice." To this Battus replied, " Oh king,
" I came to you on account of my infirmity
" of tongue; you, in return, impose upon me
" an undertaking which is impossible; for how
" can I, who have neither forces nor money, estab-
" lish a colony in Africa?" He could not, however, obtain any other answer, which, when he
found to be the case, he returned to Thera.

CLVI. Not long afterwards he, with the rest of the
Thereans, were visited by many and great calamities;
and not knowing to what cause they should impute
them, they sent to Delphi, to consult the oracle on

Battus here mentioned be confounded with the Battus whom
Mercury turned into an index, and whose story is so well told by
Ovid.—*T.*

the fubject. The Pythian informed them, that if they would colonize Cyrene in Africa, under the conduct of Battus, things would certainly go better with them; they accordingly difpatched Battus to accomplifh this, with two fifty-oared veffels. Thefe men acting from compulfion, fet fail for Africa, but foon returned to Thera; but the Thereans forcibly preventing their landing, ordered them to return from whence they came. Thus circumftanced, they again fet fail, and founded a city in an ifland contiguous to Africa, called, as we have before re-marked, Platea [154]; this city is faid to be equal in fize to that in which the Cyreneans now refide.

CLVII. They continued in this place for the fpace of two years, but finding their ill fortune ftill purfue them, they again failed to Delphi to enquire of the oracle, leaving only one of their party behind them: when they defired to know why, having eftablifhed themfelves in Africa, they had experi-enced no favourable reverfe of fortune, the Pythian made them this anfwer:—

Know'ft thou then Lybia better than the God,
Whofe fertile fhores thy feet have never trod?
He who has well explor'd them thus replies;
I can but wonder at a man fo wife!

[154] *Platea.*]—This name is written alfo *Platæa*: Stephanus Byzantinus has it both in that form, and alfo *Platæa* or *Plattia*. Pliny fpeaks of three *Plateas*, and a *Plate*, off the coaft of Troas; but they muft have been very inconfiderable fpots, and have not been mentioned by any other author. The beft editions of Herodotus read *Platæa* here; but I fufpect *Plattia* to be right, for Scylax has it fo as well as Stephanus.— The place of the ce-lebrated battle in Bœotia was Platææ.

On

On hearing this, Battus, and they who were with him, again returned; for the deity still persevered in requiring them to form a settlement in Africa, where they had not yet been: touching, therefore, at Platea, they took on board him whom they had left, and established their colony in Africa itself. The place they selected was Aziris, immediately opposite to where they had before resided; two sides of which were enclosed by a beautiful range of hills, and a third agreeably watered by a river.

CLVIII. At this place they continued six years; when at the desire of the Africans, who promised to conduct them to a better situation, they removed. The Africans accordingly became their guides, and had so concerted the matter, as to take care that the Greeks should pass through the most beautiful part of their country by night: the direction they took was westward, the name of the country they were not permitted to see was Trasa.—They came at length to what is called the fountain of Apollo [155] :—" Men of Greece," said the Africans, " the " heavens are here opened to you, and here it will " be proper for you to reside."

CLIX. During the life of Battus, who reigned forty years, and under Arcesilaus his son,

[155] *Fountain of Apollo.*]—The name of this fountain was Cyre, from which the town of Cyrène had afterwards its name. Herodotus calls it, in the subsequent paragraph, Theftis, but there were probably many fountains in this place.—*Larcher.*

who reigned fixteen, the Cyreneans remained
in this colony without any alteration with refpect to their numbers: but under their third
prince, who was alfo called Battus, and who
was furnamed the Happy, the Pythian, by her
declarations, excited a general propenfity in the
Greeks to migrate to Africa, and join themfelves to the Cyreneans. The Cyreneans, indeed,
had invited them to a fhare of their poffeffions,
but the oracle had alfo thus expreffed itfelf:

Who feeks not Libya 'till the lands are fhar'd,
Let him for fad repentance ftand prepar'd.

The Greeks, therefore, in great numbers, fettled
themfelves at Cyrene. The neighbouring Africans,
with their king Adicran, feeing themfelves injuriouf-
ly deprived of a confiderable part of their lands,
and expofed to much infulting treatment, made
a tender of themfelves and their country to
Apries, fovereign of Ægypt: this prince affembled a numerous army of Ægyptians, and
fent them to attack Cyrene. The Cyreneans
drew themfelves up at Irafa, near the fountain
Theftis, and in a fixed battle routed the Ægyptians, who till now, from their ignorance, had
defpifed the Grecian power. The battle was fo
decifive, that very few of the Ægyptians returned
to their country; they were on this account fo
exafperated againft Apries, that they revolted
from his authority.

CLX. Arcefilaus, the fon of this Battus, fucceeded

ed to the throne; he was at firft engaged in fome
conteft with his brothers, but they removed themfelves from him to another part of Africa, where,
after fome deliberation, they founded a city. They
called it Barce, which name it ftill retains. Whilft
they were employed upon this bufinefs, they endeavoured to excite the Africans againft the Cyreneans. Arcefilaus without hefitation commenced
hoftilities both againft thofe who had revolted from
him, and againft the Africans who had received
them; intimidated by which, thefe latter fled to
their countrymen, who were fituated more to the
eaft: Arcefilaus perfevered in purfuing them till
he arrived at Leuçon, and here the Africans difcovered an inclination to try the event of a battle.
They accordingly engaged, and the Cyreneans were
fo effectually routed, that feven thoufand of their
men in arms fell in the field. Arcefilaus, after this
calamity, fell fick, and was ftrangled by his brother
Aliarchus, whilft in the act of taking fome medicine. The wife of Arcefilaus, whofe name was
Eryxo [156], revenged by fome ftratagem on his murderer the death of her hufband.

CLXI. Arcefilaus was fucceeded in his authority by his fon Battus, a boy who was lame, and
had otherwife an infirmity in his feet. The Cy-

[156] *Eryxo.*]—The ftory is related at confiderable length by
Plutarch, in his treatife on the virtues of women. Inftead of
Aliarchus, he reads Learchus; the woman he calls Eryxene;
and the murderer he fuppofes to have been not the brother, but
the friend of Arcefilaus.—*T.*

reneans, afflicted by their recent calamities, sent to Delphi, desiring to know what syftem of life would most effectually secure their tranquillity. The Pythian in reply recommended them to procure from Mantinea [157], in Arcadia, some one to compose their disturbances. Accordingly, at the request of the Cyreneans, the Mantineans sent them Demonax, a man who enjoyed the universal esteem of his countrymen. Arriving at Cyrene, his first care was to make himself acquainted with their affairs; he then divided the people into three distinct tribes: the first comprehended the Thereans and their neighbours; the second the Peloponnesians and Cretans; the third all the inhabitants of the islands. He assigned a certain portion of land, with some distinct privileges, to Battus; but all the other advantages which the kings had before arrogated to themselves, he gave to the power of the people.

CLXII. In this situation things remained during the life of Battus: but in the time of his son an ambitious struggle for power was the occasion of great disturbances. Arcesilaus, son of the lame Battus, by Pheretime, refused to submit to the regulations of Demonax the Mantinean, and demanded to be restored to the dignity of his ancestors. A great tumult was excited, but the consequence was, that Arcesilaus was compelled to take refuge at Samos, whilst his mother Pheretime fled to Salamis

---

[157] *Mantinea.*]—This place became celebrated by the death of Epaminondas, the great Theban general, who was here slain. —*T.*

in Cyprus. Euelthon had at this time the government of Salamis: the fame perfon who' dedicated at Delphi a moft beautiful cenfer now depofited in the Corinthian treafury. To him Pheretime made application, intreating him to lead an army againft Cyrene, for the purpofe of reftoring her and her fon. He made her many prefents, but refufed to affift her with an army. Pheretime accepted his liberality with thanks, but endeavoured to convince him that his affifting her with forces would. be much more honourable. Upon her perfevering in this requeft, after every prefent fhe received, Euelthon was at length induced to fend her a gold fpindle, and a diftaff with wool; obferving, that for a woman this was a more fuitable prefent than an army.

CLXIII. In the mean time Arcefilaus was indefatigable at Samos; by promifing a divifion of lands, he affembled a numerous army: he then failed to Delphi, to make enquiry concerning the event of his return. The Pythian made him this anfwer: " To four Batti [158], and to as many of " the name of Arcefilaus, Apollo has granted the " dominion of Cyrene. Beyond thefe eight gene- " rations the deity forbids even the attempt. to

[158] *To four Batti.*]—According to the Scholiaft on Pindar, the Battiades reigned at Cyrene for the fpace of two hundred years. Battus, fon of the laft of thefe, endeavoured to affume the government, but the Cyreneans drove him from their country, and he retired to the Hefperides, where he finifhed his days.—*Larcher.*

" reign;

" reign: to you it is recommended to return, and
" live tranquilly at home. If you happen to find
" a furnace filled with earthen veffels, do not fuffer
" them to be baked, but throw them into the air:
" if you fet fire to the furnace, beware of entering
" a place furrounded by water. This injunction,
" if you difregard, you will perifh yourfelf, as will
" alfo a very beautiful bull."

CLXIV. The Pythian made this reply to Arcefilaus: he however returned to Cyrene with the
forces he had raifed at Samos; and having recovered
his authority, thought no more of the oracle. He
proceeded to inftitute a perfecution againft thofe
who taking up arms againft him had compelled
him to fly. Some of thefe fought and found a refuge in exile, others were taken into cuftody and
fent to Cyprus, to undergo the punifhment of death.
Thefe the Cnidians delivered, for they touched at
their ifland in their paffage, and they were afterwards tranfported to Thera: a number of them
fled to a large tower, the property of an individual
named Aglomachus, but Arcefilaus deftroyed them,
tower and all, by fire. No fooner had he perpetrated this deed than he remembered the declaration of the oracle, which forbade him to fet fire to
a furnace filled with earthen veffels: fearing therefore to fuffer for what he had done, he retired from
Cyrene, which place he confidered as furrounded
by water. He had married a relation, the daughter
of Alazir, king of Barce, to him therefore he went;
but upon his appearing in public, the Barceans, in
conjunction

conjunction with fome Cyrenean fugitives, put him
to death, together with Alazir his father-in-law.
Such was the fate of Arcefilaus, he having, de-
fignedly or from accident, violated the injunctions of
the oracle.

CLXV. Whilft the fon was thus haftening his
deftiny at Barce, Plieretime [159] his mother enjoyed
at Cyrene the fupreme authority; and amongft
other regal acts prefided in the fenate. But as foon
as fhe received intelligence of the death of Arcefilaus, fhe fought refuge in Ægypt. Her fon had
fome claims upon the liberality of Cambyfes, fon
of Cyrus; he had delivered Cyrene into his power,
and paid him tribute. On her arrival in Ægypt,
fhe prefented herfelf before Aryandes in the character of a fuppliant, and befought him to revenge
her caufe, pretending that her fon had loft his life
merely on account of his attachment to the
Medes.

CLXVI. This Aryandes had been appointed
præfect of Ægypt by Cambyfes; but afterwards,
prefuming to rival Darius, he was by him put to
death. He had heard, and indeed he had feen, that
Darius was defirous to leave fome monument of
himfelf, which fhould exceed all the efforts of his
predeceffors. He thought proper to attempt fomewhat fimilar, but it coft him his life. Darius had

[159] *Pheretime.*]—See this ftory well related in the Stratagemata of Polyænus, book viii. c. 47.—*T.*

iffued

iffued a coin [160] of the very pureft gold : the præfect of Ægypt iffued one of the pureft filver, and
called it an Aryandic. It may ftill be feen, and is
much admired for its purity. Darius hearing of
this, condemned him to death, pretending that he
had rebelled againft him.

[160] *Darius had iffued a coin.*]—" About the fame time feem
to have been coined thofe famous pieces of gold called Darics,
which by reafon of their finenefs were for feveral ages preferred before all other coin throughout the eaft: for we are told
that the author of this coin was not Darius Hyftafpes, as fome
have imagined, but a more ancient Darius. But there is no
ancienter Darius mentioned to have reigned in the eaft, excepting only this Darius, whom the fcripture calls Darius the
Median; and therefore it is moft likely he was the author of
this coin, and that during the two years that he reigned at Babylon, while Cyrus was abfent on his Syrian, Ægyptian, and
other expeditions, he caufed it to be made there out of the vaft
quantity of gold which had been brought thither into the treafury; from hence it became difperfed all over the eaft, and alfo
into Greece, where it was of great reputation: according to
Dr. Bernard, it weighed two grains more than one of our
guineas, but the finenefs added much more to its value ; for it
was in a manner all of pure gold, having none, or at leaft very
little, alloy in it ; and therefore may be well reckoned, as the proportion of gold and filver now ftands with us, to be worth twenty-
five fhillings of our money. In thofe parts of the fcripture
which were written after the Babylonifh captivity, thefe pieces
are mentioned by the name of Adarkonim ; and in the Tal-
mudifts, by the name of Darkoneth, both from the Greek Δαρ-
κοι, Darics. And it is to be obferved, that all thofe pieces
of gold which were afterwards coined of the fame weight and
value by the fucceeding kings, not only of the Perfian but alfo
of the Macedonian race, were all called Darics, from the
Darius who was the firft author of them. And there were either
whole Darics or half Darics, as with us there are guineas and
half-guineas."—*Prideaux.*

CLXVII,

CLXVII. At this time Aryandes, taking compassion on Pheretime, delivered to her command all the land and sea forces of Ægypt. To Amasis, a Maraphian, he entrusted the conduct of the army; and Badre, a Pasargadian [161] by birth, had the direction of the fleet. Before however they proceeded on any expedition, a herald was dispatched to Barce, demanding the name of the person who had assassinated Arcesilaus. The Barceans replied, that they were equally concerned, for he had repeatedly injured them all. Having received this answer, Aryandes permitted his forces to proceed with Pheretime.

CLXVIII. This was the pretence with Aryandes for commencing hostilities; but I am rather inclined to think that he had the subjection of the Africans in view. The nations of Africa are many and various; few of them had ever submitted to Darius, and most of them held him in contempt. Beginning from Ægypt, the Africans are to be enumerated in the order following.—The first are the Adyrmachidæ, whose manners are in every respect Ægyptian; their dress African. On each leg their wives wear a ring of brass. They suffer their hair to grow; if they catch any fleas upon their bodies, they first bite and then throw them away. They are the only people of Africa who do this.

---

[161] *Pasargadian.*]—There was a city in Persia called Pasargada, which doubtless gave its name to the nation of Pasargades. The place is now, in the Arabian tongue, called Databegend.—T.

It

It is also peculiar to them to present their daughters to the king just before their marriage [161], who may enjoy the persons of such as are agreeable to him. The Adyrmachidæ occupy the country between Ægypt and the port of Pleunos.

CLXIX. Next to these are the Giligammæ, who dwell towards the west as far as the island of Aphrodisias. In the midst of this region is the island of Platea, which the Cyreneans built. The harbour of Menelaus and Aziris, possessed also by the Cyreneans, is upon the continent. Silphium [162] begins

---

[161] *Before their marriage.*]—A play of Beaumont and Fletcher is founded upon the idea of this obscene and unnatural custom. The following note is by Mr. Theobald upon the "Custom of the Country." *Beaumont and Fletch.* 1778.

The custom on which a main part of the plot of this comedy is built, prevailed at one time, as Bayle tells us, in Italy, till it was put down by a prudent and truly pious cardinal. It is likewise generally imagined to have obtained in Scotland for a long time; and the received opinion hath hitherto been, that Eugenius, the third king of Scotland, who began his reign A. D. 535, ordained that the lord or master should have the first night's lodging with every woman married to his tenant or bondsman. This obscene ordinance is supposed to have been abrogated by Malcolm the third, who began his reign A. D. 1061, about five years before the Norman Conquest, having lasted in force somewhat above five hundred years.—See Blount in his Law Dictionary, under the word Mercheta. Another commentator remarks, that Sir David Dalrymple denies the existence of this custom in Scotland.—Judge Blackstone is of opinion that this custom never prevailed in England, but that it certainly did in Scotland.

[162] *Silphium.*]—Either M. Larcher or myself must be grossly mistaken in the interpretation of this passage. "The plant Silphium,"

begins where thefe terminate, and is continued from
Platea to the mouth of the Syrtes [164]. The manners

Silphium," fays his verfion, " begins in this place to be found,
and is continued," &c. This in my opinion neither agrees with
the context, nor is in itfelf at all probable. In various authors
mention is made of the Silphii, and reference is made by them
to this particular paffage of Herodotus.—T.

[164] *Syrtes.*]—The Great Syrtes muft be here meant, which is
in the neighbourhood of Barce, and nearer Ægypt than the
Small Syrtes.—*Larcher.*

There were the Greater and the Leffer Syrtes, and both
deemed very formidable to navigators. Their nature has never
been better defcribed than in the following lines from Lucan,
which I give the reader in Rowe's verfion.

> When nature's hand the firft formation try'd,
> When feas from lands fhe did at firft divide,
> The Syrts, not quite of fea nor land bereft,
> A mingled mafs uncertain ftill fhe left;
> For nor the land with fea is quite o'erfpread,
> Nor fink the waters deep their oozy bed,
> Nor earth defends its fhore, nor lifts aloft its head;
> The fcite with neither, and with each complies,
> Doubtful and inacceffible it lies;
> Or 'tis a fea with fhallows bank'd around,
> Or 'tis a broken land with waters drown'd:
> Here fhores advanc'd o'er Neptune's rule we find,
> And there an inland ocean lags behind;
> Thus nature's purpofe, by herfelf deftroy'd,
> Is ufelefs to herfelf, and unemploy'd,
> And part of her creation ftill is void.
> Perhaps, when firft the world and time began,
> Her fwelling tides and plenteous waters ran;
> But long confining on the burning zone,
> The finking feas have felt the neighbouring fun;
> Still by degrees we fee how they decay,
> And fcarce refift the thirfty god of day.

Perhaps,

ners of thefe people nearly refemble, thofe of their neighbours.

CLXX. From the weft, and immediately next to the Giligammæ, are the Afbyftæ. They are above Cyrene, but have no communication with the fea coafts, which are occupied by the Cyreneans: They are beyond all the Africans remarkable for their ufe of chariots drawn by four horfes; and in moft refpects they imitate the manners of the Cyreneans.

CLXXI. On the weftern borders of this people dwell the Aufchifæ; their diftrict commences above Barce, and is continued to the fea, near the Euefperides. The Cabales, an inconfiderable nation, inhabit towards the centre of the Aufchifæ, and extend themfelves to the fea coaft near Tauchira, a town belonging to Barce. The Cabales have the fame cuftoms as the people beyond Cyrene.

CLXXII. The powerful nation of the Nafamones border on the Aufchifæ towards the weft. This people during the fummer feafon leave their cattle on the fea coaft, and go up the country to a place called Augila to gather dates. Upon this

> Perhaps, in diftant ages 'twill be found,
> When future funs have run the burning round,
> Thefe Syrts fhall all be dry and folid ground:
> Small are the depths their fcanty waves retain,
> And earth grows daily on the yielding main.

fpot

fpot the palms are equally numerous, large, and fruitful: they alfo hunt for locufts [165], which having dried in the fun, they reduce them to a powder, and eat mixed with milk. Each perfon is allowed to have feveral wives, with whom they cohabit in the manner of the Maffagetæ, firft fixing a ftaff in the earth before their tent. When the Nafamones marry, the bride on the firft night permits every one of the guefts to enjoy her perfon, each of whom makes her a prefent brought with him for the pur-pofe. Their mode of divination and of taking an oath is this: they place their hands on the tombs [166] of thofe who have been moft eminent for their integrity and virtue, and fwear by their names,

[165] *Locufts.*]—The circumftance of locufts being dried and kept for provifion, I have before mentioned: the following appofite paffage having fince occurred to me from Niebuhr, I think proper to infert it.

On vendit dans tous les marchés des fauterelles à vil prix: car elles etoient fi prodigieufement repandues dans la plaine près de Jerim, qu'on pouvoit les prendres à pleines mains. Nous vimes un payfan qui en avoit rempli un fac, et qui alloit les fecher pour fa provifion d'hyver.

[166] *On the tombs.*]—The following fingular remark from Niebuhr feems particularly applicable in this place.

Un marchand de la Mecque me fit fur fes faints une réflec-tion, qui me furprit dans la bouche d'un Mahométan. " Il faut 'toujours à la populace," me dit-il, " un objet vifible qu'elle puiffe honorer et craindre. C'eft ainfi qu'à la Mecque tous les fermens fe font au nom de Mahomet, au lieu qu'on devroit s'adreffer à Dieu. A Molcha je ne me fierois pas à un homme qui affirmeroit une chofe en prenant Dieu à té-moin; mais je pourrois compter plutôt fur la foi de celui qui jüreroit par le nom de Schaedeli, dont la mofquée et le tom-beau font fous fes yeux."

When.

When they exercise divination, they approach the monuments of their ancestors, and there, having said their prayers, compose themselves to sleep. They regulate their subsequent conduct by such visions as they may then have. When they pledge their word, they drink alternately from each other's hands [167]. If no liquid is near, they take some dust from the ground, and lick it with their tongue.

CLXXIII. Next to the Nasamones are the Psylli [168], who formerly perished by the following accident:

[167] *Each other's hands.*]—The ancient ceremony of the Nasamenes to drink from each other's hands, in pledging their faith, is at the present period the only ceremony observed in the marriages of the Algerines.—*Shaw.*

[168] *The Psylli.*]—A measure like this would have been preposterous in the extreme. Herodotus therefore does not credit it: " I only relate," says he, " what the Africans inform me," which are the terms always used by our historian when he communicates any dubious matter. It seems very probable that the Nasamones destroyed the Psylli to possess their country, and that they circulated this fable amongst their neighbours.—See *Pliny,* book vii. chapter 2.—*Larcher.*

Herodotus makes no mention of the quality which these people possessed, and which in subsequent times rendered them so celebrated, that of managing serpents with such wonderful dexterity.—See Lucan, book ix. Rowe's version, line 1523.

Of all who scorching Afric's sun endure,
None like the swarthy Psyllians are secure.
Skill'd in the lore of powerful herbs and charms,
'Them, nor the serpent's tooth nor poison harms;
Nor do they thus in arts alone excel,
But nature too their blood has temper'd well,
And taught with vital force the venom to repel.

§

With

accident: A fouth wind had dried up all their re-
fervoirs, and the whole country, as far as the Syrtes,
was deftitute of water. They refolved accordingly,
after a public confultation, to make a hoftile expedition againft this fouth wind; the confequence
was (I only relate what the Africans inform me)
that on their arrival in the deferts, the fouth wind
overwhelmed them beneath the fands. The Pfylli
being thus deftroyed, the Nafamones took poffeffion
of their lands.

CLXXIV. Beyond thefe fouthward, in a country
infefted by favage beafts, dwell the Garamantes [169],
who avoid every kind of communication with

> With healing gifts and privileges grac'd,
> Well in the land of ferpents were they plac'd
> Truce with the dreadful tyrant, Death, they have,
> And border fafely on his realm, the grave.

See alfo Savary, vol. i. p. 63.

" You are acquainted with the Pfylli, thofe celebrated fer-
pent-eaters of antiquity, who fported with the bite of vipers, and
the credulity of the people. Many of them inhabited Cyrene,
a city weft of Alexandria, and formerly dependent on Ægypt.
You know the pitiful vanity of Octavius, who wifhed the captive Cleopatra fhould grace his triumphal car; and, chagrined
to fee that proud woman efcape by death, commanded one of
the Pfylli to fuck the wound the afpic had made. Fruitlefs
were his efforts; the poifon had perverted the whole mafs of
blood, nor could the art of the Pfylli reftore her to life."

[169] *Garamantes.*]—Thefe people are faid to have been fo
named from Garamas, a fon of Apollo.—See Virgil, vi. 794.

> Supra Garamantas et Indos
> Proferet inferium.   T.

men,

men, are ignorant of the ufe of all military weapons, and totally unable to defend themfelves.

CLXXV. Thefe people live beyond the Nafamones; but towards the fea coaft weftward are the
Macæ [170]. It is the cuftom of this people to leave
a tuft of hair in the centre of the head, carefully
fhaving the reft. When they make war, their only
coverings are the fkins of oftriches. The river
Cinyps rifes amongft thefe in a hill faid to be facred
to the Graces, whence it continues its courfe to the
fea. This hill of the Graces is well covered with
trees; whereas the reft of Africa, as I have before
obferved, is very barren of wood. The diftance
from this hill to the fea is two hundred ftadia.

CLXXVI. The Gindanes are next to the Macæ.
Of the wives of this people it is faid that they
wear round their ancles as many bandages as they
have known men. The more of thefe each poffeffes, the more fhe is efteemed, as having been
beloved by the greater number of the other fex.

CLXXVII. The neck of land which ftretches
from the country of the Gindanes towards the fea,
is poffeffed by the Lotophagi, who live entirely
upon the fruit of the lotos. The lotos is of the

---

[170] *Macæ.*]—Thefe people are thus mentioned by Silius
Italicus:

> Tum primum caftris Phœnicum tendere ritu
> Cinyphiis didicere Macæ, fquallentia barbâ
> Ora viris, humerofque tegunt velamina capri.   *T.*

fize

fize of the maftick, and fweet like the date; and the Lotophagi make of it a kind of wine.

CLXXVIII. Towards the fea, the Machlyes border on the Lotophagi. They alfo feed on the lotos, though not fo entirely as their neighbours. They extend as far as a great ftream called the Triton, which enters into an extenfive lake named Tritonis, in which is the ifland of Phla. An oracular declaration, they fay, had foretold that fome Lacedæmonians fhould fettle themfelves here.

CLXXIX. The particulars are thefe: when Jafon had conftructed the Argo at the foot of Mount Pelion, he carried on board a hecatomb for facrifice, with a brazen tripod: he failed round the Peleponnefe, with the intention to vifit Delphi. As he approached Malea, a north wind drove him to the African coaft[171]; and before he could difcover land, he got amongft the fhallows of the lake of Tritonis: not being able to extricate himfelf from this fituation, a Triton[172] is faid to have appeared to him,

[171] *To the African coaft.*]—" Some references to the Argonautic expedition," fays Mr. Bryant, " are interfperfed in moft of the writings of the ancients; but there is fcarce a circumftance concerning it in which they are agreed. In refpect to the firft fetting out of the Argo, moft make it pafs northward to Lemnos and the Hellefpont; but Herodotus fays that Jafon firft failed towards Delphi, and was carried to the Syrtic fea of Lybia, and then purfued his voyage to the Euxine. Neither can the æra of the expedition be fettled without running into many difficulties.—See the *Analyfis*, vol. ii. 491.

[172] *A Triton.*]—From various paffages in the works of Lucian,

him, and to have promised him a secure and easy
passage, provided he would give him the tripod.
To this Jason assented, and the Triton having fulfilled his engagement, he placed the tripod in his
temple, from whence he communicated to Jason
and his companions what was afterwards to happen. Amongst other things, he said, that whenever a descendant of these Argonauts should take
away this tripod, there would be infallibly an hundred Grecian cities near the lake of Tritonis [173]. The

cian, Pliny, and other authors of equal authority, it should seem
that the ancients had a firm belief of the existence of Tritons,
Nereids, &c. The god Triton was a distinct personage, and
reputed to be the son of Neptune and the nymph Salacia; he
was probably considered as supreme of the Tritons, and seems
always to have been employed by Neptune for the purpose of
calming the ocean.

> Mulcet aquas rector Pelagi, supraque profundum
> Exstantem atque humeros innato murice tectum
> Cæruleum Tritona vocat, cunctæque sonaci
> Inspirare jubet fluctusque et flumina signo
> Jam revocare dato, &c.—*Metamorph.* l. 334.   *T.*

[173] *Lake Tritonis.*]—From this lake, as we are told in some
very beautiful lines of Lucan, Minerva took her name of Tri-
tonia.—See book ix. 589; Rowe's version:

> And reach in safety the Tritonian lake.
> These waters to the tuneful god are dear,
> Whose vocal shell the sea-green Nereids hear.
> These Pallas loves, so tells reporting fame;
> Here first from heaven to earth the goddess came,
> Here her first footsteps on the brink she staid,
> Here, in the watery glass, her form survey'd,
> And call'd herself, from hence, the chaste Tritonian
>   maid.   *T.*

Africans,

Africans, hearing this prediction, are said to have concealed the tripod.

CLXXX. Next to the Machlyes live the Aufenses. The above two nations inhabit the opposite sides of lake Tritonis. The Machlyes suffer their hair to grow behind the head, the Aufenses before. They have an annual festival in honour of Minerva, in which the young women, dividing themselves into two separate bands, engage each other with stones and clubs. These rites, they say, were instituted by their forefathers, in veneration of her whom we call Minerva; and if any one die in consequence of wounds received in this contest, they say that she was no virgin. Before the conclusion of the fight they observe this custom: she who by common consent fought the best, has a Corinthian helmet placed upon her head, is clothed in Grecian armour, and carried in a chariot round the lake. How the virgins were decorated in this solemnity, before they had any knowledge of the Greeks, I am not able to say; probably they might use Ægyptian arms. We may venture to affirm, that the Greeks borrowed from Ægypt the shield and the helmet. It is pretended that Minerva was the daughter of Neptune, and the divinity of the lake Tritonis; and that from some trifling disagreement with her father she put herself under the protection of Jupiter, who afterwards adopted her as his daughter. The connection of this people with their women is promiscuous, not confining themselves to one, but living with the sex in brutal

licentioufnefs.   Every three months [174] the men
hold a public affembly, before which each woman
who has had a ftrong healthy boy produces him,
and the man whom he moft refembles is confidered
as his father.

CLXXXI. The Africans who inhabit the fea-
coaft are termed Nomades.   The more inland parts
of Africa, beyond thefe, abound with wild beafts;
remoter ftill, is one vaft fandy defart, from the
Ægyptian Thebes to the columns of Hercules [175].
Penetrating this defert to the fpace of a ten days
journey, vaft pillars of falt are difcovered, from the
fummits of which flows a ftream of water equally
cool and fweet.   This diftrict is poffeffed by the
laft of thofe who inhabit the deferts beyond the
eentre and ruder part of Africa.   The Ammonians,
who poffefs the temple of the Theban Jupiter, are
the people neareft from this place to Thebes, from

[174] *Every three months.*]—This prepofterous cuftom brings
to mind one, defcribed by Lobo, in his Voyage to Abyffinia,
practifed by a people whom he calls the Galles, a wandering
nation of Africans.   If engaged in any warlike expedition,
they take their wives with them, but put to death all the children who may happen to be born during the excurfion.   If
they fettle quietly at home, they bring up their children with
proper care.—T.

[175] *Columns of Hercules.*]—In a former note upon the columns of Hercules, I omitted to mention that more anciently,
according to Ælian, thefe were called the columns of Briareus.
This is alfo mentioned by Ariftotle.   But when Hercules had,
by the deftruction of various monfters, rendered effential fervice
to mankind, they were out of honour to his memory named
the columns of Hercules.—T.

which

which they are diftant a ten days journey. There
is an image of Jupiter at Thebes, as I have before
remarked, with the head of a goat.—The Ammonians have alfo a fountain of water, which at the
dawn of morning is warm, as the day advances it
chills, and at noon becomes exceffively cold. When
it is at the coldeft point, they ufe it to water their
gardens: as the day declines, its coldnefs dimi-
niflies; at fun-fet, it is again warm, and its warmth
gradually increafes till midnight, when it is abfo-
lutely in a boiling ftate. After this period, as the
morning advances, it grows again progreffively
colder. This is called the fountain of the Sun [176].

CLXXXII. Paffing onward beyond the Ammonians, into the defert for ten days more, another
hill of falt [177] occurs; it refembles that which is
found

[176] *Fountain of the Sun.*]—Diodorus Siculus defcribes this
fountain nearly in the fame terms with Herodotus. It is thus
defcribed by Silius Italicus:

Stat fano vicina, novum et memorabile, lympha
Quæ nafcente die, quæ deficiente tepefcit,
Quæque riget medium cum Sol accendit Olympum
Atque eadem rurfus nocturnis fervet in umbris.

Herodotus does not tell us that the Ammonians venerated
this fountain; but as they called it the fountain of the Sun, it is
probable that they did. In remoter times, men almoft univerfally worfhipped ftreams and fountains, if diftinguifhed by any
peculiar properties: all fountains were originally dedicated to
the fun, as to the firft principle of motion.—*T.*

[177] *Hill of falt.*]—I find the following defcription of the
plain of falt, in Abyffinia, in Lobo's Voyage: " Thefe plains

are

found amongſt the Ammonians, and has a ſpring of water; the place is inhabited, and called Angila, and here the Naſamones come to gather their dates.

CLXXXIII. At another ten days diſtance from the Angilæ, there is another hill of ſalt with water, as well as a great number of palms, which, like thoſe before deſcribed, are exceedingly productive: this place is inhabited by the numerous nation of the Garamantes; they cover the beds of ſalt with earth, and then plant it. From them to the Lo-tophagi is a very ſhort diſtance; but from theſe latter it is a journey of thirty days to that nation among whom is a ſpecies of oxen, which walk back-wards whilſt they are feeding; their horns [178] are ſo formed

are ſurrounded with high mountains, continually covered with thick clouds, which the ſun draws from the lakes that are here, from which the water runs down into the plain, and is there congealed into ſalt. Nothing can be more curious, than to ſee the channels and aqueducts that nature has formed in this hard rock, ſo exact, and of ſuch admirable contrivance, that they ſeem to be the work of men. To this place caravans of Abyſ-ſinia are continually reſorting, to carry ſalt into all parts of the empire, which they ſet a great value upon, and which in their country is of the ſame uſe as money."

[178] *Their horns.*]—In the Britiſh Muſeum is a pair of horns ſix feet ſix inches and a half long, it weighs twenty-one pounds, and the hollow will contain five quarts; Lobo mentions ſome in Abyſſinia which would hold ten; Dallon ſaw ſome in India ten feet long: they are ſometimes wrinkled, but often ſmooth.— *Pennant.*

Pliny, book xi. chap. 38, has a long diſſertation upon the horns

formed that they cannot do otherwife, they are
before fo long, and curved in fuch a manner, that
if they did not recede as they fed, they would ftick
in the ground; in other refpects they do not differ
from other animals of the fame genus, unlefs we
except the thicknefs of their fkins. Thefe Garamantes, fitting in carriages drawn by four horfes, give
chace to the Æthiopian Troglodytæ [179], who, of
all the people in the world of whom we have ever
heard, are far the fwifteft of foot: their food is lizards, ferpents, and other reptiles; their language
bears no refemblance to that of any other nation,
for it is like the fcreaming of bats.

CLXXXIV. From the Garamantes, it is another ten days journey to the Atlantes, where alfo
is a hill of falt with water. Of all mankind of

horns of different animals; he tells us that the cattle of the
Troglodytæ, hereafter mentioned, had their horns curved in fo
particular manner, that when they fed they were obliged to
turn their necks on one fide.—T.

[179] *Troglodytæ.*]—Thefe people have their names from τρωγλη,
a cave, and δυω, to enter; Pliny fays they were fwifter than
horfes; and Mela relates the circumftance of their feeding upon
reptiles. I cannot omit here noticing a ftrange miftake of Pliny,
who, fpeaking of thefe people, fays, " Syrbotas vocari gentem
eam Nomadum Æthiopum fecundum flumen Aftapum ad feptentrionem vergentem;" as if ad feptentrionem vergentem
could poffibly be applicable to any fituation in Æthiopia. I may
very properly add in this place, that one of the moft entertaining and ingenious fictions that was ever invented, is the
account given by Montefquieu in his Perfian Letters of the
Troglodytæs.—T.

Z 3

whom

whom we have any knowledge, the Atlantes [186] alone have no diftinction of names; the body of the people are termed Atlantes, but their individuals have no appropriate appellation: when the fun is at the higheft they heap upon it reproaches and execrations, becaufe their country and themfelves are parched by its rays. At the fame diftance onward, of a ten days march, another hill of falt occurs, with water and inhabitants: near this hill ftands mount Atlas, which at every approach is uniformly round and fteep; it is fo lofty that, on account of the clouds which in fummer as well as winter invelope it, its fummit can never be difcerned; it is called by the inhabitants a pillar of heaven. From this mountain the people take their name of Atlantes: it is faid of them, that they never feed on any thing which has life, and that they are ignorant what it is to dream.

CLXXXV. I am able to call by name all the different nations as far as the Atlantes, beyond thefe I have no knowledge. There is, however, from hence, an habitable country, as far as the co-

[186] *Atlantes.*]—Concerning the reading of this word, learned men have been exceedingly divided; Valknaer, and from him alfo M. Larcher, is of opinion that mention is here made of two diftinct nations, the Atarantes and the Atlantes; but all the peculiarities enumerated in this chapter are, by Pliny, Mela, and Solinus, afcribed to the fingle people of the Atlantes. There were two mountains, named Atlas Major and Atlas Minor, but thefe were not at a fufficient diftance from each other to folve the difficulty.—*T.*

lumns

lumns of Hercules, and even beyond it. At the regular interval of a ten days journey, there is a bed
of falt, and inhabitants whofe houfes are formed
from maffes of falt [131]. In this part of Africa it
never rains, for if it did thefe ftructures of falt
could not be durable; they have here two forts of
falt, white and purple [132]. Beyond this fandy defert, fouthward, to the interior parts of Africa, there
is a vaft and horrid fpace without water, wood, or
beafts, and totally deftitute of moifture.

CLXXXVI. Thus from Ægypt, as far as
lake Tritonis, the Africans lead a paftoral life,
living on flefh and milk, but, like the Ægyptians,
will neither eat bulls flefh nor breed fwine. The
women of Cyrene alfo efteem it impious to touch

[131] *Maffes of falt.*]—Gerrha, a town on the Perfian Gulph,
inhabited by the exiled Chaldeans, was built of falt: the falt
of the mountain Had-deffa, near lake Marks, in Africa, is
hard and folid as a ftone.—*Larcher.*

[132] *Salt, white and purple.*]—Had-deffa is a mountain entirely
of falt, fituate at the eaftern extremity of lake Marks, or lake
Tritonis of the ancients; this falt is entirely different from falts
in general, being hard and folid as a ftone, and of a red or violet
colour: the falt which the dew diffolves from the mountain
changes its colour, and becomes white as fnow; it lofes alfo
the bitternefs which is the property of rock falt.—*See Shaw's
Travels.*

One of the moft curious phænomena in the circle of natural
hiftory, is the celebrated falt-mine of Wielitfka in Poland, fo well
defcribed by Coxe: the falt dug from this mine is called green
falt, " I know not," fays Mr. Coxe, " for what reafon, for its
colour is an iron-grey."—*See Travels into Poland.*

an heifer, on account of the Ægyptian Ifis, in whofe
honour they folemnly obferve both faft-days and
feftivals. The women of Barce abftain not only
from the flefh of heifers, but of fwine.

CLXXXVII. The Africans, to the weft of lake
Tritonis, are not fhepherds, they are diftingifhed by
different manners, neither do they obferve the fame
ceremonies with refpect to their children. The
greater number of thefe African fhepherds follow
the cuftom I am about to defcribe, though I will
not fay that it is the cafe indifcriminately with them
all :—As foon as their children arrive at the age of
four years, they burn the veins either of the top of
the fcull, or of the temples, with uncleanfed wool :
they are of opinion, that by this procefs all watery
humours are prevented [183]; to this they impute the
excellent health which they enjoy. It muft be
acknowledged, whatever may be the caufe, that the
Africans are more exempt from difeafe than any
other men.—If the operation throws the children
into convulfions, they have a remedy at hand ; they
fprinkle them with goats urine [184], and they recover.

[183] *Watery humours are prevented.*]—According to Hippocrates, the Scythians apply fire to their fhoulders, arms, and
ftomachs, on account of the humid and relaxed ftate of their
bodies ; this operation dries up the excefs of moifture about the
joints, and renders them more free and active. Wcffeling remarks from Scaliger, that this cuftom ftill prevails amongft the
Æthiopian Chriftians, Mahometans, and Heathens.—*Larcher.*

[184] *Goats urine.*]—I have heard of cows urine being applied

ver.—I relate what the Africans themfelves affirm.

CLXXXVIII. As to their mode of facrifice, having cut the ear of the victim which they intend as an offering for their firft fruits, they throw it over the top of their dwelling, and afterwards break its neck: the only deities to whom they facrifice, are the fun and moon, who are adored by all the Africans; they who live near lake Tritonis venerate Triton, Neptune, and Minerva, but particularly the laft.

CLXXXIX. From thefe Africans the Greeks borrowed the veft, and the Ægis, with which they decorate the fhrine of Minerva: the vefts, however, of the African Minervas, are made of fkin, and the fringe hanging from the Ægis is not compofed of ferpents, but of leather; in every other refpect the drefs is the fame: it appears by the very name, that the robe of the ftatues of Minerva was borrowed from Africa. The women [185] of this country wear below

as a fpecific in fome dangerous obftructions; and I find in Lobo's Voyage to Abyffinia an account of goats urine being recommended in an afthmatic complaint; their blood was formerly efteemed of benefit in pleurifies, but this idea is now exploded. —*T.*

[185] *The women.*]—Apollonius Rhodius, who was an exact obferver of manners, thus defcribes the three Lybian heroines who appeared to Jafon—See Fawkes's verfion:

Attend, my friends:—Three virgin forms, who claim
From heaven their race, to footh my forrows came;
Their

below their garments goat-fkins without the hair
fringed and ftained of a red colour; from which
part of drefs the word Ægis [186] of the Greeks is
unqueftionably derived. I am alfo inclined to believe, that the loud cries [187] which are uttered in
the temples of that goddefs have the fame origin;
the African women do this very much, but not
difagreeably. From Africa alfo the Greeks borrowed the cuftom of harneffing four horfes to a
carriage.

CXC. Thefe African Nomades obferve the fame
ceremonies with the Greeks in the interment of
the dead; we muft except the Nafamones, who
bury their deceafed in a fitting attitude, and are
particularly careful, as any one approaches his end,
to prevent his expiring in a reclined pofture. Their
dwellings are eafily moveable, and are formed of

> Their fhoulders round were fhaggy goat-fkins caft,
> Which low defcending girt their flender waift.

[186] Ægis.]—From αιξ αιγος, a goat, the Greeks made
αιγις αιγιδος, which fignifies both the fkin of a goat, and the
Ægis of Minerva.

[187] Loud cries.]—See Iliad vi. 370: Pope's verfion.

> Soon as to Ilion's topmoft tower they come,
> And awful reach the high Palladian dome,
> Antenor's confort, fair Theano, waits
> As Pallas' prieftefs, and unbars the gates.
> With hands uplifted, and imploring eyes,
> They fill the dome with *fuftlicating cries*.

In imitation of which, M. Larcher remarks, Virgil ufes the
expreffion of fummoque ulularunt vertice nymphæ,

the

the afphodel fhrub, fecured with rufhes.—Such are the manners of thefe people.

CXCI. The Aufenfes, on the weftern part of the river Triton, border on thofe Africans who cultivate the earth and have houfes, they are called Maxyes; thefe people fuffer their hair to grow on the right fide of the head, but not on the left; they ftain their bodies with vermillion, and pretend to be defcended from the Trojans. This region, and indeed all the more weftern parts of Africa, is much more woody, and infefted with wild beafts, than where the African Nomades refide; for the abode of thefe latter, advancing eaftward, is low and fandy. From hence weftward, where thofe inhabit who till the ground, it is mountainous, full of wood, and abounding with wild beafts; here are found ferpents of an enormous fize, lions, elephants, bears [138], afps, and affes with horns. Here alfo are the Cynocephali, as well as the Acephali [189], who,

if

[138] *Bears.*]—Pliny pretends that Africa does not produce bears, although he gives us the annals of Rome, teftifying that in the confulfhip of M. Pifo, and M. Meffala, Domitius Ænobarbus gave during his ædilefhip public games, in which were an hundred Numidian bears.

Lipfius affirms, that the beafts produced in the games of Ænobarbus, were lions, which is the animal alfo meant by the Lybiftis urfa of Virgil: "The firft time," fays he, "that the Romans faw lions, they did not call them lions, but bears." Virgil mentions lions by its appropriate name in an hundred places; Shaw alfo enumerates bears amongft the animals which he met in Africa.—*Larcher.*

[189] *Cynocephali as well as the Acephali.*]—Herodotus mentions

a nation

if the Africans may be credited, have their eyes
in their breasts ; they have, moreover, men and,
women

a nation of this name in Lybia, and speaks of them as a race of
men with the heads of dogs. Hard by, in the neighbourhood of
this people, he places the Acephali, men with no heads at all ;
to whom, out of humanity, and to obviate some very natural
distresses, he gives eyes in the breast ; but he seems to have forgot mouth and ears, and makes no mention of a nose. Both
these and the Cynocephali were denominated from their place
of residence, and from their worship ; the one from Cahen-
Caph-El, the other from Ac-Caph-El, each of which appellations is of the same import, the right noble or sacred rock,
of the sun.—*Bryant.*

See also the speech of Othello in Shakespeare :

> Wherein of antars vast and desarts idle,
> Rough quarries, rocks, and hills whose heads touch
>   heav'n,
> It was my hint to speak, such was my process ;
> And of the cannibals that each other eat,
> The Anthropophagi ; and men whose heads
> Did grow beneath their shoulders.   *T.*

The Cynocephali, whom the Africans considered as men
with the heads of dogs, were a species of baboons, remarkble
for their boldness and ferocity. As to the Acephali, St. Augus-
tin assures us, that he had seen them himself of both sexes. That
holy father would have done well to have considered, that in
pretending to be eye-witness of such a fable he threw a stain
on the veracity of his other works. If there really be a nation
in Africa which appear to be without a head, I can give no
better account of the phænomenon, than by copying the ingenious author of Philosophic Researches concerning the Americans.

"There is," says he, "in Canibar, a race of savages who
have hardly any neck, and whose shoulders reach up to the
ears. This monstrous appearance is artificial, and to give it to
their

women who are wild and favage; and many ferocious animals whofe exiftence cannot be difputed [190].

CXCII. Of the animals above mentioned, none
are found amongft the African Nomades; they have
however pygargi [191], goats, buffaloes, and affes, not
of

their children, they put enormous weights upon their heads, fo
as to make the vertebræ of the neck enter (if we may fo fay)
the channel-bone (clavicule). Thefe barbarians, from a diftance, feem to have their mouth in the breaft, and might well
enough, in ignorant or enthufiaftic travellers, ferve to revive the
fable of the Acephali, or men without heads."—The above
note is from Larcher; who alfo adds the following remark upon
the preceding note, which I have given from Mr. Bryant.

Mr. Bryant, imagining that thefe people called themfelves
Acephali, decompofes the word, which is purely Greek, and
makes it come from the Ægyptian Ac-Caph-El, which he interprets " the facred rock of the fun." The fame author, with
as much reafon, pretends that Cynocephali comes from Cahen-
Caph-El, to which he affigns a fimilar interpretation: here, to
me at leaft, there feems a vaft deal of erudition entirely thrown
away.

In the fifth century, the name of Acephali was given to a
confiderable faction of the Monophyfites, or Eutychians, who by
the fubmiffion of Mongus were deprived of their leader.—T.

Apollonius Rhodius calls thefe people ημικυνες, or half
dogs; and it is not improbable but that the circumftance of
their living entirely by the produce of the chace, might give
rife to the fable of their having the heads of dogs.—T.

[190] Cannot be difputed.]—We may, I think, fairly infer from
this expreffion, that Herodotus gave no credit to the ftories of
the Cynocephali and Acephali.—T.

[191] Pygargi.]—Ariftotle claffes the pygargus amongft the
birds of prey; but as Herodotus in this place fpeaks only of
quadrupeds,

of that species which have horns, but a particular
kind which never drink.   They have also oryxes [12a]
of the size of an ox, whose horns are used by the
Phœnicians to make the sides of their citharæ.   In

quadrupeds, it is probable that this also was one.   Hardouin
makes it a species of.goat.—Thus far Larcher.   Ælian also
ranks it amongst the quadrupeds, and speaks of its being a very
timid animal.—See also Juvenal, Sat. xi. 138.

> Sumine cum magno, lepus atque aper, et pygargus.

See also Deuteronomy, chap. xiv. verse 5.   " The hart and
the roebuck, and the fallow deer, and the wild goat, and the
pygarg, and the wild ox, and the chamois."
It may probably be the gazelle, a species of antelope.—*T*.
[122] *Oryxes.*]—Pliny describes this animal as having but one
horn; Oppian, who had seen it, says the contrary.   Aristotle
classes it with the animals having but one horn.   Bochart thinks
it was the aram, a species of gazelle; but Oppian describes the
oryx as a very fierce animal.—The above is from *Larcher*.
The oryx is mentioned by Juvenal, Sat. xi. 140.

> Et Gætulus oryx:

And upon which line the Scholiast has this remark :
Oryx animal minus quem bubalus quem Mauri uncem vo-
cant, cujus pellis ad citoras proficit scuta Maurorum minora.—
From the line of Juvenal above mentioned it appears that they
were eaten at Rome, but they were also introduced as a ferocious
animal in the amphitheatre.   See Martial, xiii. 95.

> Matutinarum non ultima præda ferarum
>   Sævus oryx, constat quot mihi mute canum.

That it was an animal well known and very common in Africa,
is most certain ; but, unless it be what Pennant describes under
the name of the leucoryx, or white antelope, I confess I know
not what name to give it.—*T*.

this region likewife there are baffaria [193], hyenæ, por-
cupines, wild boars, dictyes [194], thoes [195], panthers,
boryes [196], land crocodiles [197] three cubits long, refembling lizards, oftriches, and fmall ferpents, hav-

[193] *Baffaria.*]—Ælian makes no mention of this animal, at
leaft under this name. Larcher interprets it foxes, and refers
the reader to the article βασσαρις, in Hefychius, which we learn
was the name which the people of Cyrene gave to the fox.
—*T.*

[194] *Dictyes.*]—I confefs myfelf totally unable to find out what
animal is here meant.

[195] *Thoes.*]—Larcher is of opinion that this is the beaft which
we call a jack-all, which he thinks is derived from the Arabian
word *chatall.* He believes that the idea of the jackall's being
the lion's provider is univerfally credited in this country; but
this is not true. The fcience of natural hiftory is too well
and too fuccefsfully cultivated amongft us to admit of fuch an
error, except with the moft ignorant. I fubjoin what Shaw
fays upon this fubject.

The black cat (fcyah ghufh) and the jackall, are generally
fuppofed to find out provifion or prey for the lion, and are therefore called the lion's provider; yet it may very much be
doubted, whether there is any fuch friendly intercourfe between
them. In the night, indeed, when all the beafts of the foreft
do move, thefe, as well as others, are prowling after fuftenance;
and when the fun arifeth, and the lion getteth himfelf away to
his den, both the black cat and the jackall have been often found
gnawing fuch carcafes as the lion is fuppofed to have fed upon
the night before. This, and the promifcuous noife which I
have heard the jackall particularly make with the lion, are the
only circumftances I am acquainted with in favour of this opinion.—*T.*

[196] *Boryes.*]—Of this animal I can find no account in any
writer, ancient or modern.

[197] *Land crocodiles,*] or κροκοδειλος χερσαιος, fo called in con-
tradiftinction from the river crocodile, which by way of eminence was called Κροκοδειλος only.—*T.*

§

ing each a single horn. Besides these animals, they
have such as are elsewhere found, except the stag
and the boar [178], which are never seen in Africa.
They have also three distinct species of mice, some
of which are called dipodes [199], others are called ze-
geries, which in the African tongue has the same
meaning with the Greek word for hills. The other
species is called the echines. There are moreover
to be seen a kind of weazel produced in Silphium,
and very much like that of Tarteflus. The above
are all the animals amongst the African Nomades,
which my moft diligent refearches have enabled me
to difcover.

CXCIII. Next to the Maxyes are the Zaueces,
whofe women guide the chariots of war.

[198] *Boar.*]—This animal muft have been carried to Africa
fince the time of Herodotus, for it is now found there: according to Shaw, it is the chief food and prey of the lion, againft
which it has fometimes been known to defend itfelf with fo
much bravery, that the victory has inclined to neither fide, the
carcafes of them both having been found lying the one by the
other, torn and mangled to pieces.—*Shaw.*

[199] *Dipodes.*]—Shaw is of opinion that this is the jerboa of
Barbary. " That remarkable difproportion," obferves this
writer, " betwixt the fore and hinder legs of the jerboa, or
δωυς, though I never faw them run, but only ftand or reft
themfelves upon the latter, may induce us to take it for one of
the διποδις, or two-footed rats which Herodotus and other writers
defcribe as the inhabitants of thefe countries, particularly (τω
Σιλφιω) of the province of Silphium." Accordingly Mr. Pennant has fet down the μυς διπυς of Theophraftus and Ælian
among the fyonyms of the jerboa.—*Hift. of An.* p. 427.
N° 291.

CXCIV.

CXCIV. The people next in order are the Zygantes, amongſt whom a great abundance of honey is found, the produce of their bees; but of this they ſay a great deal more is made by the natives [200]. They all ſtain their bodies with vermilion, and feed upon monkies, with which animal their mountains abound.

CXCV. According to the Carthaginians, we next meet with an iſland called Cyranis, two hundred ſtadia in length. It is of a trifling breadth, but the communication with the continent is eaſy, and it abounds with olives and vines. Here is a lake from which the young women of the iſland draw up gold duſt [201] with bunches of feathers beſmeared with pitch. For the truth of this I will not anſwer, relating merely what I have been told. To me it ſeems the more probable, after having ſeen at Zacynthus [202] pitch drawn from the bottom of

---

[200] *Made by the natives.*]—" I do not ſee," ſays Reiſke on this paſſage, " how men can poſſibly make honey. They may collect, clarify, and prepare it by various proceſſes for uſe, but the bees muſt firſt have made it."

I confeſs I ſee no ſuch great difficulty in the above. There were various kinds of honey, honey of bees, honey of the palm, and honey of ſugar, not to mention honey of grapes; all the laſt of which might be made by the induſtry of man.—See Lucan:

Quique bibunt tenera dulces ab arundine ſuccos.   *T.*

See Shaw's Travels, p. 339.

[201] *Gold duſt.*]—See a minute account of this in Achilles Tatius.—*T.*

[202] *Zacynthus.*]—The modern name of this place is Zante.

of the water. At this place are a number of lakes, the largeſt of which is ſeventy feet in circumference, and of the depth of two orgyiæ. Into this water they let down a pole, at the end of which is a bunch of myrtle; the pitch attaches itſelf to the myrtle, and is thus procured. It has a bituminous ſmell, but is in other reſpects preferable to that of Pieria[201]. The pitch is then thrown into a trench dug for the purpoſe by the ſide of the lake; and when a ſufficient quantity has been obtained, they put it up in caſks. Whatever falls into the lake

Its tar ſprings, to uſe the words of Chandler, are ſtill a natural curioſity deſerving notice.

The tar is produced in a ſmall valley about two hours from the town, by the ſea, and encompaſſed with mountains, except toward the bay, in which are a couple of rocky iſlets. The ſpring which is moſt diſtinct and apt for inſpection, riſes on the farther ſide near the foot of the hill. The well is circular, and four or five feet in diameter. A ſhining film, like oil mixed with ſcum, ſwims on the top: you remove this with a bough, and ſee the tar at the bottom, three or four feet beneath the ſurface, working up, it is ſaid, out of a fiſſure in the rock; the bubbles ſwelling gradually to the ſize of a large cannon-ball, when they burſt, and the ſides leiſurely ſinking, new ones ſucceed, increaſe, and in turn ſubſide. The water is limpid, and runs off with a ſmart current: the ground near is quaggy, and will ſhake beneath the feet, but is cultivated. We filled ſome veſſels with tar, by letting it trickle into them from the boughs which we immerſed, and this is the method uſed to gather it from time to time into pits, where it is hardened by the ſun, to be barrelled when the quantity is ſufficient. The odour reaches a conſiderable way.—See *Chandler's Travels*.

[201] *That of Pieria.*—This was highly eſteemed. Didymus ſays that the ancients conſidered that as the beſt which came from Mount Ida; and next to this, the tar which came from Pieria. Pliny ſays the ſame.—*Larcher*.

paſſes

paſſes under ground, and is again ſeen in the ſea, at the diſtance of four ſtadia from the lake. Thus what is related of this iſland contiguous to Africa, ſeems both conſiſtent and probable.

CXCVI. We have the ſame authority of the Carthaginians to affirm, that beyond the columns of Hercules there is a country inhabited by a people with whom they have had commercial intercourſe [104]. It is their cuſtom, on arriving amongſt them, to unload their veſſels, and diſpoſe their goods along the ſhore. This done, they again embark, and make a great ſmoke from on board. The natives, ſeeing this, come down immediately to the ſhore, and placing a quantity of gold by

[104] *Commercial intercourſe.*]—It muſt be mentioned to the honour of the weſtern Moors, that they ſtill continue to carry on a trade with ſome barbarous nations bordering upon the river Niger, without ſeeing the perſons they trade with, or without having once broke through that original charter of commerce which from time immemorial has been ſettled between them. The method is this: at a certain time of the year, in the winter, if I am not miſtaken, they make this journey in a numerous caravan, carrying along with them coral and glaſs beads, bracelets of horn, knives, ſciſſars, and ſuch like trinkets. When they arrive at the place appointed, which is on ſuch a day of the moon, they find in the evening ſeveral different heaps of gold duſt lying at a ſmall diſtance from each other, againſt which the Moors place ſo many of their trinkets as they judge will be taken in exchange for them. If the Nigritians the next morning approve of the bargain, they take up the trinkets and leave the gold duſt, or elſe make ſome deduction from the latter. In this manner they tranſact their exchange without ſeeing one another, or without the leaſt inſtance of diſhoneſty or perfidiouſneſs on either ſide.—*Shaw.*

way of exchange for the merchandise, retire. The Carthaginians then land a second time, and if they think the gold equivalent, they take it and depart; if not, they again go on board their vessels. The inhabitants return and add more gold, till the crews are satisfied. The whole is conducted. with the strictest integrity, for neither will the one touch the gold till they have left an adequate value in merchandize, nor will the other remove the goods till the Carthaginians have taken away the gold.

CXCVII. Such are the people of Africa whose names I am able to ascertain; of whom the greater part cared but little for the king of the Medes, neither do they now. Speaking with all the precision I am able, the country I have been describing is inhabited by four nations only: of these two are natives and two strangers. The natives are the Africans and Æthiopians; one of whom possess the northern the other the southern parts of Africa. The strangers are the Phœnicians and the Greeks.

CXCVIII. If we except the district of Cinyps, which bears the name of the river flowing through it, Africa in goodness of soil cannot, I think, be compared either to Asia or Europe. Cinyps is totally unlike the rest of Africa, but is equal to any country in the world for its corn. It is of a black soil, abounding in springs, and never troubled with drought. It rains in this part of Africa, but the rains, though violent, are never injurious. The produce

duce of corn is not exceeded by Babylon itself. The country alfo of the Euefperitæ is remarkably fertile; in one of its plentiful years it produces an hundred fold; that of Cinyps three hundred fold.

CXCIX. Of the part of Africa poffeffed by the Nomades, the diftrict of Cyrene is the moft elevated. They have three feafons, which well deferve admiration: the harveft and the vintage firft commence upon the fea-coaft; when thefe are finifhed, thofe immediately contiguous, advancing up the country, are ready; this region they call Buni. When the requifite labour has been here finifhed, the corn and the vines in the more elevated parts are found to ripen in progreffion, and will then require to be cut. By the time therefore that the firft produce of the earth is confumed, the laft will be ready. Thus for eight months in the year the Cyreneans are employed in reaping the produce of their lands.

CC. The Perfians who were fent by Aryandes to avenge the caufe of Pheretime proceeding from Ægypt to Barce, laid fiege to the place, having firft required the perfons of thofe who had been acceffary to the death of Arcefilaus. To this the inhabitants, who had all been equally concerned in deftroying him, paid no attention. The Perfians, after continuing nine months before the place, carried their mines to the walls, and made a very vigorous attack. Their mines were difcovered by a fmith, by means of a brazen fhield. He made a

circuit

circuit of the town; where there were no miners beneath the fhield did not reverberate, which it did wherever they were at work. The Barceans therefore dug countermines, and flew the Perfians fo employed. Every attempt to ftorm the place was vigoroufly defeated by the befieged.

CCI. After a long time had been thus confumed with confiderable flaughter on both fides (as many being killed of the Perfians as of their adverfaries) .Amafis, the leader of the infantry, employed the following ftratagem;—Being convinced that the Barceans were not to be overcome by any open attacks, he funk in the night a large and deep trench: the furface of this he covered with fome flight pieces of wood, then placing earth over the whole, the ground had uniformly the fame appearance. At the dawn of the morning he invited the Barceans to a conference; they willingly affented, being very defirous to come to terms. Accordingly they entered into a treaty, of which thefe were the conditions: it was to remain valid[205] as long as the earth upon which the agreement was made fhould retain its prefent appearance. The Barceans were to pay the Perfian monarch a certain reafonable

---

[205] *It was to remain valid.*]—Memini fimilem fœderis formulam apud Polybium legere in fœdere Hannibalis cum Tarentinis, fi bene memini.—*Reifke.*

Reifke's recollection appears in this place to have deceived him. Tarentum was betrayed to Hannibal by the treachery of fome of its citizens; but in no manner refembling this here defcribed by Herodotus.—*T.*

tribute; and the Perfians engaged themfelves to undertake nothing in future to the detriment of the Barceans. Relying upon thefe engagements, the Barceans, without hefitation, threw open the gates of their city, going out and in themfelves without fear of confequences, and permitting without reftraint fuch of the enemy as pleafed to come within their walls. The Perfians, withdrawing the artificial fupport of the earth, where they had funk a trench, entered the city in crouds; they imagined by this artifice that they had fulfilled all they had undertaken, and were brought back to the fituation in which they were mutually before. For in reality, this fupport of the earth being taken away, the oath they had taken became void.

CCII. The Perfians feized and furrendered to the power of Pheretima fuch of the Barceans as had been inftrumental in the death of her fon. Thefe fhe crucified on different parts of the walls; fhe cut off alfo the breafts of their wives, and fufpended them in a fimilar fituation. She permitted the Perfians to plunder the reft of the Barceans, except the Battiadæ, and thofe who were not concerned in the murder. Thefe fhe fuffered to retain their fituations and property.

CCIII. The reft of the Barceans being reduced to fervitude, the Perfians returned home. Arriving at Cyrene, the inhabitants of that place granted them a free paffage through their territories, from reverence to fome oracle. Whilft they were on

their

their paffage, Bares, commander of the fleet, folicited them to plunder Cyrene; which was oppofed
by Amafis, leader of the infantry, who urged that
their orders were only againft Barce. When, paffing Cyrene, they had arrived at the hill of the Lycean Jupiter [106], they expreffed regret at not having
plundered it. They accordingly returned, and endeavoured a fecond time to enter the place; but the
Cyreneans would not fuffer them. Although no
one attempted to attack them, the Perfians were
feized with fuch a panic, that returning in hafte,
they encamped at the diftance of about fixty ftadia
from the city. Whilft they remained here a meffenger came from Aryandes, ordering them to return. Upon this, the Perfians made application to
the Cyreneans for a fupply of provifions; which
being granted, they returned to Ægypt. In their
march they were inceffantly harraffed by the Africans for the fake of their clothes and utenfils. In
their progrefs to Ægypt, whoever was furprized or
left behind was inftantly put to death.

CCIV. The fartheft progrefs of this Perfian
army was to the country of the Euefperidæ. Their
Barcean captives they carried with them from
Ægypt to king Darius, who affigned them for their
refidence a portion of land in the Bactrian diftrict,
to which they gave the name of Barce; this has

---

[106] *Lycean Jupiter.*]—Lycaon erected a temple to Jupiter in
Parrhafia, and inftituted games in his honour, which the Ly-
ceans called Λυκαια. No one was permitted to enter this temple; he who did was ftoned.—*Larcher.*

within

within my time contained a great number of inhabitants.

CCV. The life, however, of Pheretima had by no
means a fortunate termination. Having gratified her
revenge upon the Barceans, fhe returned from Africa
to Ægypt, and there perifhed miferably. Whilſt
alive, her body was the victim of worms [207] : thus
it is that the gods punifh thofe who have provoked
their indignation; and fuch alfo was the vengeance
which Pheretima, the wife of Battus, exercifed upon
the Barceans.

[207] *Victim of worms.*]—This paſſage, with the reafoning of
Herodotus upon it, cannot fail to bring to the mind of the reader
the miferable end of Herod, furnamed the Great.

And he went down to Cæfarea, and there abode : and upon a
fet day Herod arrayed in royal apparel fat upon his throne,
and made an oration unto them. And the people gave a fhout,
faying, It is the voice of a god, and not of a man. And immediately the angel of the Lord fmote him, becaufe he gave not
God the glory : and he was eaten of worms, and gave up the
ghoſt.—See Lardner's obfervations upon the above hiſtorical
incident.—*T.*

ADDENDA

MELPOMENE.

WHEN the fourth book of Herodotus was nearly printed off, a small tract fell into my hands, published in Germany, under the title of Geographia Africæ Herodotea; the name of the author is Schlichthorst; and it attracted my attention, from being introduced by a preface, with the respectable name of Chr. G. Heyne. After a closer examination, I found that it contained what, to me at least, seemed worthy of attention. The geography of Africa, always obscure, has not in modern times been sufficiently investigated; much remains to be known concerning this quarter of the globe: I feel it therefore a duty to the reader to give such extracts from the tract above mentioned as appear to illuminate this intricate part of geographical science, and to make us better acquainted with the places and inhabitants of ancient Lybia.

In Chap. CLXVIII. Herodotus speaks of the Adyrmachidæ. —It is well known, that in the age which followed, the Greeks drove these Adyrmachidæ into the higher parts of Lybia, and took possession of the sea-coast. When, therefore, Ptolemy describes the Adyrmachidæ as inhabiting the interior parts of Lybia, there is no contradiction betwixt his account and that of Herodotus. The manners of this people are described by Herodotus, and they are thus mentioned by Silius Italicus:—

Verisicolor contra cetra et falcatus ab arte
Ensis Adyrmachidæ ac lævo tegmina crure;

Sed

Sed menfis afper populus, victuque maligno
Nam calida triftes epulæ torrentur arena.—

L. iii. 278.

They are again mentioned by the fame author, book ix. 223, 224.

——ferro vivere lætum
Vulgus Adyrmachidæ.

Chap. CLXIX. *Aziris.*]—See the hymn of Callimachus to Apollo, verfe 89, where this place is written Αζιλις.

Herodotus in this place fpeaks of two iflands, inhabited by the Giligammæ, Platea, and Aphrodifias; it is not certain whether the firft of thefe is what Ptolemy called Ædonis: the fecond was afterwards named Læa, and was, according to Scylax, a good harbour for fhips.

The country of the Giligammæ produced a fpecies of the filphium, called by the Latins laferpiticum, from which a medical drug was extracted; fee Pliny, Nat. Hift. xix. 3. " In the country of the Cyrene (where the beft filphium grew) none of late years has been found, the farmers turning their cattle into the places where it grew: one ftem only has been found in my time, this was fent as a prefent to Nero."

Chap. CLXXI. *Cabales.*]—This word is fometimes' written Bacales; and Wefleling hefitates what reading to prefer.

What Herodotus fays of the Nafamones, c. 173, is confirmed by Pliny, Nat. Hift. vii. c. 2; Silius Italicus, i. 408; Lucan, ix. 439, &c.

Concerning their manner of plighting troth, c. 172, Shaw tells us, that the drinking out of each others hands is the only ceremony which the Algerines at this time ufe in marriage.

The ftory which Herodotus relates of the Pfylli, 173, is told alfo by Aulus Gellius, Noct. Att. 16.—11. It feems more probable that they were deftroyed by the Nafamones.—See Pliny, Nat. Hift. viii. 1.—See alfo Hardouin ad Plin. and Larcher, vii. 312.

Concerning τα Ιρασα, called by Herodotus, 158, καλλιςος των χωρων, fee Callimach. Hymn to Apollo, 88, 89.

Tauchira.]—Called by Strabo, Ptolemy, and Pliny, Teuchira; afterwards it was known by the name of Arfinoe, and laftly by
Antony

Antony it was named Cleopatris, in honour of Cleopatra : in modern times it has been called Teukera (d'Anville) ; Trochare (de la Croix) ; Trochara (Hardouin) ; Tochara (Simlonus) ; Trochata (Dapper).

Euefperides.]—The city was afterwards named Berenice ; of this appellation fome veftiges now remain, for the place is called Bernic, Berbic, and by fome Beric.

The fertility of the contiguous country gave rife to the Grœian fable of the gardens of the Hefperides.

Chap. CLXXII. *Barce.*]—Many of the ancients believed that this place was anciently called Ptolemais, as Strabo, Pliny, Servius, and others.

Of Cyrene, about which Strabo fpeaks lefs fabuloufly than Herodotus, but few traces now remain ; they are differently mentioned under the names of Keroan, Curin, and Guirina.

Chap. CLXXIV. *Garamantes*]—Mentioned by Mela, book viii. and by him called Gamphafantes.

Chap. CLXXV. *Macæ.*]—Amongft thefe people was the fountain of Cinyps, called by Strabo and Ptolemy Κινυφος, by Pliny Cinyps ; its modern name, according to d'Anville, is Wadi-Quaham.

Chap. CLXXVI. *Girdanes.*]—This people, according to Stephanus, lived on the lotus, as well as the Lotophagi.

Chap. CLXXVII. *Lotophagi.*]—Whether from the fame lotus the Lotophagi obtained both meat and wine, is laborioufly difputed by Voffius ad Scyll. 114. and Stapel. ad Theophraft, l. iv. c. 4. p. 327. A delineation of the lotus may be feen in Shaw and De la Croix : it is what the Arabs of the prefent day call feedra, and is plentiful in Barbary, and the defarts of Barbary.

Chap. CLXXVIII. *Machlyes.*]—There were a people of this name alfo in Scythia ; the name, however, is written different ways.—See Weffeling ad Herod. 178.

The river Triton is the fame with that now called Gabs.—See Shaw.

Stephanus Byzantinus confounds the Phla of Herodotus with the ifland of Phila, which was in Æthiopia, not far from Ægypt. —See alfo Shaw on this ifland, 129, 4to. edit.

Chap. CLXXXI. *Ammonians.*]—Bochart derives the name
of

of Ammonians from Cham, the fon of Noah, who was long reverenced in the more barren parts of Africa, under the title of
Ham or Hammon, one of the names of Jupiter.

That the name of Ammon was very well known in Arabia,
and throughout Africa, we may learn from the river Ammon,
the Ammonian promontory, the Ammonians, the city Ammon,
&c.—See Strabo, Pliny, Ptolemy, &c.

Some remains of the temple of Jupiter Ammon are ftill to be
feen, if the travellers to Mecca may be believed; the place is
called Hefach-bir (or mole lapidum).

In the fame chapter Herodotus mentions η κρηνη Ηλιυ, the
temple of the fun, concerning which fee Diodorus, xvii. 528.—
See alfo Arrian, l. iii. c. 4.—Curtius, l. iv. c. 7.—Mela, l. i.
c. 8.

Chap. CLXXXII. *Angilæ.*]—Herodotus fays that this country
abounded in dates; and the Africans of the prefent day go
there to gather them.—*See Marmot,* vol. iii. p. 53.

Concerning the fituation of the Angilæ, fee Pliny, lib. v. c. 4;
and Dapper, p. 323.

Amongft all the countries of Lybia, mentioned by the ancient Greek writers, Angila is the only one which to this day
retains its primitive name without the fmalleft variation.

Chap. CLXXXIII. Of the cattle, which whilft they grazed
walked backwards, Mela fpeaks, lib. i. c. 8.—Pliny, Nat. Hift.
l. viii. c. 45.— Ariftotle Hiftory of Animals, lib. vii. c. 21.—See
alfo Voffius ad Melæ, loc. p. 41.

Chap. CLXXXIV. *Atrantes.*]—Some manufcripts read Atlantes, but this cannot be the genuine reading, which alfo is the
opinion of Salmafius, Valknaer, Weffeling, and Larcher.—See
Voffius ad Melæ, locum laudatum.

Atlantes.]—The Atlantei, mentioned by Diodorus, l. iii. 187,
if ever they exifted, muft be diftinct from the Atlantes of Herodotus. Of mount Atlas, and its extreme height, Homer fpeaks,
Odyff. i. 52, 4.

Chap. CXCV. I have defcribed at fome length the tar-
fprings of Zante, from Dr. Chandler: I did not mention that
fome account of them is alfo to be found in Antigonus Caryftius,
p. 169, and Vitruvius, l. viii. c. 3.

Cyraunis.]—The fame with the Cercinna of Strabo, now called
Querqueni,

Querqueni, or Chercheni; concerning this ifland confult Diodorus, l. v. 294; but Diodorus, we fhould remark, confounded
Cercinna with Cerne, an ifland of the Atlantic.

Chap. CXCVI. *Columns of Hercules.*]—The Libyan column
was by ancient writers called Abyla; that on the Spanifh fide,
Calpe.—*See P. Mela*, l. ii. c. 6.

Chap. CXCIX. *Cyrene.*]—About the limits of this diftrict
the ancients were not at all agreed, they are no where defined
by Herodotus: the province of Cyrene, formerly fo populous,
is the contrary now; the fea-coafts are ravaged by pirates, the
inland parts by the Arabians; fuch inhabitants as there are
are rich by the fale of the Europeans who fall into their hands
to the Æthiopians.—*See La Croix*, tom. ii. 252.

Of the abundant fertility of Cyrene, Diodorus Siculus alfo
fpeaks, p. 183, c. cxxviii.—Concerning the fountain of Cyre,
one of the Fontes Cyrenaicæ, fee Callimachus's Ode to Apollo,
88; and Juftin, lib. xñi. c. 7.

Concerning the Afbyftæ, of whom Herodotus fpeaks, c. 170,
1, Salmafius has collected much, ad Solinum, 381; fo alfo has
Euftathius, ad Dionyf. Perieg. 211.—See too Larcher, vol. vii.
43.

Of the people with whom the Carthaginians traded, beyond
the columns of Hercules, without feeing them, I have fpoken at
length, and given from Shaw the paffage introduced by Schlich-
thorft. The place, whofe name is not mentioned by Herodotus,
is, doubtlefs, what we now call Senegambia. All the part of Lybia defcribed by Herodotus is now comprehended under the
general name of Barbary, and contains the kingdoms of Morocco,
Fez, Algiers, Tunis, and Tripoli: the maritime part of Lybia,
from Carthage weftward, was unknown to Herodotus.

HERODOTUS.

HERODOTUS.

BOOK V.

TERPSICHORE.

CHAP. I.

THE Perfians who had been left in Europe by Darius, under the conduct of Megabyzus, commenced their hoftilities on the Hellefpont with the conqueft of the Perinthii [1], who had refufed to acknowledge the authority of Darius, and had formerly been vanquifhed by the Pæonians [2]. This latter people, inhabiting the banks of the

---

[1] *Perinthii.*]—Perinthus was firft called Mygdonia, afterwards Heraclea, and then Perinthus.—*T.*

[2] *Pæonians.*]—As the ancients materially differed in opinion concerning the geographical fituation of this people, it is not to be expected that I fhould fpeak decifively on the fubject. Herodotus here places them near the river Strymon ; Dio, near mount Rhodope ; and Ptolemy, where the river Haliacmon rifes. Pæonia was one of the names of Minerva, given her from her fuppofed fkill in the art of medicine.—*T.*

Strymon,

Strymon, had been induced by an oracle to make war on the Perinthians : if the Perinthians on their meeting offered them battle, provoking them by name, they were to accept the challenge; if otherwise, they were to decline all contest. It happened accordingly, that the Perinthians marched into the country of the Pæonians, and encamping before their town, sent them three specific challenges, a man to encounter with a man, a horse with a horse, a dog with a dog. The Perinthians having the advantage in the two former contests, sung with exultation a song of triumph [3]; this the Pæonians conceived to be the purport of the oracle : "Now," they exclaimed, " the oracle will be fulfilled; this " is the time for us." They attacked, therefore, the Perinthians, whilst engaged in their imaginary triumph, and obtained so signal a victory that few of their adversaries escaped.

II. Such was the overthrow which the Perin-

---

[3] *Song of triumph.*]—Larcher renders this passage " Sung the pæon;" and subjoins this note : " Of this song there were two kinds, one was chaunted before the battle, in honour of Mars, the other after the victory, in honour of Apollo; this song commenced with the words " Io Pæan." The allusion of the word Pæon to the name of the Pæonians, is obvious, to preserve which I have rendered it " sung the Pæon."—The usage and application of the word Pæan, amongst the ancients, was various and equivocal: the composition of Pindar, in praise of all the gods, was called Pæan; and Pæan was also one of the names of Apollo. To which it may be added, that Pæan, being originally a hymn to Apollo, from his name Pæan, became afterwards extended in its use to such addresses to other gods.

thians

thians received, in their conflict with the Pæonians: on the prefent occafion they fought valiantly,
in defence of their liberties, againft Megabyzus, but
were overpowered by the fuperior numbers of the
Perfians. After the capture of Perinthus, Megabyzus over-ran Thrace with his forces, and reduced
all its cities and inhabitants under the power of the
king: the conqueft of Thrace had been particularly enjoined him by Darius.

III. Next to India, Thrace is of all nations the
moft confiderable⁴: if the inhabitants were either
under the government of an individual, or united
amongft themfelves, their ftrength would in my
opinion render them invincible; but this is a thing
impoffible, and they are of courfe but feeble.
Each different diftrict has a different appellation;
but except the Getæ, the Traufi⁵, and thofe beyond Creftona, they are marked by a general fimilitude of manners.

IV. Of the Getæ, who pretend to be immortal,
I have before fpoken. The Traufi have a general
uniformity with the reft of the Thracians, except in
what relates to the birth of their children, and the
burial of their dead. On the birth of a child, he is
placed in the midft of a circle of his relations, who

----

⁴ *Moft confiderable.*]—Thucydides ranks them after the Scythians, and Paufanias after the Celtæ.—*Larcher.*

⁵ *Traufi.*]—Thefe were the people whom the Greeks called
Agathyrfi.—*T.*

lament aloud the evils which, as a human being, he muſt neceſſarily undergo, all of which they particularly enumerate[6]; but whenever any one dies, the body is committed to the ground with clamorous joy, for the deceaſed, they ſay, delivered from his miſeries, is then ſupremely happy.

V. Thoſe beyond the Creſtonians have theſe obſervances :—Each perſon has ſeveral wives; if the huſband dies, a great conteſt commences amongſt his wives, in which the friends of the deceaſed intereſt themſelves exceedingly, to determine which of them

---

[6] *Particularly enumerate.*]—A ſimilar ſentiment is quoted by Larcher, from a fragment of Euripides, of which the following is the verſion of Cicero :—

> Nam nos decebat cœtum celebrantes domus
> Lugere, ubi eſſet aliquis in lucem editus
> Humanæ vitæ varia reputatantes mala
> At qui labores morte finiſſet graves
> Hunc omni amicos laude et lætitia exſequi.

See alſo on this ſubject Gray's fine Ode on a diſtant Proſpect of Eton College :—

> Alas ! regardleſs of their doom,
> The little victims play;
> No ſenſe have they of ills to come,
> Nor care beyond to-day :
> Yet ſee how all around them wait
> The miniſters of human fate,
> And black misfortune's baleful train.
> Ah ! ſhew them where in ambuſh ſtand,
> To ſeize their prey, the murtherous band;
> Ah ! tell them they are men.—
> Theſe ſhall the fury paſſions tear ? &c.   *T.*

had

had been moſt beloved. She to whom this honour
is aſcribed is gaudily decked out by her friends,
and then ſacrificed by her neareſt relation on the
tomb of her huſband [7], with whom ſhe is afterwards

[7] *Tomb of her huſband.*]—This cuſtom was alſo obſerved by
the Getæ: at this day, in India, women burn themſelves with
the bodies of their huſbands, which uſage muſt have been continued there from remote antiquity. Propertius mentions it:

> Et certamen habent leti quæ viva ſequatur
> Conjugium, pudor eſt non licuiſſe mori
> Ardent victrices et flammæ pectora præbent
> Imponuntque ſuis ora peruſta viris.

Cicero mentions alſo the ſame fact. Larcher quotes the paſſage
from the Tuſculan Queſtions, of which the following is a tranſlation.

" The women in India, when their huſband dies, eagerly contend to have it determined which of them he loved beſt, for
each man has ſeveral wives. She who conquers, deems herſelf
happy, is accompanied by her friends to the funeral pile, where
her body is burned with that of her huſband; they who are
vanquiſhed depart in ſorrow."—The civil code of the Indians,
requiring this ſtrange ſacrifice, is to this effect: " It is proper
for a woman, after her huſband's death, to burn herſelf in the
fire with his corpſe, unleſs ſhe be with child, or that her huſband
be abſent, or that ſhe cannot get his turban or his girdle, or unleſs ſhe devote herſelf to chaſtity and celibacy: every woman
who thus burns herſelf ſhall, according to the decrees of deſtiny,
remain with her huſband in paradiſe for ever."—" This practice," ſays Raynal, " ſo evidently contrary to reaſon, has been
chiefly derived from the doctrine of the reſurrection of the dead,
and of a future life: the hope of being ſerved in the other
world by the ſame perſons who obeyed us in this has been the
cauſe of the ſlave being ſacrificed on the tomb of his maſter,
and the wife on the corpſe of her huſband; but that the Indians,
who firmly believed in the tranſmigration of ſouls, ſhould give

wards buried: his other wives esteem this an affliction, and it is imputed to them as a great disgrace.

VI. The other Thracians have a custom of selling their children, to be carried out of their country. To their young women they pay no regard, suffering them to connect themselves indiscriminately with men; but they keep a strict guard over their wives, and purchase them of their parents at an immense price. To have punctures on the skin [s] is with them a mark of nobility, to be without these is a testimony of mean descent: the most honourable life with them is a life of indolence; the most contemptible that of an husbandman. Their

way to this prejudice, is one of those numberless inconsistencies which in all parts of the world degrade the human mind."—*See Raynal*, vol. i. 91. The remark, in the main, is just, but the author, I fear, meant to insinuate that practices contrary to reason naturally proceed from the doctrines he mentions; a suggestion which, though very worthy of the class of writers to which he belongs, has not reason enough in it to deserve a serious reply.—*T*.

[s] *Punctures on their skin.*]—If Plutarch may be credited, the Thracians in his time made these punctures on their wives, to revenge the death of Orpheus, whom they had murdered. Phanocles agrees with this opinion, in his poem upon Orpheus, of which a fragment has been preserved by Stobæus. If this be the true reason, it is remarkable that what in its origin was a punishment, became afterwards an ornament, and a mark of nobility.—*Larcher*.

Of such great antiquity does the custom of tattaowing appear to have been, with descriptions of which the modern voyages to the South Sea abound.—*T*.

supreme

fupreme delight is in war and plunder.—Such are their more remarkable diftinctions.

VII. The gods whom they worfhip are Mars, Bacchus [9], and Diana : befides thefe popular gods, and in preference to them, their princes worfhip Mercury. They fwear by him alone, and call themfelves his defcendants.

VIII. The funerals of their chief men are of this kind : For three days the deceafed is publicly expofed; then having facrificed animals of every defcription, and uttered many and loud lamentations, they celebrate a feaft [10], and the body is finally either

---

[9] *Bacchus.*]—That Bacchus was worfhipped in Thrace, is attefted by many authors, and particularly by Euripides : in the Rhefus, attributed to that poet, that prince, after being flain by Ulyffes, was tranfported to the caverns of Thrace by the mufe who bore him, and becoming a divinity, he there declared the oracles of Bacchus. In the Hccuba of the fame author, Bacchus is called the deity of Thrace. Some placed the oracle of Bacchus near mount Pangæa, others near mount Hæmus.— *Larcher.*

[10] *Celebrate a feaft.*]—It appears from a paffage in Jeremiah, that this mixture of mourning and feafting at funerals was very common amongft the Jews :—

" Both the great and the fmall fhall die in this land: they fhall not be buried, neither fhall men lament for them, nor cut themfelves, nor make themfelves bald for them.

" Neither fhall men tear themfelves for them in mourning, to comfort them for the dead; neither fhall men give them the cup of confolation to drink for their father or for their mother.

" Thou

either burned or buried. They afterwards raise a mound of earth " upon the spot, and celebrate games " of various kinds, in which each particular contest has a reward assigned suitable to its nature.

IX. With respect to the more northern parts of this region, and its inhabitants, nothing has been yet decisively ascertained. What lies beyond the Ister, is a vast and almost endless space. The whole

" Thou shalt not also go into the house of feasting, to sit with them to eat and to drink."—xvi. 6, 7, 8.

The same custom is still observed in the countries of the east. —*T.*

" *Mound of earth.*]—Over the place of burial of illustrious persons, they raised a kind of tumulus of earth. This is well expressed in the " ingens aggeritur tumulo tellus," of Virgil. —*Larcher.*

The practice of raising barrows over the bodies of the deceased was almost universal in the earlier ages of the world. Homer mentions it as a common practice among the Greeks and Trojans. Virgil alludes to it as usual in the times treated of in the Æneid. Xenophon relates that it obtained among the Persians. The Roman historians record that the same mode of interring took place among their countrymen; and it appears to have prevailed no less among the ancient Germans, and many other uncivilized nations.—See *Coxe's Travels through Poland,* &c.

" *Celebrate games.*]—It is impossible to say when funeral games were first instituted. According to Pliny, they existed before the time of Theseus; and many have supposed that the famous games of Greece were in their origin funeral games. The best description of these is to be found in Homer and in Virgil. In the former, those celebrated by Achilles in honour of Patroclus; in the latter, those of Æneas in memory of his father.—*T.*

of

of this, as far as I am able to learn, is inhabited by the Sigynæ, a people who in drefs refemble the Medes; their horfes are low in ftature, and of a feeble make, but their hair grows to the length of five digits; they are not able to carry a man, but, yoked to a carriage, are remarkable for their fwiftnefs, for which reafon carriages are here very common. The confines of this people extend almoft to the Eneti [13] on the Adriatic. They call themfelves a colony of the Medes [14]; how this could be, I am not able to determine, though in a long feries of time it may not have been impoffible. The Sigynæ are called merchants [15] by the Ligurians,

[13] *Eneti,*] or rather Heneti, which afpirate, reprefented by the Æolic digamma, forms the Latin name Veneti. Their horfes were anciently in great eftimation. See the Hippolytus of Euripides, ver. 230. Homer fpeaks of their mules.—*T.*

[14] *Colony of the Medes.*]—Strabo fays that this people obferved in a great meafure the cuftoms of the Perfians: thus the people whom Herodotus calls Medes might be confidered as genuine Perfians, according to his cuftom of confounding their names, if Diodorus Siculus had not decided the matter.

[15] *Called merchants.*]—The whole of this fentence Larcher omits, giving as his opinion, that it was inferted by fome Scholiaft in the margin, and had thence found its way into the text. For my part, I fee no reafon for this; and I think the explication given by the Abbé Bellanger, in his Effais de Critique fur les Traduct. d'Herodote, may fairly be accepted. Herodotus means, fays he, to inform his reader, that Sigynæ is not an unufual word; the Ligurians ufe it for merchants, the Cyprians for fpears."—But if this be true, the following verfion by Littlebury muft appear abfurd enough: " The Ligurians," fays he, " who inhabit beyond Marfeilles, call the Sigynes brokers; and the Cyprians give them the name of javelins."—*T.*

whø

who live beyond Maffilia : with the Cyprians, Sigynæ is the name for fpears.

X. The Thracians affirm that the places beyond
the Ifter are poffeffed wholly by bees, and that a
paffage beyond this is impracticable. To me this
feems altogether impoffible, for the bee is an infect
known to be very impatient of cold [16]; the extremity of which, as I fhould think, is what renders
the parts to the north uninhabitable. The fea-coaft
of this region was reduced by Megabyzus under
the power of Perfia.

XI. Darius having croffed the Hellefpont, went
immediately to Sardis, where he neither forgot the
fervice of Hiftiæus, nor the advice of Coës of
Mitylene. He accordingly fent for thefe two perfons, and defired them to afk what they would.
Hiftiæus, who was tyrant of Miletus, wifhed for
no acceffion of power; he merely required the
Edonian [17] Myncinus, with the view of building
there

[16] *Impatient of cold.*]—This remark of Herodotus concerning bees, is in a great meafure true, becaufe all apiaries are
found to fucceed and thrive beft, which are expofed to a degree
of middle temperature : yet it would be difficult perhaps to
afcertain the precife degree of cold in which bees would ceafe
to live and multiply. Modern experiments have made it obvi-
oufly appear, that in fevere winters this infect has perifhed as
frequently from famine as from cold. It is alfo well known
that bees have lived in hollow trees in the colder parts of Ruffia.
—*T.*

[17] *Edonian.*]—This diftrict is by fome writers placed in
Thrace,

there a city: Coës, on the contrary, who was a private individual, wished to be made prince of Mitylene. Having obtained what they severally desired, they departed.

XII. Darius, induced by a circumstance of which he was accidentally witness, required Megabyzus to transport the Pæonians from Europe to Asia. Pigres and Mantyes were natives of Pæonia, the government of which became the object of their ambition. With these views, when Darius had passed over into Asia, they betook themselves to Sardis, carrying with them their sister, a person of great elegance and beauty. As Darius was sitting publicly in that division of the city appropriate to the Lydians, they took the opportunity of executing the following artifice: they decorated their sister in the best manner they were able, and sent her to draw water; she had a vessel upon her head.[13], she led

a horse

Thrace, by others in Macedonia. The *o* is used long by Virgil, and short by Lucan:

Ac velut Edoni Boreæ cum spiritus alto.

Æn. xii. 365.

Nam qualis vertice Pindi
Edonis Ogygio decurrit plena Lyæo.

Luc. i. 674. *T.*

[13] *Upon her head.*]—Nicolas Damascenus tells a similar story of Alyattes king of Sardis. This prince was one day sitting before the walls of the town, when he beheld a Thracian woman with an urn on her head, a distaff and spindle in her hand, and behind her a horse secured by a bridle. The king, astonished,

nished,

a horſe by a bridle faſtened round her arm, and ſhe
was moreover ſpinning ſome thread. Darius viewed her as ſhe paſſed with attentive curioſity, obſerving that her employments were not thoſe of a
Perſian, Lydian, nor indeed of any Aſiatic female.
He was prompted by what he had ſeen to ſend
ſome of his attendants, who might obſerve what
ſhe did with the horſe. They accordingly followed her: the woman, when ſhe came to the river,
gave her horſe ſome water, and then filled her
pitcher. Having done this, ſhe returned by the
way ſhe came; with the pitcher of water on her
head, the horſe faſtened by a bridle to her arm,
and as before employed in ſpinning.

XIII. Darius, equally ſurprized at what he heard
from his ſervants and had ſeen himſelf, ſent for the
woman to his preſence. On her appearance, the
brothers, who had obſerved all from a convenient
ſituation, came forwards, and declared that they
were Pæonians, and the woman their ſiſter. Upon

---

niſhed, aſked her who and of what country ſhe was? She replied, ſhe was of Myſia, a diſtrict of Thrace. In conſequence of this adventure, the king by his ambaſſadors deſired
Cotys prince of Thrace to ſend him a colony from that country,
of men, women, and children.—*Larcher.*

  The Myſia mentioned in the above account is called by ſome
Greek writers *Myſia in Europe,* to diſtinguiſh it from the province of that name in Aſia Minor; but Pliny, and moſt of the
Latin writers, diſtinguiſh it more effectually, by writing it
Mœſia; in which form it will be found in the maps, extending
along the ſouthern ſide of the Danube, oppoſite to Dacia: being
the tract which forms the modern Servia and Bulgaria.

this

this Darius enquired who the Pæonians were, where was their country, and what had induced themfelves to come to Sardis. The young men replied, " that as to themfelves, their only motive was a de- " fire of entering into his fervice; that Pæonia " their country was fituated on the banks of the " river Strymon, at no great diftance from the Hel- " lefpont." They added, " that the Pæonians were " a Trojan colony." Darius then enquired if all the women of their country were thus accuftomed to labour; they replied without hefitation in the affirmative, for this was the point they had particularly in view.

XIV. In confequence of the above, Darius fent letters to Megabyzus, whom he had left commander of his forces in Thrace, ordering him to remove all the Pæonians to Sardis, with their wives and families. The courier fent with this meffage inftantly made his way to the Hellefpont, which having paffed, he prefented Megabyzus with the orders of his mafter. Megabyzus accordingly loft no time in executing them; but taking with him fome Thracian guides [19], led his army againft Pæonia.

XV. The Pæonians being aware of the intentions of the Perfians, collected their forces, and advanced towards the fea, imagining the enemy would

---

[19] *Thracian guides.*]—The French tranflators of Herodotus who preceded Larcher, miftaking the Latin verfion, fumptis e Thraciâ ducibus, have rendered this paffage, " commanda aux capitaines de Thrace."—*T.*

there make their attack : thus they prepared themfelves to refift the invafion of Megabyzus : but the
Perfian general being informed that every approach
from the fea was guarded by their forces, under the
direction of his guides made a circuit by the
higher parts of the country, and thus eluding the
Pæonians, came unexpectedly upon their towns, of
which, as they were generally deferted, he took poffeffion without difficulty.   The Pæonians, informed
of this event, difperfed themfelves, and returning
to their families fubmitted to the Perfians.   Thus,
the Pæonians, the Syropæonians, the Pæoplæ,
and they who poffefs the country as far as the Prafian lake, were removed from their habitations, and
tranfported to Afia.

XVI. The people in the vicinity of mount Pangæus [10], with the Doberæ, the Agrianæ, Odomanti,
and thofe of the Prafian lake, Megabyzus was not
able to fubdue.   They who lived upon the lake, in
dwellings of the following conftruction, were the
objects of his next attempt.   In this lake ftrong
piles [11] are driven into the ground, over which planks
are thrown, connected by a narrow bridge with the
fhore.   Thefe erections were in former times made
at the public expence ; but a law afterwards paffed,
obliging a man for every wife whom he fhould marry

[10] *Pangæus.*]—This place, as Herodotus informs us in the
feventh book, poffeffed both gold and filver mines.—*T.*

[11] *Strong piles,* &c.]—Exemplum urbis in fluvio fuper tignis
et tabulatis ftructæ in America habet Teixeira.—*Reifke.*

(and

(and they allow a plurality) to drive three of thefe piles into the ground, taken from a mountain called Orbelus. Upon thefe planks each man has his hut, from every one of which a trap-door opens to the water. To prevent their infants from falling into the lake, they faften a ftring to their legs. Their horfes and cattle are fed principally with fifh[11], of which there is fuch abundance, that if any one lets down a bafket into the water, and fteps afide, he may prefently after draw it up full of fifh. Of thefe they have two particular fpecies, called papraces and tilones.

XVII. Such of the Pæonians as were taken captive were removed into Afia. After the conqueft of this people, Megabyzus fent into Macedonia feven Perfians of his army, next in dignity and eftimation to himfelf, requiring of Amyntas, in the name of Darius, earth and water. From the lake Prafis to Macedonia there is a very fhort paffage; for upon the very brink of the lake is found the mine which in after-times produced to Alexander a talent every day. Next to this mine is the Dyfian mount, which being paffed, you enter Macedonia.

XVIII. The Perfians on their arrival were admitted to an immediate audience of Amyntas, when

---

[11] *With fifh.*]—Torffæus, in his Hiftory of Norway, informs us, that in the cold and maritime parts of Europe cattle are fed with fifh.—*Weffeling.*

they

they demanded of him, in the name of Darius, earth and water. This was not only granted, but Amyntas received the meſſengers hoſpitably into his family, gave them a ſplendid entertainment, and treated them with particular kindneſs. When after the entertainment they began to drink, one of the Perſians thus addreſſed Amyntas: " Prince of Ma-
" cedonia, it is a cuſtom with us Perſians, when-
" ever we have a public entertainment, to intro-
" duce our concubines and young wives. Since
" therefore you have received us kindly, and with
" the rites of hoſpitality, and have alſo acknow-
" ledged the claims of Darius, in giving him earth
" and water, imitate the cuſtom we have men-
" tioned." " Perſians," replied Amyntas, " our
" manners are very different, for our women are
" kept ſeparate from the men. But ſince you are
" our maſters, and require it, what you ſolicit ſhall
" be granted." Amyntas therefore ſent for the women, who on their coming were ſeated oppoſite to the Perſians. The Perſians obſerving them beautiful, told Amyntas that he was ſtill defective:
" For it were better," they exclaimed, " that they
" had not come at all, than on their appearing
" not to ſuffer them to ſit near us, but to place
" them oppoſite, as a kind of torment to our
" eyes²¹." Amyntas, acting thus under compul-
ſion,

²¹ *Torment to our eyes.*]—This paſſage has been the occaſion of much critical controverſy. Longinus cenſures it as frigid. Many learned men, in oppoſition to Longinus, have vindicated

the

Gon, directed the women to fit with the Perfians.
The women obeyed, and the Perfians, warmed by
their wine, began to put their hands to their bo-
foms, and to kifs them.

the expreffion. Pearce, in his Commentaries, is of opinion that
thofe who in this inftance have oppofed themfelves to Longinus
have not entered into the precife meaning of that critic. The
hiftorian, he obferves, does not mean to fay that the beauty of
thefe females might not excite dolores oculorum, but they could
not themfelves properly be termed dolores oculorum. Pearce
quotes a paffage from Æfchylus, where Helen is called μαλθακον
ομμάτων βιλος, the tender dart of the eyes. Alexander the
Great called the Perfian women βολιδας ομματων, the darts of
the eyes. After all, to me at leaft, confidering it was ufed by
natives of Perfia, and making allowance for the warm and
figurative language of the eaft, the expreffion feems to require
neither comment nor vindication. In fome claffical lines written
by Cowley, called The Account, I find this ftrong expreffion:

> When all the ftars are by thee told,
> The endlefs fums of heavenly gold;
> Or when the hairs are reckon'd all,
> From fickly Autumn's head that fall;
> Or when the drops that make the fea,
> Whilft all her fands thy counters be,
> Thou then, and then alone, may'ft prove
> Th' arithmetician of my love.
> An hundred loves at Athens fcore;
> At Corinth write an hundred more;
> Three hundred more at Rhodes and Crete,
> Three hundred 'tis I'm fure complete,
> For arms at Crete each face does bear,
> *And every eye's an archer there*, &c.

When we confider that the Cretan archers were celebrated beyond all others, this expreffion will not feem much lefs bold or
figurative than that of Herodotus.—*T.*

XIX.

XIX. Amyntas obferved this indecency, and with great vexation, though his awe of the Perfians induced him not to notice it. But his fon Alexander, who was alfo prefent, and witneffed their behaviour, being in the vigour of youth, and hitherto without experience of calamity, was totally unable to bear it. " Sir," faid he to Amyntas, being much incenfed, " your age is a fufficient ex-" cufe for your retiring; leave me to prefide at the " banquet, and to pay fuch attention to our guefts " as fhall be proper and neceffary." Amyntas could not but obferve that the warmth of youth prompted his fon to fome act of boldnefs; he accordingly made him this reply : " I can plainly fee " your motive for foliciting my abfence; you de-" fire me to go, that you may perpetrate fomewhat " to which your fpirit impels you; but I muft in-" fift upon it²⁴, that you do not occafion our ruin " by molefting thefe men; fuffer their indignities " patiently.— I fhall however follow your advice, " and retire." With thefe words Amyntas left them.

XX. Upon this Alexander thus addreffed the Perfians : " You are at liberty, Sirs, to repofe your-" felves with any or with all of thefe females; I

²⁴ *Infift upon it.*]—The reader will in this place, I prefume, be naturally fufpicious that the good old king Amyntas was well aware what his fon Alexander intended to perpetrate. If he fufpected what was about to be done, and had not wifhed its accomplifhment, he would probably, notwithftanding his age, have ftayed and prevented it.—*T.*

have

" have only to require, that you will make your
" choice known to me. It is now almoſt time to
" retire, and I can perceive that our wine has had
" its effect upon you. You will pleaſe therefore
" to ſuffer theſe women to go and bathe them-
" ſelves, and they ſhall afterwards return." The
Perſians approved of what he ſaid, and the women
retired to their proper apartments; but, in their
room, he dreſſed up an equal number of ſmooth-
faced young men, and arming each with a dagger, he introduced them to the company. " Per-
" ſians," ſaid he, on their entering, " we have given
" you a magnificent entertainment, and ſupplied
" you with every thing in our power to procure.
" We have alſo, which with us weighs more than
" all the reſt, preſented you with our matrons and
" our ſiſters, that we might not appear to you in
" any reſpect inſenſible of your merits; and that
" you may inform the king your maſter with what
" liberality a Greek and prince of Macedonia has
" entertained you at bed and at board." When
he had thus ſaid, Alexander commanded the Macedonians, whom he addreſſed as females, to ſit by
the ſide of the Perſians; but on their firſt attempt
to touch them, the Macedonians put every one of
them to death.

XXI. Theſe Perſians with their retinue thus
forfeited their lives; they had been attended on this
expedition with a number of carriages and ſervants,
all of which were ſeized and plundered. At no
great interval of time, a ſtrict inquiſition was made

by the Perſians into this buſineſs; but Alexander, by his diſcretion, obviated its effects. To Bubaris[25], a native of Perſia, and one of thoſe[26] who had been ſent to enquire into the death of his countrymen, he made very liberal preſents, and gave his ſiſter in marriage. By theſe means the aſſaſſination of the Perſian officers was overlooked and forgotten.

XXII. Theſe Greeks were deſcended from Per-diccas: this they themſelves affirm, and indeed I myſelf know it, from certain circumſtances which I ſhall hereafter relate. My opinion of this matter is alſo confirmed by the determination of thoſe who preſide at the Olympic games[27]: for when Alexander,

with

---

[25] *Bubaris.*]—It appears from book the ſeventh, chap. 21, of our author, that this Bubaris was the ſon of Megabyzus. —*T.*

[26] *One of thoſe.*]—It is contended by Valknaer, and who is anſwered by Larcher, in a very long note, that inſtead of τῶν ϛϱατηγῶν, it ſhould be τῷ ϛϱατηγῳ, that is in fact, whether it ſhould be "one of thoſe," &c. or "chief of thoſe," &c. Which of theſe is the more proper reading, is not, I think, of ſufficient importance to warrant any haſty ſuſpicion, not to ſay alteration of the text. That Bubaris was a man of rank we know, for he was the ſon of Megabyzus; that he was the chief of thoſe employed on this occaſion, may be preſumed, from his receiving from Alexander many liberal preſents, and his own ſiſter in marriage.—*T.*

[27] *Preſide at the Olympic games.*]—The judges who preſided at the Olympic games were called Hellanodicæ; their number varied at different times; they were a long time ten, ſometimes more, ſometimes leſs, according to the number of the Elean tribes; but it finally reverted to ten. They did not all judge promiſcuouſly at every conteſt, but only ſuch as were deputed to

de

with an ambition of diftinguifhing himfelf, expreffed a defire of entering the lifts, the Greeks, who were his competitors, repelled him with fcorn, afferting, that this was a conteft, not of Barbarians, but of Greeks; but he proved himfelf to be an Argive, and was confequently allowed to be a Greek. He was then permitted to contend, and was paired with the firft combatant [28].

do fo. Their decifions might be appealed from, and they might even be accufed before the fenate of Olympia, who fometimes fet afide their determinations. They who were elected Hella-nodicæ were compelled to refide ten months fucceffively in a building appropriated to their ufe at Olympia, and named from them the Hellanodicæon, in order to inftruct themfelves, pre-vious to their entering on their office.—*Larcher.*

[28] *With the firft combatant.*]—See Lucian, Hermotimus, vol. i. p. 782-3.—Hemfterhufius.

Lycinus.—Do not, Hermotimus, tell me what anciently was done, but what you yourfelf have feen at no great diftance of time.

Hermotimus.—A filver urn was produced facred to the god, into which fome fmall lots of the fize of beans were thrown: two of thefe are infcribed with the letter A, two more with B, two others with G, and fo on, according to the number of com-petitors, there being always two lots marked with the fame letter. The combatants then advanced one by one, and call-ing on the name of Jupiter, put his hand into the urn, and drew out a lot. An officer ftood near with a cudgel in his hand, and ready to ftrike if any one attempted to fee what letter he had drawn. Then the Alytarch, or one of the Hellanodicæ, obliging them to ftand in a circle, paired fuch together as had drawn the fame letter. If the number of competitors was not equal, he who drew the odd letter was matched againft the victor, which was no fmall advantage, as he had to enter the lifts quite frefh againft a man already fatigued.

C c 2   XXIII.

XXIII. I have related the facts which happened. Megabyzus, taking the Pœonians along with him, passed the Hellespont, and arrived at Sardis. At this period, Histiæus the Milesian was engaged in defending with a wall the place which had been given him by Darius, as a reward for his preserving the bridge; it is called Myncinus [29], and is near the river Strymon. Megabyzus, as soon as he came to Sardis, and learned what had been done with respect to Histiæus, thus addressed Darius: "Have you, Sir, done wisely, in permitting a "Greek of known activity and abilities to erect a "city in Thrace? in a place which abounds with "every requisite for the construction and equip- "ment of ships; and where there are also mines of "silver? A number of Greeks are there, mixed "with Barbarians, who, making him their leader, "will be ready on every occasion to execute his "commands. Suffer him therefore to proceed no "farther, lest a civil war be the consequence. Do "not, however, use violent measures; but when "you shall have him in your power, take care to "prevent the possibility of his return to Greece."

XXIV. Darius was easily induced to yield to the arguments of Megabyzus, of whose sagacity he entirely approved. He immediately therefore sent him a message to the following purport: "His- "tiæus, king Darius considers you as one of the

---

[29] *Myncinus.*]—This place in some books of geography is written Myncenus.—*T.*

"ablest

" ableſt ſupports of his throne, of which he has
" already received the ſtrongeſt teſtimony. He
" has now in contemplation. a buſineſs of great
" importance, and requires your preſence and ad-
" vice." Hiſtiæus believed the meſſenger, and,
delighted with the idea of being invited to the
king's councils, haſtened to Sardis, where on his
arrival Darius thus addreſſed him : " Hiſtiæus,
" my motive for ſoliciting your preſence is this ;
" my not ſeeing you at my return from Scythia
" filled me with the extremeſt regret ; my deſire to
" converſe with you continually increaſed, being
" well convinced that there is no treaſure ſo great
" as a ſincere and ſagacious friend, for of your truth
" as well as prudence I have received the moſt ſa-
" tisfactory proofs. You have done well in coming
" to me ; I therefore intreat that, forgetting Miletus,
" and leaving the city you have recently built in
" Thrace, you will accompany me to Suſa ; you
" ſhall there have apartments in my palace, and
" live with me, my companion and my friend."

XXV. Darius having thus accompliſhed his
wiſhes, took Hiſtiæus with him, and departed for
Suſa. Artaphernes, his brother by the father's
ſide, was left governor of Sardis ; Otanes was entruſted with the command of the ſea-coaſt. Si-
ſamnes, the father of the latter, had been one of the
royal judges ; but having been guilty of corruption in the execution of his office, was put to
death by Cambyſes. By order of this prince, the
entire ſkin was taken from his body, and fixed over the

tribunal

tribunal [10] at which he formerly prefided. Cambyfes
gave the office of Sifamnes to his fon Otanes, commanding him to have conftantly in memory in what
tribunal he fat.

XXVI. Otanes having at firft the above appointment, fucceeded afterwards to the command of Megabyzus, when he reduced Byzantium and Chalcedon. He took alfo Lamponium [11] and Antandros [12], which latter is in the province of Troy.
With the affiftance of a fleet from Lefbos, he made
himfelf mafter of Lemnos and Imbros, both of
which were then inhabited by Pelafgi.

XXVII. The Lemnians fought with great bravery, and made a long and vigorous refiftance, but
were at length fubdued. Over fuch as furvived the
conflict the Perfians appointed Lycaretus governor; he was the brother of Mæander, who had

---

[10] *Fixed over the tribunal.*]—This it feems was a common
cuftom in Perfia; and corrupt judges were fometimes flayed
alive, and their fkins afterwards thus difpofed. Larcher quotes
a paffage from Diodorus Siculus, which informs us that Artaxerxes punifhed fome unjuft judges precifely in this manner.
—*T.*

[11] *Lamponium.*]—Pliny, and I believe Strabo, call this place
Lamporea. It was an ifland of the Cherfonefe.

[12] *Antandros.*]—

Claffemque fub ipfa
Antandro et Phrygiæ molimur montibus Idæ.
Virg. Æn. iii. 5.

This place has experienced a variety of names, Affos, Apollonia, and now Dimitri—*T.*

reigned

reigned at Samos, but he died during his government. All the above-mentioned people were reduced to fervitude: it was pretended that fome had been deferters in the Scythian expedition, and that others had harraffed Darius in his retreat. Such was the conduct of Otanes in his office, which he did not long enjoy with tranquillity.

XXVIII. The Ionians were foon vifited by new calamities, from Miletus and from Naxos [13]. Of all the iflands, Naxos was the happieft; but Miletus might be deemed the pride of Ionia, and was at that time in the height of its profperity. In the two preceding ages it had been confiderably weakened by internal factions, but the tranquillity of its inhabitants was finally reftored by the interpofition of the Parians [14], whom the Milefians had preferred on this occafion to all the other Greeks.

XXIX.

---

[13] *Naxos.*]—This place was firft called Strongyle, afterwards Dia, and then Naxos; there was a place of this name alfo in Sicily. The Naxos of the Ægean is now called Naxia; it was anciently famous for its whetftones, and Naxia cos became a proverb. In claffical ftory, this ifland is famous for being the place where Thefeus, returning from Crete, forfook Ariadne, who afterwards became the wife of Bacchus: a very minute and fatisfactory account of the ancient and modern condition of this ifland, is to be found in Tournefort. Stephens the geographer fays, that the women of Naxos went with child but eight months, and that the ifland poffeffed a fpring of pure wine.—*T.*

[14] *Parians.*]—The inhabitants of Paros have always been accounted people of good fenfe, and the Greeks of the neigh-

bouring

XXIX. To heal the diforders which exifted amongft them, the Parians applied the following remedy :—Thofe employed in this office were of confiderable diftinction; and perceiving, on their arrival at Miletus, that the whole ftate was involved in extreme confufion, they defired to examine the condition of their territories : wherever, in their progrefs through this defolate country, they obferved any lands well cultivated, they wrote down the name of the owner. In the whole diftrict, however, they found but few eftates fo circumftanced. Returning to Miletus, they called an affembly of the people, and they placed the direction of affairs in the hands of thofe who had beft cultivated their lands; for they concluded, that they would be watchful of the public intereft who had taken care of their own : they enjoined all the Milefians who had before been factious, to obey thefe, and they thus reftored the general tranquillity.

XXX. The evils which the Ionians experienced from thefe cities were of this nature :—Some of the more noble inhabitants of Naxos were driven by the common people into banifhment; they fought a refuge at Miletus ; Miletus was then governed by Ariftagoras, fon of Molpagoras, the fon-in-law and coufin of Hiftiæus, fon of Lyfagoras, whom Darius detained at Sufa : Hiftiæus was

bouring iflands often make them arbitrators of their difputes.
—See Tournefort, who gives an excellent account of this ifland.

prince of Miletus, but was at Sufa when the Naxians arrived in his dominions. Thefe exiles petitioned Ariftagoras to affift them with fupplies, to enable them to return to their country: he immediately conceived the idea, that by accomplifhing their return, he might eventually become mafter of Naxos. He thought proper, however, to remind them of the alliance which fubfifted betwixt Hiftiæus and their countrymen; and he addreffed them as follows: "I am not mafter of adequate force "to reftore you to your country, if they who are "in poffeffion of Naxos fhall think proper to op- "pofe me: the Naxians, I am told, have eight "thoufand men in arms, and many fhips of war'; "I, neverthelefs, wifh to effect it, and I think it "may be thus accomplifhed—Artaphernes, fon of "Hyftafpes, and brother of Darius, is my particu- "lar friend; he has the command of all the fea- "coaft of Afia, and is provided with a numerous "army, and a powerful fleet; he will, I think, do "all that I defire." The Naxians inftantly intrufted Anaxagoras with the management of the bufinefs, intreating him to complete it as he could: they engaged to affift the expedition with forces, and to make prefents to Artaphernes; and they expreffed great hopes that as foon as they fhould appear before the place, Naxos, with the reft of the iflands, would immediately fubmit; for hitherto none of the Cyclades were under the power of Darius.

XXXI. Ariftagoras went immediately to Sardis, where

where meeting with Artaphernes, he painted to
him in flattering terms the iſland of Naxos, which,
though of no great extent, he repreſented as exceedingly fair and fertile, conveniently ſituated with
reſpect to Ionia, very wealthy, and remarkably populous.—" It will be worth your while," ſaid he,
" to make an expedition againſt it, under pretence
" of reſtoring its exiles ; to facilitate this, I already
" poſſeſs a conſiderable ſum of money, beſides
" what will be otherwiſe ſupplied. It is proper
" that we who ſet the expedition on foot ſhould
" provide the contingent expences ; but you will
" certainly acquire to the king our maſter, Naxos
" with its dependencies, Paros and Andros, with
" the reſt of the iſlands called the Cyclades : from
" hence you may eaſily attempt the invaſion of
" Eubœa [15], an iſland large and fertile, and not at
" all inferior to Cyprus ; this will afford you an
" eaſy conqueſt, and a fleet of an hundred ſhips
" will be ſufficient to effect the whole." To this
Artaphernes replied, " What you recommend
" will, unqueſtionably, promote the intereſt of the
" king, and the particulars of your advice are rea-
" ſonable and conſiſtent ; inſtead of one hundred, a
" fleet of two hundred veſſels ſhall be ready for you
" in the beginning of ſpring ; it will be proper,

---

[15] *Eubœa.*]—This large iſland is now commonly called Ne-
gropont or Negrepont, by the Europeans ; which is a corruption
of its proper appellation *Egripo :* anciently it had, at different
times, a great variety of names, Macris, Chalcis, Aſopis, &c.
At Artemiſium, one of its promontories, the firſt battle was
fought betwixt Xerxes and the Greeks.—*T.*

" however,

" however, to have the fanction of the king's au-
" thority."

XXXII. Pleafed with the anfwer he received,
Ariftagoras returned to Miletus. Artaphernes fent
immediately to acquaint Darius with the project of
Ariftagoras, which met his approbation ; he accordingly fitted out two hundred triremes, which he
manned partly with Perfians and partly with their
allies : Megabates had the command of the whole,
a Perfian of the family of the Achæmenides, related
to Darius and himfelf, whofe daughter, if report
may be credited [16], was, in fucceeding times, be-
trothed to Paufanias the Lacedæmonian, fon of
Cleombrotus, who afpired to the fovereignty of
Greece. Thefe forces, under the direction of this
Megabates, were fent by Artaphernes to Ariftag-
goras.

XXXIII. Megabates embarking at Miletus,
with Ariftagoras, a body of Ionians, and the Naxians, pretended to fail towards the Hellefpont ; but
arriving at Chios, he laid-to near Caucafa [17],
meaning,

---

[16] *If report may be credited.*]—It appears by this, that when
Herodotus compofed this work, he had no knowledge of the
letter in which Paufanias demanded of Xerxes his daughter in
marriage.—It may be feen in Thucydides.—*Larcher.*

[17] *Near Caucafa.*]—This paffage has been erroneoufly rendered,
by the French tranflators of Herodotus who preceded Larcher,
as well as by our countryman Littlebury, " over-againft mount
Caucafus;" but whoever will be at the pains to attend to
the

meaning, under the favour of a north wind, to pass
from thence to Naxos. The following circumstance, however, happened, as if to prove that it
was not ordained for the Naxians to suffer from
this expedition:—Megabates, in going his rounds,
found a Myndian vessel deserted by its crew; he
was so exasperated, that he commanded his guards
to find Scylax, who commanded it, and to bind
him in such a situation, that his head should appear
outwardly from the aperture through which the oar
passed, his body remaining in the vessel. Aristagoras being informed of the treatment which his
friend the Myndian had received, went to Megabates to make his excuse, and obtain his liberty;
but as his expostulations proved ineffectual, he went
himself and released Scylax. Megabates was much
incensed, and expressed his displeasure to Aristagoras; from whom he received this reply: "Your
"authority," said Aristagoras, "does not extend
"so far as you suppose; you were sent to attend
"me, and to sail wherever I should think expe-
"dient;—you are much too officious." Megabates took this reproach so ill, that at the approach
of night he dispatched some emissaries to Naxos, to
acquaint the inhabitants with the intended inva-
sion.

the geographical distances of mount Caucasus and the islands
of the Ægean sea, Chios and Naxos, will easily perceive that
the place here meant must be some strait in the island of Chios,
or some small island in its vicinity.—See the Essais de Critique
sur les Traductions d'Herodote, by the Abbé Bellanger.—
T.

XXXIV.

XXXIV. Of this attack the Naxians had not. the remoteft expectation; but they took the advantage of the intelligence imparted to them, and provided againft a fiege, by removing their valuables from the fields to the town, and by laying up a, ftore of water and provifions, and, laftly, by repairing their walls; they were thus prepared againft every emergence, whilft the Perfians, paffing over from Chios to Naxos, found the place in a perfect ftate of defence. Having wafted four months in the attack, and exhaufted all the pecuniary refources which themfelves had brought, together with what Ariftagoras fupplied, they ftill found that much was wanting to accomplifh their purpofe; they erected, therefore, a fort for the Naxian exiles, and returned to the continent greatly difappointed.

XXXV. Ariftagoras thus found himfelf unable to fulfil his engagements with Artaphernes; and he was alfo, to his great vexation, called upon to defray the expence of the expedition: he faw, moreover, in the perfon of Megabates, an accufer, and he feared that their ill fuccefs fhould be imputed to him, and made a pretence for depriving him of his authority at Miletus; all thefe motives induced him to meditate a revolt. Whilft he was in this perplexity, a meffenger arrived from Hiftiæus, at Sufa, who brought with him an exprefs command to revolt; the particulars of which were impreffed in

legible

legible characters upon his scull [18]. Histiæus was de-
sirous to communicate his intentions to Aristagoras,
but as the ways were strictly guarded, he could devise
no other method; he therefore took one of the most
faithful of his slaves, and inscribed what we have mentioned upon his scull, being first shaved; he detained
the man till his hair was again grown, when he sent
him to Miletus, desiring him to be as expeditious
as possible; and simply requesting Aristagoras to
examine his scull, he discovered the characters
which commanded him to commence a revolt. To
this measure Histiæus was induced, by the vexation

---

[18] *Upon his scull.*]—Many curious contrivances are on record, of which the ancients availed themselves to convey secret
intelligence. Ovid mentions an example of a letter inscribed
on a person's back:

  Caveat hoc custos, pro charta, conscia tergum
  Præbeat, inque suo corpore verba ferat.

The circumstance here mentioned by Herodotus is told at
greater length by Aulus Gellius, who says that Histiæus chose
one of his domestics for this purpose who had sore eyes, to cure
which he told him that his hair must be shaved, and his head
scarified; having done which, he wrote what he intended on
the man's head, and then sent him to Aristagoras, who, he told
him, would effect his cure by shaving his head a second time.
Josephus mentions a variety of stratagems to effect this purpose; some were sent in coffins, during the Jewish war, to convey intelligence; others crept out of places disguised like dogs;
some have conveyed their intentions in various articles of food:
and in bishop Wilkin's Mercury, where a number of examples
of this nature are collected, mention is made of a person, who
rolled up a letter in a wax candle, bidding the messenger inform
the party that was to receive it, that the candle would give him
light for his business.—*T.*

he

he experienced from his captivity at Sufa. He flattered himfelf, that as foon as Ariftagoras was in action he fhould be able to efcape to the fea-coaft; but whilft every thing remained quiet at Miletus, he had no profpect of effecting his return.

XXXVI. With thefe views Hiftiæus difpatched his emiffary; the meffage he delivered to Ariftagoras was alike grateful and feafonable, who accordingly fignified to his party, that his own opinions were confirmed by the commands of Hiftiæus: his intentions to commence a revolt met with the general approbation of the affembly, Hecatæus the hiftorian being the only one who diffented. To diffuade them from any act of hoftility againft the Perfian monarch, he enumerated the various nations which Darius had fubdued, and the prodigious power he poffeffed: when he found thefe arguments ineffectual, he advifed them to let their fleet take immediate poffeffion of the fea, as the only means by which they might expect fuccefs. He confeffed that the refources of the Milefians were but few; but he fuggefted the idea, that if they would make a feizure of the wealth depofited by Crœfus the Lydian in the Branchidian temple [19], they might promife themfelves thefe two advanta-

---

[19] *Branchidian temple.*]—For an account of the temple of Branchidæ, fee vol. i. p. 47. " If Ariftagoras," fays Larcher, " had followed the prudent counfel of Hecatæus, he would have had an increafe of power againft the Perfian, and deprived Xerxes of the opportunity of pillaging this temple, and employing its riches againft Greece."—*T.*

ges;

ges; they would be able to make themselves mafters of the sea, and by thus using thefe riches themfelves would prevent their being plundered by the
enemy.—That thefe riches were of very confiderable value, I have explained in my firft book. This
advice, however, was as ill received, although the
determination to revolt was fixed and univerfal: it
was agreed, that one of their party fhould fail to
the army, which, on its return from Naxos, had
difembarked at Myus [40], with the view of feizing
the perfons of the officers.

XXXVII. Iatragoras was the perfon employed
in this bufinefs; who fo far fucceeded, that he cap-
tured Oliatus the Mylaffenfian, fon of Ibanolis, Hiftiæus of Termene [41], fon of Tymnis, Coës the fon
of Erxander, to whom Darius had given Mitylene,
together with Ariftagoras the Cymæan, fon of Heraclides, with many others. Ariftagoras thus commenced a regular revolt, full of indignation againft

[40] *Myus.*]—This city was given to Themiftocles, to furnifh
his table with fifh, with which the bay of Myus formerly
abounded: the bay, in procefs of time, became a frefh-water
lake, and produced fuch fwarms of gnats, that the inhabitants
deferted the place, and were afterwards incorporated with the
Milefians. Chandler, who vifited this place, complains that the
old nuifance of Myus tormented him and his companions exceedingly, and that towards the evening the infide of their
tent was made quite black by the number of gnats which infefted them.—*T.*

[41] *Termene.*]—Larcher remarks on this word, that no fuch
place exifted in Caria as Termere, which is the common reading: it certainly ought to be Termene.—*T.*

Darius.

Darius. To engage the Milefians to act in concert with him, he eftablifhed among them a republican form of government. He adopted a fimilar conduct with refpect to the reft of Ionia; and to excite a general prejudice in his favour, he expelled the tyrants from fome places, and he alfo fent back thofe who had been taken in the veffels which ferved againft Naxos, to the cities to which they feverally belonged.

XXXVIII. The inhabitants of Mitylene had no fooner got Coës into their hands, than they put him to death, by ftoning him. The Cymeans fent their tyrant back again; and the generality of thofe who had poffeffed the fupreme authority being driven into exile, an equal form of government was eftablifhed: this being accomplifhed, Ariftagoras the Milefian directed magiftrates [41], elected by the people, to be eftablifhed in the different cities; after which he himfelf failed in a trireme to Lacedæmon, convinced of the neceffity of procuring fome powerful allies.

XXXIX. Anaxandrides, fon of Leontes, did not then fit upon the throne of Sparta; he was deceafed, and his fon Cleomenes had fucceeded him, rather on account of his family than his virtues: Anaxan-

---

[41] *Magiftrates.*]—The original is στρατηγος, which, as M. Larcher remarks, does not in this place mean the leader of an army, but a magiftrate, correfponding with the archons of Athens, &c.—*T.*

drides

drides had married his niece, of whom he was exceedingly fond, though she produced him no children; in consequence of which the ephori thus
expostulated with him: " If you do not feel for your-
" self, you ought for us, and not suffer the race of
" Eurysthenes to be extinguished. As the wife which
" you now have is barren, repudiate her and marry
" another, by which you will much gratify your
" countrymen." He replied, that he could not comply with either of their requests, as he did not think
them to be justified in recommending him to divorce
an innocent woman, and to marry another.

XL. The ephori consulted with the senate, and
made him this reply : " We observe your excessive
" attachment to your wife; but if you would avoid
" the resentment of your countrymen, do what we
" advise : we will not insist upon your repudiating
" your present wife,—behave to her as you have
" always done ; but we wish you to marry ano-
" ther, by whom you may have offspring."—To
this Anaxandrides assented, and from that time had
two wives [41], and two separate dwellings, contrary
to the usage of his country.

XLI. At no great interval of time the woman
whom he last married produced him this Cleome-

[41] *Two wives.*]—" He was the only Lacedæmonian," says
Pausanias, " who had two wives at the same time, and had
two separate dwellings."—*See Pausanias, Lacon.* lib. iii. chap. 3.
211.—*T.*

nes,

nes, the presumptive heir of his dominions; about the same period his former wife, who had hitherto been barren, proved with child. Although there was not the smallest doubt of her pregnancy, the relations of the second wife, vexed at the circumstance, industriously circulated a report, that she had not conceived, but intended to impose upon them a supposititious child. Instigated by these insinuations, the ephori distrusted and narrowly observed her; she was, however, delivered first of Dorieus, then of Leonidas [44], and lastly of Cleombrotus; by some it has been affirmed, that Leonidas and Cleombrotus were twins. The second wife, who was the daughter of Prinetades, and grand-daughter of Demarmenus, had never any other child but Cleomenes.

XLII. Of Cleomenes it is reported, that he had not the proper use of his faculties, but was insane; Dorieus, on the contrary, was greatly distinguished by his accomplishments, and trusted to find his way to the throne by valour and by merit. On the death of Anaxandrides [45], the Lacedæmonians, agreeably to the custom of their nation, preferred Cleomenes [46], as eldest, to the sovereignty. This

greatly

[44] *Leonidas.*]—This was the Leonidas who died with so much glory at the straits of Thermopylæ.—*T.*

[45] *Anaxandrides.*]—An apophthegm of this Anaxandrides is left by Plutarch: being asked why they preserved no money in the exchequer; "That the keepers of it," he replied, " might not be tempted to become knaves."—*T.*

[46] *Cleomenes..*]—This Cleomenes, as is reported by Ælian,

greatly difgufted Dorieus, who did nòt choofe to
become the dependant of his brother; taking with
him, therefore, a number of his countrymen, he
left Sparta, and founded a colony : but fo impetu-
ous was his refentment, that he neglected to enquire
of the Delphic oracle where he fhould fix his refidence; nor did he obferve any of the ceremonies [47] ufual on fuch occafions. Under the conduct
of fome Thereans, he failed to Africa, and fettled
on the banks of a river near Cinyps [48], one of the
moft

ufed to fay that Homer was the poet of the Lacedæmonians,
and Hefiod the poet of the Helots : one taught the art of war,
the other of agriculture.—*T.*

[47] *Of the ceremonies.*]—Amongft other ceremonies which they
obferved, when they went to eftablifh a colony, they took fome
fire from the Prytaneum of the metropolis ; and if in the colony
this ever was extinguifhed, they returned to the metropolis to
re-kindle it.—*Larcher.*

[48] *Cinyps.*]—The vicinity of this river abounded in goats,
and was celebrated for its fertility.—See Virgil :

> Nec minus interea barbas, incanaque menta
> Ciniphii tondent hirci.

It may be proper to obferve, that this paffage, quoted from
Virgil, has been the occafion of much literary controverfy.—See
Heyne on Georgic. lib. iii. 312.

The fertility of the places adjoining to the Cinyps, is thus
mentioned by Ovid :

> Ciniphiæ fegetis citius numerabis ariftas.

This river is in the diftrict belonging to the modern Tripoli.

The Cinyps fell into the fea, near Leptis, in Proper Africa ;
Claudian has called it *Vagus,* without much appropriation of
his epithet ; for its courfe is fhort, and not wandering :

Quos

moſt delightful ſituations in that part of the world ᵪ in the third year of his reſidence, being expelled by the joint efforts of the Maci,. Afri, and Carthaginians, he returned to the Peloponneſe.

XLIII. Here Antichares of Elis adviſed him, in conformity to the oracles of Laius [49], to found Heraclea in Sicily; affirming, that all the region of Eryx was the property of the Heraclidæ, as having belonged to Hercules [50]: he accordingly went to Delphi to conſult the oracle, whether the

> Quos Vagus humeċtat Cinyps, et proximus hortis
> Heſperidum Triton, et Gir notiſſimus amnis,
> Æthiopum, ſimili mentitus gurgite Nilum.—
>   *De Laud. Stil.* 251.—*T.*

[49] *Oracles of Laius.*]—The Greek is εκ των Λαιυ χϱησμων:— this M. Larcher has rendered " the oracles declared to Laius." —*T.*

[50] *Belonged to Hercules.*]—When Hercules came into the country of Eryx, Eryx the ſon of Venus, and Bula the king of the country, challenged Hercules to wreſtle with him : both ſides propoſed the wager to be won and loſt. Eryx laid to ſtake his kingdom, but Hercules his oxen : Eryx at firſt diſdained ſuch an unequal wager, not fit to be compared with his country; but when Hercules, on the other ſide, anſwered, that if he loſt them, he ſhould loſe his immortality with them, Eryx was contented with the condition, and engaged in the conteſt; but he was overcome, and ſo was ſtripped of the poſſeſſion of his country, which Hercules gave to the inhabitants, allowing them to take the fruits to their own uſe, till ſome one of his poſterity came to demand it, which afterwards happened; for, many ages after, Dorieus the Lacedæmonian, ſailing into Sicily, recovered his anceſtor's dominion, and there built Heraclea.— *Booth's Diodorus Siculus.*

country where he was about to reside would prove
a permanent acquisition.   The reply of the Pythian
being favourable, he embarked in the same vessels
which had accompanied him from Africa, and sailed to Italy.

XLIV. At this period, as is reported, the Sybarites, under the conduct of Telys their king, meditated an attack upon the inhabitants of Crotona ;
apprehensive of which, these latter implored the
assistance of Dorieus ; he listened to their sollicita-
tions, and joining forces, he marched with them
against Sybaris [51], and took it [52].   The Sybarites
say,

[51] *Sybaris*,]—was founded by the Achæans, betwixt the
rivers Crathis and Sybaris ; it soon became a place of great
opulence and power; the effeminacy of the people became proverbial : see Plutarch.—" It is reported," says he, in his Banquet of the Seven Wise Men, " that the Sybarites used
to invite their neighbours wives a whole twelvemonth before
their entertainments, that they might have convenient time to
dress and adorn themselves."—See also Athenæus, book xii.
c. 3. by whom many whimsical things are recorded of the Sybarites.   Their attendants at the bath had fetters, that they
might not by their careless haste burn those who bathed ; all
noisy trades were banished from their city, that the sleep of the
citizens might not be disturbed ; for the same reason, also, they
permitted no cocks to be kept in their city.   An inhabitant of
this place being once at Sparta, was invited to a public entertainment, where, with the other guests, he was seated on a wooden
bench : " Till now," he remarked, " the bravery of the Spartans has excited my admiration ; but I no longer wonder that
men living so hard a life should be fearless of death."   This
place was afterwards called Thurium.—*T.*

[52] *And took it.*]—The cause of the war, according to Diodo-

say, that Dorieus' and his companions did this; but the people of Crotona deny that in their contest with the Sybarites they availed themselves of the assistance of any foreigner, except Callias of Elis, a priest of the family of the Iamidæ [53]. He had fled from Telys, prince of Sybaris, because on some solemn sacrifice he was not able from the entrails of the victim to promise success against Crotona.— The matter is thus differently stated by the two nations.

XLV. The proofs of what they severally assert are these:—The Sybarites shew near the river Crastis, which is sometimes dry, a sacred edifice, built, as they affirm, by Dorieus after the capture of his city, and consecrated to the Crastian [54] Minerva. The death of Dorieus himself is another, and with

rus Siculus, was this; "Telys persuaded the Sybarites to banish five hundred of their most powerful citizens, and to sell their effects by public auction; the exiles retired to Crotona. Telys sent ambassadors to demand the fugitives, or in case of refusal to denounce war; the people were disposed to give them up, but the celebrated Pythagoras persuaded them to engage in their defence: Milo was very active in the contest, and the event was so fatal to the Sybarites, that their town was plundered and reduced to a perfect solitude.—*Larcher.*

[53] *Iamidæ.*]—To Iamus and his descendants, who were after him called Iamidæ, Apollo gave the art of divination.—See the fifth Olympic of Pindar.

[54] *Crastian.*]—The city Crastis, or, as it is otherwise called, Crastus, was celebrated for being the birth-place of the comic poet Epicharmus, and of the courtesan Lais.—*T.*

them

them the ftrongeft teftimony, for he Poft his life
whilft acting in oppofition to the exprefs commands of the oracle. For if he had confined his
exertions to what was the avowed object of his expedition, he would have obtained, and effectually
fecured, the poffeffion of the region of Eryx, and
thus have preferved himfelf and his followers. The
inhabitants of Crotona are fatisfied with exhibiting
certain lands, given to the Elean Callias, in the diftrict of Crotona, which even within my remembrance the defcendants of Callias poffefs: this
was not the cafe with Dorieus, nor any of his pofterity. It muft be obvious, that if this Dorieus, in
the war above mentioned, had affifted the people of
Crotona, they would have given more to him than
to Callias. To the above different teftimonics,
every perfon is at liberty to give what credit he
thinks proper.

XLVI. Amongft thofe who accompanied Dorieus, with a view of founding a colony, were
Theffalus, Paræbates, Celees, and Euryleon, all of
whom, Euryleon excepted, fell in an engagement
with the Phœnicians and Ægiftans, on their happening to touch at Sicily: this man, collecting fuch
as remained of his companions, took poffeffion of
Minoas, a Selinufian colony, which he delivered
from the oppreffion of Pythagoras. Euryleon, putting the tyrant to death, affumed his fituation and
authority. Thefe, however, he did not long enjoy,
for the Selinufians rofe in a body againft him, and

flew

flew him before the altar of Jupiter Forenfis [55], where he had fled for refuge.

XLVII. Philip [56], a native of Crotona, and fon of Butacides, was the companion of Dorieus in his travels and his death : he had entered into engagements of marriage with a daughter of Telys of Sybaris, but not choofing to fulfil them, he left his country, and went to Cyrene ; from hence alfo he departed, in fearch of Dorieus, in a three-oared veffel of his own, manned with a crew provided at his own expence : he had been victorious in the Olympic games, and was confeffedly the handfomeft man in Greece. On account of his accomplifh-ments of perfon [57], the people of Ægeftus diftin-guifhed

---

[55] *Jupiter Forenfis.*]—That is to fay, in the public forum, where the altar of this god was erected.—T.

[56] *Philip.*]—" There feems in this place," fays Reifke, " to be fomething wanted : how did Philip come amongft the Ægeftans ; or how did he obtain their friendfhip ; or, if he was killed with Dorieus, in Italy, how did he efcape in a battle with the Ægeftans ? Thefe," concludes Reifke, " are difficulties which I am totally unable to reconcile."

[57] *Accomplifhments of perfon.*]—For καλλος in this place, fome are for reading κλεος ; but Euftathius quotes the circumftance and paffage at length, a ftrong argument for retaining the reading of καλλος :—" Defignatur," fays Weffeling, " quid fieri folebat Egeftæ :" but that it was ufual in various places to honour perfons for their beauty, is evident from various paffages in ancient authors. A beautiful paffage from Lucretius, which I have before quoted in this work, fufficiently attefts this, —Καθιςων δε κ̣ πολλοι τας καλλιςες βασιλεας : many nations affign the fovereignty to thofe amongft them who are the moft beautiful,

guished him by very unusual honours; they erected a monument over the place of his interment, where they offered sacrifices as to a divinity.

XLVIII. We have above related the fortunes and death of Dorieus. If he could have submitted to the authority of his brother Cleomenes, and had remained at Lacedæmon, he would have succeeded to the throne of Sparta. Cleomenes, after a very short reign, died, leaving an only child, a daughter, of the name of Gorgo [58].

XLIX. During the reign of Cleomenes, Aristagoras, prince of Miletus, arrived at Sparta: the Lacedæmonians affirm, that desiring to have a conference with their sovereign, he appeared before him with a tablet of brass in his hand, upon which was inscribed every known part of the habitable world, the seas, and the rivers. He thus addressed the Spartan monarch: " When you know my bu-
" siness, Cleomenes, you will cease to wonder at
" my zeal in desiring to see you. The Ionians,

---

tiful, says Athenæus. Beauty, declares Euripides, is worthy of a kingdom—πρωτον μεν ειδος αξιον τυραννιδος.—See a very entertaining chapter on this subject in Athenæus, book xiii. c. 2. —*T*.

[58] *Gorgo.*]—She married Leonidas. When this prince departed for Thermopylæ, Gorgo asked him what commands he had for her; " Marry," says he, " some worthy man, and become the mother of a valiant race."—He himself expected to perish. This princess was remarkable for her virtue, and was one of the women whom Plutarch proposed as a model to Eurydice.— *Larcher.*

" who

" who ought to be free, are in a ſtate of ſervitude,
" which is not only diſgraceful, but alſo a ſource
" of the extremeſt ſorrow to us, as it muſt alſo be
" to you, who are ſo pre-eminent in Greece.—I
" intreat you, therefore, by the gods of Greece,
" to reſtore the Ionians to liberty, who are con-
" nected with you by ties of conſanguinity. The
" accompliſhment of this, will not be difficult; the
" Barbarians are by no means remarkable for
" their valour, whilſt you, by your military virtue,
" have attained the ſummit of renown. They ruſh
" to the combat armed only with a bow and a
" ſhort ſpear [59]; their robes are long, they ſuffer their
" hair to grow, and they will afford an eaſy con-
" queſt; add to this, that they who inhabit the
" continent are affluent beyond the reſt of their
" neighbours. They have abundance of gold, of
" ſilver, and of braſs; they enjoy a profuſion of
" every article of dreſs, have plenty of cattle, and
" a prodigious number of ſlaves [60] : all theſe, if you
" think

[59] *Bow and a ſhort ſpear.*]—A particular account of the military habit and arms of the oriental nations, is given in the ſeventh book of Herodotus, in which place he minutely deſcribes the
various people which compoſed the prodigious army of Xerxes.
It may not be improper to add, that the military habits of the
Greeks and Romans very much reſembled each other.—*T*.

[60] *Number of ſlaves.*]—The firſt ſlaves were doubtleſs captives taken in war, who were employed for menial purpoſes;
from being ſought after for uſe, they finally were purchaſed and
poſſeſſed for oſtentation. A paſſage in Athenæus informs us,
that he knew many Romans who poſſeſſed from ten to twenty
thouſand ſlaves. According to Tacitus, four hundred ſlaves
were

" think proper, may be yours. The nations by
" which they are furrounded I fhall explain : next
" to thefe Ionians are the Lydians, who poffefs a
" fertile territory, and a profufion of filver." Saying this, he pointed on the tablet in his hand, to the
particular diftrict of which he fpake. " Contigu-
" ous to the Lydians," continued Ariftagoras, " as
" you advance towards the eaft, are the Phrygians,
" a people who, beyond all the nations of whom I
" have any knowledge, enjoy the greteft abundance
" of cattle, and of the earth's produce. The
" Cappadocians, whom we call Syrians, join to the
" Phrygians ; then follow the Cilicians, who pof-
" fefs the fcattered iflands of our fea, in the vicinity
" of Cyprus : thefe people pay annually to the
" king a tribute of five hundred talents. The Ar-
" menians, who have alfo great plenty of cattle,
" border on the Cilicians. The Armenians have
" for their neighbours the Matieni, who inhabit

were difcovered in one great man's houfe at Rome, all of whom
were executed for not preventing the death of their mafter.
Some nations marked their flaves like cattle ; and in Menjan's
hiftory of Algiers, the author reprefents a Turk faying fcorn-
fully to a Chriftian, " What, have you forgot the time when a
Chriftian at Algiers was fcarce worth an onion ?" We learn
from Sir John Chardin, that when the Tartars made an incurfion into Poland, and carried away as many captives as they
could, perceiving they would not be redeemed, they fold them
for a crown a head. To enter into any elaborate difquifition on
the rights of man, would in this place be impertinent ; and the
reader will perceive that I have rather thrown together fome
detached matters on this interefting fubject, perhaps not fo generally known.

§

" the

" the region contiguous to Ciffia : in this latter dif-
" trict, and not far remote from the river Choafpes,
" is Sufa, where the Perfian monarch occafionally
" refides, and where his treafures are depofited.
" —Make yourfelves mafters of this city, and you
" may vie in affluence with Jupiter himfelf. Lay
" afide, therefore, the conteft in which you are en-
" gaged with the Meffenians, who equal you in
" ftrength, about a tract of land not very extenfive,
" nor remarkably fertile. Neither are the Arca-
" dians, nor the Argives, proper objects of your
" ambition, who are deftitute of thofe precious
" metals [61], which induce men to brave dangers
" and death : but can any thing be more defira-
" ble, than the opportunity now afforded you, of
" making the entire conqueft of Afia ?" Ariftago-

[61] *Precious metals.*]—I have always been much delighted
with the following paffage in Lucretius, wherein he informs his
readers that formerly brafs was fought after and valued, and
gold held in no eftimation, becaufe ufelefs.

> Nam fuit in pretio magis æs, aurumque jacebat
> Propter inutilitatem hebeti mucrone retufum
> Nunc jacet æs, aurum in fummum fucceffit honorem
> Sic volvenda ætas commutat tempora rerum
> Quod fuit in pretio, fit nullo denique honore :
> Porro aliud fuccedit et e contemptibus exit
> Inque dies magis appetitur, floretque repertum
> Laudibus, et miro 'ft mortaleis inter honore.

Again,

> Tunc igitur pelles, nunc aurum et purpura curis
> Exercent hominum vitam belloque fatigant.   *T.*

ras here finifhed. " Milefian friend," replied Cleomenes, " in the fpace of three days you fhall have
" our anfwer."

L. On the day, and at the place. appointed,
Cleomenes enquired of Ariftagoras, how many
days journey it was from the Ionian fea to the
dominions of the Perfian king. Ariftagoras, though
very fagacious, and thus far fuccefsful in his views,
was here guilty of an overfight. As his object was
to induce the Spartans to make an incurfion into
Afia, it was his intereft to have concealed the
truth, but he inconfiderately replied, that it was a
journey of about three months. As he proceeded
to explain himfelf, Cleomenes interrupted him;,
" Stranger of Miletus," faid he, " depart from
" Sparta before fun-fet : what you fay cannot be
" agreeable to the Lacedæmonians, defiring to lead
" us a march of three months from the fea."
Having faid this, Cleomenes withdrew.

LI. Ariftagoras taking a branch of olive [61] in his
hand, prefented himfelf before the houfe of Cleomenes, entering which as a fuppliant, he requefted

an

---

[61] *Branch of olive.*]—It would by no means be an eafy tafk
to enumerate the various ufes to which the olive was anciently.
applied, and the different qualities of mind of which it was the
fymbol. It rewarded the victors at the Olympic games ; it was
facred to Minerva, and fufpended round her temples ; it was the

emblem

an audience, at the fame time defiring that the
prince's daughter might retire; for it happened
that Gorgo, the only child of Cleomenes, was prefent, a girl of about eight or nine years old: the
king begged that the prefence of the child might
be no obftruction to what he had to fay. Ariftagoras then promifed to give him ten talents, if he

emblem of peace; it indicated pity, fupplication, liberty, hope,
&c. &c. The invention of it was imputed to Minerva.

> Oleæque Minerva
> Inventrix.

Statius calls it fupplicis arbor olivæ.—Directions for the
mode of planting them had place amongft the inftitutes of Solon:
he who pulled up for his own private ufe more than two olives
in the year, paid a fine of one hundred drachmæ. They were
not known till a very late period at Rome, but when introduced
their fruit became an indifpenfable article of luxury, and was
eaten before and after meals. See Martial:

> Inchoat atque eadem finit oliva dapes.

It fhould feem from a paffage in Virgil, that the fuppliant
carried a wreath of olive in his hands:

> Præferimus manibus vittas et verba precantum.

Of its introduction into the weftern world, Mr. Gibbon
fpeaks thus: " The olive followed the progrefs of peace, of
which it was confidered as the fymbol. Two centuries after
the foundation of Rome both Italy and Africa were ftrangers
to that ufeful plant; it was naturalized in thofe countries, and
at length carried into the heart of Spain, and Gaul. The timid
errors of the ancients, in fuppofing that it required a certain
degree of heat, and could only flourifh in the neighbourhood
of the fea, were infenfibly exploded by induftry and experience."—T.

would

would accede to his requeſt. As Cleomenes refuſed, Ariſtagoras roſe in his offers to fifty talents ;
upon which the child exclaimed, " Father, unleſs
" you withdraw, this ſtranger will corrupt you."
The prince was delighted with the wiſe ſaying of
his daughter, and inſtantly retired. Ariſtagoras
was never able to obtain another audience of the
king, and left Sparta in diſguſt.

LII. In that ſpace of country about which Cleomenes had enquired, the Perſian king has various
ſtathmi, or manſions, with excellent inns [61]; theſe
are all ſplendid and beautiful, the whole of the
country is richly cultivated, and the roads good and
ſecure. In the regions of Lydia and Phrygia,
twenty of the above ſtathmi occur, within the ſpace
of ninety paraſangs and a half. Leaving Phrygia,
you meet with the river Halys, where there are gates
which are ſtrongly defended, but which muſt be neceſſarily paſſed. Advancing through Cappadocia, to

[61] *Excellent inns.*]—There can be little doubt, but that
theſe are the ſame with what are now called caravanſeras, and
which abound in all oriental countries; theſe are large ſquare
buildings, in the centre of which is a ſpacious court. The
traveller muſt not expect to meet with much accommodation in
theſe places, except that he may depend upon finding water:
they are eſteemed ſacred, and a ſtranger's goods, whilſt he remains in one of them, are ſecure from pillage.

Such exactly are alſo the *choultries* of Indoſtan, many of
which are buildings of great magnificence, and very curious
workmanſhip. What the traveller has there to expect is little
more than mere ſhelter.—*T*.

the

the confines of Cilicia, in the fpace of one hundred and four parafangs, there are eight-and-twenty ftathmi. At the entrance of Cilicia are two necks of land, both well defended; paffing beyond which through the country, are three ftathmi in the fpace of fifteen parafangs and a half: Cilicia, as well as Armenia, are terminated by the Euphrates, which is only paffable in veffels. In Armenia, and within the fpace of fifty-fix parafangs and a half, there are fifteen ftathmi, in which alfo are guards: through this country flow the waters of four rivers, the paffage of which is indifpenfable, but can only be effected in boats. Of thefe the firft is the Tigris; by the fame name alfo the fecond and the third are diftinguifhed, though they are by no means the fame, nor proceeding from the fame fource: of thefe latter the one rifes in Armenia, the other from amongft the Matieni. The fourth river is called the Gyndes, which was formerly divided by Cyrus into three hundred and fixty channels. From Armenia to the country of the Matieni, are four ftathmi: from hence, through Ciffia, as far as the river Choafpes, there are eleven ftathmi, and a fpace of forty-two parafangs and a half. The Choafpes is alfo to be paffed in boats, and beyond this Sufa is fituated. Thus it appears, that from Sardis to Sufa are one hundred and eleven [64] ftations, or ftathmi.

LIII.

---

[64] *One hundred and eleven.*]—According to the account given by Herodotus in this chapter.

LIII. If this meafurement of the royal road by
parafangs, be accurate, and a parafang be fuppofed equal to thirty ftadia, which it really is, from
Sardis to the royal refidence of Memnon are thirteen thoufand five hundred ftadia, or four hundred
and fifty parafangs: allowing, therefore, one hundred and fifty ftadia to each day, the whole diftance
will be a journey of ninety entire days.

LIV. Ariftagoras was, therefore, correct in telling Cleomenes the Lacedæmonian, that it was a
three months march to the refidence of the Perfian
monarch. For the benefit of thofe who wifh to
have more fatisfactory information on the fubject,
it may not be amifs to add the particulars of the
diftance betwixt Sardis and Ephefus. From the
Greek fea to Sufa, the name by which the city of
Memnon [65] is generally known, is fourteen thou-
                                                  fand

	Stathmi.	Parafangs.
In Lydia and Phrygia are	20	94½
In Cappadocia	28	104
In Cilicia	3	15½
In Armenia	15	56½
In the country of the Matieni	4	
In Ciffia	11	42½

So that here muft evidently be fome miftake, as inftead of 111
ftathmi, we have only 81; inftead of 450 parafangs, only 313.
Wefeling remarks on the paffage, that if the numbers were accurate, much advantage might be derived from knowing the
exact proportion of diftance between a ftathmus and a parafang. The fame defect is obfervable in the Anabafis of Xenophon, which Hutchinfon tries in vain to explain.—T.

[65] *Of Memnon.*]—Strabo fays that Sufa was built by Titron,
                                                  the

fand and forty ſtadia: from Epheſus to Sardis is five hundred and forty ſtadia; thus three days muſt be added to the computation of the three months.

LV. From Sparta Ariſtagoras went to Athens, which at this period had recovered its liberty: Ariſtogiton and Harmodius [66], who were Gephyreans

the father of Memnon; Herodotus alſo, in another place, calls Suſa the city of Memnon.

[66] *Ariſtogiton and Harmodius.*]—To the reader of the moſt common claſſical taſte the ſtory of theſe Athenians muſt be too familiar to require any repetition in this place. An extract from a poem of Sir William Jones, in which the incident is happily introduced, being leſs common, may not perhaps be unacceptable. It is entitled,

Julii Meleſigoni ad Libertatem
Carmen.

Virtus renaſcens quem jubet ad ſonos
Spartanam avitos ducere tibiam?
Quis fortium cætus in auras
Athenias juvenum ciebit;

Quos Marti amicos, aut hyacinthinis
Flava in palæſtra conſpicuos comis
Aut alma libertas in undis
Egelidis agiles videbat,

Plauſitque viſos? Quis modulabitur
Excelſa plectro carmina Leſbio,
Quæ dirus Alcæo ſonante
Audiit, et tremuit dynaſtes?

E e 2

Quis

reans by defcent, had put to death Hipparchus, fon of Pififtratus, and brother of Hippias the tyrant. We are informed that Hipparchus had received intimation in a vifion [67] of the difafter which afterwards

Quis myrteâ enfem fronde reconditum
Cantabit ? Illum civibus Harmodi
Dilecte fervatis, nec ullo
Interiture die tenebas :

Vix fe refrœnat fulmineus chalybs,
Mox igne cœlefti emicat, exilit
Et cor reluctantis tyranni
Perforat ictibus haud remiffis.

O ter placentem Palladi victimam, &c.

The reader will perceive that Julii Melefigoni is an anagram of William Jones.

A more particular account of thefe deliverers of their country may be found in Thucydides, book vi. c. 12. Paufanias, book i. and in Suidas.—*T.*

[67] *In a vifion.*]—'The ancients imagined that a diftinct dream was a certain declaration of the future, or that the event was not to be averted, but by certain expiatory ceremonies. See the Electra of Sophocles, and other places.—*Larcher.*

One method which the ancients had of averting the effects of difagreeable vifions, was to relate them to the Sun, who they believed had the power of turning afide any evils which the night might have menaced.—*T.*

From Larcher's prolix note on the fubject of Ariftogiton and Harmodius, I extract fuch particulars as I think will be moft interefting to an Englifh reader.

Harmodius is reported to have infpired the tyrant Hipparchus with an unnatural paffion, who loving and being beloved by Ariftogiton, communicated the fecret to him, and joined with him in his refolution to deftroy their perfecutor. This is
fufficiently

afterwards befel him; though for four years after his death the people of Athens fuffered greater oppreffion than before.

LVI. The particulars of the vifion which Hipparchus faw are thus related: in the night preceding the feftival of the Panathenæa[68], Hipparchus beheld

fufficiently contradicted, with refpect to the attachment betwixt Harmodius and Ariftogiton, which appears to have been the true emotions of friendfhip only.

The courtezan Leæna, who was beloved by Harmodius, was tortured by Hippias, to make her difcover the accomplices in the affaffination of Hipparchus. Diftrufting her own fortitude, fhe bit off her tongue. The Athenians, in honour of her memory, erected in the veftibule of the citadel a ftatue in bronze of a lionefs without a tongue.

Thucydides feems willing to impute the action which caufed the death of Hipparchus to a lefs noble motive than the love of liberty; but the cotemporaries of the confpirators, and pofterity, have rendered Harmodius and Ariftogiton the merit which was their due.

Popular fongs were made in their honour, one of which is preferved in Athenæus, book xv. chap. 15. It is alfo to be feen in the Analecta of Brunck, i. 155. This fong has been imputed to Alcæus, but falfely, for that poet died before Hipparchus.

The defcendants of the confpirators who deftroyed the tyrant were maintained in the Prytaneum at the public expence.

One of the pofterity of Harmodius, proud of his birth, reproached Iphicrates with the meannefs of his family: "My nobility," anfwered Iphicrates, "commences with me, yours terminates in you." In the very time of the decline of Athens, the love of liberty was there fo hereditary and indelible, that they erected ftatues to the affaffins of Cæfar.

[68] *Panathenæa.*]—On this fubject I give, from different writers, the more interefting particulars.

The

beheld a tall and comely perfonage, who addreffed him in thefe ambiguous terms :

> Brave lion, thy unconquer'd foul compofe
> To meet unmov'd intolerable woes :
> In vain th' oppreffor would elude his fate,
> The vengeance of the gods is fure, though late.

As foon as the morning appeared, he difclofed what he-had feen to the interpreters of dreams. He however flighted the vifion, and was killed in the celebration of fome public feftival.

LVII. The Gephyreans, of which nation were the affaffins of Hipparchus, came, as themfelves affirm, originally from Eretria. But the refult of my enquiries enables me to fay that they were Phœnicians, and of thofe who accompanied Cadmus into the region now called Bœotia, where they fettled, having the diftrict of Tanagria affigned them by lot. The Cadmeans were expelled by the Argives; the Bœotians afterwards drove out the Gephyreans, who took refuge at Athens. The Athenians en-

The feftival was in honour of Minerva. There were the greater and leffer Panathenæa. The leffer originated with Thefeus ; thefe were celebrated every year in the month Hecatombeon; the greater were celebrated every five years. In the proceffion on this occafion old men, felected for their good perfons, carried branches of olive. There were alfo races with torches both on horfe and foot ; there was alfo a mufical contention. The conqueror in any of thefe games was rewarded with a veffel of oil. There was alfo a dance by boys in armour. The veft of Minerva was carried in a facred proceffion of perfons of all ages, &c. &c.—T.

rolled

rolled them amongft their citizens, under certain
reftrictions of trifling importance.

LVIII. The Phœnicians who came with Cadmus, and of whom the Gephyreans were a part,
introduced during their refidence in Greece various
articles of fcience; and amongft other things letters [69], with which, as I conceive, the Greeks were
before

---

[69] *Amongft other things letters.*]—Upon the fubject of the invention of letters, it is neceffary to fay fomething; but fo much
has been written by others, that the tafk of felection, though
all that is neceffary, becomes fufficiently difficult.

The firft introduction of letters into Greece has been generally affigned to Cadmus; but this has often been controverted,
no arguments on either fide have been adduced fufficiently
ftrong to be admitted as decifive. It is probable that they
were in ufe in Greece before Cadmus, which Diodorus Siculus
confidently affirms. But Lucan, in a very enlightened period of
the Roman empire, without any more intimation of doubt, than
is implied in the words famæ fi creditur, wrote thus:

> Phœnices primi, famæ fi creditur, aufi
> Manfuram rudibus vocem fignare figuris
> Nondum flumineas Memphis contexere biblos
> Noverat, et faxis tantum, volucrefque feræque
> Sculptaque fervabant magicas animalia linguas.

> Phœnicians firft, if ancient fame be true,
> The facred myftery of letters knew;
> They firft by found, in various lines defign'd,
> Expreft the meaning of the thinking mind,
> The power of words by figures rude convey'd,
> And ufeful fcience everlafting made.
> Then Memphis, ere the reedy leaf was known,
> Engrav'd her precepts and her arts in ftone;
> While animals, in various order plac'd,
> The learned hieroglyphic column grac'd.   *Rowe.*

before unacquainted. Thefe were at firft fuch as the Phœnicians themfelves indifcriminately ufe; in procefs of time, however, they were changed both in found and form [70]. At that time the Greeks

To this opinion, concerning the ufe of hieroglyphics, bifhop Warburton accedes, in his Divine Legation of Mofes, who thinks that they were the production of an unimproved ftate of fociety, as yet unacquainted with alphabetical writing. With refpect to this opinion of Herodotus, many learned men thought it worthy of credit, from the refemblance betwixt the old Eaftern and earlieft Greek characters, which is certainly an argument of fome weight.

No European nation ever pretended to the honour of this difcovery; the Romans confeffed they had it from the Greeks, the Greeks from the Phœnicians.

Pliny fays the ufe of letters was eternal; and many have made no fcruple of afcribing them to a divine revelation. Our countryman Mr. Aftle, who has written perhaps the beft on this complicated fubject, has this expreffion, with which I fhall conclude the fubject.

" The vanity of each nation induces them to pretend to the 'moft early civilization; but fuch is the uncertainty of ancient hiftory, that it is difficult to determine to whom the honour is due. It fhould feem, however, that the conteft may be confined to the Ægyptians, Phœnicians, and Cadmeans."—T.

[70] *In found and form.*]—The remark of Dr. Gillies on this paffage feems worthy of attention,

" The eaftern tongues are in general extremely deficient in vowels. It is, or rather was, much difputed whether the ancient orientals ufed any characters to exprefs them : their languages therefore had an inflexible thicknefs of found, extremely different from the vocal harmony of the Greek, which abounds not only in vowels but in diphthongs. This circumftance denotes in the Greeks organs of perception more acute, elegant, and difcerning. They felt fuch faint variations of liquid founds as efcaped the dulnefs of Afiatic ears, and invented marks to exprefs them. They diftinguifhed in this manner not only their articulation, but their quantity, and afterwards their mufical intonation."

moft

moſt contiguous to this people were the Ionians, who learned theſe letters of the Phœnicians, and, with ſome trifling variations, received them into common uſe. As the Phœnicians firſt made them known in Greece, they called them, as juſtice required, Phœnician letters. By a very ancient cuſtom, the Ionians call their books diphteræ or ſkins, becauſe at a time when the plant of the biblos was ſcarce [71], they uſed inſtead of it the ſkins of goats and ſheep. Many of the barbarians have uſed theſe ſkins for this purpoſe within my recollection.

LIX. I myſelf have ſeen, in the temple of the Iſmenian Apollo, at Thebes of Bœotia, theſe Cadmean letters inſcribed upon ſome tripods, and having a near reſemblance to thoſe uſed by the Ionians. One of the tripods has this inſcription [72]:

Amphytrion's

---

[71] *Biblos was ſcarce.*]—Je ne parlerai point ici de toutes les matieres ſur leſquelles on a tracé l'écriture. Les peaux de chevre et de mouton, les differens eſpeces de toile furent ſucceſſivement employées: on a fait depuis uſage du papier tiſſu des couches interieures de la tige d'une plante qui croit dans les marais de l'Egypte, ou au milieu des eaux dormantes que le Nil laiſſe apres ſon inondation. On en fait des rouleaux, a l'extremité, deſquels eſt ſuſpendre une etiquette contenant le titre du livre. L'écriture n'eſt tracée que ſur une des faces de chaque rouleau; et pour en faciliter la lecture, elle s'y trouve diviſée en pluſieurs compartimens ou pages, &c.—*Voyage du Jeune Anacharſis.*

Every thing neceſſary to be known on the ſubject of paper, its firſt invention, and progreſſive improvement, is ſatisfactorily diſcuſſed in the edition of Chambers's Dictionary by Rees.—*T.*

[72] *This inſcription.*]—Some curious inſcriptions upon the ſhields of the warriors who were engaged in the ſiege of the

capital

Amphytrion's prefent from Teleboan fpoils.

This muft have been about the age of Laius, fon of Labdacus, whofe father was Polydore, the fon of Cadmus.

LX. Upon the fecond tripod, are thefe hexameter varfes :—

> Scæus, victorious pugilift, beftow'd
> Me, a fair offering, on the Delphic god.

This Scæus was the fon of Hippocoon, if indeed it was he who dedicated the tripod, and not another perfon of the fame name, cotemporary with Œdipus the fon of Laius.

LXI. The third tripod bears this infcription in hexameters :—

> Royal Laodamas to Phœbus' fhrine
> This tripod gave, of workmanfhip divine.

Under this Laodamas, the fon of Eteocles, who had the fupreme power, the Cadmeans were expelled by the Argives, and fled to the Encheleans [71]. The Gephyræans were compelled by the Bœotians to retire to Athens [74]. Here they built

capital of Eteocles, are preferved in the " Seven againft Thebes of Æfchylus," to which the reader is referred.

[73] *Encheleans.*]—The Cadmeans and Encheleans of Herodotus are the Thebans and Illyrians of Paufanias.

[74] *To Athens.*]—They were permitted to fettle on the borders of the Cephiffus, which feparates Attica from Eleufis; there they built a bridge, in order to have a free communication on both fides. I am of opinion that bridges, γεφυραι, took their

name

built temples for their own particular ufe, refembling in no refpect thofe of the Athenians, as
may be feen in the edifice and myfteries of the
Achæan Ceres.

LXII. Thus have I related the vifion of Hipparchus, and the origin of the Gephyreans, from
whom the confpirators againft Hipparchus were defcended : but it will here be proper to explain more
at length the particular means by which the Athenians recovered their liberty, which I was beginning
to do before. Hippias had fucceeded to the fupreme authority, and, as appeared by his conduct,
greatly refented the death of Hipparchus. The
Alcmæonidæ, who were of Athenian origin, had
been driven from their country by the Pififtratidæ :
they had, in conjunction with fome other exiles,
made an effort to recover their former fituations,
and to deliver their country from its oppreffors, but
were defeated with confiderable lofs. They retired
to Lipfydrium beyond Pæonia, which they fortified, ftill meditating vengeance againft the Pififtratidæ. Whilft they were thus circumftanced, the
Amphictyons [75] engaged them upon certain terms

to

name from thefe people. The author of the Etymologicum
Magnum pretends that the people were called Gephyreans from
this bridge ; but it is very certain that they bore this name before they fettled in Attica.—*Larcher*.

[75] *Amphictyons.*]—The Amphictyons were an affembly compofed of deputies from the different ftates of Greece. Each
ftate fent two deputies, one to examine into what related to
the ceremonies of religion, the other to decide difputes betwixt
individuals.

to conftruct that which is now the temple of Delphi [76], but which did not exift before.   They were
not deficient in point of wealth; and, warmed with
the generous fpirit of their race, they erected a
temple far exceeding the model which had been
given, in fplendour and in .beauty.   Their agreement only obliged them to conftruct it of the ftone
of Porus [77], but they built the veftibule of Parian
marble.

LXIII. Thefe men, as the Athenians relate,
during their continuance at Delphi bribed the Py-

individuals.   Their general refidence was at Delphi, and they
determined difputes betwixt the different ftates of Greece.
Before they proceeded to bufinefs, they facrificed an ox cut
into fmall pieces; their decifions were facred, and without
appeal.   They met twice in the year, in fpring and in autumn.
In fpring at Delphi, in autumn at Thermopylæ.

This council reprefented but a certain number of. the ftates
of Greece; but thefe were the principal and moft powerful.
Demofthenes makes mention of a decree where the Amphic-
tyonic council is called το κοινον των Ελληνων συνεδριον; and Cicero alfo calls them commune Græciæ concilium.—*T.*

[76] *Temple of Delphi.*]—The temple of Delphi was in its origin no more than a chapel made of the branches of laurel
growing near the temple.   One Pteras of Delphi afterwards
built it of more folid materials: it was then conftructed of
brafs; the fourth time it was erected of ftone.—*Larcher.*

[77] *Stone of Porus.*]—This ftone refembled the Parian marble
in whitenefs and hardnefs; but, according to Pliny and Theophraftus, it was lefs ponderous.   Of the marble of Paros I
have fpoken elfewhere.   Larcher remarks that Phidias, Praxiteles, and the more eminent fculptors of antiquity, always preferred it for their works.   Tournefort without hefitation prefers the marbles of Italy to thofe of Greece.

thian

thian to propofe to every Spartan who fhould confult her, in a private or public capacity, the deliver-
ance of Athens.   The Lacedæmonians, hearing inceffantly the fame thing repeated to them, fent an
army under the conduct of Anchimolius, fon of
After, a man of a very popular character, to expel
the Pififtratidæ from Athens.   They in this refpect
violated fome very ancient ties of hofpitality ; but
they thought it better became them to liften to
the commands of Heaven, than to any human confideration.   Thefe forces were difpatched by fea,
and being driven to Phalerus, were there difembarked by Anchimolius.   The Pififtratidæ being
aware of this, applied for affiftance to the Theffalians, with whom they were in alliance.   The people of Theffaly obeyed the fummons, and fent them
a thoufand horfe [78], commanded by Cineas their
king;

[78] *Thoufand horfe.*]—The cavalry of Theffaly were very famous.—See *Theocritus, Id.* xviii. 30.

Η καπω κυπαρισσος, η αρματι Θεσσαλος ιππος
Ωδι και ροδοκρως Ελινα Λακιδαιμονι κοσμος;

As the cyprefs is an ornament to a garden, as a Theffalian
horfe to a chariot, fo is the lovely Helen the glory of Lacedæmon.—*Larcher.*

Amongft other folemnities of mourning which Admetus prince
of Theffaly orders to be obferved in honour of his deceafed
wife, he bids his fubjects cut the manes of all the chariot
horfes:

Τιθριππα τι ζευγινσθι κ μοναμπυκας;
Πωλυς σιδηρω τεμνιτ αυχινων φοβην.

From which incident it may perhaps be inferred, that the
Theffalians held their horfes in no fmall eftimation: the fpeech
of Admetus being as much as to fay, " All that belongs to me.
all

king, a native of Coniæus: on the arrival of their
allies, the Pififtratidæ levelled all the country about
Phalerus, and thus enabling the cavalry to act, they
fent them againft the Spartans.   They accordingly
attacked the enemy, and killed feveral, amongft
whom was Anchimolius.   Thofe who efcaped were
driven to their veffels.   Thus fucceeded the firft
attempt of the Lacedæmonians: the tomb of Anchimolius is ftill to be feen near the temple of Hercules, in Cynofarges[79], in the diftrict of Alopece[80],
in Attica.

LXIV.

all that have any fhare of my regard, fhall aid me in deploring
my domeftic lofs.''—See vol. i. 215.—T.

[79] *Cynofarges.*]—This place gave name to the fect of the
Cynics. It was a gymnafium, or place for public exercifes, annexed to a temple, and fituated near one of the gates of Athens.
The origin of its appellation *Cynofarges* is thus related: an
Athenian named Didymus was performing a facrifice in his
houfe, but was interrupted by a large white dog, which coming
in unexpectedly, feized the victim, carried it off, and left it in
another place. Much difturbed by an accident fo inaufpicious,
Didymus confulted the oracle in what manner he might avert
the omen; he was told to build a temple to Hercules in the
place where the dog had depofited the victim: he did fo, and
called it *Cynofarges,* απο τυ κυνος αργυ, from the *white dog,*
which that name expreffes. When Antifthenes founded his
fect, he hired this place as conveniently fituated for his lectures;
and from the name of the place, added to the confideration of
the fnarling doggifh nature of thofe philofophers, was derived
the appellation *Cynic,* which means *doggifh.* Antifthenes himfelf was fometimes called απλοκυων, *mere* or *genuine dog.* The
expreffion ad Cynofarges was proverbial.—See this explained
at length in the Adagia of Erafmus; it fignified the fame as
abi ad cervos, ad malam rem, &c.—T.

[80] *Alopece.*]—This place was appropriated to the tribe of

Antiochis,

LXIV. The Lacedæmonians afterwards sent a greater body of forces against Athens, not by sea but by land, under the direction of their king Cleomenes, son of Anaxandrides. These, on their first entrance into Attica, were attacked by the Thessalian horse, who were presently routed[81], with the loss of forty of their men : the remainder retired without any further efforts into Thessaly. Cleomenes advancing to the city, was joined by those Athenians who desired to be free; in conjunction with whom he besieged the tyrants in the Pelasgian citadel.

LXV. The Lacedæmonians would have found themselves finally inadequate to the expulsion of the Pisistratidæ, for they were totally unprepared for a siege, whilst their adversaries were well provided with necessaries. After therefore continuing the blockade for a few days, they were about to return to Sparta, when an accident happened, as fatal to one party as favourable to the other. The children of the Pisistratidæ in their attempts privately to escape, were taken prisoners : this incident reduced them to extreme perplexity, so that finally, to recover their children, they submitted to such terms

Antiochis, and according to Diogenes Laertius, was celebrated for being the birth-place of Socrates.—T.

[81] *Presently routed.*]—Frontinus, in his Stratagemata, relates that Cleomenes obstructed the passage of the Thessalian horse, by throwing branches of trees over the plain. This delivery of the Athenians by Cleomenes, is alluded to by Aristophanes, in his play called Lysistratus.—*Larcher.*

as

as the Athenians impofed, and engaged to leave
Attica within five days. Thus, after enjoying the
fupreme authority for thirty-fix years, they retired
to Sigeum beyond the Scamander. They were in
their defcent Pylians, of the family of Peleus; they
were by birth related to Codrus and Melanthus,
who had alfo arrived at the principality of Athens,
though ftrangers like themfelves. In memory of
which Hippocrates, the father of Pififtratus, had
named his fon from the fon of Neftor. The Athenians were thus delivered from oppreffion; and it
will now be my bufinefs to commemorate fuch
profperous or calamitous events as they experienced
after they had thus recovered their liberties, before
Ionia had revolted from Darius, and Ariftagoras the
Milefian had arrived at Athens to fupplicate affiftance.

LXVI. Athens was confiderable before, but, its
liberty being reftored, it became greater than ever. Of
its citizens, two enjoyed more than common reputation: Clifthenes, of the family of the Alcmæonidæ,
who according to the voice of fame had corrupted
the Pythian; and Ifagoras, fon of Tifander, who was
certainly of an illuftrious origin, but whofe particular defcent I am not able to fpecify. The individuals of this family facrifice to the Carian Jupiter [12]: thefe two men, in their contention for fuperiority,

---

[11] *Carian Jupiter.*]—The Carians were exceedingly con-
temned, and they were regarded as flaves, becaufe they were
the

riority, divided the ſtate into factions: Cliſthenes, who was worſted by his rival, found means to conciliate the favour of the people. The four tribes [13], which were before named from the ſons of Ion, Geleon, Ægicores, Argades, and Hoples, he divided into ten, naming them according to his fancy, from

the firſt who let out troops for hire; for which reaſon they were expoſed to the moſt perilous enterprizes. This people had a temple common to themſelves, with the Lydians and Myſians; this was called the temple of the Carian Jupiter. They who ſacrificed to the Carian Jupiter acknowledged themſelves to have been originally from Caria. Plutarch does not omit this opportunity of reproaching Herodotus; and indeed this is amongſt the very few inſtances of his having juſtice on his ſide. As early as in the time of Homer, the following proverb was current:

—— τιω δε μιν εν Καρος αιση,

I value him no more than a Carian. *Larcher.*

This interpretation has, however, been juſtly conſidered as doubtful. See Dr. Clarke's excellent note on that paſſage. *Il.* ix. 378.—*T.*

[13] *The four tribes.*]—The names of the four ancient tribes of Athens varied at different times: they were afterwards, as in this place repreſented, multiplied into ten; two others were then added. Each of theſe ten tribes, like ſo many different republics, had their preſidents, officers of police, tribunals, aſſemblies, and different intereſts. Fifty ſenators were elected as repreſentatives of each tribe, which of courſe made the aggregate repreſentation of the ſtate of Athens amount to five hundred. The motive of Cliſthenes in dividing the Athenians into ten tribes, was a remarkable inſtance of political ſagacity; till then any one tribe uniting with a ſecond muſt have rendered any conteſt equal. The names here inſerted have been the ſubject of much learned controverſy. See the Ion of Euripides, ver. 1576, and the commentators upon it. An inſcription publiſhed by Count Caylus has at length removed many of the difficulties.—*T.*

the heroes of his country. One however he called after Ajax [34], who had been the neighbour and ally to his nation.

LXVII. In this particular, Clisthenes seems to me to have imitated his grandfather of the same name by his mother's side, who was prince of Sicyon: this Clisthenes having been engaged in hostilities with the Argives, abolished at Sicyon the poetical contests of the rhapsodists [35], which he

was

---

[34] *Ajax.*] —Ajax, son of Telamon, had been prince of Ægina, an island in the neighbourhood of Attica.—*Larcher.* This is a most remarkable mistake in Larcher: Ajax was of Salamis, not of Ægina. See the well-known line in Homer:

Αιας δ'εκ Σαλαμινος αγεν δυοκαιδεκα νας.

[35] *Rhapsodists.*]—This word is compounded either of ραπτω, to sew, or ραβδος, a rod or branch, and ῳδη, a song or poem. According to the first derivation it signifies a poet, author of various songs or poems which are connected together, making one poem, of which the different parts may be detached and separately recited. According to the second, it signifies a singer, who holding in his hand a branch of laurel, recites either his own compositions or those of some celebrated poet.

Hesiod inclines to the former etymology. Homer, Hesiod, &c. were rhapsodists in this sense; they composed their poems in different books and parts, which uniting together made one perfect composition. The ancient poets went from country to country, and from town to town, to instruct and amuse the people by the recital of their verses, who in return treated them with great honours and much liberality. The most ancient rhapsodist on record is Phemius, whom Homer, after being his disciple, immortalizes in his Odyssey. The most probable opinion is, that in singing the verses which they themselves composed, they carried in their hand a branch of laurel. The rhapsodists of the second kind were invited to feasts and public sacrifices, to sing the poems of Orpheus, Musæus, Hesiod, Archilochus,

was induced to do, becaufe in the verfes of Homer, which were there generally felected for this purpofe, Argos and its inhabitants were fuch frequent objects of praife. From the fame motive he was folicitous to expel the relics of Adraftus, an Argive, the fon of Talaus, which were depofited in the forum of Sicyon[86]; he went therefore to enquire of the Delphic oracle, whether he might expel Adraftus. The Pythian faid in reply, that Adraftus was a prince of Sicyon, whilft he himfelf was a robber. Meeting with this repulfe from the oracle, he on his

chilochus, Mimnermus, Phocylides, and in particular of Homer. Thefe were fatisfied with reciting the compofitions · of others, and certainly carried a branch of laurel, which particularly has been difputed with refpect to the firft.

They were alfo called Homerides or Homerifts, becaufe they generally recited verfes from Homer.

They fung fitting on a raifed chair, accompanying their verfes with a cithera or fome other inftrument, and in return a crown of gold was given them. In procefs of time the words rhapfodift and rhapfody became terms of contempt, from the abufe which the rhapfodifts made of their profeffion; and at the prefent day the term rhapfody is applied to a number of vile pieces ill put together.—*Larcher.*

The note above given from Larcher will neceffarily bring to the mind of the Englifh reader the character and office of our ancient bards, whom the rhapfodifts of old in many re-fpects refembled. Of the two, the bards were perhaps the more honourable, as they confined themfelves to the recital of the valorous actions of heroes, and of fuch fentiments as in-fpired bravery and virtue. In our language alfo, rhapfody is now always ufed in a bad fenfe; but it was not fo with our more ancient writers, and our poets in particular.—*T.*

[86] *Forum of Sicyon.*]—Dieutychidas relates that Adraftus was buried at Megara, and that at Sicyon there was only a cenotaph of this hero. See Scholiaft to Pindar. ad Nem. 30.— *Larcher.*

return

return concerted other means to rid himself of A-
draftus. Thinking he had accomplished this, he
sent to Thebes of Bœotia to bring back Melanippus[87], a native of Sicyon, and son of Astacus.
By the consent of the Thébans, his request was
granted; he then erected to his honour a shrine in
the Prytaneum, and deposited his remains in a place
strongly fortified. His motive for thus bringing
back Melanippus, which ought not to be omitted,
was the great enmity which subsisted betwixt him
and Adraftus, and farther, becaufe Melanippus had
been acceffary to the deaths of Meciftes the brother,
and Tydeus the son-in-law of Adraftus. When the
shrine was completed, Clifthenes affigned to Melanippus the facrifices and feftivals which before had
been appropriated to Adraftus, and folemnized by
the Sicyonians with the greateft pomp and magnificence. This diftrict had formerly been under the
fovereignty of Polybus, who dying without children, had left his dominions to Adraftus, his grandson by a daughter. Amongft other marks of honour which the Sicyonians paid the memory of
Adraftus, they commemorated in tragic chorufes[88]
his

---

[87] *Melanippus.*]—When the Argives attacked Thebes, this
warrior flew Tydeus and Meciftus, the brother of Adraftus,
whilft he himfelf perifhed by the hands of Amphiaraus.

[88] *Tragic chorufes.*]—It may be inferred, fays Larcher, from
this paffage, that Thefpis was not the inventor of tragedy;
and he quotes Themiftius as faying, " The Sicyonians were the
inventers of tragedy, but the Athenians brought it to perfection."
Suidas alfo, at the word Θεσπις, fays, that Epigenes of Sicyon
was the firft tragedian, and Thefpis only the fixteenth.   M.
Larcher

his perfonal misfortunes, to the neglect even of
Bacchus. But Clifthenes appropriated the chorufes
to Bacchus, and the other folemnities to Melanippus.

LXVIII. He changed alfo the names of the Doric tribes, that thofe of the Sicyonians might be
altogether different from thofe of the Argives, by
which means he made the Sicyonians extremely
ridiculous. He diftinguifhed the other tribes by

Larcher is of a contrary opinion, but avoids any difcuffion of
the argument, as beyond the propofed limits of his plan.

To exhibit a chorus, was to purchafe a dramatic piece of an
author, and defray the expence of its reprefentation. This at
Athens was the office of the archon, at Rome of the ædiles.
The following paffage from Lyfias may ferve to explain the
ancient chorus with regard to its variety and expence.

" When Theopompus was archon, I was furnifher to a tragic
chorus, and I laid out 30 minæ—afterwards I got the victory
with the chorus of men, and it coft me 20 minæ. When Glau-
cippus was archon, I laid out eight minæ upon the pyrrichifts;
when Diocles was archon, I laid out upon the cyclian chorus
three minæ; afterwards, when Alexias was archon, I furnifhed
a chorus of boys, and it coft me fifteen minæ; and when Eu-
clides was archon, I was at the charge of fixteen minæ on the
comedians, and of feven upon the young pyrrichifts."

From which it appears that the tragic was the moft expenfive
chorus, and its fplendour in after-times became fo extravagant,
that Horace complains the fpectators minded more what they
faw than what they heard:

Dixit adhuc aliquid, nil fane, quid placet ergo
Lana Tarentino violas imitata veneno.

The bufinefs of the chorus at its firft inftitution was to fing dithyrambic verfes in honour of Bacchus. How it afterwards
became improved and extended, has been too often and too well
difcuffed to require any elaborate difcuffion in this place.—T.

F f 3   the

the words Hys and Onos [19], fuperadding only their refpective terminations: to his own tribe he prefixed the word Arche, expreffive of authority; thofe of his own tribe were therefore termed Archelaens; of the others, fome were called Hyatæ, fome Oneatæ, others Chæræatæ. The Sicyonians were known by thefe appellations during the time of Ciifthenes, and for fixty years afterwards. After this period, in confequence of a confultation held amongft themfelves, they changed thefe names to Hylleans, Pamphylians, and Dymanatæ. To thefe they added a fourth tribe, which in honour of Ægialeus, fon of Adraftus, they called Ægialeans.

LXIX. Such was the conduct of Clifthenes of Sicyon. The Clifthenes of Athens, grandfon of the former by a daughter, and named after him, was, as it appears to me, defirous of imitating him from whom he was called. To fhew his contempt of the Ionians, he would not fuffer the tribes of Athens to bear any refemblance to thofe of Ionia. Having conciliated his countrymen, who had before been averfe to him, he changed the names of the tribes, and increafed their number. Inftead of four phylarchi he made ten, into which number of tribes he alfo divided the people; by which means he fo conciliated their favour, that he obtained a decided fuperiority over his opponents [90].

LXX,

---

[19] *Hys and Onos.*]—Literally, a fwine and an afs.

[90] *Over his opponents.*]—Clifthenes and Ifagoras had no intention of becoming tyrants, and were united to expel the Pififtratidæ from Athens: but they were not at all the more harmonious on this account. The firft defired to eftablifh a democracy,

LXX. Ifagoras, though overcome, endeavoured to recover his importance; he accordingly applied to Cleomenes the Spartan, with whom he had formed the tie of hofpitality whilft he was befieging the Pififtratidæ, and who has been fufpected of an improper connection with Ifagoras's wife. The Lacedæmonian prince, fending a herald before him, pronounced fentence of expulfion againft Clifthenes, and many other Athenians, on pretence of their being polluted by facrilegious murder. Ifagoras prevailed upon him to make this his excufe, becaufe the Alcmæonidæ, with thofe of their party, had been guilty of a murder, in which neither Ifagoras nor any of his followers were concerned.

LXXI. The reafon why thefe Athenians were called polluted [91], was this: Cylon, a native of Athens, who had obtained the prize in the Olympic games, had been convicted of defigns upon the government, for, having procured a number of young men of the fame age with himfelf, he endeavoured to feize the citadel; difappointed in his hopes, he with his companions placed themfelves

cracy, and to accomplifh it he gave the people more authority than they ever poffeffed before, by diftributing them into a greater number of tribes, making them by thefe means lefs eafy to be gained. Ifagoras, on the contrary, wifhed to eftablifh an ariftocracy; and as he could not poffibly fucceed in his views, unlefs by force, he therefore invited the Lacedæmonians to affift him.—*Larcher.*

91 *Polluted.*]—Literally *Enagees,* that is, polluted by their crime, and therefore devoted to the curfe of the goddefs whom they had offended: the term implies a facrilegious offence.—*T.*

F f 4 before

before the fhrine of Minerva, as fupplïants. The
Prytanes of the Naucrari [91], who then governed
Athens, perfuaded them to leave this fanctuary,
under a promife that their lives fhould not be forfeited. Their being foon afterwards put to death [93]

was

[91] *The Prytanes of the Naucrari.*]—I fhall endeavour, as concifely as poffible, to make this intelligible to the Englifh
reader.

The magiftrates of Athens were compofed of the Archons,
the Areopagites, and the fenate of five hundred. When the
people of Athens confifted only of four tribes, one hundred
were elected by lot from each tribe; when afterwards they
were divided into ten, fifty were chofen from each tribe; thefe
were the Prytanes, and they governed the city by turns. Each
body of fifty, according to Solon's eftablifhment, ruled for the
fpace of thirty-five days, not all at once, but in regular divifions
of their body for a certain limited time. To expatiate on the
fubject of the Prytanes, the particulars of their duty, and their
various fubdivifions into other refponfible magiftracies, would
require a long differtation.

Of the Naucrari, or, as it is fometimes written, Naucleri, what
follows may perhaps be fufficient.

To the ten tribes of Clifthenes, two more were afterwards
added; thefe twelve were divided into Δημοι, or boroughs, who
anciently were named Naucrariæ: of thefe the magiftrates
were called Naucrari; each Naucraria furnifhed for the public fervice two horfemen and one veffel. Each Athenian bo-
rough had anciently its own little fenate; thus the Prytanes of
the Naucrari were a felect number, prefiding in each of thefe
fenates. With refpect to the paffage before us, " Many," fays
Larcher, " are of opinion that Herodotus ufes the expreffion
of Prytanes of the Naucrari in a particular fenfe, meaning by
Naucrari the Athenians in general; and by Prytanes, the Archons.—*T*.

[93] *Put to death.*]—The particulars of this ftrange bufinefs
are related at length by Thucydides; much alfo concerning it
may be found in the Sera numinis vindicta of Plutarch, and in

the

was generally imputed to the Alcmæonidæ.—Thefe events happened before the time of Pififtratus.

LXXII. Cleomenes having thus ordered the expulfion of Clifthenes, and the other *Enagees*, though Clifthenes had privately retired [94], came foon afterwards to Athens with a fmall number of attendants. His firft ftep was, to fend into exile as polluted feven hundred Athenian families [95], which Ifagoras pointed out to him. He next proceeded to diffolve the fenate, and to entruft the offices of government with three hundred of the faction of Ifagoras. The fenate exerted themfelves, and pofitively refufed to acquiefce in his projects; upon which Cleomenes, with Ifagoras and his party,

the Life of Solon. The detail in this place would not be interefting; the event happened 612 years before the Chriftian æra.—*T*.

[94] *Voluntarily retired.*]—We are told by Ælian, that Clifthenes, having introduced the law of the oftracifm, was the firft who was punifhed by it. Few Englifh readers will require to be informed, that the oftracifm was the Athenian fentence of banifhment, determined by the people writing the name of the perfon to be banifhed on an oyfter-fhell.

The punifhment itfelf was not always deemed difhonourable, for the victim, during the term of his banifhment, which was ten years, enjoyed his eftate. A perfon could not be banifhed by the oftracifm, unlefs an affembly of fix thoufand were prefent. —*T*.

[95] *Athenian families.*]—This expreffion is not fo unimportant as it may appear to a carelefs reader. There were at Athens many domefticated ftrangers, who enjoyed all the rights of citizens, except that they could not be advanced to a ftation of any authority in the ftate.—*Larcher*.

feized

feized the citadel: they were here, for the fpace of two days, befieged by the Athenians in a body, who took the part of the fenate. Upon the third day certain terms were offered, and accepted, and the Spartans all of them departed from Athens: thus was an omen which had happened to Cleomenes accomplifhed. For when he was employed in the feizure of the citadel, he defired to enter the adytum and confult the goddefs; the prieftefs, as he was about to open the doors, rofe from her feat, and forbade him in thefe terms: " Lacedæmonian, re-" turn, prefume not to enter here, where no ad-" mittance is permitted to a Dorian." " I," re-turned Cleomenes, " am not a Dorian, but an " Achean." This omen, however, had no influ-ence upon his conduct; he perfevered in what he had undertaken, and with his Lacedæmonians was a fecond time [96] foiled. The Athenians who had joined themfelves to him were put in irons, and condemned to die; amongft thefe was Timefi-theus of Delphi, concerning whofe gallántry and fpirit I am able to produce many teftimonies.—Thefe Athenians were put to death in prifon.

LXXIII. The Athenians having recalled Clif-thenes, and the feven hundred families expelled by

[96] *Second time.*]—See chapter lxiv. and lxv.—See alfo the Lyfiftratus of Ariftophanes, verfe 273.

" Non memini," fays Reifke, " de primo Cleomenis irrito co-natu Athenas occupandi in fuperioribus legere. Nam quod, p. 308, narravit non Cleomeni, fed Anchimolio id evenit."

Cleomenes,

Cleomenes, fent ambaffadors to Sardis, to form an alliance with the Perfians; for they were well convinced that they fhould have to fupport a war againft Cleomenes and Sparta. On their arrival at Sardis, and explaining the nature of their commiffion, Artaphernes, fon of Hyftafpes, and chief magiftrate of Sardis, enquired of them who they were, and where they lived, defiring to become the allies of Perfia. Being fatisfied in this particular, he made them this abrupt propofition: if the Athenians would fend to Darius earth and water, he would form an alliance with them, if not, they were immediately to depart. After deliberating on the fubject, they acceded to the terms propofed, for which, on their return to Athens, they were feverely reprehended.

LXXIV. Cleomenes knowing that he was reproached, and feeling that he was injured by the Athenians, levied forces in the different parts of the Peloponnefe, without giving any intimation of the object he had in view. He propofed, however, to take vengeance on Athens, and to place the government in the hands of Ifagoras, who with him had been driven from the citadel: with a great body of forces he himfelf took poffeffion of Eleufis, whilft the Bœotians, as had been agreed upon, feized Oenoë and Hyfias [97], towns in the extremity

---

[97] *Hyfias.*]—Larcher thinks that Hyfias never conftituted a part of Attica, and therefore, with Wefſeling, wifhes to read Phyle.—See Wefſeling's note.

of

of Attica: on another fide the Chalcidians laid
wafte the Athenian territories. The Athenians,
however, perplexed by thefe different attacks, deferred their revehge on the Bœotians and Chalcidians, and marched with their army againft the
Peloponnefians at Eleufis.

LXXV. Whilft the two armies were prepared
to engage, the Corinthians firft of all, as if confcious of their having acted an unjuftifiable part,
turned their backs and retired. Their example was
followed by Demaratus, fon of Arifton, who was
alfo a king of Sparta, had conducted a body of
forces from Lacedæmon, and till now had feconded Cleomenes in all his meafures. On ae-
count of this diffenfion between their princes, the
Spartans paffed a law, forbidding both their kings
to march with the army at the fame time. They
determined alfo, that one of the Tyndaridæ [98]
fhould remain with the prince who was left at
home, both of whom, till now, had accompanied
them on foreign expeditions. The reft of the confederates at Eleufis, perceiving this difunion of the
princes, and the feceffion of the Corinthians, returned to their refpective homes.

[98] *One of the Tyndaridæ.*]—It may perhaps be inferred from
this paffage, that the fymbol or image reprefenting Caftor and
Pollux, which before was one piece of wood, was feparated into
two diftinct emblems. See Abbé Winckelman:—" Chez les La-
cedæmoniens Caftor et Pollux avoient la forme de deux mor-
ceaux de bois parallcles, joints par deux baguettes de traverfe ;
et cette ancienne figure s'eft confervée jufqu'à nous par le
figne Ⅱ, qui denote ces frères gemeaux du zodiaque.—*T*.

LXXVI.

LXXVI. This was the fourth time that the Dorians had entered Attica, twice as enemies, and twice with pacific and friendly views. Their firſt expedition was to eſtabliſh a colony at Megara, which was when Codrus [99] reigned at Athens. They came from Sparta the ſecond and third time to expel the Piſiſtratidæ. The fourth time was when Cleomenes and the Peloponneſians attacked Eleuſis.

LXXVII. The Athenians, obſerving the adverſary's army thus ignominiouſly diminiſh, gave place to the deſire of revenge, and determined firſt to attack the Chalcidians, to aſſiſt whom the Bœotians advanced as far as the Euripus [100]. On ſight of them the Athenians reſolved to attack them before

[99] *Codrus.*]—Of this Codrus the following ſtory is related :—The Dorians of the Peloponneſe, as here mentioned, marched againſt the Athenians, and were promiſed ſucceſs from the oracle of Delphi, provided they did not kill Codrus the Athenian prince. Cleomantis of Delphi gave intimation of this to the Athenians; upon which Codrus left his camp, in the habit of a beggar, mingled with the enemy's troops, and provoked ſome amongſt them to kill him; when the Athenians ſent to demand the body of their prince, the Peloponneſians, on hearing the incident, retreated.—*T.*

[100] *Euripus.*]—This was the name of the very narrow ſtreight between Bœotia and Eubœa, where the ſea was ſaid by the ancients to ebb and flow ſeven times a day. It was rendered more memorable, becauſe Ariſtotle was reported here to have deſtroyed himſelf from mortification, being unable to explain the cauſe of this phænomenon. It afterwards became an appellation for any ſtreight of the ſea.

The

fore the Chalcidians : they accordingly gave them
battle, and obtained a complete victory, killing a
prodigious number, and taking seven hundred prisoners.   On the same day they passed into Euboea,
and fought the Chalcidians ; over these also they
were victorious, and they left a colony to the number of four thousand on the lands of the Hippobotæ [101], by which name the most opulent of the
Chalcidians were distinguished.   Such of these as
they took prisoners, as well as their Bœotian captives, they at first put in irons, and kept in close confinement : they afterwards suffered them to be ran-
somed at two minæ a man, suspending their chains
from the citadel.   These were to be seen even
within my memory, hanging from the walls which
were burnt by the Medes, near the temple facing
the west.   The tenth part of the money produced
from the ransom of their prisoners was consecrated,
with it they purchased a chariot of brass [102] for four
horses : it was placed at the left hand side of the
entrance of the citadel, with this inscription :—

The circumstance of the ebb and flow of the sea in this place
happening seven times a day, is thus mentioned in the Hercules
of Seneca :

Euripus undas flectit instabilis vagas
Septemque cursus volvit et totidem refert
Dum lassa Titan mergat oceano juga.   *T*.

[101] *Hippobotæ*]—literally means keepers of horses, from ιππος,
a horse, and βοσκω, to feed.

[102] *Chariot of brass.*]—From the tenth of the spoils of the
Bœotians, and of the people of Chalcis, they made a chariot of
brass.—*See Pausanias, Attic.* chap. xxviii.

Her

Her arms, when Chalcis and Bœotia tried,
Athens in chains and darkneſs quell'd their pride:
Their ranſom paid, the tenths are here beſtow'd,
A votive gift to fav'ring Pallas ow'd.

LXXVIII. The Athenians continued to en-
creaſe in number and importance: not from their
example alone, but from various inſtances, it may be
made appear that an equal form of government is
the beſt. Whilſt the Athenians were in ſubjection
to tyrants, they were ſuperior in war to none of their
neighhours, but when delivered from their oppreſ-
ſors, they far ſurpaſſed them all; from whence it is
evident, that whilſt under the reſtraint of a maſter,
they were incapable of any ſpirited exertions, but
as ſoon as they obtained their liberty, each man
zealouſly exerciſed his talents on his own account.

LXXIX. The Thebans after this, deſirous of
obtaining revenge, ſent to conſult the oracle. In
reply, the Pythian aſſured them, that of themſelves
they would be unable to accompliſh this. She recommended them to conſult their popular aſſembly,
and to apply to their neareſt neighbours [101] for aſſiſtance. Thoſe employed in this buſineſs called on
their return an aſſembly of their countrymen, to
whom they communicated the reply of the oracle.
Hearing that they were required to aſk aſſiſtance of
their neighbours, they deliberated amongſt them-

[101] *Neareſt neighbours.*]—The term των αγχιτα is ambiguous,
and may be underſtood either of neighbours or relations.

ſelves.

felves. " What," faid fome of them, "do not the Ta-
" nagræi [104], the Coronæi [105], and the Thefpians [106],
" who are our neighbours, conftantly act in con-
" cert with us; do they not always affift us in war,
" with the moft friendly and fpirited exertions?
" To thefe there can be no occafion to apply; the
" oracle muft therefore have fome other mean-
" ing."

LXXX. Whilft they were thus debating, fome
one amongft them exclaimed, " I think that I am
" able to penetrate the meaning of the oracle; Afo-
" pus [107] is reported to have had two daughters,
                                               " Thebe,

---

[104] *Tanagræi.*]—The country of Tanagra, according to
Pliny and others, was very celebrated for a breed of fighting
cocks.—Jam ex his quidam (galli) ad bella tantum et prœlia
affidua nafcuntur quibus etiam patrias nobilitarunt Rhodum ac
Tanagram.—*Pliny*, x. 21.

Its modern name is Anatoiia.—*T.*

[105] *Coronæi.*]—Of Coronea a very fingular circumftance is
related, that whereas all the reft of Bœotia abounded with moles,
not one was ever feen in Coronea.—*T.*

[106] *Thefpians.*]—Thefpia was one of thofe cities confidered
by the ancients as facred to the mufes, whence one of their names
Thefpiades.—*T.*

[107] *Afopus.*]—Oceanus and Tethys, as the ftory goes, amongft
other fons after whom rivers were named, had alfo Peneus and
Afopus; Peneus remained in the country now called Theffaly,
and gave his name to the river which waters it. Afopus refiding at Phlyus, married Merope, the daughter of Laden, by
whom he had two fons, Pelafgus, and Ifmenus, and twelve
daughters, Cencyra, Salamis, Ægina, Pirene, Cleone, Thebe,
Tanagra, Thefpia, Afopis, Sinope, Ænia, and Chalcis. Ægina
                                                            was

" Thebe and Ægina; as thefe were fifters, I am
" inclined to believe that the deity would have us
" apply to the Æginetæ, to affift us in obtaining
" revenge." The Thebans not being able to de-
vife any more plaufible interpretation, thought that
they acted in conformity to the will of the oracle,
by fending to the Æginetæ for affiftance, as to their
neareft neighbours, who, in return, engaged to fend
the Æacidæ [108] to their aid.

LXXXI. The Thebans, relying on the affiftance
of the Æacidæ, commenced hoftilities with the
Athenians, but they met with fo ill a reception, that
they determined to fend back the Æacidæ, and to
require the aid of fome troops. The application
was favourably received, and the Æginetæ, confident
in their riches, and mindful of their ancient enmity
with the Athenians, began hoftilities againft them,
without any formal declaration of war. Whilft
the forces of Athens were folely employed againft
the Bœotians, they paffed over with a fleet into
Attica, and not only plundered Phaleros [109], but

was carried away by Jupiter to the ifland which was called
after her.

Afopus, informed of this by Sifyphus, purfued her; but Jupiter ftruck him with his thunder.—*Diodorus Siculus.*

[108] *Æacidæ.*]—M. Larcher, comparing this with a paragraph
in the following chapter, is of opinion that Herodotus here
fpeaks not of any perfons, but of images reprefenting the Æacidæ, which the Æginetæ lent the Thebans.

[109] *Phaleros.*]—This place is now called Porto Leone.—*T.*

almoſt all the inhabitants of the coaſt; by which the Athenians ſuſtained conſiderable injury.

LXXXII. The firſt occaſion of the enmity between the Ægineta and the Athenians was this:—
The Epidaurians being afflicted by a ſevere and
continued famine, conſulted the Delphic oracle;
the Pythian enjoined them to erect ſtatues to
Damia and Auxeſia [110], promiſing that their ſituation would then be amended. The Epidaurians
next enquired, whether they ſhould conſtruct theſe
ſtatues of braſs or of ſtone. The prieſteſs replied, of
neither, but of the wood of the garden olive. The
Epidaurians, in conſequence, applied to the Athenians for permiſſion to take one of their olives,
believing theſe of all others the moſt ſacred; indeed
it is ſaid, that at this period olives were no where
elſe to be found [111]. The Athenians granted their
requeſt, on condition that they ſhould every year

[110] *Damia and Auxeſia.*]—Theſe were the ſame as Ceres and
Proſerpine: theſe goddeſſes procured fertility, and had a temple
in Tegea, where they were called Carpophoræ. Pauſanias
relates the ſame fact as Herodotus, except that he calls the two
goddeſſes Auxeſia and Lamia.

They were alſo worſhipped at Trœzene, but for different reaſons: Damia was the Bona Dea of the Romans; ſhe was, alſo,
according to Valcnaer, the ſame as the Roman Maia.—*Larcher.*

[111] *To be found.*]—This aſſertion was by no means true, and, as
Larcher remarks, Herodotus knew it, but not chooſing to hurt
the pride of the Athenians, he admits the report, qualifying it
with, " it is ſaid."

furniſh

furnish a sacrifice to Minerva Pólias [112], and to Erectheus [113]. The Epidaurians acceding to these terms, constructed of the Athenian olive the figures which had been enjoined, and as their lands immediately became fruitful, they punctually fulfilled their engagements with the Athenians.

LXXXIII. At and before this period, the Æginetæ were so far in subjection to the Epidaurians, that all subjects of litigation betwixt themselves and the people of Epidaurus were determined among the latter. In process of time they built themselves a fleet, and revolted from their allegiance; becoming still more powerful, they made themselves masters of the sea, and plundered their former masters, carrying away the images of Damia and Auxesia. These they deposited in the centre of their own territories, in a place called Œa, about twenty stadia from their city: having done this, they instituted sacrifices in their honour, with ludicrous choruses of women [114], assigning to each of these

---

[112] *Minerva Polias.*]—Patroness of the city, for the same reason she was called Poliouchos.

[113] *Erectheus.*]—Was the sixth king of Athens, in whose reign Ceres came to Athens, and planted corn; not only he, but his daughters were received into the number of the gods.

Nostri quidem publicani cum essent in Bæotiâ deorum immortalium excepti lege censoria negabant immortales esse ullos qui aliquando homines fuissent.—Sed si sunt hi dii, est certe Erectheus cujus Athenis et delubrum vidimus et sacerdotem.—*Cic. de Nat. Deor.* iii. 19.

[114] *Ludicrous choruses of women.*]—If Herodotus, where he

says

thefe goddeffes ten men, who were to prefide over
the chorufes. Thefe chorufes did not infult any
male, but the females of the country. The Epidaurians had dances fimilar to thefe, with other
ceremonies which were myfterious.

LXXXIV. From the time of their lofing thefe
images, the Epidaurians ceafed to obferve their
engagements with the Athenians, who fent to re-
monftrate with them on the occafion. They made
reply, that in this refpect they were guilty of no in-
juftice, for as long as they poffeffed the images, they
had fulfilled all that was expected from them; having loft thefe, their obligation became void, devolv-
ing from them to the Æginetæ. On receiving this
anfwer, the Athenians fent to Ægina to demand
the images, but the Æginetæ denied that the Athenians had any bufinefs with them.

LXXXV. The Athenians relate, that after this
refufal of their demand, they fent the perfons before
employed in this bufinefs in a veffel to Ægina. As
thefe images were made of the wood of Athens,
they were commiffioned to carry them away from
the place where they ftood; but their attempt to

---

fays that the Epidaurians honoured the goddeffes Damia and
Auxefia, χοροισι γυναικηϊοισι κερτομοισι, with chorufes of women,
that ufed to abufe and burlefque the women of the country, had
called them χοροισι κωμικοισι, comical chorufes, he had faid nothing unworthy of a great hiftorian; becaufe thofe chorufes of
women, were much of the fame fort that were afterwards called
comical.—*Bentley on Phalaris.*

do this not prevailing, they endeavoured to remove them with ropes: in the midſt of their efforts they were alarmed by an earthquake, and loud claps of thunder; thoſe employed were ſeized with a madneſs, which cauſed them to kill one another; one only ſurvived, who immediately fled to Phaleros.

LXXXVI. The above is the Athenian account. The Æginetæ affirm, that this expedition was not made in a ſingle veſſel, for the attacks of one, or even of many veſſels, they could eaſily have repelled, even if they had poſſeſſed no ſhips of their own; but they ſay that the Athenians invaded them with a powerful fleet; in conſequence of which they retired, not chooſing to hazard a naval engagement. It is, however, by no means evident, whether they declined a ſea-fight from a want of confidence in their own power, or whether they retired voluntarily and from deſign. It is certain that the Athenians, meeting with no reſiſtance, advanced to the place where the images ſtood, and not able to ſeparate them from their baſes, they dragged them along with ropes; during which, both the figures did what ſeems incredible to me, whatever it may to others [115]. They aſſert, that they

---

[115] *Whatever it may to others.*]—This is one of the numerous examples in Herodotus, which concur to prove, that the character of credulity, ſo univerſally imputed to our hiſtorian, ought to be ſomewhat qualified. For my own part, I am able to recollect very few paſſages indeed, where, relating any thing marvellous, or exceeding credibility, he does not at the ſame time intimate, in ſome form or other, his own ſuſpicions of the fact.—*T.*

both

both fell upon their knees, in which attitude they have ever fince remained. Such were the proceedings of the Athenians. The people of Ægina, according to their own account, hearing of the hoftile intentions of the Athenians, took care that the Argives fhould be ready to affift them. As foon, therefore, as the Athenians landed at Ægina, the Argives were at hand, and unperceived by the enemy, paffed over from Epidaurus to the ifland, whence intercepting their retreat to their fhips, they fell upon the Athenians; at which moment of time an earthquake happened, accompanied with thunder.

LXXXVII. In their relation of the above circumftances, the Æginetæ and the Argives concur. The Athenians acknowledge, that one only of their countrymen returned to Attica; but this man, the Argives fay, was the fole furvivor of a defeat, which they gave the Athenians; whilft thefe affirm, that he efcaped from the vengeance of the divinity, which, however, he did not long elude, for he afterwards perifhed in this manner: when he returned to Athens, and related at large the deftruction of his countrymen, the wives of thofe who had been engaged in the expedition againft Ægina were extremely exafperated that he alone fhould furvive; they accordingly furrounded the man, and each of them afking for her hufband, they wounded him with the clafps [116] of their garments, till he died.

This

---

[116] *With the clafps.*]—The Greeks called the clafp or buckle
with

This behaviour of their women was to the Athenians more afflicting than the misfortune which preceded it; all however they could do was to make them afterwards assume the Ionian dress. Before this incident, the women of Athens wore the Doric vest, which much resembles the Corinthian; that they might have no occasion for clasps, they obliged them to wear linen tunics,

with which they fastened their garments, περονη, and sometimes πορπη; the Latins for the same thing used the word fibula. Various specimens of ancient clasps or buckles may be seen in Montfaucon, the generality of which resemble a bow that is strung. Montfaucon rejects the opinion of those who affirm, that the buckles of which various ancient specimens were preserved, were only styli, or instruments to write with.—" The styli," he adds, " were long pins, and much stronger than the pins with which they fastened the buckles anciently." When Julius Cæsar was assassinated, he defended himself with his stylus, and thrust it through the arm of Casca. When the learned Frenchman says, that the ancient clasps or buckles could not possibly serve for offensive weapons, he probably was not acquainted with the fact here mentioned by Herodotus. An elegant use is made by Homer, of the probability of a wound's being inflicted by a clasp: when Venus, having been wounded by Diomed, retires from the field, Minerva says sarcastically to Jupiter,

> Permit thy daughter, gracious Jove, to tell
> How this mischance the Cyprian queen befell;
> As late she tried with passion to inflame
> The tender bosom of a Grecian dame,
> Allur'd the fair with moving thoughts of joy,
> To quit her country for some youth of Troy;
> The clasping zone, with golden buckles bound,
> Razed her soft hand with this lamented wound. *T.*

G g 4 LXXXVIII

LXXXVIII. It seems reasonable to believe, that this vest was not originally Ionian but Carian: formerly the dress of the Grecian females was universally the same with what we now call Dorian. It is reported, that the Argives and the Æginetæ, in opposition to the above ordinance of the Athenians, directed their women to wear clasps, almost twice as large as usual, and ordained these to be the particular votive offering made by the women, in the temples of the above divinities. They were suffered to offer there nothing which was Attic, even the common earthen vessels were prohibited, of which they were allowed to use none but what were made in their own country. Such, even to my time, has been the contradictory spirit of the women of Argos and Ægina, with respect to those of Athens, that the former have persevered in wearing their clasps larger than before.

LXXXIX. This which I have related, was the origin of the animosity between the people of Athens and Ægina. The latter still having in mind the old grievance of the statues, readily yielded to the solicitations of the Thebans, and assisted the Bœotians, by ravaging the coasts of Attica. Whilst the Athenians were preparing to revenge the injury, they were warned by a communication from the Delphic oracle, to refrain from all hostilities with the people of Ægina for the space of thirty years: at the termination of this period, they were to erect a fane to Æacus, and might then commence offensive operations against the Æginetæ with success;

cefs; but if they immediately began hoftilities, although they would do the enemy effential injury, and finally fubdue them, they would in the interval fuffer much themfelves. On receiving this communication from the oracle, the Athenians erected a facred edifice to Æacus [117], which may now be feen in their forum; but notwithftanding the menace impending over them, they were unable to defer the profecution of their revenge for the long period of thirty years.

XC. Whilft they were thus preparing for revenge, their defigns were impeded by what happened at Lacedæmon. The Spartans having difcovered the intrigues between the Alcmæonidæ and the Pythian, and what this laft had done againft the Pififtratidæ and themfelves, perceived that they were involved in a double difappointment. Without at all conciliating the Athenians, they had expelled from thence their own friends and allies. They were alfo ferioufly impreffed by certain ora-

[117] *Æacus.*]—The genealogy of Æacus is related in Ovid, book xiii. The circumftance of Jupiter, at the requeft of Æacus, turning ants into men, who were called from thence Myrmidons, may be found in Ovid, book vii.—

> Myrmidonafque voco, nec origine nomina fraudo;
> Corpora vidifti, mores quos ante gerebant
> Nunc quoque habent, parcum genus eft patienfque
>   laborum,
> Quæfitique tenax, et qui quæfita refervent.

The word Myrmidons has been anglicifed, and is ufed to exprefs any bold hardy ruffians, by no lefs authority than Swift —*T.*

cles,

cles, which taught them to expect from the Athenians many and great calamities. Of these they
were entirely ignorant, till they were made known
by Cleomenes at Sparta. Cleomenes had difcovered and feized them in the citadel of Athens,
where they had been originally depofited by the
Pififtratidæ, who, on being expelled, had left them
in the temple.

XCI. On hearing from Cleomenes the above
oracular declarations, the Lacedæmonians obferved
that the Athenians increafed in power, and were
but little inclined to remain fubject to them ; they
farther reflected, that though when oppreffed by
tyrants, the people of Athens were weak and fub-
miffive, the poffeffion of liberty would not fail to
make them formidable rivals. In confequence of
thefe deliberations, they fent for Hippias the fon of
Pififtratus, from Sigeum on the Hellefpont, where
the Pififtratidæ had taken refuge. On his arrival,
they affembled alfo the reprefentatives of their other
allies, and thus expreffed themfelves : " We con-
" fefs to you, friends and allies, that under the im-
" preffion of oracles, which deceived us, we have
" greatly erred. The men who had claims upon
" our kindnefs, and who would have rendered
" Athens obedient to our will, we have banifhed
" from their country, and have delivered that city
" into the power of an ungrateful faction. Not
" remembering that to us they are indebted for
" their liberty, they are become infolent, and have
" expelled difgracefully from amongft them, us and

" our king. They are endeavouring, we hear, to
" make themselves more and more formidable;
" this their neighbours the Bœotians and Chalci-
" dians have already experienced, as will others
" also who may happen to offend them. To atone
" for our past errors and neglect, we now profess
" ourselves ready to assist you in chastising them:
" for this reason, we have sent for Hippias, and
" assembled you; intending, by the joint opera-
" tions of one united army, to restore him to
" Athens, and to that dignity of which we for-
" merly deprived him."

XCII. These sentiments of the Spartans were
approved by very few of the confederates. After
a long interval of silence, Sosicles of Corinth made
this reply: " We may henceforth certainly expect
" to see the heavens take the place of the earth [118],
" the earth that of the heavens; to see mankind
" existing in the waters, and the scaly tribe on
" earth, since you, oh Lacedæmonians, meditate
" the subversion of free and equal governments, and
" the establishment of arbitrary power; than which

---

[118] *Take the place of the earth.*]—With a sentiment similar to
this, Ovid commences one of his most beautiful elegies:

In caput alta suum labentur ab æquore retro
    Flumina, conversis solque recurret equis,
Terra feret stellas, cœlum findetur aratro,
    Unda dabit flammas et dabit ignis aquas;
Omnia naturæ præpostera legibus ibunt,
    Parsque suum mundi nulla tenebit iter.
Omnia jam fient, fieri quæ posse negabam,
    Et nihil est de quo non sit habenda fides.   *T*.

" surely

" surely nothing can be more unjuft in-itfelf, or
" more fanguinary in its effects. If you confider
" tyranny with fo favourable an eye, before you
" think of introducing it elfewhere, fhew us the
" example, and fubmit firft to a tyrant yourfelves :
" at prefent, you are not only without a tyrant,
" but it fhould feem, that in Sparta, nothing can be
" guarded againft with more vigilant anxiety ; why
" then wifh to involve your, confederates in what
" to you appears fo great a calamity ; a calamity
" which like us if you had known, experience
" would doubtlefs have prompted a more fagacious
" counfel. The government of Corinth was for-
" merly in the hands of a few ; they who were
" called the Bacchiadæ '¹⁹ had the adminiftration of
" affairs. To cement and confirm their authority,
" they were careful to contract no marriages but
" amongft themfelves. One of thefe, whofe name
" was Amphion, had a daughter called Labda '²⁰,
                                      " who

¹¹⁹ *Bacchiadæ*]—Paufanias and Diodorus Siculus are a
little at variance with our author in their accounts of the Bacchiadæ. The matter however feems from them all to be this :
Bacchis was one of the Heraclidæ, and prince of Corinth ; on
account of his fplendid character and virtues, his defcendants
took the name of Bacchiadæ, which with the fovereignty of
Corinth, they retained till they were expelled by Cypfelus.—*T.*

¹²⁰ *Labda.*]—This, fays M. Larcher, was not her real name,
but was given her on account of the refemblance which her
lamenefs m de her bear to the letter L, or Lambda. Anciently
the letter Lambda was called Labda. It was a common cuftom
amongft the ancients to give as nicknames the letters of the
alphabet. Æfop was called Theta, by his mafter Iadmus, from
his fuperior acutenefs, Thetes being alfo a name for flaves.
Galerius Craffus, a military tribune under the Emperor Ti-
                                      berius,

" who was lame. As none of the Bacchiadæ were
" willing to marry her, they united her to Eetion, fon
" of Echecrates, who, though of the low tribe of
" Petra, was in his origin one of the Lapithæ [121],
" defcended from Cæneus [122]. As he had no children
" by this or by any other wife, he fent to Delphi to
" confult the oracle on this fubject. At the mo-
" ment of his entering the temple, he was thus ad-
" dreffed by the Pythian:—

" Eetion, honour'd far below thy worth;
" Know Labda fhall produce a monftrous birth,
" A ftone, which, rolling with enormous weight,
" Shall crufh ufurpers, and reform the ftate.

" This prediction to Eetion came by accident to
" the ears of the Bacchiadæ. An oracle had before
" fpoken concerning Corinth, which though dark

berius, was called Beta, becaufe he loved Beet (poirée). Or-
pyllis, a courtefan of Cyzicum, was named Gamma; Anthe-
nor, who wrote the hiftory of Crete, was called Delta; Apollonius who lived in the time of Philopater, was named Epfilon,
&c.—*Larcher.*

[121] *Lapithæ.*]—The Lapithæ were celebrated in antiquity, as
being the firft people who ufed bridles and harnefs for horfes:

Fræna Pelethronii Lapithæ gyrofque dedere
Impofiti dorfo.   *Virgil.*

[122] *Cæneus.*]—The ftory of Cæneus is this: Cænis was a virgin, and was ravifhed by Neptune, who afterwards, at her requeft,
turned her into a man, and caufed her to be invulnerable. After
this change of fex his name alfo was changed to Cæneus; he
then fought with the Lapithæ againft the Centaurs, who not able
otherwife to deftroy him, overwhelmed him beneath a pile of
wood. Ovid fays he was then turned into a bird; Virgil, on
the contrary, afferts, that he refumed his former fex.—*T.*

3   " and

" and obſcure, was evidently of the ſame tendency
" with that declared to Eetion: it was this :—

" Amidſt the rocks an eagle [121] ſhall produce
" An eagle, who ſhall many knees unlooſe,
" Bloody and ſtrong: guard then your meaſures
   " well,
" Ye who in Corinth and Pirene [124] dwell!

" When this oracle was firſt delivered to the Bacchi-
" adæ, they had no conception of its meaning ; but
" as ſoon as they learned the particulars of that given
" to Eetion, they underſtood the firſt from the laſt.
" The reſult was, that they confined the ſecret to
" themſelves, determining to deſtroy the future child
" of Eetion. As ſoon as the woman was delivered,
" they commiſſioned ten of their number to go to
" the place where Eetion lived, and make away with
" the infant. As ſoon as they came to where the tribe
" of Petra reſided, they went to Eetion's houſe, and
" aſked for the child : Labda, ignorant of their in-
" tentions, and imputing this viſit to their friendſhip
" for her huſband, produced her infant, and gave it
" to the arms of one of them.   It had been con-
" certed, that whoever ſhould firſt have the child in
" his hands, was to daſh it on the ground : it hap-
" pened, as if by divine interpoſition, that the infant
" ſmiled in the face [125] of the man to whom the mo-
                                             " ther

[121] *An eagle.*]—Eetion is derived from the Greek word
ἀετος, an eagle.

[124] *Pirene.*]—This fountain was ſacred to the muſes, and remarkable for the ſweetneſs of its waters.

[125] *Smiled in the face.*]—The effects of an infant ſmiling in
                                             the

" ther had entrufted it. He was feized with an emo-
" tion of pity, and found himfelf unable to deftroy it;
" with thefe feelings, he gave the child to the perfon
" next him, who gave it to a third, till thus it paffed
" through the hands of all the ten : none of them
" was able to murder it, and it was returned to the
" mother. On leaving the houfe, they ftopped at the
" gate, and began to reproach and accufe each other,
" but particularly him who firft receiving the child,
" had failed in his engagements. After a fhort inter-
" val, they agreed to enter the houfe again, and jointly
" deftroy the child : but fate had determined that the
" offspring of Eetion fhould ultimately prove the de-
" ftruction of Corinth. Labda, ftanding near the gate,
" had overheard their difcourfe, and fearing that as
" their fentiments were changed, they would infal-
" libly, if they had opportunity, murder her infant,
" fhe carried it away, and hid it in a place little ob-
" vious to fufpicion, namely in a corn-meafure [116].
" She

the face of rude untutored men, is delightfully expreffed in part
of an ode on the ufe and abufe of poetry, preferved by Warton,
in his Effay on the Genius and Writings of Pope.

Father of peace and arts—he firft the city built;
No more the neighbour's blood was by his neighbour fpilt;
He taught to till and feparate the lands ;
He fix'd the roving youths in Hymen's myrtle bands,
 Whence dear domeftic life began,
 And all the charities that foftened man :
 The babes that in their fathers faces fmil'd,
 With lifping blandifhments their rage beguil'd,
 And tender thoughts infpired.

[116] *In a corn meafure.*]—The defcription of this cheft, which
was preferved in the temple of Juno at Olympia, employs feveral chapters in the fifth book of Paufanias. He tells us that
       the

" She was satisfied, that on their return they would
" make a strict search after the child, which accord-
" ingly happened : finding however all their dili-
" gence ineffectual, they thought it only remained for
" them to return and acquaint their employers, that
" they had executed their commission. When the
" son of Eetion grew up, he was called Cypselus, in
" memory of the danger he had escaped in the
" 'corn-measure,' the meaning of the word Cypsela.
" On his arrival at manhood, he consulted the Del-
" phic oracle : the answer he received was ambi-
" guous ; but confident of its favourable meaning,
" he attacked and made himself master of Corinth.
" The oracle was this :—

" Behold a man whom fortune makes her care,
" Corinthian Cypselus, Eetion's heir ;
" Himself shall reign, his children too prevail,
" But there the glories of his race must fail.

" When Cypselus had obtained possession of the go-
" vernment, he persecuted the inhabitants of Co-
" rinth, depriving many of their wealth, and more
" of their lives. After an undisturbed reign of thirty
" years, he was succeeded by his son Periander,
" who at first adopted a milder and more mode-
" rate conduct ; but having by his emissaries formed
" an intimate connection with Thrasybulus, sove-

the chest was made of cedar, and that its outside was enriched
with animals, and a variety of historical representations in
cedar, ivory, and gold. " It is not likely," says M. Larcher,
" that the chest described by Pausanias was the real chest in
which Cypselus was preserved, but one made on purpose to
commemorate the incident."—*T.*

" reign

" reign of Miletus he even exceeded his father in
" cruelty. The object of one of his embaffies was
" to enquire of Thrafybulus what mode of govern-
" ment would render his authority moft fecure and
" moft honourable. Thrafybulus conducted the
" meffenger to a corn-field without the town,
" where, as he walked up and down, he afked fome
" queftions of the man relative to his departure from
" Corinth; in the mean while, wherever he dif-
" cerned a head of corn taller than the reft [127], he
" cut it off, till all the higheft and the richeft were
" levelled with the ground. Having gone over the
" whole field in this manner, he retired, without
" fpeaking a word to the perfon who attended him.
" On the return of his emiffary to Corinth, Perian-
" der was extremely anxious to learn the refult of
" his journey, but he was informed, that Thrafybu-
" lus had never faid a word in reply; that he even
" appeared to be a man deprived of his reafon, and
" bent on the deftruction of his own property. The
" meffenger then proceeded to inform his mafter of
" what Thrafybulus had done. Periander immedi-
" ately conceived the meaning of Thrafybulus to be,
" that he fhould deftroy the moft illuftrious of his
" citizens. He in confequence exercifed every
" fpecies of cruelty, till he completed what his fa-

[127] *Taller than the reft.*]—A fimilar ftory is told of Tarquin
the Proud, and his fon Sextus, who ftriking off the heads of
the talleft poppies in his garden, thus intimated his defire that
his fon fhould deftroy the moft eminent characters of Gabii, of
which he was endeavouring by ftratagem to make himfelf mafter.—See *Livy*, b. i. ch. 54. It is remarkable that Ariftotle in
his Politics twice mentions this enigmatical advice as given by
Periander to Thrafybulus.—*T.*

VOL. II.   H h   " ther

" ther Cypſelus had begun, killing ſome, and driv-
" ing others into exile. On account of his wife
" Meliſſa, he one day ſtripped all the women of
" Corinth of their cloaths. He had ſent into Theſ-
" protia near the river Acheron, to conſult the
" oracle of the dead * concerning ſomething of
" value which had been left by a ſtranger. Meliſſa
" appearing, declared that ſhe would by no means
" tell where the thing required was depoſited, for
" ſhe was cold and naked; for the garments in
" which ſhe was interred were of no ſervice to her,
" not having been burned. In proof of which ſhe
" aſſerted, that Periander had ' put bread into a
" cold oven;' Periander, on hearing this, was ſa-
" tisfied of the truth of what ſhe ſaid, for he had
" embraced Meliſſa after her deceaſe. On the re-
" turn therefore of his meſſengers, he commanded
" all the women of Corinth to aſſemble at the tem-
" ple of Juno. On this occaſion the women came
" as to ſome public feſtival, adorned with the great-
" eſt ſplendour. The king having placed his guards
" for the purpoſe, cauſed them all to be ſtripped,
" free women and ſlaves, without diſtinction. Their
" cloaths were afterwards diſpoſed in a large trench,
" and burned in honour of Meliſſa, who was ſolemn-
" ly invoked on the occaſion. When this was done,
" a ſecond meſſenger was diſpatched to Meliſſa, who

---

* *The oracle of the dead.*]—Νικυομαρτηϊον, a place where divination was carried on by calling up the dead with magical
rites. Pauſanias places this oracle at Aornos in Theſprotia.
The ſuperſtitions of Italy ſeem to have been borrowed from that
country ; hence Cicero mentions an oracle of the ſame kind at
the lake Avernus in Italy.—*Tuſc.* i. 16.

" now

" now vouchſafed to ſay where the thing required
" might be found.—Such, oh men of Sparta, is a
" tyrannical government, and ſuch its effects. Much
" therefore were we Corinthians aſtoniſhed, when
" we learned that you had ſent 'for Hippias; but
" the declaration of your ſentiments ſurpriſes us ſtill
" more. We adjure you therefore, in the names of
" the divinities of Greece, not to eſtabliſh tyranny
" in our cities. But if you are determined in your
" purpoſe, and are reſolved in oppoſition to what
" is juſt, to reſtore Hippias, be aſſured that the Co-
" rinthians will not ſecond you."

XCIII. Soſicles, the deputy of the Corinthians,
having delivered his ſentiments, was anſwered by
Hippias. He having adjured the ſame divinities,
declared, that the Corinthians would moſt of all
have occaſion to regret the Piſiſtratidæ, when the
deſtined hour ſhould arrive, and they ſhould groan
under the oppreſſion of the Athenians. Hippias
ſpoke with the greater confidence, becauſe he was
beſt acquainted with the declarations of the oracles.
The reſt of the confederates, who had hitherto been
ſilent, hearing the generous ſentiments of Soſicles,
declared themſelves the friends of freedom, and fa-
vourers of the opinions of the Corinthians. They
then conjured the Lacedæmonians to introduce no
innovations which might affect the liberties of a
Grecian city.

XCIV. When Hippias departed from Sparta,
Amyntas the Macedonian prince offered him for a
reſidence Anthemos, as did the Theſſalians Iol-

cos;

cos [118]; but he would accept of neither, and returned to Sigeum, which Pisistratus had taken by
force from the people of Mitylene. He had appointed Hegesistratus, his natural son by a woman
of Argos, governor of the place, who did not retain his situation, but after much and violent contest. The people of Mitylene and of Athens issuing,
the one from the city of Achillea [119], the other from
Sigeum, were long engaged in hostilities. They of
Mitylene insisted on the restoration of what had
been violently taken from them; but it was answered, that the Æolians had no stronger claims upon the territories of Troy than the Athenians themselves, and the rest of the Greeks, who had assisted
Menelaus in avenging the rape of Helen.

XCV. Among their various encounters it happened, that in a severe engagement, in which the
Athenians had the advantage, the poet Alcæus [120]

fled

---

[118] *Iolcos.*]—This place is now called Iaco; we learn from
Horace, that it was formerly famous for producing poisonous
plants:

> Herbasque quas Iolcos atque Iberia
> Mittit venenorum ferax.

[119] *Achillea.*]—In the fourth book, Herodotus calls this place
the Course of Achilles. Its modern name is Fidonisi.—*T.*

[120] *Alcæus.*]—Was a native of Mitylene, in the island of
Lesbos; he was cotemporary with Sappho, and generally is
considered as the inventor of lyric poetry. Archilochus,
Alcæus, and Horace, were all unsuccessful in their attempts to
distinguish themselves as soldiers; and all of them ingenuously
acknowledged their inferiority in this respect. Bayle doubts
whether Horace would have confessed his disgrace, if he had
not been sanctioned by the great examples above-mentioned.
However that may be, he writes thus of himself:

Tecum

fled from the field. The Athenians obtained his arms, and suspended them at Sigeum, in the temple of Minerva. Alcæus recorded the event in a poem which

> Tecum Philippos et celerem fugam
> Sensi, relicta non bene parmula
> Quum fracta virtus et minaces
> Turpe solum tetigere mento.

Of Alcæus we have very few remains; but it is understood that Horace in many of his odes minutely imitated him. The principal subjects of his muse seem to have been the praise of liberty and a hatred of tyrants. The ancient poets abound with passages in his honour, and his memory receives no disgrace from the following apostrophe by Akenside, in his ode on lyric poetry:

> Broke from the fetters of his native land,
> Devoting shame and vengeance to her lords,
> With louder impulse and a threatening hand
> The Lesbian patriot smites the sounding chords.
>   Ye wretches, ye perfidious train,
>   Ye cursed of gods and free-born men,
>   Ye murderers of the laws,
>   Tho' now ye glory in your lust,
>   Tho' now ye tread the feeble neck in dust,
> Yet time and righteous Jove will judge your dreadful cause.

After all, Alcæus does not appear to have been one of the fairest characters of antiquity, and has probably received more commendation than he deserved. His house, we learn from Athenæus, was filled with military weapons, his great desire was to attain military glory; but in his first engagement with an enemy, he ignominiously fled. The theme of his songs was liberty, but he was strongly suspected of being a secret friend to some who meditated the ruin of their country. I say nothing of his supposed licentious overture to Sappho, thinking with Bayle, that the verses cited by Aristotle have been too hardly construed. Of these verses the following is an imperfect translation;

Hh 3   ALCÆUS.

which he fent to Mitylene, explaining to a friend named Melanippus the particulars of his misfortune. Periander the fon of Cypfelus at length reunited the contending nations: he being chofen arbiter, determined that each party fhould retain what they poffeffed. Sigeum thus devolved to the Athenians.

XCVI. Hippias, when he left Sparta, went to Afia, where he ufed every effort to render the Athenians odious to Artaphernes, and to prevail on him to make them fubject to him and to Darius. As foon as the intrigues of Hippias were known at Athens, the Athenians difpatched emiffaries to Sardis, intreating the Perfians to place no confidence in men whom they had driven into exile. Artaphernes informed them in reply, that if they wifhed for peace, they muft recal Hippias. Rather than accede to thefe conditions, the Athenians chofe to be confidered as the enemies of Perfia.

XCVII. Whilft they were refolving on thefe meafures, in confequence of the impreffion which had been made to their prejudice in Perfia, Arif-tagoras the Milefian, being driven by Cleomenes

ALCÆUS.

I wifh to fpeak, but ftill thro' fhame conceal
The thoughts my tongue moft gladly would reveal.

SAPPHO.

Were your requeft, oh bard, on virtue built,
Your cheeks would wear no marks of fecret guilt;
But in prompt words the ready thought had flown,
And your heart's honeft meaning quickly fhewn.

I give them, with fome flight alteration, from Bayle.—*T*.

from Sparta, arrived at Athens, which city was then powerful beyond the reſt of its neighbours. When Ariſtagoras appeared in the public aſſembly, he, enumerated, as he had done at Sparta, the riches which Aſia poſſeſſed, and recommended a Perſian war, in which they would be eaſily ſucceſsful againſt a people uſing neither ſpear nor ſhield [131]. In addition to this, he remarked that Miletus was an Athenian colony, and that conſequently it became the Athenians to exert the great power they poſſeſſed in favour of the Mileſians. He proceeded to make uſe of the moſt earneſt intreaties and laviſh promiſes, till they finally acceded to his views. He thought, and as it appeared with juſtice, that it was far eaſier to delude a great multitude than a ſingle individual; he was unable to prevail upon Cleomenes, but he won to his purpoſe no leſs than thirty thouſand [132] Athenians. The people of A-

[131] *Spear nor ſhield.*]—A particular account of the military habit and arms of the oriental nations may be found in the ſeventh book of Herodotus, where he ſpeaks of the nations which compoſed the prodigious armament of Xerxes.—*T.*

[132] *Thirty thouſand.*]—Herodotus is the only ancient author who makes the aggregate of the Athenians amount to more than twenty-one thouſand individuals. Is this, inquires M. Larcher, a fault of the copyiſts, or were the Athenians more populous before the Perſian and Peloponneſian wars? " The narrow policy," obſerves Mr. Gibbon, " of preſerving, without any foreign mixture, the pure blood of the ancient citizens, had checked the fortune, and haſtened the ruin of Athens and Sparta. The aſpiring genius of Rome ſacrificed vanity to ambition, and deemed it more prudent as well as honourable, to adopt virtue and merit for her own, whereſoever they were found, among ſlaves or ſtrangers, enemies or barbarians."

thens accordingly agreed to fend to the affiftance of
the Ionians, twenty veffels of war, of which Me-
lanthius, a very amiable and popular character, was
to have the command. This fleet was the fource
of the calamities [133] which afterwards enfued to the
Greeks and Barbarians.

XCVIII. Before their departure, Ariftagoras returned to Miletus, where he contrived a meafure
from which no advantage could poffibly refult to
the Ionians. Indeed, his principal motive was to
diftrefs Darius. He difpatched a meffenger into
Phrygia, to thofe Pæonians who from the banks of
the Strymon had been led away captive by Megabyzus, and who inhabited a diftrict appropriated
to them. His emiffaries thus addreffed them:—
" Men of Pæonia, I am commiffioned by Arifta-
" goras, prince of Miletus, to fay, that if you will
" follow his counfel, you may be free. The whole
" of Ionia has revolted from Perfia, and it becomes
" you to feize this opportunity of returning to your
" native country. You have only to appear on
" the banks of the ocean; we will provide for the

[133] *Source of the calamities.*]—This is another of the examples
which Plutarch adduces in proof of the malice of Herodotus.
" He has the audacity," fays Plutarch, " to affirm, that the
veffels which the Athenians fent to the affiftance of the Ionians,
who had revolted from the Perfians, were the caufe of the evils
which afterwards enfued, merely becaufe they endeavoured to
deliver fo many, and fuch illuftrious Grecian cites from fervitude." In point of argument, a weaker tract than this of Plutarch was never written, and this affertion in particular is too
abfurd to require any formal refutation.—*T.*

" reft,"

" reft." The Pæonians received this information with great fatisfaction, and with their wives and children fled towards the fea. Some, however, yielding to their fears, remained behind. From the fea-coaft they paffed over to Chios: here they had fcarce difembarked, before a large body of Perfian cavalry, fent in purfuit of them, appeared on the oppofite fhore. Unable to overtake them, they fent over to them at Chios, foliciting their return. This however had no effect: from Chios they were tranfported to Lefbos, from Lefbos to Dorifcus [134], and from hence they proceeded by land to Pæonia.

XCIX. At this juncture, Ariftagoras was joined by the Athenians in twenty veffels, who were alfo accompanied by five triremes of Eretrians. Thefe latter did not engage in the conteft from any regard for the Athenians, but to difcharge a fimilar debt of friendfhip to the Milefians. The Milefians had formerly affifted the Eretrians againft the Chalcidians, when the Samians had united with them againft the Eretrians and Milefians. When thefe and the reft of his confederates were affembled, Ariftagoras commenced an expedition againft Sardis: he himfelf continued at Miletus, whilft his brother Charopinus commanded the Milefians, and Hermophantus had the conduct of the allies.

---

[134] *Dorifcus.*]—Dorifcus is memorable for being the place where Xerxes numbered his army.—*T.*

C. The

C. The Ionians arriving with their fleet at Ephefus, difembarked at Coreffus, a place in its vicinity.
Taking fome Ephefians for their guides, they advanced with a formidable force, directing their
march towards the Cayfter [115]. Paffing over mount
Tmolus, they arrived at Sardis, where meeting no
refiftance, they made themfelves mafters of the
whole of the city, except the citadel. This was
defended by Artaphernes himfelf, with a large body
of troops.

CI. The following incident preferved the city
from plunder: the houfes of Sardis [116] were in general conftructed of reeds; fuch few as were of
brick had reed coverings. One of thefe being fet
on fire by a foldier, the flames fpread from houfe to
houfe, till the whole city was confumed. In the
midft of the conflagration, the Lydians, and fuch
Perfians as were in the city, feeing themfelves furrounded by the flames, and without the poffibility of
efcape, rufhed in crowds to the forum, through the
center of which flows the Pactolus. This river

[115] *Cayfter.*]—This river was very famous in claffic ftory.
It anciently abounded with fwans, and from its ferpentine
courfe has fometimes been confounded with the Mæander; but
the Mæander was the appropriate river of the Milefians, as
was the Cayfter of the Ephefians. The name the Turks now
give it is Chiny.—*T.*

[116] *Sardis.*]—The reader will recollect that Sardis was the
capital of Crœfus, which is here reprefented as confifting only
of a number of thatched houfes, a proof that architecture had as
yet made no progrefs.—*T.*

brings,

brings, in its defcent from mount Tmolus, a quantity of gold duft [117] ; paffing, as we have defcribed,
through Sardis, it mixes with the Hermus, till both
are finally loft in the fea. The Perfians and Lydians thus reduced to the laft extremity, were compelled to act on the defenfive. The Ionians feeing
fome of the enemy prepared to defend themfelves,
others advancing to attack them, were feized with
a panic, and retired to mount Tmolus [118], from
whence, under favour of the night, they retreated to
their fhips.

CII. In the burning of Sardis, the temple of
Cybele, the tutelar goddefs of the country, was totally deftroyed, which was afterwards made a pretence by the Perfians for burning the temples of
the Greeks. When the Perfians who dwell on this
fide the Halys were acquainted with the above invafion, they determined to affift the Lydians. Following the Ionians regularly from Sardis, they came
up with them at Ephefus. A general engagement
enfued, in which the Ionians were defeated with

[117] *Gold duft.*]—It had ceafed to do this in the time of Strabo,
that is to fay, in the age of Auguftus.—*Larcher.*

[118] *Tmolus.*]—Strabo enumerates mount Tmolus amongft the
places which produced the moft excellent vines. It was alfo celebrated for its faffron.—See Virgil,

Nonne vides croceos ut Tmolus odores, &c.

It was alfo called Timolus. See Ovid,

Deferuere fui nymphæ vineta Timoli.

It is now named Timolitze.—*T.*

great

great slaughter. Amongst others of distinction who
fell, was Eualcis, chief of the Eretrians: he had
frequently been victorious in many contests, of
which a garland was the reward, and had been
particularly celebrated by Simonides of Ceos [119].
They who escaped from this battle took refuge in
the different cities.

CIII. After the event of the above expedition,
the Athenians withdrew themselves entirely from
the Ionians, and refused all the solicitations of Aristagoras by his ambassadors, to repeat their assistance.
The Ionians, though deprived of this resource, continued with no less alacrity to persevere in the hostilities they had commenced against Darius. They
sailed to the Hellespont, and reduced Byzantium,
with the neighbouring cities: quitting that part
again, and advancing to Caria, the greater part of

[119] *Simonides of Ceos.*]—There were several poets of this
name; the celebrated satire against women was written by another and more modern Simonides. The great excellence of
this Simonides of Ceos was elegiac composition, in which
Dionysius Halicarnassus does not scruple to prefer him to Pindar.
The invention of local memory was ascribed to him, and it is
not a little remarkable, that at the age of eighty, he contended
for and won a poetical prize. His most memorable saying was
concerning God. Hiero asked him what God was? After many
and reiterated delays, his answer was, "The longer I meditate
upon it, the more obscure the subject appears to me." He is
reproached for having been the first who prostituted his muse
for mercenary purposes. Bayle seems to have collected every
thing of moment relative to this Simonides, to whom for more
minute particulars, I refer the reader.—*T*,

§

the

the inhabitants joined them in their offenfive operations. The city of Caunus, which at firft had refufed their alliance, after the burning of Sardis added itfelf to their forces.

CIV. The confederacy was alfo farther ftrengthened by the voluntary acceffion of all the Cyprians, except the Amathufians [140]. The following was the occafion of the revolt of the Cyprians from the Medes : Gorgus prince of Salamis, fon of Cherfis, grandfon of Siromus, great grandfon of Euelthon, had a younger brother, whofe name was Onefilus ; this man had repeatedly folicited Gorgus to revolt from the Perfians ; and on hearing of the feceffion of the Ionians, he urged him with ftill greater importunity. Finding all his efforts ineffectual, affifted by his party, he took an opportunity of his brother's making an excurfion from Salamis to fhut the gates againft him : Gorgus, thus deprived of his city, took refuge amongft the Medes. Onefilus ufurped his ftation, and perfuaded the Cyprians to rebel. The Amathufians, who alone oppofed him, he clofely befieged.

CV. At this period, Darius was informed of the burning of Sardis by the Athenians and Ionians, and that Ariftagoras of Miletus was the principal

[140] *Amathufians.*]—From Amathus, which was facred to Venus, the whole ifland of Cyprus was fometimes called Amathufia.—According to Ovid, it produced abundance of metals ;

Gravidamque Amathunta metallis. *T.*

inftigator

inftigator of the confederacy againft him. On firft
receiving the intelligence, he is faid to have treated
the revolt of the Ionians with extreme contempt,
as if certain that it was impoffible for them to
efcape his indignation; but he defired to know who
the Athenians were? on being told, he called for
his bow, and fhooting an arrow into the air, he exclaimed:—" Suffer me, oh Jupiter, to be revenged
" on thefe Athenians." He afterwards directed one
of his attendants to repeat to him three times every
day, when he fat down to table, " Sir, remember
" the Athenians."

CVI. After giving thefe orders, Darius fummoned
to his prefence Hiftiæus of Miletus, whom he had
long detained at his court. He addreffed him thus:
" I am informed, Hiftiæus, that the man to whom
" you entrufted the government of Miletus, has
" excited a rebellion againft me; he has procured
" forces from the oppofite continent, and feduced
" the Ionians, whom I fhall unqueftionably chaftife,
" from their duty. With their united affiftance,
" he has deftroyed my city of Sardis. Can fuch a
" conduct poffibly meet with your approbation?
" or unadvifed by you, could he have done what
" he has? Be careful not to involve yourfelf in a
" fecond offence againft my authority." " Can
" you, Sir, believe," faid Hiftiæus in reply, " that
" I would be concerned in any thing which might
" occafion the fmalleft perplexity to you? What
" fhould I, who have nothing to wifh for, gain by
" fuch conduct? Do I not participate all that you
" yourfelf

" yourſelf enjoy; and have I not the honour of
" being your counſellor and your friend? If my
" repreſentative has acted as you alledge, it is en-
" tirely his own deed; but I cannot eaſily be per-
" ſuaded that either he, or the Mileſians, would
" engage in any thing to your prejudice. If, ne-
" vertheleſs, what you intimate be really true, by
" withdrawing me from my own proper ſtation,
" you have only to blame yourſelf for the event.
" I ſuppoſe that the Ionians have taken the oppor-
" tunity of my abſence, to accompliſh what they
" have for a long time meditated. Had I been
" preſent in Ionia, I will venture to affirm, that not
" a city would have revolted from your power:
" you have only therefore to ſend me inſtantly to
" Ionia, that things may reſume their former ſitu-
" ation, and that I may give into your power the
" preſent governor of Miletus, who has occaſioned
" all this miſchief. Having firſt effected this, I
" ſwear by the deities of Heaven, that I will not
" change the garb in which I ſhall ſet foot in Ionia,
" without rendering the great iſland of Sardinia [141]
" tributary to your power."

[141] *Sardinia.*]—It has been doubted by many, whether on
account of the vaſt diſtance of Sardinia from the Aſiatic continent, the text of Herodotus has not here been altered. Rollin
in particular is very incredulous on the ſubject; but as it appears by the preceding paſſages of our author, that the Ionians
had penetrated to the extremities of the Mediterranean, and
were not unacquainted with Corſica, all appearance of improbability in this narration ceaſes.—*T.*

CVII.

CVII. Hiſtiæus made theſe proteſtations to delude Darius. The king was influenced by what he
ſaid, only requiring his return to Suſa as ſoon as
he ſhould have fulfilled his engagements.

CVIII. In this interval, when the meſſenger
from Sardis had informed Darius of the fate of that
city, and the king had done with his bow what we
have deſcribed; and when, after conferring with
Hiſtiæus, he had diſmiſſed him to Ionia, the following incident occurred: Oneſilus of Salamis being engaged in the ſiege of Amathus, word was
brought him that Artybius, a Perſian officer, was
on his way to Cyprus with a large fleet, and a formidable body of Perſians. On hearing this, Oneſilus ſent meſſengers to different parts of Ionia, ex-
preſſing his want and deſire of aſſiſtance. The
Ionians, without heſitation, haſtened to join him
with a numerous fleet. Whilſt they were already at
Cyprus, the Perſians had paſſed over from Cilicia,
and were proceeding by land to Salamis. The
Phœnicians in the mean time had paſſed the promontory which is called the Key of Cyprus.

CIX. Whilſt things were in this ſituation, the
princes of Cyprus aſſembled the Ionian chiefs, and
thus addreſſed them:—" Men of Ionia, we ſubmit
" to your own determination, whether you will en-
" gage the Phœnicians or the Perſians. If you
" rather chuſe to fight on land and with the Per-
" ſians, it is time for you to diſembark, that we
" may go on board your veſſels, and attack the
                                        " Phœnicians.

" Phœnicians.—If you think it more adviſeable to
" encounter the Phœnicians, it becomes you to do
" ſo immediately.—Decide which way you pleaſe,
" that as far as our efforts can prevail, Ionia and
" Cyprus may be free." " We have been com-
" miſſioned," anſwered the Ionians, " by our coun-
" try, to guard the ocean, not to deliver up our
" veſſels unto you, nor to engage the Perſians by
" land.—We will endeavour to diſcharge our duty
" in the ſtation appointed us ; it is for you to diſ-
" tinguiſh yourſelves as valiant men, remembering
" the oppreſſions you have endured from the
" Medes."

CX. When the Perſians were drawn up before
Salamis, the Cyprian commanders placed the forces
of Cyprus againſt the auxiliaries of the enemy, ſelecting the flower of Salamis and Soli to oppoſe the
Perſians : Oneſilus voluntarily ſtationed himſelf
againſt Artybius the Perſian General.

CXI. Artybius was mounted on a charger,
which had been taught to face a man in complete
armour : Oneſilus hearing this, called to him his
ſhield-bearer, who was a Carian of great military
experience, and of undaunted courage:—" I hear,"
ſays he, " that the horſe of Artybius, by his feet
" and his teeth, materially aſſiſts his maſter againſt
" an adverſary ; deliberate on this, and tell me
" which you will encounter, the man or the horſe."
" Sir," ſaid the attendant, " I am ready to engage
" with either, or both, or indeed to do whatever

" you command me; I fhould rather think it will
" be more confiftent for you, being a prince and a
" general, to contend with one who is a prince
" and general alfo.—If you fhould fortunately
" kill a perfon of this defcription, you will acquire
" great glory, or if you fhould fall by his hand,
" which heaven avert, the calamity is fomewhat
" foftened by the rank of the conqueror: it is for
" us of inferior rank to oppofe men like ourfelves.
" As to the horfe, do not concern yourfelf about
" what he has been taught; I will venture to fay,
" that he fhall never again be troublefome to any
" one."

CXII. In a fhort time afterwards, the hoftile forces engaged both by fea and land; the Ionians, after a fevere conteft, obtained a victory over
the Phœnicians, in which the bravery of the Samians was remarkably confpicuous. Whilft the armies were engaged by land, the following incident
happened to the two generals:—Artybius, mounted
on his horfe, rufhed againft Onefilus, who, as he
had concerted with his fervant, aimed a blow at
him as he approached: and whilft the horfe reared
up his feet againft the fhield of Onefilus, the Carian
cut them off with an ax.—The horfe, with his
mafter, fell inftantly to the ground.

CXIII. In the midft of the battle, Stefenor,
prince of Curium, with a confiderable body of
forces, went over to the enemy (it is faid that the
Curians are an Argive colony); their example was
followed

followed by the men of Salamis, in their chariots of war[142]; from which events the Perſians obtained a deciſive victory. The Cyprians fled. Amongſt the number of the ſlain was Oneſilus, ſon of Cherſis, and principal inſtigator of the revolt; the Solian prince, Ariſtocyprus, alſo fell, ſon of that Philocyprus[143], whom Solon of Athens, when at Cyprus, celebrated in verſe amongſt other ſovereign princes.

CXIV. In revenge for his beſieging them, the Amathuſians took the head of Oneſilus, and carrying it back in triumph, fixed it over their gates: ſome time afterwards, when the inſide of the head was decayed, a ſwarm of bees ſettling in it, filled it with honey. The people of Amathus conſulted the oracle on the occaſion, and were directed to bury the head, and every year to ſacrifice to Oneſilus as to an hero. their obedience involved a promiſe of future proſperity; and even within my

---

[142] *Chariots of war.*]—Of theſe chariots, frequent mention is made in Homer: they carried two men, one of whom guided the reins, the other fought.—Various ſpecimens of ancient chariots may be ſeen in Montfaucon.—*T.*

[143] *Philocyprus.*]—Philocyprus was prince of Soli, when Solon arrived at Cyprus; Solis was then called Æpeia, and the approaches to it were ſteep and difficult, and its neighbourhood, unfruitful.. Solon adviſed the prince to rebuild it on the plain which it overlooked, and undertook the labour of furniſhing it with inhabitants. In this he ſucceeded, and Philocyprus, from gratitude, gave his city the name of the Athenian philoſopher. Solon mentions this incident in ſome verſes addreſſed to Philocyprus, preſerved in Plutarch.—*Larcher.*

remembrance

remembrance, they have performed what was required of them.

CXV. The Ionians, although fuccefsful in the naval engagement off Cyprus, as foon as they heard of the defeat and death of Onefilus, and that all the cities of Cyprus were closely blockaded, except Salamis, which the citizens had reftored to Gorgus, their former fovereign, returned with all poffible expedition to Ionia. Of all the towns in Cyprus, Soli made the longeft and moft vigorous defence; but of this, by undermining the place, the Perfians obtained poffeffion after a five months fiege.

CXVI. Thus the Cyprians, having enjoyed their liberties for the fpace of a year, were a fecond time reduced to fervitude. All the Ionians who had been engaged in the expedition againft Sardis were afterwards vigoroufly attacked by Daurifes, Hymees, Otanes, and other Perfian generals, each of whom had married a daughter of Darius: they firft drove them to their fhips, then took and plundered their towns, which they divided amongft themfelves.

CXVII. Daurifes afterwards turned his arms againft the cities of the Hellefpont, and in as many fucceffive days made himfelf mafter of Abydos, Percotes, Lampfacus [144], and Pæfon. From this

latter

[144] *Lampfacus.*]—This place was given to Themiftocles to furnifh

latter place he proceeded to Parion, but learning on his march, that the Carians, taking part with the Ionians, had revolted from Perfia, he turned afide from the Hellefpont, and led his forces againft Caria.

CXVIII. Of this motion of Daurifes the Carians had early information, in confequence of which they affembled at a place called the white columns, not far from the river Marfyas, which, paffing through the diftrict of Hidryas, flows into the Mæander. Various fentiments were on this occafion delivered; but the moft fagacious in my eftimation was that of Pixodarus, fon of Maufolus; he was a native of Cindys, and had married the daugh-of Syennefis, prince of Cilicia. He advifed, that paffing the Mæander, they fhould attack the enemy, with the river in their rear; that thus deprived of all poffibility of retreat, they fhould from compulfion ftand their ground, and make the greater exertions of valour. This advice was not accepted; they chofe rather that the Perfians fhould have the Mæander behind them, that if they vanquifhed the enemy in the field, they might afterwards drive them into the river.

CXIX. The Perfians advanced, and paffed the Mæander; the Carians met them on the banks of

furnifh him wine, and was memorable in antiquity for producing many eminent men.—Epicurus refided here a long time. —*T.*

the

the Marfyas, when a fevere and well fought conteft enfued. The Perfians had fo greatly the advantage in point of number, that they were finally
victorious; two thoufand Perfians, and ten thoufand Carians fell in the battle; they who efcaped
from the field fled to Labranda, and took refuge in
a facred wood of planes, furrounding a temple of
Jupiter Stratius [145]. The Carians are the only people, as far as I have been able to learn, who facrifice
to this Jupiter. Driven to the above extremity,
they deliberated amongft themfelves, whether it
would be better to furrender themfelves to the Perfians, or finally relinquifh Afia.

CXX. In the midft of their confultation, the
Milefians with their allies arrived to reinforce them;
the Carians refumed their courage, and again prepared for hoftilities; they a fecond time advanced
to meet the Perfians, and after an engagement more

[145] *Jupiter Stratius—(or Jupiter the warrior.)*—The Carians were the only people, in the time of Herodotus, who worfhipped Jupiter under this title. He was particularly honoured
at Labranda, and therefore Strabo calls him the Labrandinian
Jupiter. He held a hatchet in his hand, and Plutarch (in his
Greek Queftions) relates the reafon; he was afterwards worfhipped in other places under the fame appellation. Amongft
the marbles at Oxford, there is a ftone which feems to have
ferved for an altar, having an ax, and this infcription; ΔΙΟΣ
ΛΑΒΡΑΥΝΔΟΥ ΚΑΙ ΔΙΟΣ ΜΕΓΙΣΤΟΥ—Of the Labraindian
Jupiter and of the very Great Jupiter. It was found in a
Turkifh cemetery, between Aphrodifias and Hieropolis, and con-
fequently in Caria, though at a great diftance from Labranda.
—*Larcher.*

obftinate

obftinate than the former, fuftained a fecond defeat, in which a prodigious number, chiefly of Milefians, were flain.

CXXI. The Carians foon recruited their forces, and in a fubfequent action, fomewhat repaired their former loffes. Receiving intelligence that the Perfians were on their march to attack their towns, they placed themfelves in ambufcade, in the road to Pidafus. The Perfians by night fell into the fnare, and a vaft number were flain, with their generals Daurifes, Amorges, and Sifimaces; Myrfes, the fon of Gyges, was alfo amongft the number.

CXXII. The conduct of this ambufcade was entrufted to Heraclides, fon of Ibanolis, a Mylaffian. —The event has been related. Hymees, who was engaged amongft others in the purfuit of the Ionians, after the affair of Sardis, turning towards the Propontis, took Cios, a Myfian city. Receiving intelligence that Daurifes had quitted the Hellefpont, to march againft Caria, he left the Propontis, and proceeded to the Hellefpont, where he effectually reduced all the Æolians of the Trojan diftrict; he vanquifhed alfo the Gergithæ, a remnant of the ancient Teucri. Hymees himfelf, after all thefe fucceffes, died at Troas.

CXXIII. Artaphernes, governor of Sardis, and Otanes, the third in command, received orders to lead their forces to Ionia and Æolia, which is contiguous

ous to it; they made themselves masters of Clazo-
menæ in Ionia, and of Cyma an Æolian city.

CXXIV. After the capture of these places, Aristagoras of Miletus, though the author of all the con-
fusion in which Ionia had been involved, betrayed
a total want of intrepidity; these losses confirmed
him in the belief, that all attempts to overcome Darius would be ineffectual; he accordingly determined to seek his safety in flight. He assembled
his party, and submitted to them whether it would
not be adviseable to have some place of retreat, in
case they should be driven from Miletus. He left
it to them to determine, whether, they should establish a colony in Sardinia, or whether they should
retire to Myrcinus, a city of the Edonians, which
had been fortified by Histiæus, to whom Darius
had presented it.

CXXV. Hecatæus the historian, who was the
son of Hegasander, was not for establishing a colony at either of these places; he affirmed, that if
they should be expelled from Miletus, it would be
more expedient for them to construct a fort in the
island of Leros, and there to remain till a favourable opportunity should enable them to return to
Miletus.

CXXVI. Aristagoras himself was more inclined
to retire to Myrcinus; he confided therefore the
administration of Miletus to Pythagoras, a man exceedingly

ceedingly popular, and taking with him all thofe who thought proper to accompany him, he embarked for Thrace, where he took poffeffion of the diftrict which he had in view. Leaving this place, he proceeded to the attack of fome other, where both he and his army fell by the hands of the Thracians, who had previoufly entered into terms to refign their city into his power [146].

[146] I cannot difmifs this book of Herodotus without remarking, that it contains a great deal of curious hiftory, and abounds with many admirable examples of private life. The fpeech of Soficles of Corinth, in favour of liberty, is excellent in its kind; and the many fagacious, and indeed moral fentiments, which are fcattered throughout the book, cannot fail of producing both entertainment and inftruction.—*T*.

END OF THE SECOND VOLUME.